Ula
By: J.R. Erickson
ISBN: 978-1-927134-71-9

Bluewood Publishing Ltd
Christchurch, 8441, New Zealand
www.bluewoodpublishing.com

For news of, or to purchase this or other books please visit.

www.bluewoodpublishing.com

Ula

by

J.R. Erickson

Dedication

For my parents and my husband Will – the loves of my life.

Chapter 1

Abby turned the wheel and pointed her small Cavalier down her Aunt Sydney's long, wooded driveway, relieved to be done with the drive, but terrified at what lay ahead. Had she really just abandoned her entire life?

She could smell Lake Michigan before she saw it – like liquid earth filling the car. The sun pierced the windshield and splashed a metallic glare into her eyes. She lifted a hand to shield her face, but caught it midway as an unfamiliar shape emerged from the brilliance. The shape, a narrow black car, was parked in the small circular drive near Sydney's house, but the trunk stood open.

The driveway should have been empty. Abby had chosen her Aunt Sydney's home largely for that reason. Sydney mostly lived with Rod, her young lover, recently turned husband, in his studio apartment downtown. The couple had booked a trip to the Cayman Islands, and Abby had intended to leave Nick (and her life) when Sydney returned so that she would have a confidante. But that morning, after Nick had loaded his golf clubs and pecked her quickly on the forehead, Abby had heard a voice in her mind say 'Go'. She did not question it. She packed a duffel bag, hit the ATM for cash and fled.

It was not exactly an impulsive decision, but one that had been months in the making. Abby had tried to snuff it out, justify her unhappiness as lack of job satisfaction, or hormones out of whack. But in the end, desperation always won, and that morning Abby had felt desperate. So desperate that she did not say goodbye to her parents, specifically her mother, who would most likely implode at the news. Nor did she call her boss, return her library books or even change the kitty litter.

Now, four hours after her departure, she was already facing a kink in her poorly executed plan.

The screen door on the back of the house swung open. Her eyes followed the line of a man's foot and then his leg. The stranger did not look much older than Abby's own twenty-three years. Dark curls fell over his tan face, obscuring his eyes and nose. She could see his lips, swollen and red, sunburned. He wore a Pink Floyd t-shirt and blue shorts that stopped just above his knee. He was barefoot and carrying a cardboard box, the lid taped shut with a thick line of electrical tape.

Abby thought to back out of the driveway and go, but where?

She started to shift the car into reverse, silently whispering a plea that the stranger would not hear the crunch of gravel beneath her wheels. He did. He looked up and then stumbled, nearly dropping his box.

Abby squinted at him; he'd moved into the sun and looked large and shadowy. He was waving.

"Shit," she whispered.

Forcing a calm that she did not feel, she pressed her foot on the gas, and the Cavalier shot forward, too hard. The stranger jumped back and flattened himself against his car.

"Sorry," Abby called out her window, parking next to him. "Sorry," she said again, climbing out and getting a better look.

His blue eyes narrowed on her face, surprised, but a smile cracked his lips.

"Abby?" he asked.

She searched for his face in her internal Rolodex, but came up empty.

"I'm sorry, do I know you?" She held up a hand to block the sun.

"No, you don't, actually." He cocked his head to one side and held out his hand. "I'm Sebastian. I know you because Sydney keeps about a billion pictures of you in there." He jerked his head toward the house.

Abby nodded and shook his hand. Sydney did have a thing about taking photos. In fact, the hallway that led up the main stairwell was a giant mosaic of Abby. There were pictures of her birth, her childhood and her awkward adolescence. Sydney had spent an entire summer cutting and pasting the photos on her wall, against the wishes of her then husband, Harold, who by that time had lost all favor with his wild wife.

"I loved the potty training one," Sebastian laughed. "You looked very determined."

Abby blushed, but did not turn away. She felt vaguely suspicious of Sebastian.

"How do you know Sydney, then?" she asked, a bit hostile.

He set the box in his trunk, closed the lid and balanced his hip on the edge.

"Well." He brushed a hand through his black curls. "My grandmother knew your grandmother."

Abby scrunched her face. "Grandma Arlene?"

Abby barely remembered her Grandma Arlene. The woman had only visited her twice as a child because she traveled the world, much to the resentment of her daughter Becky, Abby's mom. Sydney talked of her often, envied her really, but Abby knew her mostly through photos and stories. She had died when Abby was only five.

"Yeah." Sebastian nodded. "Arlene and my grandmother were good friends. My mom, Julia, was a childhood friend of Sydney's. I think she knew your mom, too. Becky, right?"

Abby nodded. His discussion of her family tree made

him significantly less threatening.

"Yes, Becky," Abby said, ignoring the guilt that flamed at her mother's name. "But I don't think I've ever met your mom."

"My mom passed away quite a few years ago."

Abby grimaced and inwardly chastised herself. "Oh, I'm so sorry. I didn't mean to pry."

"No apologies." Sebastian held up a hand to silence her. "It's only logical that you would ask. Anyway," he continued, "I've been visiting Sydney on and off since I was about three."

Abby nodded and remembered something. Sydney had once shown her a photo of two little kids; both had black curls and bright blue eyes. She called them something, but Abby could not remember what. Her special children maybe?

"As for why I'm here now," Sebastian went on, "I just got back from Panama and Sydney said her house was vacant, so…"

"Oh," Abby said, flustered. Now where was she going to stay?

"But, hey, there's plenty of room. I'm in the guest room, and Sydney's room is open."

"Yeah, maybe." Abby looked back down the driveway. She didn't have extra money for a hotel room, and she really wanted to be on the lake.

"Please?" Sebastian asked kindly. "It would actually be nice to have some company."

"Okay," she said quickly, overriding her natural inclination to say no.

"Great." He clapped his hands together. "Need help with your stuff?"

She shook her head. "I only have a duffel bag. Pretty easy to carry myself." She opened the passenger door, pulled out her bag and slung it over her shoulder. "So, why were you in Panama?"

"Well, it's a long story, but I've spent most of the last year traveling. Just trying to…find things."

He scratched his arm, and when his t-shirt lifted, Abby saw a tattoo on his bicep – it looked like initials.

"What kinds of things?" she asked, carrying her bag to the house.

He followed her, but stopped short of the door. "Life. Trying to find out about life."

He didn't say more, and Abby sensed that he didn't want to talk. She smiled and walked inside.

* * * *

Sydney threw her head back and laughed from the stomach, bent over as Rod modeled his new cut-off shorts. 'Nut-cutters,' he called them.

She could almost see his pubic hair, 'almost' being the operative word, since he intended to pack and wear them on their upcoming trip to the Cayman Islands.

"And I want you to wear this." He skipped across the loft, stopping before Sydney who lay sprawled on their enormous round bed, a wet towel bunched at her waist.

Rod held up a thong bikini, a red one that he'd purchased the previous week at an expensive lingerie store.

She rolled her eyes and leaned back on her elbows. "Aren't my boobs a bit saggy for that thing?" she joked, secretly wondering if they were. She had just turned fifty, after all. Her days of smooth, creamy skin had given way to the overly soft pools of flesh that she spent hours in the gym attempting to mold into place.

"Baby, you got the best boobs around." Rod leaned in and kissed her, jumping away when she tried to grab the bikini out of his hand.

He stuffed the bikini in her suitcase and continued pillaging the closet for their vacation wardrobe.

Sydney usually stayed in Trager during the summer. Northern Michigan peaked during June, July and August, but this year she looked forward to a break from the tourist-clogged town. When Rod had found cheap plane tickets online, she'd jumped at the chance. Cayman Islands, all-inclusive for two weeks? "Hell, yeah," she'd said.

Since the previous year, when Sydney moved into Rod's place, a newly built downtown loft, she'd started noticing the tourists more. Her home, a spacious Cape Cod located on a strip of woods jutting into Lake Michigan, was very private, and for years Sydney knew the tourists only by the sounds of their motor homes ambling by. Now she saw them up close and personal every day. Whether she and Rod were running downstairs for a coffee or walking to the nearby grocery, the-out-of-towners clogged the space. The homemade donuts disappeared from the café each day by nine am, and Sydney hated to wake up before ten. She despised popping in to the party store to buy toothpaste and waiting fifteen minutes behind vacationers loaded down with aloe vera gel and fudge. But she had promised herself that she would give Rod's loft a chance and not just run home to her lakefront paradise that Rod insisted was too isolated.

Rod slipped off his jean shorts and slid into a pair of white linen pants – modeling them in front of the full-length mirror that leaned along a brick wall. He looked good, too good, and Sydney smiled at her good fortune. Well, really, fortune had nothing to do with it. When Sydney wanted something, she got it. Not because she was a bulldozer either. The world just seemed to shift for her. It had always been that way. When she was a child, she needed only to think of things, and they would miraculously appear. Not money or toys or anything of that sort, but images and people.

During the summer of her twelfth birthday, Sydney's sister Becky went to summer camp. Sydney had been elated, originally, but two days into their separation, she missed her terribly. She had no one to scavenge the woods with. That night, Sydney's parents received a call that Becky had poison ivy and had to come home. It might have been a coincidence, but Sydney knew better. She just had a way of making things happen.

Rod went into the bathroom to gather toiletries. Sydney had met Rod two years earlier. Met him after she imagined him. It was summer, and she and Harold, her then husband, were having a pool built at their Lake Michigan home. During the winter, she and Harold lived in a spacious house in Grand Rapids that Sydney loathed. It was too big, too clean and too white. Every one of Harold's stockbroker friends had one just like it. They also each owned their very own skinny, blond wife. Sydney failed at all wifely expectations, but Harold, quite frankly, just failed. Workaholic did not a husband make, so when Sydney started dreaming about a young, handsome man to steal her away from her wealthy, boring life, Rod simply appeared.

Sydney had already been considering leaving Harold. She simply wasn't the type to stick around and kick a dead horse, but when Harold proposed an indoor pool for their summer home, she became so distracted with the preparations that she put her divorce plans on hold. Then Rod arrived one morning, pool plans in hand, his red mesh shorts barely hiding his gray boxer briefs. Sydney knew him instantly, she'd been dreaming of him for weeks.

Within three days, she and Rod were having sex in the bow of her Mastercraft, and within a month, she'd left Harold and moved to Trager City to pursue her affair full time. Harold, true to his indifferent nature in all matters but financial, barely blinked an eye. When she had told him that she wanted a divorce – he nodded, scratched his chin and said, "Well, it does look like GE's going up…" And that had been that.

"Hey, Abby's gonna meet Sebastian."

"Shit," Sydney muttered, looking at the clock. She had forgotten that Sebastian was staying at the house.

"Maybe they'll get it on, and she'll dump that square, Rick."

"Nick."

"Yeah, whatever."

* * * *

That evening, Abby sat Indian style on Sydney's bed and stared out the wide window at the lake. Twilight textured the sky, and the clouds had divided into frothy layers of pink and blue. The sun, a red glare, slipped below the humid veil of Lake Michigan and disappeared.

Sebastian was gone, citing a desperate need for internet access, and Abby wandered Sydney's house like a lost soldier. Nothing much had changed in the years since Sydney and Harold bought the summer retreat, but everything felt different. Of course, the house had changed a bit when Sydney left Harold for Rod, but that had been two years ago and had nothing to do with the strangeness that Abby felt walking along the house's familiar corridors. Abby looked at photos and furniture with new eyes. For the previous two years, everything was filtered through the lens of Nick and Abby. What do Nick and Abby like to eat—drink—do? Abby and Nick even visited Sydney a few times at the lake house. The first visit ended badly when Nick refused to go in the water because the PGA tour was on. The second trip involved Nick's incessant complaints about the heat, the fish flies and Rod's clothing choices. Abby vowed that she would never bring him back.

She walked up and down the steps, admiring the carpet, the lamps and the wine. The smell of knotty pine brought back childhood memories, so she retired to Sydney's room to pilfer through old shoeboxes of pictures. In a DKNY box she found the photo of the two curly haired kids. She now felt sure that Sebastian stared out from the Polaroid, his blue eyes mischievous, a black curl cutting down his forehead. The other child, a girl, looked younger than Sebastian. She wore a black and purple striped one-piece, and her freshly tanned skin turned her blue eyes into shining marbles.

In another box she found a picture of herself and Nick, taken the previous summer. They were standing on Sydney's dock, holding hands, but her body was turned away and his smile was tight and angry. She studied her long, frizzy waves, short now, and wished she had not taken Nick's advice to cut it. She reached a hand up and felt the tips, already fraying to split ends. Short hair made her heart shaped face look too wide, she thought, but knew it no longer mattered.

Abby's cell phone vibrated and she glanced down – her mother. Her mom had called three times. Nick had called seventeen times. She didn't answer, but leaned her head back on a pillow and squeezed her eyes closed. Fear leapt through her veins like fire, and only deep breaths and strong rationalizations kept her from picking up the phone.

It was amazing how the unknown could cause physical distress. Abby was in no imminent danger. Her decision to flee did not destine her for failure or unhappiness or pain. But still the stress seeped out from her brain and made each muscle taut like she might have to spring from the bed at any moment and run to freedom.

She returned the boxes to the closet and slipped on a long t-shirt, climbing into Sydney's bed. Outside, the hazy

August day kept the mercury climbing, but Abby shivered beneath the heavy comforter.

Chapter 2

In the morning Abby tried not to wake Sebastian. In her socked feet, she slid from the bottom stair, through the lower level hall and into the living room.

Sebastian lay open-mouthed on the couch, a soft snore trembling his lower lip. His right leg dangled from the red suede sofa, and his Pink Floyd t-shirt was twisted around his waist, revealing a thin trail of black hair from his navel into his jeans.

She crept past him, stepping over his discarded tennis shoes and around the pile of blankets he'd thrown off during the night.

She slid her feet noiselessly into her sandals and shoved a Detroit Tigers ball cap over her unbrushed brown hair. Hair that needed washing, since she'd skipped a shower the previous day in her rush to get out of Lansing. The chipped, pink polish on her toenails looked ragged as she stepped into the bright morning. The August sun, already a blistering orange, made her squint.

From the front porch she watched the rippling water of Lake Michigan, the streaks of iridescent blue as the sun washed the lingering morning fog from the air. She felt good, and for the first time in months had awoken that morning starved. The previous spring Abby had lost her appetite. She started waking up to a stomach twisted in knots. She tried vitamins, probiotics and eggs. Nick bought her real cranberry juice and lectured her on cutting dairy out of her diet, but nothing worked. She simply could not eat. She did, eventually, but every food tasted bland, and every bite went down with scratchy reluctance. After a few weeks, she'd given up trying to remedy the problem despite a weight loss that left her swimming in her pants.

She rested a hand on her stomach and felt the rumbling within. The hunger seemed like an affirmation, proof that she had made the right choice. She still felt scared and a bit lonely, but those emotions paled in comparison to the vibrant quaking freedom that pulsated in her blood.

She wanted—needed—to walk, and decided to use hunger as her excuse. Good Times Party Store, a small grocery store that she'd been visiting since childhood, was only a mile from Sydney's house, and a pastry was calling to her.

She turned off the road and into the trees, cutting along a deer path, a short cut. She trailed her fingers over the tall weeds, but watched her footing carefully. Several bouts of poison ivy had made Abby a wary woods traveler. Wary, but not absent. She loved the forest around Sydney's house and knew its geography as surely as her parents' backyard.

During her childhood, Abby stayed with her Aunt Sydney for two weeks every July. Abby loved Sydney and loved to escape from her overbearing mother. Becky had always over-packed for Abby, stuffing a red suitcase with totally ridiculous items like long underwear and cue-tips.

Abby looked forward to her mother's over-packing because she knew that she and Sydney would laugh about it later.

Abby's mother, Becky, and her Aunt Sydney were night and day, the 'dichotomous duo' Sydney claimed their mother used to call them. Physically, they looked nothing alike. Becky was short, just over five feet tall and petite, her thin body often sheathed in baggy sweaters and loose jeans. Her shoulder-length brown hair ratted easily, and she wore it back in a mousy ponytail that made her pointed features even more angular. Her skin was pale, her eyes brown and her thin lips often betraying the large front teeth hiding beneath.

Sydney, on the other hand, looked like a Bond girl, or that's what Harold had always called her. She, too, was short, but had waist-length blond hair that she wore down her back. Her blue eyes shone beneath long black lashes. Her wardrobe included tight and skin tight, and the boob job that Harold bought her looked real – at least to Abby, who at fourteen had not understood why someone like Sydney would need new boobs. Becky told Abby that Sydney was trying to simulate the engorged feeling of breast milk because she was barren, which Abby had understood to be a jab.

Becky's world included knitting, the home shopping network and housework. Sydney left a mess, considered 'swinging' to be the relationship of the future and refused to turn on the TV in any season except winter.

Abby stooped to smell a bush of white lilacs. She savored the sweet scent and plucked a few petals. Abby had inherited her mother's looks—mostly. She was short, skinny and flat-chested. Her hair, now at her shoulders, was a lighter shade of brown than her mother's, but snarled easily and puffed up like an angry cat during humidity. She learned when young that hats were her friends. Her lips were plump like Sydney's, but she had her mother's brown eyes and small, pointed nose. She considered herself average, and most of the men she met labeled her 'cute,' not a very inspiring brand.

Nick did not stand apart in this category. The first time she met him, while studying at MSU's business library, he called her 'sweet'. At the time, it seemed like a huge compliment, considering it was finals week, she had a mouthful of Chili Cheese Fritos, and she had not bothered to brush her hair in two days.

Nick had been average looking with broad shoulders and blond hair buzzed close to his head. He asked her out, she complied, and their relationship became as predictable as

13

a Danielle Steel novel. Abby's mother loved Nick.

Initially, Abby liked him too. She liked his ambition to become an attorney. In the first six months of their relationship, she enjoyed spending weekends visiting his law school friends, who talked politics and boasted about their insomnia. He was still courting her then, trying to win her over. He brought flowers and burned her CDs. He cooked dinner, gave her massages and called her incessantly.

But after their one-year anniversary, she found the footing beneath their relationship starting to slip. Grad school was taking its toll, and Nick lived and breathed statutes and contracts. He got angry easily, brushed off her hurt feelings and started to lecture her on being a supportive partner. She realized that any future with him would look strangely like her mother's. Not that Abby's dad was an attorney; he was a real estate agent, but his wife treated him like the Pope. She washed, scrubbed, ironed and cooked her way to his heart. She expected Abby to do the same, and when Abby complained that Nick had changed, her mother looked at her with such disgust that Abby never brought it up again.

She walked into a thin netting of spider-webs and stopped, pulling the silky threads from her face and neck. The deer path, buried beneath weeds, had practically disappeared. She wished for tennis shoes rather than flip-flops. Twigs and leaves found their way into the crevice between her foot and sandal, and she leaned down, pulling them free. The sun, hot and getting hotter, drove rays through the thick leaves overhead. A chipmunk darted past her and paused, turning to stare from a nearby tree stump. He twittered and sped away, over the trunk and into a thick bed of nettles.

Abby wished she had worn socks or taken the road, anything to save her sensitive skin from the various pricking plants lurking nearby. She had slipped on one of Sydney's red windbreakers, but her legs, below her shorts, were bare.

She leaned close to the ground, found the deer path and continued forward, stepping around a tall bull thistle popping with hairy purple flowers, and remembered her mother scolding her for touching one of the sharp plants as a child.

Beyond the thistle, more color caught her eye, and she veered from the path. A piece of fabric, tattered and blue, clung on a low tree branch, like a long forgotten flag, meaningless without its worshippers. Abby stretched out, touched it and pulled away disgusted. The fabric was wet, slimy even, and she reached to wipe her fingers on her shorts, but stopped. A smear of red painted her pale fingertips. It was not the red of paint, nor chalk or marker. It was a deep red, brown and thick. She did not need to move her face closer to smell the coppery scent; the air hung with the metallic tinge of the cloth. She dropped it and stepped back.

She began to turn away, to disregard the startling find, but curiosity stole her good sense. She looked down over glistening green ferns and mossy branches. Her eyes landed on a sliver of white flesh, as stark as the moon, bedded in the browns around it. The flesh grew larger as she walked, trancelike, towards it. Painted toenails, a red-orange color like the inside of a papaya, came into view. From feet caked with dirt, Abby's gaze moved higher up bare legs. She saw the woman fully then, her naked torso splotched with blood, leaves tangled in her pubic hair.

A black, oily crow took flight near the head of the body and Abby gasped and stumbled back, hooking her arm on a young tree and clinging to it for balance. The body—the woman—stared vacantly, her lips parted. Streams of red hair framed her face, twigs caught in the thick tendrils. Abby could see her; she could see the corpse, the young woman's body. She also felt her, felt more than the dead thing waiting for the woods to devour it.

A whisper stole across her cheek, a warning, and Abby ran. She twisted away from the grave and sprinted through the trees, holding her arms up to shield the branches that scraped against her. Too numb to feel the nettles and picker bushes, she did not pause when her flip-flop caught on a patch of brush and stayed behind. Instead, she tore from the woods and back onto pavement.

Beyond the trees, the sky opened to piercing white light in a sea of blue and Abby slowed, panting.

She limped, one sandal lost, along the pocked road. Her Tigers cap was gone, her bare foot ached, and her heart was rapid in her ears.

Sound was muted and distant, an invisible wall muffling everything except the slap of her single flip-flop on the paved road. Her hands shook and to her horror she saw the streak of blood still coating her fingertips. She started to wipe it away and then realized that the blood was evidence – she couldn't touch it. She may have already contaminated the scene. Her mouth hung open, her tongue dry and thick, and she swallowed, but nothing slipped down the dusty channel of her throat.

She turned down Sydney's driveway and then ran, banging through the front door. The house, silent, greeted her.

Sebastian, still on the couch, sat up, startled.

"There's a dead body in the woods!" Abby shrieked, scaring herself and Sebastian both.

He didn't move, perhaps wondering if Sydney's niece was insane.

"A body, a girl, she's…she's dead."

Comprehension dawned slowly and he stood up, disoriented, sleep shrinking his pupils.

"Wait, wait." He held up a hand and then his eyes

traveled from her face to the blood on her hand – to the single sandal on her foot. He shook his head from side to side, believing, but still too tired to grasp the situation fully.

"I have to call the police," she stammered, moving to the living room where a gray house phone sat coiled in its cord.

She picked up the receiver, using her left hand—the one not smeared with blood—and punched 9-1-1.

The operator picked up. Sebastian walked to the kitchen, filled a glass with water and returned it to Abby.

She balanced the phone against her shoulder and drank.

"I'm sorry, honey, what'd you say?" the operator asked again.

Abby gritted her teeth and repeated that she had discovered a dead body.

"A dead body? Here in Trager City?"

"Yes," Abby cried, nearly overcome with rage at the operator's incompetence. "Yes, a dead body, DEAD!"

Finally, the operator began asking legitimate questions, and Abby started to calm down.

She hung up and leaned back against the couch, squeezing her eyes closed.

"What can I do?" Sebastian asked, standing beside the couch and looking agitated.

Abby sat motionless, her palms up. "I have no idea, no idea." She blinked and tried to convey some meaning in her words. "I have to go back. They said I should wait for the police." She gestured toward the door, sick at the thought of returning to the body.

"I'll come with you," Sebastian declared, finding his sandals and slipping them on. He brought her a pair of tennis shoes and helped her tie them as she held her bloody hand away from the arms of the couch.

* * * *

When they stepped out of the woods, Sebastian looked as shocked as Abby felt. He had stared at the body for a long time and then abruptly turned and left. Abby had to struggle to keep up with him as he lit out of the trees. Back in the sunlight, he found a patch of grass and sat down roughly. Abby took a seat beside him, tucking her knees beneath her.

An assembly of birds sang from the trees, and Abby could imagine the tourists as they roused from their tents to cold cereal and showers in the lake. A station wagon, packed with kids, ambled by, their faces plastered against the windows. Abby watched them go and felt a stab of homesickness. For the first time since her departure, she missed her mother. She wanted someone to hug her, to stroke her hair and whisper that all those gruesome images floating in her brain were fiction.

On any other Sunday, Abby would have been sprawled out on the living room floor, drinking coffee and flipping through the newspaper, while Nick meticulously dusted all their furniture. The image of Nick with his dust rag was enough to reassure her that she had made the right choice. She could not spend her life—her youth—with a man who spent every Sunday spring-cleaning, who forced her onto the couch with her paper and coffee so that he could vacuum the pristine carpet. What a giant leap Sebastian was from Nick. Amazing that they were the same sex at all.

Sebastian leaned against a tree, silent. After several minutes, he spoke, his eyes still closed. "Are you okay?" he asked.

Abby stared at her hand. She'd placed a plastic baggie over it at Sydney's, and some of the blood had smeared onto the plastic. "Yes," she replied, looking at the trees across the street. "Relatively speaking."

He nodded and opened his eyes, looking at her. His eyes, beneath the sun, looked like twin shining pebbles, his black pupils narrow blemishes on an otherwise flawless stone. He picked a dandelion and rubbed the yellow across his hand, leaving a mustard streak. "Death is terrible. That kind of death—" He hooked a thumb at the woods behind them "—is indescribable."

Abby agreed. She could not have conjured a portrait of the dead woman before seeing her. Death for Abby was a shallow pool of grandparents that she barely knew laid out in satin-lined beds and sheathed beneath layers of thick foundation. Beyond that, death belonged to slasher movies and television dramas.

* * * *

Several minutes passed, and Abby relaxed against a white birch, feeling the frayed bark tickling her scalp. Across the street, the woods were dense, their boughs colliding in the strangled space. She let her eyes dip and soar along the tree trunks, not really looking for anything more than a fixation. As her gaze trailed left, she caught movement among the branches, nothing drastic, just a shift in shadows. She moved onto her knees and then stood, squinting into the forest.

Sebastian fidgeted next to her. "What is it?" he asked, standing.

"I don't know, nothing maybe."

"Where?"

She pointed a finger, trembling – she saw, but did not feel confident that she pointed at anything more than a crow nesting in the leaves. Still, something prickled along her skin and the fine hairs of her neck stood erect. If a crow peered out from those trees, he must have been staring at her very intently because she could feel eyes like fingers dancing over her.

Sebastian's face pinched as he stared, his blue eyes narrowing and then his head jerking with movement.

A dark shape had disembarked from the trees. Abby saw a flash of black hood and then nothing.

Chapter 3

Abby started to say, "The police will be here soon." But Sebastian was gone, sprinting across the street, a billow of dust alighting on the roadside around him. He disappeared into the brush, his body crashing through branches and his arms up to shield his face.

"What just happened?" Abby asked aloud to no one. Had Sebastian really just run into the woods? Most likely scaring the daylights out of some wayward hiker who'd simply wandered off the beaten path. She could hear the muffled sounds of snapping twigs and mashing weeds and wondered if maybe he had found someone back there.

A police cruiser, lights flashing, pulled off the road in front of her. Abby ran over, ready to send him into the woods to save Sebastian.

A stocky officer heaved himself from the car, his navy blue uniform taut against his thick belly.

"I'm Officer Gray." He thrust a meaty hand towards her.

"We don't have time for that," she spat, ignoring his hand. "My friend…" She turned, pointing to the woods, but Sebastian was there. He exited the trees and jogged over, leaves burrowed in his curls. His eyes looked wild and he gave Abby a long, significant stare before turning to the officer.

"What were you saying, Miss?" Officer Gray asked, hiking his pants up unsuccessfully. They continued to sag below his belly.

Abby swallowed and shook her head slowly. "Umm, just that, she's there in the woods behind us."

He looked at her for a moment and then nodded

21

abruptly. Apparently he assumed all witnesses to dead bodies
acted irrationally.

"What's goin' on with your hand there?" he asked.

"Oh." She held it up as if she too had forgotten the
blood smeared on her hand. "It's from the woods. I touched
something, a piece of cloth…" She trailed off.

He stared at it a moment longer and then nodded
slowly. "And which of you called in the report?" His watery
eyes moved toward the line of trees.

"I did," Abby said, ignoring Sebastian's gaze.

"I'll need you to go ahead and show me the way." He
pulled a radio off his belt, calling for an ambulance and
backup.

Abby turned but shot a furtive glance at Sebastian. He
nodded that she should go ahead.

She followed the familiar path and stopped short, this
time pointing toward the body, but preferring not to look
again. The officer moved in, holding his breath in nervous
anticipation. He moaned, a little painfully, and pulled his
radio back out as the body came into view. Abby listened as
he radioed a description. She turned nervously and scanned
the woods around her. Had Sebastian seen someone?

Not sure whether to stay or walk back to the road, she
sat down on a decaying log that crumbled slightly, revealing
layers of bark turned ashy. The trees hovered, their green
leaves lush and thick with life. A red squirrel fled across the
branches, leaping great stretches and clutching flimsy
perches with his tiny feet.

She closed her eyes and imagined how he felt,
envisioning her own body sailing effortlessly through the
trees.

The officer hooked his radio back on his hip and turned
to face her. "Just head on back out to the road there and wait.
I'll have somebody along to talk to ya pretty soon."

Dismissed, Abby made her way out of the forest. Sebastian sat on the ground. A small group of onlookers had gathered. One or two cars were pulled off the road, and an older woman asked Sebastian questions through her car window.

"I really don't know anything, ma'am. I'm just waiting for my friend," he lied to her, relief flushing his face as Abby walked out.

"What's goin' on in there, Missy?" The nosy woman directed the question at Abby, her eyes narrowing.

"I can't really say…" Abby told her, watching uncomfortably as more cars slowed behind the woman.

"What happened?" Abby whispered, settling onto a patch of grass to Sebastian's left.

He rubbed his jaw and stared at the spot in the forest where he had run in.

"He was in there," he whispered.

Abby looked at him, confused. "Who? The killer?"

"Yes," Sebastian insisted. "Yes, the killer."

Abby wanted to ask more, but two more police cruisers pulled up, parking behind the first. An ambulance quickly followed.

Soon the area crawled with cops and onlookers, and Abby lost her chance to question Sebastian. The cops strung yellow tape around the forest perimeter, and a younger female officer dodged questions as she forced people back towards the road. Abby felt tired, but was told to stay put, so she and Sebastian watched the scene unfold.

"Pretty crazy," he sighed, nodding at a family of five walking past and peering into the woods.

"Yeah." She rubbed her temples where a throbbing ache had begun.

The female officer broke from the chaos and jogged over to Abby and Sebastian. "Hi." Her face was flushed beneath her halo of golden hair. Her eyes were giant blue saucers, and she was petite, as short as Abby. "I'm Officer Tina Hamilton."

"Abby," Abby told her politely, thrusting a trembling hand forward. "And this is Sebastian."

"Hi," he said curtly, scanning the woods behind her. "Listen, is anyone planning on searching those woods?"

"Should they?"

"Well, yeah. I'm pretty sure there was someone in there."

Tina glanced toward the woods. "Sure, we'll have someone look into it," she said dismissively.

Sebastian looked like he wanted to say more, but Tina had walked away, shooing two cyclists back toward the road.

"Cops are the worst," Sebastian muttered.

"Well, maybe it wasn't anything," Abby offered, preferring nothing to a killer watching them from the leafy cover.

"Yeah, but maybe it was…"

Tina returned, looking distracted and anxious. "I'm going to need to take the two of you to the station. The Chief will have some questions."

* * * *

Chief Caplan scratched his chin, razor-burned and red, and stared in horror at the report before him. Less than four months to retirement and a damned murder in his town. A murder! In his thirty-four years on the force, fifteen in Trager City, he'd only worked two murders, and both were domestic disputes with a clear killer, the husband. This—this catastrophe—had 'cold case' written all over it. How could he end his career with an unsolved murder?

He stood and paced to the pane of glass that looked into

the precinct. Every desk was occupied, and police and secretaries stood in huddled groups talking heatedly. They all wanted details, but no one knew what to do with them. Soon they would turn to him for answers and what could he give them, but the same blank look that had been plastered on his face since the call came in?

The outer door swung in, and he watched Tina hustle in two kids, no more than twenty-five. The girl looked scared and shocked, the one who found the body, apparently. The other looked like a hippy with long, black, curly hair and a clear disdain for authority etched into the set of his jaw. Caplan did not want to talk to them. He wanted to assign the task to some young officer hoping to climb the ranks. He would consider Tina, but she had such a chip on her shoulder, she might smack the hippy and end up getting Trager's police department sued. He scanned the other faces, looking for a suitable option, but knew he could not give it away. What would his superiors say? Especially if they couldn't find the perp?

He lifted his coffee mug, a gift from his wife that said, "If you think I'm neurotic, look at my dog" in green block letters, and drained the last of his sooty coffee. It didn't matter if he got the first cup from the pot, he still ended up with a trail of grounds that he choked down with disgust. He set it back on his desk, and the light on his phone beeped mechanically. He picked it up, happy for another distraction.

* * * *

After an older man wearing a white lab coat carefully swabbed her hand and took the baggie away for evidence, Abby sat in a stiff plastic chair. Her hands were shoved between her knees, which shook violently when not clamped tightly together. The station stank of sweat and coffee and something sugary like yeast. Men and women, mostly men, shuffled about the room, their faces pressed in worry.

Murder did not happen in Trager City. Abby could see the disintegration of that belief in their worried faces, their stressed scowls. They were responsible, accountable, and they didn't have a clue what to do about it.

Sebastian paced back and forth in front of her chair, his expression a changing mask of anxiety, fury and indifference. She wanted to talk to him, to pat the chair next to her, to apologize for getting him involved, but her tongue stuck to the roof of her mouth, and her lips were like a sealed envelope.

Given time to think, Abby had grown increasingly scared and upset. The image of the dead body kept popping into her mind like a terrible dream that she couldn't shake.

How quickly a living body could be stolen of its self, turned from living flesh into a flaccid shell. Abby had never been particularly interested in death. She had not obsessed over it as some people did, locking themselves away to create some false sense of security. Though she was also not overly adventurous and rarely sought out the adrenaline rush that so many young people coveted – no skydiving on her calendar of achievements. However, she suddenly wished for those thrills, for a long, rolling list of daring expeditions. Why had she not lived more, lived every second of every day?

"Chief Caplan, please. I just called."

The voice, magnetic, startled Abby, and she looked up, eyes connecting with a rail-thin man in an expensive silver suit. He was tall and reminded her of a praying mantis, with arms too short for his body. His handsome face scanned the room, deep-set brown eyes beneath pencil thin black eyebrows. His bald head shone with a recent shave.

He crossed the precinct in five steps, his legs like stilts, his suit barely shifting with his swagger. The office din died with his arrival, and several heads turned to watch as he strode through the room.

Sebastian's eyes locked on the man and did not leave him.

Abby shifted in her seat, clearing her throat to get Sebastian's attention, but he only ignored her, continuing to stare at the well-dressed stranger as he disappeared into a large, rectangular office.

It was the Police Chief's office. Abby knew by the small, faux gold doorplate, scuff marks visible under the hot lights. Navy blue blinds dropped over the single window in the office, and Abby could see no more.

For several long minutes, they waited. A heavy secretary with a frizzy red perm brought them each a tar-like cup of coffee in small Styrofoam cups. Abby drank hers greedily, parched and thankful for any liquid to coat her sticky gums. Sebastian barely noticed his, pausing for several minutes with the cup partially raised to his lips. Abby watched him, the firm set of his jaw and a nervous habit of licking his lips. They looked red, and Abby absently started to search for her chapstick, realizing that she was wearing Sydney's jacket, not her own.

All thoughts of her life at home had diminished beneath the weight of the day's events. Death trumped all. Only Sebastian still commanded a shard of her attention because his nervous energy banged off of her like a ping-pong ball ricocheting around the room.

The Police Chief's door squeaked open, and the Chief stepped out. He looked tired, the lines of his face especially stark against what looked like a recent sunburn. His silvery hair was cropped close to his head, and his uniform fit loosely on his sagging shoulders and tightly around his waist, where his belly protruded. He seemed disoriented, and Abby thought of the burden of the dead girl. To Abby, the Chief looked like somebody's grandfather, a man who wore knitted sweaters and putted in his living room. She felt bad for him.

He walked to Abby and Sebastian, waving Abby back down when she started to stand.

"No need, dear," he told her with forced calm. "The two of you are free to go."

"You don't have any questions?" Sebastian asked, dumbfounded. He had seemed irritated at the idea of being questioned, but now appeared equally irritated that no questioning would occur.

"No, young man, though I greatly appreciate your cooperation. Now, just head on home, and if we need to follow up, we'll be in contact with you."

"Wait." Sebastian put a hand on the Chief's arm, but he barely noticed it.

"Hmm...yes?" he asked, his eyes vacantly scanning the room.

"Who is the guy in your office?"

The Chief returned his gaze to Sebastian, frowning slightly. "He's a detective. He'll be working the case and may need to call you kids, but—"

"But, what?" Abby shrilled, unnerved by the Chief's flaky behavior.

"Oh, but nothing. Sorry about your luck, Miss. We'll be in touch."

Sebastian started to say more, but already the Chief had turned and hurried back to his office, closing the door firmly behind him.

* * * *

Tina dropped them off at Sydney's mailbox. They walked up the long driveway, their feet crunching on gravel.

"What are you thinking?" Abby asked Sebastian, who looked jived up. He kept bobbing his head to his thoughts.

"Destiny, I'm thinking destiny."

"I'm sorry, what does that mean, Aristotle?" she asked.

"Do you believe in fate, Abby? In things aligning themselves to guide you?"

Hmm, did she? No, not really. She believed in choices and action and socialized expectations that sometimes seemed like destiny, but actually felt like doom.

"Not especially," she said, matting her brown hair back into her ponytail holder.

"I see," he said dismissively.

"That's it? I see?"

He stopped walking and faced her. "How can I speak to you in a language that you don't understand?"

"Fine, never mind," she quipped, too tired to decipher his code. She hurried ahead of him to the house, not bothering to hang her coat or remove her shoes. She went straight to Sydney's bedroom, sliding her clothes off once she was beneath the covers. She feared that her disturbed mind, full to capacity, would prevent sleep, but she quickly slipped out of her living nightmare and into the safety of her dreams.

* * * *

Sebastian pushed into the guest bedroom and closed and locked the door behind him. Half a dozen boxes lined the wall next to the bed. Boxes filled with photos, journals, books and so many scraps of paper that Sebastian had stopped looking in them several months earlier.

Had he given up? No, not exactly, but he had begun to doubt himself—to doubt the man that he hunted, even to doubt his sister and her abilities.

When he had stood at the airport in Panama, finally ready to give up his crusade, dealing with the reality of a million dead leads, Sydney's house had popped into his mind like a beacon in the fog. Had he known then where it would lead him? No, no, his intuition always felt a little bit like guessing. But he had come, and now there was a dead body—a dead girl in the woods. A dead girl that did not look like Claire, but felt like her.

When Abby had led him to the body, he was not expecting the jolt of familiarity that assailed him. The position of her body, the energy that lingered in the space where she lay. Claire's death had rushed back with such force that he lost his place for a moment and stood suspended in space and time. He stood looking down at Claire's body; at her long, black hair caught in the weeds. In death, Claire was the fragile sister of his childhood. She was no longer the powerful witch of her transformation. She was merely a body, an empty space where flesh and blood could no longer live.

But still, he could not be sure that his feelings were more than his mind's invention. Until he saw the detective, though he did not know him in that capacity; the detective with the long body and stunted arms who Sebastian had seen before.

Sebastian dug through three boxes before he found the photo. In the image, he saw the woods where Claire's body was discovered, the same weedy trail that led into the nature preserve that no one ever used. The nature preserve where they had taken Claire and murdered her. A dozen people stood in the photo; law enforcement, a few spectators and one man near the back. A man with a stick figure's body, a ball cap pulled over his head, partially obscuring his eyes. The man was looking toward the woods, a half smile on his face, his arms hanging at his sides. They barely reached his waist; they were strange enough that Sebastian had noticed them years ago when he first developed the photos. Peculiar enough that he remembered them today when the man strode into the Trager City precinct and poured whatever poison into the Chief's ear that stopped him questioning Abby.

'Vepars', they were called, the witch killers who took Claire. They had taken another, and the man, the detective, was involved. Sebastian did not know how, but he would find out. Finally, the chapters of this saga—this obsession—were filing into place.

He shoved the photo into his pocket and glanced at the door. Abby slept a single wall away, and he considered. He should not drag her into his mess, but he felt drawn to Sydney's house and Abby, for whatever reason, had discovered the body. She played a part, somehow. He had learned to read the signs, to take nothing for granted and so he must keep her close. He must ensure that she continued to provide him with answers even if she had not yet found them herself.

Chapter 4

Abby woke with a single moan of terror. Her eyes flipped open to the empty room. She was alive, safe, in Sydney's bed. Her breath slowed, and she took in the golden dusk of the bedroom. The shades, only partially drawn, revealed the swiftly setting sun and its final glow before succumbing to the night. She sat up, tilted her head back and to each side, feeling the tiny creaks that had wedged from the morning's anxiety. Sydney's captain bed was tall, but a little wooden ladder butted to the side. She rolled over and crawled woozily down the steps.

She sniffed at the air, noticing the first traces of something delectable. Her stomach snarled with yearning, and she realized that it had been nearly twenty-four hours since she had eaten.

Her longing to look decent slightly outweighed her hunger and she hurried to the bathroom to survey the damage. Her hair, matted to the left side of her face, needed a brushing, and she scraped a toothbrush across her furry teeth, happy to remove a layer of film. She applied lip-gloss and tried to enliven her red-rimmed brown eyes with a spot of mascara. She lingered for a moment before the mirror and stared.

She felt foolish for caring. Nothing like a dead body to make everything else trivial, but Sebastian hovered in her mind. He was very attractive after all, albeit a bit strange, and though she didn't feel ready to even consider a new boyfriend, she didn't want to look like a swamp rat around him. With Nick, appearance had been easy. He liked plain, he liked when she wore long gray skirts and sweaters that her mother knitted, and it was not the kind of 'like' that came with accepting people as they were and loving them in sweats and all that nonsense. It was the 'like' derived from the security of having a conformist girlfriend who fit into the happy wife Jell-O mold of his life.

In Sydney's closet she found a pair of worn blue jeans, a gaping hole in the right kneecap, and struggled into them, grunting with the effort of dressing while only half awake.

She dug through a pile of shirts, and her hand flicked over a pointed corner. She wrestled it free and found herself looking at the smiling faces of her mother and Sydney. The sisters must have been only sixteen or seventeen, but even then their distinct personalities were evident in their clothing choices. Abby's mother wore tapered khakis that hung on her narrow waist and a crisp white blouse. Sydney was dressed in a purple velvet mini dress, the plunging neckline revealing her bronzed and perky cleavage. They stood, arms linked, in front of Sydney's car, a shiny, black Stingray Corvette that Sydney had gushed to Abby about on more than one occasion. Becky's smile was pinched and uncomfortable, her thin lips and horsey teeth almost homely next to Sydney's wide, red-lipped grin. In the background, Abby spotted her grandmother, Arlene.

Abby slipped the photo back into the clothes and pulled out a loose fitting gray cashmere sweater. Quickly yanking the sweater over her head, her stomach won the battle over beauty, and she lurched out of the room in search of dinner.

The smell of spaghetti, a childhood favorite, pervaded the hallway as she hurried down the stairs.

Sebastian whisked through the kitchen, humming along to an internal tune, a pink apron with pig ears tied snugly around his waist.

She unsuccessfully muffled a laugh and he turned towards her.

"Ah, she wakes." He grinned, holding a tomato-covered spatula in the air. "Sit, sit." He hurried around the counter and pulled out a stool.

He didn't say anything about their strange and stunted conversation from earlier, and she was grateful.

"I think you need a drink." He produced a crystal wineglass and poured her a hefty portion of red wine.

"I don't think that's a serving," she mumbled, surveying the enormous goblet.

"No, you're right." He filled the glass to the top and laughed, sliding it carefully across the counter to her. She had to bend down and sip from the edge to stop it from spilling over.

He went back to his cooking, hustling around the kitchen to stir the sauce, examine the garlic bread and strain the noodles. She could see that he was a liberal garlic user and made a mental note to find mints.

She sipped her wine, initially cringing at the bitter flavor as it hit her tongue. She did not often drink, but hoped that it might chase away the images bobbing on the surface of her thoughts.

In the living room, the telephone rang, and Sebastian slipped away to answer it.

"Abby, it's for you," he called.

She groaned aloud, realizing that only two people would have thought to track her down at Sydney's – Nick and her mother.

Sebastian held the phone out; she took it dubiously, her mind racing for an excuse.

"Abby, is that you?" Nick's voice seethed through the line, and Abby flinched. Sebastian lingered.

Are you okay? he mouthed, pointing at the receiver.

She nodded meekly and started to speak, then thought better of it. Instead, she dropped the phone back into its cradle, shocked by her nerve. Before its shrill ring could start again, she reached back and unplugged the cord, shrugging

34

her shoulders in response to Sebastian's questioning gaze.

"Long story," she told him simply and returned to the kitchen, avoiding his stare.

She settled back onto her stool and traced her fingers along the marbled counter top. Had she really just hung up on Nick?

"So, how are you?" Sebastian asked, returning to the stove, his brows furrowed as if the spaghetti sauce had just become immensely more complex. He continued to stare into the metal pan, his spoon weaving in giant, sloppy circles.

"I don't know," she sighed, pressing the wine glass to her warm forehead. "Shocked, a little sick."

He nodded, but did not respond, choosing instead to don a massive crab claw oven mitt and pull out the garlic bread.

She felt another wave of hunger, her stomach's growls giving way to a full-blown wail.

"Whoa, we better feed that thing." He grinned, sliding the hot pan onto the counter.

Her cheeks flushed and she took another sip of wine, deepening the flush and igniting a wave of lightheadedness.

"This yours?" he asked, holding up the crab claw mitt.

"No, thank you very much," she snapped, and reached for a scalding piece of garlic bread.

"How about the porch?" Sebastian asked, while he scooped spaghetti onto massive dinner plates.

She followed him out, and they set their plates on the round glass patio table that stood in the center of Sydney's back porch.

Night had fallen over the colossal lake sky, the spell of stars stretched hand in hand across the black heavens. The warm air, split by a faint breeze, washed the last of the sleep from her eyes. They ate in silence, the slowly lapping waves and frenzied crickets a musical backdrop that lulled them

35

both into their thoughts.

Abby thought of her parents and Nick. The probable conversations between her mother and Nick as they plotted her capture and return to captivity. Or perhaps that was too harsh. Nick was a person after all, a person who thought he'd found his future wife, a sensible girl who would accompany him to elegant law dinners and iron his button downs. The type of girl who would someday make a fine mother, wife, and not quite domestic servant. She knew that Nick imagined their wedding day, he could picture their unborn children, and he reveled in Sunday dinners with her parents.

At that moment, she felt more disconnected from Nick than she ever had before. In only a day, her world had transformed. In spite of the fear nibbling gently at her mind, she felt hopeful, which quickly brought her thoughts around to the girl or the woman, whatever she was. Abby did not know how to distinguish the two, even for herself. Was she a girl? A girl, who listened to her mother, catered to her boyfriend and followed the lines carefully drawn in for her? Or a woman who turned her back on convention and ran like hell for whatever freedom she could find?

Abby looked at the palm of her hand, the delicate crisscross of lines etched there. She'd heard of palm reading, dissecting a future through the length of lifelines and love lines. What did a murder look like on the palm of a hand? Had this girl's lifeline come to a steep halt? Or had her death been a shock even to the fates that attempted to foresee such things? Abby's hands were small, the lines shallow, she searched the tiny map there and wondered if it had changed the day that she fled Lansing. Had some tiny atomic shift appeared, too minute for her eyes to see?

She looked up at Sebastian then, his blue eyes stuck to hers for a split second before she broke away. She knew that she should speak, say something witty, but her mouth felt papery. She opted for another sip of wine, swishing it over her gums before she swallowed.

A sprinkling of boat lights flickered distantly in the lake. As a child, Sydney had often taken Abby on the lake at night. They crept out while Sydney's husband slept, blankets wrapped tight around their shoulders. Sydney liked the speedboat because it had a large, wrap-around bow with cushy seats, and would bring a bottle of wine for herself and a bottle of carbonated apple juice for Abby. They drank directly from the bottles and shone flashlights into the water in search of fish.

"Have you flown the coop?" Sebastian asked, pulling Abby from her thoughts.

"The coop?" She blinked hard, rubbing away the memories.

"Here, now, your body?"

"I would if I could."

"Feel like sharing?" He leaned back in his chair, tilting his head to the side.

She watched the curve of his lips as he smiled. He had nice full lips, and she lifted a finger to her own self-consciously.

"Perhaps, in a while."

He nodded and then a look of inspiration marked his gaze. "I know what we need." He stood and slipped into the house. She watched his back as he disappeared through the glass door.

She felt a pang of guilt at the rumblings of desire he inspired, as though even her thoughts were monitored and policed, the sanctuary of her brain just another space for control. She had no cause for guilt, she'd done nothing, but she found him alluring, a mysterious attraction that buzzed in the back of her mind. The realization sent another shiver down her spine and the flesh of her arms prickled. It was not

J.R. Erickson

simply his looks, though he was quite a sight, the desire laid more in his freedom. He moved like a man who did and said and thought whatever he pleased. No internal mechanism clamped down on his brain, no alarm system screeched that his actions were rebellious.

The low sound of Billie Holiday's scratchy voice wafted out the door as Sebastian returned to the porch, his arms piled with votive candles. He laid them across the table, quickly lighting them all with a single match.

"Don't worry," he said quickly at the surprised look on her face. "It's all about setting. I'm not trying to take your clothes off."

She laughed uncomfortably and took another sip of wine.

"How about a dance? Something to ease your troubles." He held out his hand.

She stared for a moment, incredulous at his offer. Dance? Could she dance? As she mulled over the possibility, the absurdity of her hesitation struck her. She had packed up and left her whole life, how could she fear a dance?

She thrust her sweaty palm into his, and he pulled her from her seat, keeping her at a safe distance. She felt the stiffness of her posture, obvious against his graceful sway, a piece of plywood to his silk sheet.

His warm hands snaked through her fingers, and she struggled to squeeze tighter. He stood a foot taller than her, staring out at the black night, while she snuck glances at his face. When she'd met him the day before, he'd intimidated her. Not because he behaved arrogantly or with condescension. No, it stemmed from his singleness. He acted as if he belonged only to himself and that no other factor, familial or societal, swayed his choices. There were physical things, too. Abby had grown accustomed to Nick, who wore pleated slacks and button down shirts, even while watching television. Sebastian, on the other hand, was logging day two in his ratty t-shirt and ripped jeans. His hair was uncombed, his face rough with stubble and his eyes like brilliant blue orbs that folded back her flesh and peered far beyond the blood and bone of her body.

"So, this has been like the vacation from Hell for you, huh?" He broke the silence.

"Vacation?"

"Aren't you on vacation?"

Ha, vacation! She laughed aloud at the idea and then shook her head firmly.

"This is not a vacation for me," she told him, pulling away and stuffing her hands into her pockets. "This is a…"

"Sabbatical? Leave of absence? Soul searching expedition?"

She laughed and nodded, appreciating his humor and his company more than she could tell him.

"All of the above and, after today, none of the above."

He nodded and his smile faded, both of their thoughts drifting to death—to the girl.

"It feels bad to laugh," she said quietly.

He sighed and closed his eyes for a long moment. When he opened them, they looked far away, the pupils receding to tiny points.

"Are you okay?" she asked.

He forced a smile, a weak one. "Are we ever okay?"

How true. She didn't feel okay, she felt confused and lost. She wanted to confide in Sebastian, to tell him everything and let him pass some kind of judgment on her, but that was old Abby. The Abby that needed approval and direction, this one was fighting hard to keep it all between her own two ears.

"Where is home, Abby?" he asked suddenly.

"Lansing. Ever been there?"

He grimaced. Obviously, he'd been there. "Passed through a few times, lots of shopping centers."

"Yes, so you can see why I'd rather be here instead."

"Easily, but I still don't understand."

She chewed her lip and tried to imagine a glamorous way to describe abandoning her life. "Well, I kind of ran away." The words flopped out lifelessly, and she immediately regretted them, how juvenile they sounded. "I ran away from my life. It was suffocating me. My boyfriend, my parents, my job…I kept having this nightmare that I was really old, living in my parents' house and sewing booties for Nick's and my prize schnauzers."

He laughed, holding up his hand to stop her. "I'm sorry, it's not funny, but really? Booties for schnauzers? I would have left too."

"Yeah, well, the booties were the least of it."

"Was that him tonight on the phone, Nick?"

"Yeah," Abby sighed, vaguely guilty. "I haven't talked to him yet, weird, huh?"

"Weird is my calling card," Sebastian said, craning his neck back to look at the stars. "Maybe they led you here."

Abby looked up. "The stars?"

"Sure, paths laid out celestially and all that."

Abby cocked an eyebrow at him. "Are you serious?"

"Nah." He shook his head and wandered off the porch, kicking his sandals off at the edge of the grass where the yard ended and the beach began.

She nodded, wondering if her reaction had upset him.

They walked toward the lake. Her bare feet sank into the dewy grass that poked between her toes. She thought about continuing, purging herself of the gory details of her departure, but found the silence comforting. How nice to walk alone with a man and not feel the pressure to make idle small talk.

Though Sydney's house stood on a peninsula, to the east her beach gave way to a several mile expanse of public beach rarely occupied. Behind the beach lay the thick expanse of forest that Abby had wandered only that morning. If they walked far enough along the sandy shore, they could turn into the trees and return to the site of the body. Not that she wanted to—of course not—but…something gnawed there—some pull. Probably just another macabre fantasy, the attraction to a scene of horror, like vultures to road kill.

Together they walked, their feet sinking into the soft, floury sand, still warm from the sun. It felt good to Abby, barefoot, the nearly full moon casting a tunnel of light around them. They might have been lovers on vacation or two strangers finding each other on a seaside walk. His closeness, as they moved, felt deliberate, their arms occasionally brushing and sending sporadic flutters of anxiety along Abby's spine.

Normally, she would have talked. Her fear of silence would be so encompassing that she might have blabbed until she ran out of words in the English language, but instead the silence felt good—too good. In the past, she rarely pursued romantic notions like soul mates or love at first sight, but Sebastian triggered all of these sentiments within her. Not speaking felt like a small step in preserving the moment, encapsulating it by the shroud of silence that acted like a shield around them.

The water drifted lazily like a ribbon undulating along the beach's edge. It played with their toes as they sank into the mushy wetness, pulling away with clumps of sand caked along their feet.

Abby's mind wandered, and she fought back the needling thoughts of her abandoned life, but could not stave off the images of the girl. The girl, the girl, like a thunderstorm hovering over her, electric and frightening and enticing all at once.

"What do you think we should do?" Abby asked.

"About what?"

"The dead girl."

Sebastian paused and stared out at the lake. Abby followed his gaze to the invisible horizon.

"What do *you* want to do?"

She didn't know, but something. She did not feel like a random witness who'd discovered a body. The events of the morning, now seemingly light years away, filled the rooms of her mind. Every door swung open to that patch of woods, to that white naked flesh, to the swirls of red hair.

"Anything, something. I mean, right?"

He looked at her, his eyes bore into her, and he seemed to be contemplating her question very seriously.

"Investigate?" he asked, pulling his feet from the sand and continuing down the beach.

"Yes," she said urgently, excited and scared at the prospect. "Yes. I just, I feel like we should." She caught herself on 'we' and paused. "Not that you have to get involved," she amended quickly, hurrying to keep up with him.

He stopped again, looking worried. "Of course we," he answered roughly. "It would have to be the two of us because…"

"Because what? I'm a girl?" Abby snapped and then laughed at her own overreaction.

"No, because great minds think alike."

She smiled and nodded vigorously. Surely, together they could help. Maybe they could even find the murderer.

"Why do you want to do this?" he asked.

She chewed anxiously on a strand of hair and searched for a brilliant answer that would wipe away any lingering doubts that either of them had.

"No idea," she declared, but with enthusiasm.

He smiled.

Beside them, the water changed. Though no wind had risen, small crests started to roll in the previously calm lake. The tide shot further up the beach, soon swelling around their ankles.

"Strange," Sebastian whispered, breaking the quiet.

They stopped and turned to face the water. Its turbulent swells grew larger into folding white caps. Abby had never seen anything like it, the lake transforming so quickly. It was more than the waves, however. It hung in the air like a softly buzzing energy. She could almost feel her hair lifting with the static electricity surging around them.

Sebastian grinned at her. "This is amazing," he laughed and threw his head back.

As if on cue, the sky opened above them, a deluge of water pouring forth from a bulbous gray cloud that, she could have sworn, had not been there only moments before. Sebastian opened his mouth to the flood of rain.

"Run," he yelled over the besieging storm, and they did. They raced back along the beach, their feet slow in the giving sand, their bodies instantly soaked.

Chapter 5

Abby crawled out of bed and smiled in spite of herself. Streaks of the morning sun ushered across the bedroom floor and warmed her legs.

Downstairs, she found the couch empty, Sebastian's blankets neatly folded at one end, a sticky note on his pillow.

Had some errands, will be back in a couple of hours – *S*, the message read in sloppy cursive.

Errands? She grimaced and crumpled the note. She wanted to get down to business, and now her partner had vanished. Of course, she needed to think of it that way – business. Because how could she think of their plan in any human terms? Murder was not a game of Clue. The images in her mind, the sinking weight of death as it dragged her beneath the surface and forced her eyes wide, her mouth open, was not at all glamorous. On the contrary, the mere thought of the girl's body made her heart thump wildly with fear and rage and guilt.

She brewed coffee and retreated to the living room to watch the news, knowing that facts might chase away the veil of mystery plaguing her. No information allowed for infinite possibilities: rape, cults, disgruntled boyfriends, family feuds. How could she begin to understand why murder happened? But with evidence, with facts, maybe…

A voluptuous blonde reporter stood in front of the forest, microphone held to her lips, as she waved a slender arm back towards the sun filled trees. Her hot pink pantsuit looked out of place on the tree-lined road.

"The name of the woman found in the woods has not been released to the public. However, my sources indicate that she is a local woman, and her death is being investigated as a homicide."

Abby strained toward the television, but the reporter was gone, replaced by an advertisement for bottled water.

She decided to begin her search without Sebastian.

She considered calling the precinct, but then imagined getting Tina on the line and dismissed it as an option.

Her purse sat on the counter, and she dug out her cell phone, battery dead. She could use Sydney's phone, but worried about caller ID. She searched for a pen, and her fingers flicked across the unopened bottle of antidepressants that sat snugly in a zippered pocket. She had picked up the prescription four weeks earlier, but had not taken a single pill. The tiny green and cream capsules stared out at her, and she frowned back at them. A part of her blamed the pills, not for any specific thing, but for years of ambivalence. Only when she stopped consuming them did she finally get the courage to leave the life that she hated. If Nick or her mother had known that she was skipping her Prozac, they would have balked.

She walked the bottle to the sink, unscrewed the cap and poured them into the garbage disposal, smiling in delight as the metal teeth crunched them into oblivion.

She returned to her investigation and flipped idly through the phone book. Scanning the pages she passed C and beneath that Coroner. Bingo. She found a phone number for Cherry Road Coroner's Office and decided to call.

"You've reached Seth at Cherry Road Coroners. How may I help you?" a boy's prepubescent voice cracked.

"Hi, Seth, this is Officer Smith," Abby lied. "I just have a few questions about the body, if you've got a second."

She felt like a horrible imposter, but if it worked she was a genius.

"Oh, yes, of course, Officer. What do you need? My dad's back there right now with the Chief."

45

"Yes, Chief Caplan, he's great, isn't he?" she blurted and then scrunched her forehead and took a deep breath. "I just need to get the exact spelling of the deceased's name." Her voice wavered, and she feared that she had blown her cover.

"Yep, hold on just a sec."

She waited, her stubby fingernails drumming on the counter. Seconds passed, and she wondered if he had to ask his dad, igniting the Chief's suspicions.

"Okay, it looks like her first name is spelled D-E-V-I-N. Last name is B-L-A-K-E. Anything else?" he asked, eager to please.

Abby scribbled the name quickly. "No, that's all I need, thanks."

She hung up the phone and stared at the name: Devin Blake. It sounded masculine, not what she might have attributed to the red haired beauty.

Sydney did not have a computer, claiming that its absence made the lake house woodsy. Well, woodsy in Sydney's version, but that didn't stop her from decking the place out in every other modern convenience imaginable. It was more likely that Sydney kept computers out because she didn't know how to use them and didn't want to feel dated.

Abby ripped off the sheet of paper and walked to her car. She drove the to the public library, taking what Sydney called the 'scenic route' to avoid getting stuck in the traffic jam most likely occurring outside of the crime scene.

The library occupied a squat, brick building that smelled of mothballs. The librarian was probably not a librarian at all, but a local girl who got paid peanuts to point wayward patrons to fiction vs. nonfiction or shelve big boxes of books according to their ridiculously long numbers, something like ATR4539YTu. Abby knew because she had worked at a library for two years during college, and despite her love of books, hated every minute of it.

The girl at the desk held a tattered copy of *Rose Madder* inches from her face, her brown eyes magnified behind thick-lensed glasses. Tempted to ask the young librarian if she knew the dead girl, Abby veered to the nearest shelf and peeked at her from between the books. She looked about twenty, but if Abby gave out Devin's name she might arouse suspicion. She decided to ask for help without any specifics.

"Hi," Abby said politely, approaching the girl who looked up, surprised.

"How can I help you?" the girl squeaked, sliding her book beneath the desk.

"I was wondering if you keep local yearbooks here?" Abby tried to feign only mild interest.

"Absolutely," the girl chirped, jumping down from her chair.

She came around the desk, and Abby followed. They turned into a well-lit backroom where shelves were lined with newspapers, yearbooks, and magazines.

"The little yellow stickers give the graduation date," the girl told her, pointing to the tiny yellow tabs. "Anything else?"

"No, this is perfect."

The girl retreated to the front, eager to return to her book, and Abby walked the rows of neatly shelved yearbooks, searching for 2004 and 2005, assuming that Devin would have graduated in one of these years. She flipped through the books, her fingers brushing the glossy pages as she scanned columns of student names. The 2005 book had no Blakes at all, nor did the 2004. She opened them back up, deciding to look through faces of each graduating class. Again, the 2005 book revealed nothing. However, as she peered at the faces in 2004, she stopped. Devin was pictured, but the name printed was Devin Kent, not Blake. Why had the coroner given her the name Devin Blake? Could she have been married? She seemed so young.

The redhead gazed back at her, poised in front of a towering birch tree. Although her face was slightly out of focus, Abby recognized the mass of red curls that fell over her right shoulder. She wore long, black, billowy pants and a tight, black corset that laced up the front in purple ribbon; her head was cocked at an angle as she stared at the overflowing branches above her. Her lips, painted reddish-black, were blood-like against her milky skin. Devin did not look like an average teenager smiling vainly at the camera. Instead, she looked regal, as if the photo belonged in the history text of some long dead royal family. Unlike the other graduating students, Devin did not have a trailing list of sports and activities. Only one group appeared below her name: 'Trager High Club for the Arts.'

Abby found two more listings for Kent: Danny Kent and Eliza Kent. She flipped to their pictures. Danny, listed as a junior, looked nothing like Devin. He had short, spiky black hair and a large Roman nose. The girl, Eliza, was a freshman who also did not resemble Devin. She was plump and her thick brown hair was pulled over each shoulder, partially obscuring her round face.

Abby wrote down the two names and the art club, contemplating where to go next in her search. She could probably track down a phone number, maybe even an address, but what if the family did not know of her death? If they did and were grieving, they might be angry for Abby's disruption. At the same time, she felt that her investigation would be stalled without speaking to the girl's family. She wished that Sebastian could help and wondered if he had returned to the house.

* * * *

Back at Sydney's, where there was still no sign of Sebastian, Abby searched through the yellow pages and found five Kent listings in Trager. She tried to rehearse her questions, but they sounded hollow and insincere. Finally, she just dialed the first number.

The call went straight to the voicemail of Donald Kent, who was in Barbados until October. The next clicked to an operator who informed Abby that the phone number was disconnected. On the third call, she got an answer.

"What?" The young voice, rude and unapologetic, startled Abby into silence.

"Umm, hi, sorry, I'm from the *Lansing News*..." She trailed off, hoping that she had gotten the right number.

"Listen, I've already talked to the police. What do you want?"

Jackpot. Her hand trembled, and she leaned her elbow on the table to steady it.

"Yes, I'm very sorry for your loss. I was hoping to ask you a few questions about Devin."

The listener sighed, and Abby feared the click of his receiver.

"There ain't much to tell. Devin hasn't lived here fer two years and even when she did, she hated it. Once she got started tryin' to find her birth parents, we just became a pile of trash hold'n her back."

Well, that explained her name change.

"I understand, and you are Devin's brother, then?"

He snorted loudly and laughed. "Uh, yeah, I guess you could say that."

He didn't add more and Abby hurried on. "So, where was Devin living for the last two years?"

"Listen, lady, I'm not her babysitter, okay. I already

49

told the police I don't know. I heard she had a boyfriend, but I ain't ever saw him."

Abby scribbled furiously, wishing that she had made a list of questions after all.

"How about your parents? Are they at home?"

"No, they ain't at home. And for your information, it's parent. My ma's been dead for ten years."

"I'm very sorry to hear that, Danny. It is Danny, right?"

"Yeah, it was Danny, but I can't talk no more."

Click.

Abby held the receiver in her hand, realizing that her vice-like grip had caused her flesh to turn stark white. She dropped the phone back into its cradle and stared at her scrawled comments, trying to make sense of them.

Danny, far from distraught, didn't even sound sad. Apparently, not a very happy home at the Kents'. Scanning each word, she wondered how she could find the boyfriend.

Sydney's clock, a giant black cat with whiskers for hands, showed almost four pm. Still no Sebastian, but Abby didn't mind – she could feel the wheels turning.

She wondered briefly if her desire to solve the murder arose from a need to distract. She refused the thought and returned to her notes – they looked a bit blurry. She needed a break. A quick run to the grocery store would give her one, then she could make Sebastian dinner. She considered leaving him a message, but decided not to; it seemed too formal, writing notes back and forth like an estranged married couple.

* * * *

The small grocery store bustled with the talk of death. Abby listened to the stories as tourists and locals circled the shelves, stocking up on marshmallows and hot dogs. She made a beeline for the rack of gourmet items, looking at jars of imported olives and Spanish chocolates. She was not a great cook, not even a mediocre cook, but she persisted anyway.

She picked up a small plastic basket and loaded it with makeshift gourmet options: chocolate truffles, basil, lemon, asparagus, salmon, capers, and a bottle of merlot. On second thought, Sydney kept the wine pantry stocked at all times, so she put the merlot back and grabbed a baguette instead.

As she continued through the store, she perked up at the name Devin, barely audible in the cereal aisle. She wanted to peek around the corner, but didn't dare, fearing that the talkers might see her.

"Yes, I told you, my boyfriend's little brother is best friends with Seth, who is the son of the coroner, and he said it was Devin Kent or whatever her name is now..." The female voice, gossipy, came out in a harsh whisper.

"I cannot believe it. I mean she was weird, but who would want to kill her?" A huskier female voice responded.

They both grew silent, and Abby could hear a customer's cart squeak noisily down the aisle, boxes of cereal plunking in. A short, round woman in a polka dot sundress walked from between the shelves, her squeaking cart continually veering to the left as she tried to wrestle it towards the checkout lane.

The girls carried on, sounding much closer to where Abby stood, her head strained in their direction.

"I heard she joined a cult, probably something that guy she was dating started..."

"What was his name? Todd or Tommy or something?"

"Yeah, something like that. I never actually saw him, so she probably just made him up."

The girls turned the corner, crashing smack into Abby, who barely caught her basket before dumping the contents onto the floor. The girls, both in their late teens, rolled their eyes in irritation and walked on. The shorter one, her dark, bobbed curls bouncing rhythmically, turned once to glare at Abby before they moved into the frozen aisle. Abby looked down, embarrassed, and headed for the counter.

She stood in line listening to snippets of conversations. Campers, afraid that it was a night stalker; the cashier claiming that she saw a strange van parked on the street just days earlier. One man talked loudly about Big Foot and despite the several, *shut up, Jerry's* that came from his severe-looking wife, he continued in earnest. Each theory sounded ridiculous, but Abby hung on every word.

As she waited, determining what mess she might create with her basket of unrelated ingredients, she tallied in her mind the day's clues. She knew that the body was a young woman, Devin, and that she had a boyfriend named Tommy or Todd. Devin was adopted, her brother seemed unhappy, and someone wanted to murder her.

A sharp look from the woman in front of her made Abby realize that she'd been murmuring under her breath, an embarrassing habit of hers.

"Don't think out loud, Abigail," her mother used to scold her. "You'll get sent away!"

She clamped her teeth closed and stared at the ground before her, wishing that the line would hurry up.

A puff of breath slid across Abby's neck, and she shifted uncomfortably. Why did people have to stand so close in checkout lines? She felt it again, cold and wet, more like air from the freezer than breath. Moving ahead, she looked down and backwards, but saw no feet planted on the dirty linoleum. She turned fully, scanning the candy racks to her right, but behind her the line was empty. Along the nape of her neck, she felt goose-bumps pulling her skin taut and knew that she had not imagined the breath.

She scanned the store, eyes moving quickly across heads and over carts. They caught on a dark patch, blurred because the person stood behind a freezer. The man, it had to be a man, he looked so tall, stood in the frozen aisle, but a wide freezer displaying microwave pizzas blocked him. Abby did not want to look at him directly because she could feel his gaze slicing through the glass and across the store, landing on her. Her skin crawled, and she pretended to examine a magazine. 'Lose Ten Pounds in Ten Days,' it said. She slid her eyes off the glossy cover and back toward the man, searching for his dark shape, but the space stood empty.

"Next, please. *Next,* please." The irritated voice of the cashier broke into Abby's thoughts, and she jerked her head around. The cashier, a middle-aged woman with soft pools of skin beneath her eyes, glared at Abby and waved impatiently.

Abby heaved her basket onto the belt and scuttled forward, shooting a final glance behind her at the empty aisle where the man had stood. She wondered if the figure was simply an ordinary patron picking up a pizza. She shook her head *no* at the thought; she had felt his eyes on her.

"Like someone walking over your grave," Sydney used to say, when Abby got the chills. The thought made her shudder anew.

Had Devin noticed chills in recent weeks as people traipsed through the woods, carelessly stomping where her body would lie?

"Cash or check?" the cashier snapped, staring Abby down across the counter, her stiff polo shirt ballooning out to make her chest look enormous.

Abby handed her cash and smiled, wondering about the mystery man who'd been watching her.

Chapter 6

Sebastian's small black car sat in Sydney's driveway.

"Hi, there," he called to her as she trotted up the porch steps.

"Hey," she gushed, grabbing the lawn chair next to his. "I did some research today."

His lithe body was stretched across a padded lawn chair, his arm hanging over the edge and a tall Margarita at his fingertips.

"Yeah?" He sat up and swung his legs around, planting his bare feet on the deck.

"Yes." Abby pulled her notes from her back pocket and folded them on the chair next to her. "Her name was Devin Kent or Blake. She was adopted, so she changed it, but…"

"Whoa, tiger," he said, holding up a hand and then taking a long swig from his Margarita. "I was thinking Mexican."

Abby sniffed at the air, catching the first whiff of salsa and cheese.

"Oh, great," she moaned, holding up the groceries.

"Hey, no worries." He grinned, his laugh followed by a blast of hot tequila breath. Abby shrank away from him.

"Are you drunk?" she asked, surprised.

He raised an eyebrow and licked the rim of his glass, salt flecking his lower lip. "That depends. Will you love me anyway?" He stood shakily from his chair, leaning hard on the backrest and nearly stumbling over. "I'm fine, don't worry, I'm fine." He laughed, teetered a bit, then found his balance and wandered into the house. "Let's eat."

She watched him, half in awe and half in horror. She wanted to fill him in on Devin and force him to concentrate, but could clearly see he'd made some progress on his

Margaritas, plural. Following him into the house, she watched as he piled his plate with tacos. Cheese and lettuce fell in clumps onto the hardwood floor.

"Oops," he laughed.

"I'm gonna run upstairs and change," she told him, escaping to Sydney's bedroom.

She sat on the bed and stared at her notes, finally folding the sheet of paper and setting it on the bedside table. She didn't mind that he was drunk, in fact, she could understand why he wanted to be, but still, she felt slightly rebuked. Hadn't they planned to investigate—together?

She dug in Sydney's closet and found a knee length red sweater dress. Not, by any means, Abby's normal attire, but all the more appealing because of it. She slid it on and admired herself in the mirror, pulling the sides of her brown hair half up and clipping them with a small green barrette.

"Eat your heart out, Sebastian," she laughed, blushing at her boldness.

In Sydney's bathroom, she dotted pale, pink lipstick on her lips, puckering and smiling. Her skin looked pasty beneath the fluorescent bathroom globes, but her eyes sparkled.

Coffee. She would brew a pot of coffee and force Sebastian to sober up, so they could get to work.

"Nice," Sebastian whistled when she returned to the kitchen.

"Thanks," she mumbled and grabbed a plate.

"No, no, not like that." Sebastian took her sparsely stocked plate. He laid the tortillas flat and loaded them with chicken, lettuce, tomato, cheese and sour cream, carefully folding them and sticking toothpicks in the centers.

Abby watched, tempted to protest, she didn't much care for cheese, but allowed him to continue. He licked his fingers as he worked, humming a tune that Abby didn't recognize, and taking frequent sips from an open bottle of Tequila.

"Let's call it quits on this," she said, grabbing the bottle and screwing the cap on.

"Huh?" He looked up at her bleary eyed, glanced at the bottle and then shrugged. "To the porch!" He held her plate high and walked out the door.

She set the coffee maker and followed him to the patio table, rushing forward to grab her plate when he nearly dumped it on his chair as he struggled to pull it out.

In the center of the table stood a fat cobalt vase filled with red flowers, their petals bleeding orange in the candlelight. She looked at him and then at the flowers, but he only stared dazedly at his food, finally taking a sloppy bite, spilling cheese down his shirt.

"Beautiful," she said, leaning in to smell them as he swiped at the falling food. "What are these?" She pointed to a prickly looking flower with a red tip and yellow base, hoping to start a conversation that might pull him from his drunken reverie.

"Those are red hot pokers," he murmured, running his fingers over the spiky surface. "And the others are geraniums and red nasturtiums."

She smiled, surprised. She had expected something less coherent.

"All red, huh?" she teased. "Got a thing for redheads?"

"Actually, I'm partial to brunettes," he told her, pulling back from the flowers and staring at her. "These flowers are said to protect."

"Protect what?" she asked, though her mind was still stuck on the brunettes comment and the way his red-rimmed eyes burned into her.

"Oh, I don't know, it's just superstition, nothing serious. So, tell me about your day." He stopped eating and folded his hands on the table in front of him, shaking his head once, hard, as if a fog had gathered there.

"Don't worry. Coffee is brewing," she said.

"A necessary evil."

"Yes, less evil than other vices though, I'm sure."

"Uh, oh, the alcohol police?" he asked, lolling his head to the side quizzically.

"No." She yawned, stretching her arms overhead and admiring the rosy sky as evening trickled in. "I just thought that we were going to talk about…"

"The girl."

"Yes."

"So, talk then. What did you discover, Sherlock?"

She bristled at his sarcastic tone and considered not telling him anything, suddenly angry that he was drunk and feeling confused about their relationship.

"Never mind," she said, lifting her own Margarita and nearly draining it. Her brain screamed as the icy drink needled into its center, but she bit back her scowl of pain.

His eyes softened, and he leaned forward, balancing his elbows clumsily on the table.

"Hey, I'm sorry, really. Tequila creeps you up. On you. Up on you."

She laughed and shrugged, ready to forgive. She didn't, after all, have anyone else to talk to, and she liked Sebastian, drunk or not.

"Tell me what you found."

"Well," she started, not bothering to retrieve her notes. "Devin was her name, and she was adopted by a family named Kent. She had an adopted brother and sister, but apparently she was looking for her biological family."

Sebastian nodded, considering. "That it?"

"No, she also had a boyfriend, whose name started with a T and she was local, went to Trager High School."

"Name started with a T?"

"Yep."

He traced circles on the table, but didn't speak. His eyes went in and out of focus, and Abby wondered if he would remember their conversation tomorrow.

"Tobias? Did you hear that name at all?"

Abby thought back to the grocery store. "No, Tommy or Todd was what these girls said. No Tobias."

"Coffee," Sebastian said suddenly, standing up and walking through the screened door to the kitchen.

* * * *

Abby finished her taco, wiped a napkin along her lips, and waited. She could hear Sebastian in the kitchen, coffee mugs clanking together. The sound of crunching gravel drew her eyes away from the house. Headlights illuminated the porch and momentarily blinded her.

When she heard footsteps advancing across the driveway and onto the porch, she thought of Sydney and jumped from her chair in excitement. But the silhouette was too large, too broad shouldered, and as Nick's face come into view, she gasped and stumbled backward, her hand striking the vase of flowers, which tipped and shattered. Glass and water dripped through the wrought-iron table, red petals splayed across the dark metal, their dinner plates pooled with the spilled water.

Sebastian ran out of the house, coffee slopping from his mug. He stopped abruptly, eyes trained on Nick, whose fists were balled at his sides.

"What the hell is going on here?" Nick snarled, his eyes on Abby, but shifting repeatedly to Sebastian.

Abby stood paralyzed, registering Nick's rage, Sebastian's shock and the red flowers, dead, wasted.

"Nick," she stammered, finding a child's voice instead of her own.

Sebastian stepped to Abby's side, facing Nick and arrogantly appraising him.

"Everything okay here?" He touched Abby's elbow lightly.

Nick's eyes narrowed in on the small gesture, and he took a reactionary step forward.

Nick, usually cool and collected, looked disheveled. His short, blond hair stood in spiky tufts around his head, and his clothes were rumpled. His meticulously dry-cleaned slacks showed creases from sitting too long, and Abby noticed a distinct smear of something brown on his left knee.

"Yes, fine," she said, quickly moving away from Sebastian and toward Nick, who regarded her with a mingled look of disgust and alarm.

Sebastian understood and backed away, turning to the table to unsuccessfully mop up the mess with their napkins.

Abby took Nick's hand, which shook in her own, and pulled him toward the house.

"Let's talk inside," she said as he twisted to glare at Sebastian a final time.

Nick did not speak, but pulled a chair out from the counter and sat down heavily. His green eyes were spotted with small bursts of red veins, and the usually smooth skin of his face was rough with blond stubble. He shaved every morning, every single morning, but today, clearly, he had not.

Abby searched for words, perhaps an apology, while pulling down two mugs and filling them with coffee. The scalding fluid released tendrils of steam into the air, little phantoms eavesdropping on their conversation, and Abby wished for the power to send them across the room and whisk Nick away into the night.

"Please, speak," Nick demanded, cupping his hands around the mug as if the ceramic were not blistering. "Your mother is worried sick. Do you know that? Do you even care?"

Did she even care? She didn't know. Leaving had been the hardest part and once that was over she felt renewed, freed, but now here was Nick reminding her that he still remained, as did her mother and the long snaking threads of her old life, continually trying to pull her back in, to force her into the pattern and make her disappear forever.

Abby sipped from her mug. She could see Sebastian on the porch, his head still as if he were listening.

Nick noticed. "Who the fuck is that?" He pointed his finger angrily at Sebastian, and she felt small and hated him for it.

"None of your business."

Nick's eyes widened in surprise, and he stood roughly from his chair, knocking it backward onto the hardwood floor. It clattered, and Sebastian moved close to the screen door.

"Just stop, okay," Abby snapped, walking around and grabbing the chair, putting it upright.

She held her ground against Nick, who stood a foot taller than her, his square face pinched angrily.

She knew that he had not expected this. Not expected his sweet little Abby to stand up to him, and now he didn't know how to react. He paced away from her, stuffing his hands into his pockets, finally spinning around to confront her again. "Fine, you're unhappy, explain. Enlighten me, Abby, okay, what makes your life so miserable?"

She hated his tone, his patronizing stare, and could not figure out how she had lasted two years with Nick; Nick and his obsessive cleaning, his infinite expectations, and most of all, his criticism, carefully woven into his every thought, word and action.

"You know what, Nick?" Abby said, suddenly tired. "I'm sick of you. I'm sick of our life. I'm sick of your fake personality and your bullshit friends. I am so sick—" She moved towards him then, glad when he started to back away "—of everything that you represent. I'm finished."

He stared at her, and she watched the raging façade crack. His pupils shrank, and the set of his jaw slid down, drooping beneath his mouth, which was turned in painfully. He took his hands from his pockets and held them out flat.

As he crumbled on the outside, she felt a mean little flower bloom in her chest.

"Abby, wait." He swallowed hard, and his eyes pooled with tears. He braced a hand on the wall next to him and looked down, his face flaring again angrily.

Abby realized that his gaze had alighted on a pile of clothes on the floor, Sebastian's and hers, their laundry from the previous day. It looked bad; she could see Sebastian's green boxer briefs nestled against her shorts.

"No." He shook his head, slowly, sickly, and looked up at her, his eyes searching her face.

She started to deny the accusation and then stopped. The petals unfurled beneath her ribs.

"What?" she asked. "That—" She jerked her head toward the clothes "—is none of your business."

He squatted down and fingered the fabric of her shorts. She leaned forward and ripped them away.

"Leave," she said.

He looked up, wounded and pitiful.

Jolts of shock and guilt coursed through her, but the flower continued to open and fill the cavity where Nick used to live. He started to cry, and a cruel laugh bubbled inside her. She tried to contain it, but could not. The laugh erupted and poured over his down-turned head. This time, he did not look at her with shock. A change had come over him; a recognition that Abby, his Abby, was gone.

Chapter 7

After Nick's taillights disappeared down the long driveway, Abby returned to the porch where Sebastian sat, gulping his second mug of coffee.

She sat on the step next to him.

"Cheers," he said, clanging their cups together.

Her coffee had grown cold.

"The famous Nick," she said, staring out at the water, dark now, except for an orange moon rising behind the trees.

"Quite charming, especially the murderous glint in his eye," Sebastian joked, stretching his legs out long before him. He set his mug on the step and slapped at a mosquito that landed on his calf.

"Yes," Abby murmured, but didn't have the heart to re-hash Nick. Already, she didn't want to face her viciousness towards him. The bud of cruelty that she'd nurtured, and still felt, throbbed in her chest. Never in their two years had Abby been spiteful towards Nick. Their fights fizzled quickly because she never took him on. If he got angry, she relented, it was easier that way.

Sebastian rifled in his pocket and pulled out some lint, two quarters and a rock. "Quarter for your thoughts? Or a rock?"

She took the rock and looked at it closely, running her fingers along the rough edges.

"Sandstone," he said.

"And you carry it because…?"

"Because I am a rock collector, clearly."

"Really?"

"No, but my back seat will make you believe that I'm lying. I have a thing for picking up interesting rocks."

"Hmm." She rubbed the rock along her palm. It left a rusty streak.

"Keep it. Might help calm you down."

"I'm calm," she said quickly, handing the rock back.

"No, really." He folded her fingers around it. "Rocks are more powerful than you think."

She considered it, turning the diamond shaped sandstone over. She liked the idea of something so small, so seemingly insignificant, being powerful.

"No pockets," she said, setting the rock on the porch.

"Do you need to talk about this?" Sebastian asked.

She pursed her lips and let her eyes wander along the shore. The water was a flat mirror, black with an expanding cone of light as the moon rose higher in the sky, its red body growing yellow and eventually white.

She didn't want to talk, not about herself anyway.

"Let's talk about you," she said, turning so that her knees brushed against his.

"What's to know?"

"Everything."

"We'll be here for ten years just covering how Randy Mull used to kick my ass in kindergarten."

Abby laughed, watching Sebastian as he hopped up and retrieved their Margaritas from the patio table.

"Don't worry, I picked the glass out," he joked.

"I thought we were off Tequila and on coffee."

He grinned. "Coffee was fine for dinner, but we're having relationship therapy now."

"Ha." She took a drink and grimaced, as this one was stronger than her last. "My love life will not be tonight's feature."

"Oh, curse it," he moaned. "Fine, just tell me then, what you saw in Jack the Jock, I mean other than his rippling muscles."

Abby pulled her dress down, trying to cover her white thighs peeking from beneath the fabric. She searched for the answer, but knew how deeply buried the truth was, and she had no energy for digging.

"No, you've gotten a first-hand look at the disaster that is my life. Tell me about yours, preferably something nasty that makes mine seem better in comparison."

"That calls for more Tequila."

He ran inside and out again, carefully holding two shot glasses and the fifth of alcohol.

"Let's make a game of this, eh? One shot gets one answer, for you and me both."

Abby's lip curled as she looked at the amber liquid. She had only a single memory of Tequila shots, and they involved Nick, several of his hoity-toity law school friends and Abby vomiting on the dinner table. Not only did she ruin dessert—cherry cheesecake—but also Nick chastised her every time she had a glass of wine for months afterward.

"Hey, try to contain your excitement," he laughed, setting the liquor on the table and pulling Abby to her feet. He yanked her chair out, and she settled into it, staring at the bottle like an evil Genie might pour forth at any moment. "I'll go first."

He poured himself a shot, the Tequila sloshing over the tiny glass. The fumes rose in the air and tickled Abby's nostrils.

"What is your favorite movie?" He held the shot high and then downed it. "You have to answer because I already took the shot."

"Fine," she said, giving in and pulling her own glass towards her. "My favorite movie is Jaws."

She poured a shot, a much smaller one and held it up.

"You cheated me," he said, laughing. "I need some explanation. Why Jaws?"

"That wasn't the question. Now, my turn, where are you from exactly?"

"Drink."

"No, answer me and then I'll drink."

He groaned and leaned his chair back, scrambling forward when he nearly tipped over.

"I am from Ohio." He scratched his chin. "A boring town by the name of Grimville, yes, the name says it all."

"Go on."

"That's it. Grimville, the suburbs, population twelve humans and seven thousand cows. Now drink!"

She took the shot, fighting her gag reflex, and immediately followed it with a gulp of bitter coffee. It burned all the way down, maybe hotter than the bile waiting to dissolve it.

"My turn." He poured another shot. "Why did you leave home?" He choked a bit on his drink, some dribbling down his chin, and used the collar of his t-shirt to sop it up.

"Specifics, too, please, otherwise we're going to finish the bottle before I find out your last name."

"I left home because…" She paused, the shot already blurring the concrete images in her mind. Why had she left home? "Because everything felt wrong."

"How so?"

"Well, I hated my job, my mother got weekly updates from my boyfriend on my behavior, and my boyfriend, well, you met him. He thought I was a naughty puppy who needed constant supervision."

Sebastian nodded and licked his lips. "Yeah, he seemed a bit controlling."

"He was, but it wasn't just him. I mean it wasn't him at all really. It was me. A few weeks ago, I'd just had enough, and every day became the longest, worst day of my life."

"I've been there," he said.

Abby filled her glass. "When?"

Sebastian smiled and nudged the shot towards her.

She took it. "When?"

"When? Well, a couple times." His eyes glazed, and he focused hard on his hands. "The first time was when my parents were killed in a car accident."

Abby inhaled loudly and started to apologize, but Sebastian interrupted her.

"And the second time was when my sister got murdered."

Abby felt a stab of guilt, a sudden shrinking as she considered her own, much smaller, problems. She reached a hand out to his, pressing hard on his fingers.

"I'm sorry, I…" She hesitated, searching, but the alcohol made it less real, death and pain and loss. How could she comfort him? How could anyone?

"Listen," he spoke loudly, his drunkenness becoming obvious again. "Tit for tat, no apologies here."

She nodded and almost stopped him when he poured another shot, gulping it immediately.

"Do you want to go swimming?"

"That's your question?" she asked.

"Yes, there's nothing that squelches thought like the weight of the sea."

She turned toward the lake, remembering night swims with Sydney. Wading out into the dark water, blind to the creatures swimming beneath the surface. She even swam a few times in the lake alone, stripping her bikini off in the water and drifting lazily, her tight skin exposed to the moon.

"That looks like a yes," he said excitedly, standing.

"Wait." She held up a hand. "Are you sure you're fine to swim?"

He laughed, grabbed the bottle and took another long drink. "Better than fine."

He jumped off the porch and raced across the yard. She watched him fling off his shirt and shorts as he ran, splashing into the water in his boxers.

She ran inside and up the stairs, ripping off Sydney's dress and leaving it in a heap on the floor. Feeling like a kid again, she pulled on a black and white polka dot one-piece and sprinted back outside. She did not hesitate or second-guess herself as she dashed into the water. He was a bit further out, but swam towards her, kicking giant splashes that rained over her head. She squealed and splashed him back, cupping her hands and catapulting water bombs that mostly fell short of his laughing face.

He lay on his back and scissored a plume of water towards her, which she dodged, diving below the surface. Every muscle and fiber of her body surged with energy, and she played. Played in a way that she had never done, even as a child under the apprehensive eyes of her mother.

She belly flopped next to him, sending a wave of water cascading over his dark curls. He ran to the beach and down Sydney's dock, flying off the end into a loose cannon ball. She grinned and followed suit, her cannonball making a much smaller dent in the shiny water. Back and forth they went, swan dives, back smackers – Sebastian even did a front flip. For a while every other thought, memory and pain was forced beneath the water and held there, gone from sight and mind.

The faint echo of the telephone called from the house, but they both ignored it, continuing their reckless excursion.

"Race ya," he screamed and began a ferocious freestyle deep into the lake.

Abby, always a strong swimmer, kept pace, a much faster pace than even she was used to. Apparently all those boring days in the office hadn't killed her aerobic capacity after all. She felt her lungs straining, but she thrust forward, her thighs and shoulders burning. He finally stopped, paddling in place and they both leaned back in the water, waving their arms in circles as they stared at the tinsel flecked sky. Abby could feel the ripples of water that his body made, hear the rapid, shallow breaths as his heart-rate returned to normal. The Tequila buzz continued, but the cool water had blurred its edge.

"And back," he yelled, startling her as he drove himself toward the shore in a floppy butterfly swim that reminded her of a drowning seagull.

Rather than follow, Abby watched. She saw Sebastian climb onto the dock, backing up to gain running speed. She trod water, loving the smooth glide as her legs scissored beneath her. She bobbed below the surface and opened her eyes. The moon streamed into the water like light bullets, casting streaks of shining green on her legs and torso. She dived deeper, then deeper still, until she must have swum fifteen feet straight down. She reached the sandy bottom, beyond the moon's probing fluorescent fingers, but strangely, she could still see. Thick vines of seaweed grew towards the nighttime sun, their bodies shifting as she displaced the water around them. As she swam, her vision became more and more clear, her eyes seeking out small fish further into the lake and opalescent shells smothered by tiny white zebra muscles.

Not out of breath, though she should have been, she kicked off the lake floor and shot toward the surface. She felt a vicious pull on her head and was raked from the water, a hand thrust deep into her hair.

Panic seized her. "Ouch! Stop! Ow!" she screamed, beating at her captor.

For a moment, the struggle ensued, Abby clawing at her attacker while trying to swim away.

"Relax! Stop, you're panicking!" Sebastian screamed

J.R. Erickson

in her ear, pulling his hand free of her hair and forcing it under her armpit and across her chest.

"I am not panicking," she spat, prying his arm loose.

She swam into chest deep water and turned to face him.

"What the hell do you think you're doing?" Her head ached where he had pulled her hair.

"I'm sorry," he sputtered, looking confused as he moved towards her in the water. "You were under for so long. I thought you were drowning."

His normally tan face glowed sickly white, and Abby could see the fear draining from his features. She had been beneath the water a long time, but it couldn't have been too long. She was still alive, after all. The shock had sobered them both, and she rubbed the heels of her hands into her eyes, fuzzy from opening them beneath the water.

"I'm sorry." She shook her head and reached up gingerly to the soft spot on her scalp. "I was under a long time."

"I didn't mean to hurt you." He gestured toward her head. "I freaked out."

He waded toward her and together they walked to the beach, collapsing on the sand. They lay side by side, allowing their breath to slow. She felt the heat of his arm pressed against her own.

He rolled on his side. "How did you do that?"

His body blocked the moonlight, and she could only see the shadow of his features. She wondered if he was still upset.

"I'm not sure," she told him, perplexed. "I just had a lot of air, I guess."

He did not speak, chewing silently on her uncertain answer. Abby knew that the moment had vanished, and their carefree feelings were as lost as the sand she absently cupped in her fingers.

"Abby, that seemed impossible." He spoke slowly, placing his words carefully, and she got the feeling that he was waiting for a disclosure.

"Well, it was obviously not impossible," she said hotly. Then, apologetic, "I mean, I did it. I'm not like a sea monster or anything." Though she suddenly felt like one, as if Sebastian's image of her had changed in the last several minutes.

"Listen, I'm not trying to make you feel bad," he soothed, tugging her arm until she sat up. "It shocked me, is all."

She sat on the sand facing him, the water massaging their feet and calves. The worry lines had disappeared from his face, and he smiled sheepishly.

"Forgive me?" he asked.

She nodded and ran a hand through her hair, fingering the knots free. He reached up and took it, pressing his cold lips against the thin flesh of her knuckles.

His lips were hot, and she shivered, closing her eyes as warm shoots rippled through the rest of her body.

"I'm beat," he said suddenly, struggling to his feet and swiping the sand from his boxers.

She started to argue with him. She hated to see the night end, and they hadn't even talked about Devin, but she stopped, seeing the drawn look on his face. She had scared him badly.

They cleaned the patio table in silence, both eating a final taco to absorb the Tequila and saying a quick goodnight.

In bed, she watched the shadows twist across the ceiling. Her body felt overheated, and she tossed, pushing the blankets off, then pulling them up, only to shove them off again. The alcohol, the conversation and the swim had jazzed her up. She wanted to talk about Devin or go for a walk or run in circles until she collapsed, exhausted. But she also felt the need to rein herself in. His lips left a burned imprint on her body, and she wanted to press all of her against him. A ridiculous notion considering she'd been apart from Nick for barely a few days. Still, the body wanted what it wanted, and her mind had little say in the matter.

She slipped off the bed and padded to the window, watching the moonlit lake. The dark tree line beckoned to her, and she considered returning to the forest. She had never been especially frightened of the woods at night, but had not exactly frolicked through them. She could imagine making her way along the shadows of the road, knowing that she'd found the right spot when the yellow tape appeared streaming from the trees. She could find her path back in, her feet moving slowly over the brittle twigs, holding her arms out so that she didn't twist an ankle. And then what? She didn't know, probably get so frightened that she would run screaming back to Sydney's and dive under the covers like a child.

She pushed her face close to the glass, sensing movement before she saw it. A figure moved across the backyard, staying near the forest line, but sliding closer to the water's edge. She squinted at the shape of the dark hood pressed over his head. As she watched, the head turned. She dived to the floor, but knew that whoever it was had seen her. Was it Sebastian out for a stroll? A wandering tourist? Or someone much more sinister? Devin's killer, whoever he or she was, had not been found or even identified. Perhaps he was killing off witnesses. She crawled to the door and stood up, pressing her back along the wall, out of view of the large bay window. Moving slowly down the stairs, her limbs locked in fear, she cursed herself for not having locked the doors and windows before bed. At any moment, she might hear the kitchen door creak open and soft steps on the tile floor.

She could see the faint glow of the television in the living room. She peeked in, hoping to alert Sebastian, but the couch was empty. Of course, it was only Sebastian. He must have been as revved up as she and had taken a walk.

At the front door, she pressed a palm against the cherry wood, feeling the smothered splinters beneath the lacquer finish. She longed for his return, imagining him opening the door at that exact moment, their eyes fiercely connecting beneath the breath of air between them and then instantly felt terrified at the thought.

As she stood at the door, ridiculing her troubled longings, Abby did not sense the hooded figure standing behind it.

He felt her, though. He smelled her, and could— almost—taste her beneath the bitter polyurethane and seedy lake air. For several seconds, they stood that way, only a pane of wood apart.

A toilet flushed, and Abby panicked. Sebastian was not outside. She ran, muffling each footfall. On the stairs, she crawled, grimacing when the third stair groaned beneath her. She heard the bathroom door click as if he also wanted to be quiet. Had he heard her? At the top of the stairway, she waited, listening to his naked feet on the floor and the hushed groan as he settled onto the couch.

Abby did not remember the cloaked figure until she climbed into Sydney's bed, flicking off the bedside lamp. As darkness fell, the image rose in her mind and she sat up, the blankets clenched in her fist. Across the room, pale shafts of moonlight leached in, haunting the shadows. Her mind returned to the grocery store and the man behind the freezer.

"It was nothing," she whispered to herself, twice and

then three times until she was sure that it really had been nothing; a tree, a bush, a trick of moonlight, all totally plausible culprits.

Chapter 8

Abby, too tired to stand, pulled a stool over to the counter and made coffee, sitting. Her night had been a restless one, tormented by dreams of Devin lost in a forest of bleeding trees. Twice she woke to the black room, convinced that someone stood nearby, watching her. When dawn finally made an appearance, Abby edged off the bed, happy to face the day with the night behind her.

The coffee pot sputtered and whined as it neared its finish. Abby filled two enormous mugs and carried them to the living room, where Sebastian stirred.

"Morning," he yawned, struggling to sit up. He took his mug and eyed the contents warily. "No cream or sugar? I need to see the manager."

"Send him a letter," Abby mumbled, choking down her own scalding coffee and leaning into the couch. Her head swam with images from her dreams.

"Long night?"

"To say the least. You?"

"I slept like a fat cat." He brushed a hand through his hair. It got stuck and he frowned, exasperated. "I guess it's shower time."

"Good idea," she told him, fumbling the remote from the coffee table and switching the television on.

Sebastian heaved off the couch and disappeared into the bathroom.

She flipped idly through the channels, searching for news. Amazing how perky the QVC woman seemed, selling "absolutely authentic, and did I mention, real mother of pearl earrings," at eight o'clock in the morning.

Abby found the morning news. Weather looked good,

J.R. Erickson

sunny and mid-eighties, which meant another bad hair day for Abby. She lifted a hand to her head and felt the frizz already forming at the mention of humidity. She would have to hit the shower after Sebastian.

Beneath commercials for fancy cat food in crystal bowls and hair implants for men, Abby could hear Sebastian doing a bad rendition of *Bad to the Bone*.

"Buh, buh, buh, bad to the bone," he crooned, and Abby turned up the volume.

The local news started, and a grim-faced reporter announced that Trager Police had arrested a suspect in the homicide of local woman Devin Blake, previously Devin Kent.

In the bathroom, the shower spray slowed and then died.

"Authorities have not released a motive. However, Police Chief Caplan identified the suspect as the victim's own brother, Danny Kent."

"Holy shit, Sebastian, look at this!" Abby called, plopping to her knees near the screen.

Sebastian hurried in, a towel draped around his waist and his wet curls leaking over his shoulders. Abby paused, caught off guard, and then pointed at the television.

"Look."

The camera changed to an image of Chief Caplan at a press conference outside the precinct. In the background, Abby saw Tina, her face smug and unsmiling, and the strange insect-like detective from their previous visit to the police station. He stood near the building, his dark eyes trained on the camera as if they saw through it.

"He's creepy," Abby said. "That detective."

Sebastian didn't speak, but when Abby glanced up at him, his face was hard and unsmiling.

"Hey, are you okay?" she asked, distracted by his tight

76

jaw and fists, opening and closing at his sides.

"It wasn't him," Sebastian said gruffly, walking closer to the television.

"Who? Danny, her brother? How do you know?"

"We have to go to the woods."

"What woods? The woods?"

"Yes, get dressed."

Sebastian left without another word, slamming the bathroom door behind him. Abby sat for another minute, dumbfounded and watching the TV as the report changed to a local bookstore facing bankruptcy. She didn't understand.

She stopped outside the bathroom door, tempted to knock, but decided to humor him. In Sydney's bedroom, she slipped into red jogging pants and a black athletic tank, pulling her hair into a ponytail.

Downstairs, Sebastian stood by the door. He looked impatient, his eyes darting toward the television, which now blared a commercial about 'Blast Off', a great new energy drink that provided men with that extra oomph to "go all night long." Abby started to crack a joke about erectile dysfunction, but stopped at Sebastian's deepening frown.

They took the beach, but walking on the sand was slow and frustrating. Abby wanted to ask questions, but Sebastian only offered curt replies and seemed lost in his thoughts.

Summer tourists clogged the lake. Abby watched a brightly colored Baja bounce by, tossed on the climbing waves. Several bikini clad girls sat dangerously on the motor lid, screaming with each swell. Abby stared at them for a moment longer, transfixed with horror. Her mother had once slapped her for sitting on that wide platform at the rear of Sydney's boat. "You'll get chopped in the motor," she said, wiping her red hand on her yellow shorts as if Abby's skin had rubbed off.

"I think this is it." Sebastian stopped at a dense thicket

of woods. No trail led from the beach in, but Abby knew that he was right. The curve of the beach matched the curve of the road on the other side of the woods, and they were pretty closely aligned with the murder site.

"Are you sure about this?" Abby asked, suddenly scared.

"Completely."

Sebastian started into the woods. Despite the heat, he'd worn long sleeves. He held up his forearms to block the scratching branches, careful to hold them aside so that they didn't fling back and hit Abby in the face. Twigs cracked loudly beneath them, and ferns crunched underfoot, but the dense brush muffled the noise, and Abby knew that it sounded louder in her own mind than it actually was.

A quarter mile in, Sebastian stopped. "Shh," he whispered and shot an arm out to block Abby from going further.

Voices, still a few yards ahead, drifted back to them.

Sebastian gripped Abby's forearm as they moved forward, stopping again when the voices grew louder.

"Do you think he did it?" a man asked.

"The Chief doesn't mess up." Abby recognized Tina, her tone defensive.

"Ah, come on, Bridge, just cause you're layin' the old man doesn't mean he ain't made a few mistakes," said a different male voice, this one much deeper.

A radio crackled loudly, but Abby could not make out the words.

"Fuck you, Kinsey," Tina snapped.

"Really, though," the first man said again. "What are we doing out here if they've already got Kent in jail?"

"Seems to me, the Chief's got nothing to do with Kent being in jail. That Detective Alva's runnin' the show around here," Kinsey replied. He spat loudly, and Tina cursed at him.

Sebastian tilted his head toward the voices, and they moved closer, concealed behind a wall of vines that had brought several trees sloping to accommodate them. Abby looked down, surprised to see that she had been digging her fingernails into the palm of her hand. She released her hold, and tiny moon-shaped welts creased the flesh.

"What kind of name is Alva, anyway?" Kinsey asked, loudly sucking phlegm from his throat and spitting it.

"Just do your goddam job, Kinsey, so we can get the hell outta here," Tina growled.

Sebastian and Abby waited, breath held as the three cops moved around the woods. The radio crackled again, and this time, Tina responded.

"Yes, Chief, we're just wrappin' it up. See you in ten." The static disappeared. "Chief says to pack it in," she told the others.

The forest was hot. Abby pulled the tank away from her skin, but its tightness made fanning herself impossible. Sebastian looked hot as well. His gray shirt was like a Rorschach Ink Blot Test. She could distinctly see a butterfly on his shoulder blades and a swan in the center of his back. She wondered what those perceptions said about her personality.

"I think they're gone," Sebastian whispered after the sound of several car doors slamming.

"Now, what?"

"Now, we investigate."

"Investigate, how?"

"I don't know."

She walked beside him as they moved around the perimeter of the vine wall toward the clearing, where police had hacked away bushes.

Abby did not have high hopes. The ground had been

razed almost to the earth. Pockets of dirt, cleared of all leaves and twigs, greeted them. Her eyes trailed the barren floor and, though it looked different, immediately recognized the spot where Devin's body had been. The decaying stump still stood nearby, its surface scraped heavily.

She shuddered as Sebastian walked directly to the dead tree, dropping to his knee and brushing his fingers over the soil. He picked something up.

Abby moved next to him and saw that he pinched a single red hair between his thumb and forefinger.

"Useless cops," he muttered.

The hair was foreboding, and Abby wished that he hadn't found it.

"So, what do we look for, Sebastian? I'm feeling pretty lost here."

"Look for markings in the dirt or weird materials, you know, like rope or something."

Abby nodded but did not feel confident. She squatted down and peered at the dirt, occasionally picking up a rock or branch that looked strange.

She wanted to help find Devin's killer, too, but why would the police arrest Danny if he didn't do it?

"Any chance we're beating a dead horse here?" she asked Sebastian, who had dropped onto his belly and stared at the ground from only centimeters above it.

He jerked his head toward her, and she recoiled. His face was scrunched and angry, his eyes narrowed at her like she'd punched him in the back, not asked a simple question.

"You can leave any time you want," he snapped.

Abby paused, surprised by his tone.

Forget it, she thought, but as she clambered to her feet, she remembered Sebastian's sister.

"Hey, listen," she said, returning to the ground on her knees, hoping that she didn't tear a hole in Sydney's pants. "I understand why this is so important to you…"

He shuffled along the forest floor, propelling himself with his pointed toes and shooting her a cold look. "No, you don't, but that doesn't matter because we're both here, aren't we?"

"Fine," she said, standing and wiping her hands on her pants. "You're on your own."

She started to walk away.

"Bingo," he whispered.

"What?" She turned as he scrambled to his feet.

He walked over and held open his hand where a small piece of worn leather, no more than an inch in length, lay.

"What is it?" She tried to keep the annoyance from her voice. It didn't look like much.

"It's a clue."

"To what, though? I mean how can you find significance in this when you haven't even been investigating?"

He stared at her funnily and then blinked hard. "I have been, without you."

She shrugged; he might have told her as much the day before. "Well, let's go bust this guy, Pinkerton," she joked.

"It's not funny."

"Fine, it's not funny, Sebastian. What do you want me to say? Eureka, you found a tiny piece of leather that might have been lying in these woods for a century?"

"We need to continue, Abby."

She rolled her eyes and settled back on the ground. They searched for another half hour, sweating and not speaking. The normally cool forest held the heat; even the leaves drooped miserably. After a seeming eternity, Sebastian stood and announced that they should leave.

A motorcycle roared by on the road. They couldn't see it, but its engine created a tunnel of noise around them. When it was gone, the silence was thick, and despite the sun streaming through, vaguely terrifying. Abby felt her skin prickle again, sensing something watching them. Sebastian paused and then spun around, his eyes narrowing in on the woods.

"Do you see someone?" Abby whispered.

"No, but I feel someone," he said gruffly. "We'll take the road back."

This time, he walked behind her, turning circles to scan the trees around them.

* * * *

Abby slipped on the one-piece swimsuit from the previous night, still damp, and plodded across the lawn to the beach edge. The hot sand burned the soles of her feet, and she sprang on toes to the water, relieved at the coolness and relishing the soft swells that broke over her ankles. She walked waist deep and then dived, closing her eyes and allowing a wave to crash over her head. The public beaches would have Red Flags flying today because of the rough waters, but Abby didn't mind. She always swam when the waves were high.

She felt the undertow, strong, liquid hands grasping her ankles, but swam against it, staying close to the shore where her knees scraped the sand. She thought of Sebastian's find but still could not make sense of it. A hair and an old piece of leather did not seem like much, though Sebastian seemed transfixed by his discoveries. When they'd returned to Sydney's on foot, he'd complained of a headache and disappeared into the guest bedroom upstairs. Abby wondered if he faked the headache, but didn't say as much.

As she stood, a large swell overcame her, and she sucked in a mouthful of water. She pitched to the side and was thrust beneath the surface. The liquid hands took hold and pulled her out, scraping her body along the lake-floor. She panicked and gulped another mouthful of water, her nose and throat burning as it raced down her trachea and into her lungs. Her hands reached the bottom, fingers clawing the sand and stone, but found nothing to grab hold of. The undertow continued to pull, holding her body below the surface and spinning her wildly around.

The sun streaked into the lake, and she kicked and heaved upward, but could not break from the cyclone. Her breath was gone, and she sucked in more water, her limbs going slack beneath her.

* * * *

Abby opened her eyes heavily and stared into nothing. The darkness was suffocating, and she spun in a circle ready to flee the death that had descended upon her. She moved left and struck a rock wall, slippery on her face and hands. Breathing, counting back from one hundred, she waited, and, finally, her eyes adjusted. An outline emerged. She was standing in a cave. Solid, slimy rock rose around her, and she stood too deep for any natural light to penetrate. Still, gradually, she could see. The air was gelatinous, but her body felt light, as buoyant as a soap bubble. The dim tunnel focused—still dark—but increasingly visible. She was definitely in a cave, and though brain damage crossed her mind, she dismissed it. She expected confusion or fear, but they did not come, only a longing to move forward, deeper into the darkness ahead.

She sensed a cold dampness but could not feel it on her skin. In fact, she felt almost nothing, no rapid heartbeat or sweating palms. She was an observer in her body.

The jagged rock walls spread out beside her, and she

advanced. The cave shifted to a downward slope, and she picked up speed. Was she walking? No, not exactly, more like floating, swimming without movement. The tunnel narrowed, darkness stooped to meet her with low ceilings and close walls. Psychological claustrophobia threatened her, but again it could not find a place for its frantic fingers. The cave descended like a spiral into the center of the earth; she followed – mesmerized.

The tunnel forked into three passages, each glowing as if lit from a different source. She chose the path on her right where long, orange shadows sliced along the craggy walls like serpent tongues. The path tightened, barely more than an arm's length across, and appeared to end abruptly, but as she drifted forward, she saw that it was an illusion. The tunnel turned sharply. She continued around the bend where the cave yawned into a massive round room, ceiling-less. A black vacuum of night sky, stars like fireflies buzzing in its face, gaped overhead.

In the center of the room, a group of figures surrounded a blazing fire that crackled, sending flaming embers into the dark space overhead. A figure broke from the group and advanced towards her. The woman had a single pale arm stretched from beneath her black cloak. Two glowing, green eyes peered from the pocket of darkness beneath the woman's hood, and her hair, as black as her cloak, danced on her shoulders electrically. In her palm, Abby saw a small, swirling ball of blue light. It spun and contorted, gradually forming a shape. The blue fell away, and an object emerged – an intricate silvery castle with turrets stretching upward like arrowheads.

Abby reached forward, overwhelmed with a desire to touch the castle, to feel the tangible body of an object conjured from nothing. Before her fingers could settle on the tiny fortress, it shimmered and then faded, like a hologram losing its light source.

The other figures detached from the fireside and moved around her, forming a circle. Abby felt a twinge of fear and a graying at the edges of her vision.

The figures began to chant and sway. A sea of black cloth billowed around her. Unconsciously, Abby tilted with them, her body drifting to their rhythm. Hands reached out from the cloaks and grasped her—flesh, but not flesh— embraced her, and then she began to dissolve into them. They all did: their cloaks fell to the floor as they merged into a single blue ball of energy, growing as they faded into her, became her, and she became them.

Chapter 9

Lips, wet and warm, pressed against her. A mouth, soft and giving, pushed in and then breath, fast like a balloon that's popped, exploded into her mouth and lungs. Abby choked, water spewed from her mouth, and then hands, rough on her shoulders, forced her sideways. Sand dug into her right bicep, along her hip and down her leg. She coughed and choked and opened her eyes to the beach, blazing in the midday sun. Sebastian's face hovered above hers, terrified.

He lifted her to his chest, her wet face on his hot, bare skin.

"You're okay, you're okay," he murmured again and again, a mantra. He lifted her, like a child, over his outstretched legs and slapped her back. More water trickled from her mouth. Her nose and throat felt like she'd snorted battery acid. She swallowed once, but it hurt too much to try again.

"Water," she croaked, and Sebastian turned her back over, his eyes moving to her face like she might die anyway. "I'm okay."

"Holy shit," he whispered finally, realizing that Abby was conscious, that she was alive.

He stood and grasped her firmly, pulling her to her feet and then half carrying her, with his arm around her waist, back to the house.

Inside, she gulped two glasses of ice water on the couch, where he'd propped a pillow beneath her feet.

"You shouldn't have been swimming," he muttered, more to himself, than to her. "Those waves are huge today."

"I think I died," she said flatly, the vision of the cave coming back to her fully. She could feel the energy of the blue light, her energy, but not only hers, the others as well.

"Why?" He looked concerned and not at all skeptical.

"I was in a cave with all these figures, but it was so real, and then I turned into this blue energy, and we all became, like one entity."

He stared at her and said nothing.

"It didn't feel like a dream, it felt real."

She massaged her throat, sore and still burning, but less so than on the beach.

"Maybe it wasn't death," Sebastian said, finally.

She thought about what else it might have been: a dream, a hallucination, perhaps a journey to another dimension. It felt too heavy for her brain. She didn't have the energy to go there.

"You need to rest." He grabbed a blanket from the couch-end.

She stretched out, and he tucked the blanket around her. She shivered in spite of the heat and nestled her head into the pillow that he'd been using the previous few nights. It smelled like him, and the scent comforted her.

* * * *

Sebastian closed the guest bedroom door quietly – not wanting to disturb Abby, who, he hoped, slept soundly downstairs. He felt nauseated, and the headache he'd faked earlier had come on passionately. He popped four painkillers in his mouth and chased them with a cup of green tea, propping the glass on his bedside table.

Had she nearly died? He didn't think so, some gut instinct told him, "no." And her vision, her near-death dream, rang all too familiar. He knew that he had read about it before, that Claire had written about something similar in her journal.

He pulled a box, one of many, across the floor, and peeled back the cardboard flaps. Claire had kept several journals, all in cheap dime-store notebooks, which were tattered from his overzealous searches through their pages. The words, mostly written in pencil, were smeared in some spots, and he'd tried to touch them up with pen. He intended to type it all, at some point, but there was never time.

He found the green notebook, one of her first, and carefully turned the pages, touching only the corners to keep the oils from his fingers from tainting the loopy cursive of Claire's hand. He had read most of the journals, though not all of them. After her death, it took months to even get them out, to look at the words without tears splattering and ruining her carefully documented experiences.

He found the excerpt:

Adora gave me a wonderful gem of knowledge yesterday and put to rest a concern that has plagued me for months. The dream that I had, the dream that acted almost as a catalyst to this newfound power, was an initiation of sorts. Adora called it 'The Majestic Rite' and said that we all experienced it at the onset of our powers. She said that, during the rite, three things occurred: suffering, death and rebirth. She asked about the dream, and I told her that it happened when I was very ill. I had a high fever and thought I was dying. Sebastian was worried sick. I thought that the dream was a result of my fever, but the cave had been real. I woke from it knowing that I was more than this, more than this physical body, and that the light, the blue light, made me one of them, the figures around the fire. Adora said that I was right and now I have a name for it: 'The Majestic Rite'.

Sebastian closed the journal and leaned back against the bed, resting his head on the wood frame. He closed his eyes against the pain of remembering Claire, the sharp stabs that arose whenever he looked at her journals and found himself back in the past, when she still lived.

Abby. Now he had Abby, and each passing hour seemed to dump another load of evidence into his lap. Evidence that she was special, that he had found her for a reason. Was she one of them? Or simply experiencing the dreams vicariously through him, somehow? He put the journal back and returned the box to the others.

He needed to think, which meant he needed to drive. The drum of the wheels on the road had soothed him ever since his parents' death. He used to take Claire for drives. In the beginning, the drives were necessary. She refused to get in the car for months after the accident, but he coaxed her. At first, they just drove around the block – eventually making wider loops until their drives were hours long and they'd visited cities far outside of their own. He taught Claire to drive, and sometimes he napped in the passenger seat while she drove to Chicago or Michigan or just miles into farm country.

He didn't leave Abby a note, assuming that she would sleep for a while, and pulled out of Sydney's driveway looking for a long stretch of open road.

* * * *

The phone shrilled in Abby's ear. Her head, sunk deeply into the pillow, was only inches from the gray plastic as it shook. Abby opened her eyes groggily. Her lips stuck together and made a loud smacking noise when she opened her mouth fully, trying to wake up, but continuing to hang between this world and the last. The back of her eyelids projected visions of the dead girl, the dead woman, the dead thing that wanted to drag her into the lake.

She shook her head and moaned. The phone, louder than ever, shrieked again near the top of her head. Not thinking, or maybe thinking that anything was better than that dead thing, she fumbled, grasped the receiver, and thrust it to her ear.

"H'lo?" she mumbled, almost too quiet to hear in her raspy voice.

"Abigail? Abigail, is that you?" Abby's mother's voice came like a sharp kick to the side of her head.

She grimaced, pulled the phone away and forced her eyes open all the way. Sydney's living room slowly materialized. Abby stared down at the checkered blanket rumpled across her legs, her white feet poking out. The suede couch felt sticky beneath her, sweat sticky, and she struggled to sit up.

"Mom?" she asked, not really asking, but too fuzzy to say anything else.

"Abigail Daniels, what in the name of the good Lord is going on? I have been absolutely worried sick about you. Do you hear me, missy? Abigail?"

"Abby, Mom, okay? Abby."

"What's wrong with your voice? Are you taking drugs?"

Abby snorted and covered the phone, too late.

"Are you laughing at me, Abigail Daniels?"

"No, Mom, I sneezed, and I swallowed some water in the lake, that's why my voice is scratchy."

"Oh, yes, I'm sure that you just swallowed some lake water. Nick's let me know exactly what you're up to, and I'm telling you that the buck stops here. I am going to call Sydney and give her a piece of my mind for letting this go on under her roof. What is she running? A brothel up there?"

"Are you finished?"

"Am I finished?" her mother seethed, and Abby imagined her standing in her narrow kitchen, twisting the phone cord frantically around her wrist while the shopping network blared from the living room.

"This," Abby snapped, "is why I didn't call you, Mother. Because I knew that if I tried to be honest and let you know I was unhappy, you'd just torment me until I stayed."

"How dare you speak to me that way? After all I've done for you, Abigail. You must stop this, immediately!" She enunciated every word. If they were written, it would be all caps with giant exclamation points after each syllable.

"I CAN-NOT DO THIS RIGHT NOW!" Abby yelled into the phone, and then reached behind her and smashed it onto its base.

She was now fully awake and filled with a blind rage that left her momentarily frozen on the couch, back stiff and hands clenched on her knees like they were stress balls and not sensitive joints filled with bone and cartilage. She forced a few deep breaths and then thirstily drank the last of the water that Sebastian had left on the coffee table.

Abby shoved off the couch, her mother's words ringing in her ears. Normally, her mother was an expert emotional blackmailer, but this time Abby had stood up for herself. In fact, it had not even crossed her mind to bow down to her mother's rant. Her mother, who considered suffocation and love to be synonymous, had finally been forced back.

From a small child, Abby's mother had played her like a puppeteer plays her dummies. "Dance," she'd say, and Abby danced. She danced and sewed and ice-skated. She took anti-depressants, attended college close to home, and even cut her hair the way her mother—and Nick— recommended. She stayed with Nick, long after their relationship had curdled, largely because her mother adored him.

Suddenly, she was liberated from the maternal talons that had been clutching her spine since birth.

In the kitchen, she drank another glass of water and then dug out bread and cheese, which she munched angrily as she mentally blacked out every piece of advice her mother had ever given her. "Abigail, your fingernails are ghastly," her mother used to say. "Wipe off that paint right now." And she would wipe it off. She skipped navel piercing, tattoos and parties at her mother's command.

How many Friday nights had she spent carefully supergluing porcelain faces on little doll bodies stuffed with cotton? Even as a child, Abby had hated dolls and yet she dedicated half of her adolescence to assembling the freakish things and piling them on her bedspread, exactly as her mother liked them. They never stopped, the dolls, arriving in gleaming white trucks, ordered from some infomercial or magazine ad. They came in wooden boxes, stiff with packing straw, their glass eyes staring out from disembodied heads. 'Suzie, Sissy, Madeleine, Ginger, Heather'. Her mother named every one. She named three of them Abigail, insisting that they looked like her daughter with their thick, frizzy curls and empty brown eyes.

Abby reached up and touched her hair, crinkled where she'd lain on it. It smelled like lake water. She pulled a long butcher knife from the wooden block next to Sydney's sink, reached for a clump of hair and sliced. The blade did not cut easily; it grated back and forth on the strands, a stylist's worst nightmare, but Abby hacked away, ignoring the clumps of brown that fell at her feet. She did not stop until her hair stood in ear length strands, bits brushed her cheek and others stood erect, too short to lay flat on her scalp. She dropped the knife; it clattered in the sink where she left it.

In Sydney's closet, she found tight black stretch pants and a glittery red tank top that said *Jamaica* in leather block letters. She dug out a bottle of nail polish and painted her toes and fingernails red, not bright red, but a darker one, the color of blood. She put on red lipstick and scared herself when she glanced in the mirror. Who was that face looking back? Her cheeks were bone white, her lips looked like she'd been kissing a bloody carcass and gotten her teeth involved in the process. She opened her mouth wide and licked the lipstick off her teeth, grinning. Her brown hair could have belonged to a Chia Pet who'd spent the day with a group of five year olds. She sprayed some mousse in her hand and fluffed it up, somehow making it better and worse, as it stiffened into a helmet of spirals.

She kept waiting to hear Sebastian clunking around downstairs, but when she looked out the window, she saw that he had left. Had he left for good? Had she scared him away?

She barely entertained the thought as she pushed open the guest bedroom door. A blue duffel bag lay open on the bed and in the corner half a dozen boxes were stacked.

She did not consider Sebastian's privacy as she walked boldly into the room, shuffling the clothes in his suitcase. He appeared to own only two types of clothing: t-shirts and jeans, all torn and unwashed. She lifted an orange Bob Marley shirt to her face and sniffed. It stank of sweat and aftershave, but she liked it and carefully smoothed it on the bed, tracing her fingers along the collar.

Moving to the boxes, she crouched and looked for labels, but none were marked. She picked one out, pulled the flaps open and peered inside. Loose leaf papers were stuffed at various angles, some water marked and coffee stained. She dug beneath the papers, and her fingers brushed leather. Trying to move the papers aside without damaging them further, she lifted out a heavy, leather-bound book. The words *Astral Coven* were engraved in the upper left corner and stained red. The book looked and smelled old, its heavy thickness balancing on her knees. She slid her hands along the cover, the smooth leather cold to the touch.

She did not have a plan or even a thought as she dived into Sebastian's personal life. She had only a hunger for power, for knowledge.

She slipped her index finger beneath the bulky shield, opening it gingerly. The pages were old, fragile, and reminded her of the crumbling bodies of B-grade mummy flicks. She wondered if Sebastian was carting around ancient family heirlooms and felt vaguely disappointed that it was not his journal. The first page held a long list of names, each written in French cursive, the letters elegantly and painstakingly placed on the page. She hunched over the book, squinting at each tiny name, barely legible after years of fading. She recognized none, but realized that the list went on and on, ten pages, at least, of the packed identities, most likely long ago dead and buried. Beyond the names came another section that listed various recipes, some in English, others scrawled in languages that Abby did not recognize. She peered closely at a recipe titled 'Darken The Moon'. The recipe, which looked more like a poem, read:

Shining Mother in divinest night
Drip down the wax of thy candlelight
Bleed forth your luminescent fire
Leave these woods in shadowed streaks
We ask you hasten quick to cloak
For blessed blackness you evoke

Beneath the poem, more words were scattered without any apparent rhyme or reason. Rosemary, black snake, river stones, one double yoke egg and Indian cane.

She flipped deeper into the book, and several sheets of loose paper fluttered to the floor. Different than the thick parchment of the other pages, these appeared to be yellowed newspaper clippings, their edges stiff and cracking.

Abby spread the pages flat on the carpet and crouched

over them. The first clipping depicted a fire ravaging a dense forest. Even on the withered pages, Abby could see the intensity of the blaze as it leaped across the desperate leaves. The caption below read 'Ebony Woods Destroyed At Last.' She found the date, 10th of August 1908, and was amazed that the clipping was still in one piece.

She pulled out the next newspaper article, staring incredulously at the blown up picture staring back it her. It was Devin, or someone who so closely resembled her that, for a moment, Abby was sure that she was seeing a ghost. August 8, 1908, only two days before the burning of the Ebony Woods. A short article followed the photo of the Devin look-a-like standing in front of a small cabin, a single wildflower clutched in her palm. Like Devin, her hair was wild, her skin a pearly white. She wore a long, dark dress buttoned high up her neck.

Aubrey Blake Stands Accused

Com. vs. Aubrey Blake: The defendant in this case is the single living child of the deceased Nathan and Susan Blake. Complainant is one Jonas Herman of the upper end of the city. The defendant threatened revenge against Herman and his family after her mule took ill. Upon the mule's death, Herman's single son, Solomon came ill with the Black Death and died three short days later. Aubrey Blake is accused of having dealings with the devil and performing witch behavior to infect Solomon Herman. Aubrey Blake resides in the Ebony Woods. Proceeding is scheduled for the Monday after next.

Abby stared at the picture until her eyes swam. She shut them tight and tried to block it out, to force the face of Aubrey—Devin's face—from her mind. Slowly, the picture dissolved, but Sebastian's took its place. She saw him the first day, the surprised look on his face when she pulled into the driveway, the box he quickly placed in his trunk. She wanted to justify the clippings, to pretend that this was all part of his separate investigation, but she knew better.

"No, no, no, no." She realized that she'd been murmuring aloud, and she clamped her teeth together, putting a hand on the floor to brace herself. She stared at the newspaper clipping again, at the face smiling out. Devin's face, Aubrey's face, Devin's face, Aubrey's face, they swirled in her mind, became an inferno scorching her eyes, a fire like the one in Ebony Woods, a fire that could burn you alive.

"Abby?" Sebastian's voice startled her and she shot to her feet, staring at him with wild eyes. Terror streaked up her spine and screamed that she *RUN!*

She tried to streak past him, but he caught her around the waist, heaving his body back to balance the thrust of her own. He pinned her against the doorway, forcing her arms to her sides, and she cranked her head away, refusing to look into his face.

"What the hell is going on? Why are you freaking out?"

Her mind reeled for an excuse, for a logical explanation, but how could there be one? How could she explain what she'd discovered and still get away?

"I, umm, I was looking for your phone. I thought I heard a cell phone."

Sebastian's eyes narrowed into hers, reading her, and she concentrated on her heart, on steady beats that might bring the color back to her face.

"What happened to your hair?" He smiled and she shrank away from him.

"Ha," she laughed weakly. "I cut it."

He reached his hand up and touched it, bouncing his fingers on the stiff curls. "Yes, you did."

He looked past her into the room, and she saw his eyes

shift down. They paused on the leather book and the newspaper clippings. "Were you going through my stuff?" He didn't sound angry, just surprised and curious.

"No, I mean, not exactly. It sounded like a phone was in that box, so I just, you know, looked around, but I didn't see anything," she added quickly.

"Well, we need to talk about all of that anyway," he told her, the smile dropping from his face. He released her arms and moved further into the room, sinking onto the edge of the bed. He patted the space next to him. "Wanna chat?"

Her eyes darted from him to the bed, and, without thinking, she rushed into the hallway and slammed the door behind her. She fled down the steps, ripped her purse from the kitchen table and raced across the driveway to her car, sure that any second his hands would reach out and take hold. Nearly ripping the door from its hinge, she dived inside and hit the lock button, starting the engine and reversing faster than she could control, which sent the car into a tailspin in the gravel drive. She pointed the nose towards the road and lurched forward, gunning the engine. As she pulled away, she caught a glimpse of Sebastian standing on Sydney's porch, a questioning gaze on his face.

Chapter 10

She drove recklessly, her foot skidding from gas to break as she sped down the tree-lined road towards town. She looked in her mirror more than she looked at the road and twice had to slam on her brakes when cars slowed in front of her.

"Go, dammit, go," she cursed out loud, tears streaming. The tears had begun when she pulled from the drive, and realizing that Sebastian had not followed her, had time to grasp the magnitude of her discovery. Sebastian was a murderer. He had killed Devin. Why else would he have pictures of Devin? Of her family? Why would he pretend not to know her, while carting around her family keepsakes? Maybe he had murdered her and then stolen the boxes. Maybe they were filled with Devin's valuables, and Sebastian thought that he could hock the old book as an antique.

She thought these things on one plane, but just below that another river of thought ran. Who had been in the woods when she showed him the body? Why did he insist that Devin's brother wasn't the murderer?

She sped into town, swearing at every red light, and nearly mowing down a group of tourists rollerblading on the side of the road. She pulled into the police station and cut the engine, turning fully in her seat to scan for Sebastian's car through every window. When she was sure he was nowhere in sight, she jumped from the car and ran into the precinct.

"Hi, I need to speak to Chief Caplan," she said urgently to a middle-aged woman perched behind a wide, mahogany desk.

"Do you have an appointment?" the woman asked,

taking off her glasses and rubbing them on her tropical themed blouse. The blouse, a hideous umbrella-like thing, was smothered by parrots and crocodiles.

"No, no, but it's urgent. I have to see him right now." She almost said, "it's about a murder," but stopped when she noticed several officers eavesdropping nearby.

"Well, honey, he's gone for the day."

Abby gaped at the woman before her, ready to scream or grab the lady by her bloody looking blouse and shake her until she understood.

"Well, can you call him? It's very important."

The woman rolled her eyes and started to speak, but was interrupted.

"Hello, miss," a man said behind Abby, and she spun around.

The scary detective, the Praying Mantis, was silhouetted in the doorway. He leaned toward Abby and drooped his head, looking directly into her face and smiling a wide, white grin. Up close he looked fake, like one of her old porcelain dolls, and she backed away from him, stopping when her back hit the receptionist's desk.

"I'm covering for the Chief today. You can talk to me," he said in a strange drawl that made every word long, like an echo that continued in Abby's head, rolling in circles around her skull.

She followed him, partially out of fear, but also because she felt mesmerized, like he had all the answers, like he could help her with anything.

He shut the door in the Chief's office and beckoned her to a chair. When she sat down, he continued to stand behind her, his long, bony fingers on the chair back. She tried to sit forward, but he gripped her shoulders and pulled her back.

"Here, now, just relax, young lady. Just take a deep breath."

She did take a deep breath and then another. The florescent lights of the office had seemed harsh at first, but they began to appear dimmer, soothing even, and she leaned her head fully back.

He stepped in front of her, walked behind the Chief's desk and sat down, lacing his fingers in front of him.

His eyes sought hers, and he looked and looked, his black pupils enlarging and then shrinking, narrowing to tiny points that she could feel. They didn't land on the outside; instead, they penetrated her own pupils, travelling along the optic nerve and into her brain. She shook her head, feeling dizzy and sleepy. Sebastian didn't seem like such a big deal anymore, nothing did. She just wanted a nap.

"It's okay, dear, just rest. That's it. It's warm in here, close your eyes."

He stood up, walked to the office's single window and lowered the shades, flicking the wand to close them completely.

He took a chair close to hers, allowing his knee to brush her own – she felt a shock like she'd been electrocuted. She jerked, and her chair yelped on the rubbery floor. The room focused, and she realized that the detective was leaning towards her, his eyes closed, sniffing at the air.

Go!

The command was so loud that she turned, looking for the source, before she realized that it had risen in her own mind. She paused for another second, frozen with fear and wanting to bolt, but afraid that she couldn't reach the door in time.

The detective opened his eyes, and they seemed to be searching her again, as if he'd lost his connection and wanted desperately to get it back.

"I'm gonna grab a coffee," she said, too loud, but better than the whisper she had feared.

He stared at her for another second, his head cocked to the side, and then a smile slid over his face, revealing the straight, sharp teeth beneath his thin lips.

Concentrating on a steady step, she walked across the office, opened the door and stepped back into the precinct. The lights buzzed and cops milled about, talking and laughing. A few looked her way but paid little attention. She stumbled forward and looked back. The Chief's office had become a tomb and the lights hurt her eyes. She felt foggy, but dared not slow as she hurried through the building and back into the parking lot. She was sure that she had not been in the building long, but already her car seats were hot. She cranked the air conditioner and pulled back onto the street, searching for a place to go.

* * * *

Sebastian veered off the road, maneuvering his car down a two track clogged with weeds, but still visible in the dense woods. He cut the engine and leaned his head back on his seat, seeking refuge in his mind. Claire had taught him a few things, not powers exactly, but more like a sixth sense. A sense that had to be found within and strengthened with mediation, which he rarely had the time or concentration for.

He didn't know what he wanted to accomplish. He knew why Abby had left and he didn't blame her, the newspaper clippings had stunned him as completely as they'd shocked her. He had been carrying around the book, *The Astral Coven*, for two years and yet he'd never seen the clippings. He'd leafed through it a few times and read some of the spells. It had been difficult enough trying to get through Claire's journals; the book had fallen by the wayside. Could he have prevented Devin's death? He didn't know. Claire had stressed reading the *signs*, paying attention to every detail. "There are no coincidences," she once said, but that had been her world, not his, or so he thought.

Now he had to remember, he had to seek that power within.

"It is your spirit dwelling, a cave or lagoon or house," Claire had said. "It is different for each of us. There is you, Sebastian, the human, the man produced by your biology and your environment, and then there is your spirit. Not wholly separate, but separated by your decision to ignore the spirit voice and make decisions based on this material world." Claire had been rhapsodizing all that evening about the importance of finding his source of power. Sebastian, drunk on wine and candlelight, had drifted in and out of her lecture, listening, but also daydreaming.

"To go to the place where your spirit dwells, you must detach from this world, blank your mind and concentrate completely on that place. Focus on the image that comes to you. Is it a cave? If it is, then hold only that image in your mind's eye. See it from your forehead, from here." She had leaned toward him, the long, thin chain around her neck dangling on the cushions beneath them, and brushed her fingers across his forehead, in the space just above and between his eyes. "This is your third eye. From here you can venture into yourself. It is the voice of your spirit that must guide you. Your mind will fixate on fear, it will rationalize, and it will guide you toward destruction. Ignore the mind and listen to the soul."

He slowly released the memory of that night, one of the last he spent with her, and pushed all of his energy into his third eye, imagining, not a cave, but a glacial crevice, a deep tear in an icy mountain, a place that he had gone before. He closed his eyes, tuned out the material world and sank deeper into that split in the mountain, seeing and feeling, not cold, but great warmth, as he grew closer to his spirit and further from his physical being.

Then he drifted, cut off from his worldly perceptions. When the wind rose and branches scraped the hood of his car, he heard nothing. His eyelids fluttered, his face impassive except for their twitching.

Sebastian sat on a wide, flat rock, his hands clasped in his lap as he watched a shape move down the icy crevice above him. Claire did not land, she'd not been flying, she simply moved from above to beside him, her own being perched on the rock.

"I need help," he told her, flooded by grief and love at the sight of her. He did not know if she was real, but he thought not. Instead, he believed that she took on the form of a spiritual guide for him because she had become that in his physical life. On the rock, he commanded himself to concentrate. It was easy to lose the vision. Too much thought would return him to reality.

"Not my help," Claire said, laying back on the rock, her long, white robes too thin for the cold, which did not seem to bother her. "Her help."

"Abby? I need Abby's help?"

"Do you?"

"Don't play with me, Claire."

"Then don't play with yourself." She giggled and blew puffs of icy air out from her lips. They crystallized and formed little shapes, like clouds.

"Where is she? Do you know?"

"She is finding herself and then she will find you."

"Find me where? Should I go back to the house? She thinks I'm a murderer."

"Not a murderer," Claire said, sitting back up and brushing her dark hair over her shoulder. She braided her fingers through it, turning her wide blue eyes up at the sky. "She thinks you're deceiving her, and you are."

"What choice do I have?"

"You have a choice, and you made a choice. Sometimes, we have to take them back and start again."

"How?"

She didn't answer, and Sebastian felt a bead of sweat roll from his hairline, down his forehead. He reached up to catch it as it slid from his nose, and in that instant, the crevice dissolved, and he found himself back in the car.

"Thank you," he said aloud, to no one.

* * * *

Driving without direction reminded Abby, rather dismally, of her escape from Lansing only days earlier. How had it all gotten so screwed up?

She left downtown Trager, wanting to put distance between the detective and herself. Her head felt funny, like the Praying Mantis had picked through her brain with a rusted nail, and she had a rotten taste in her mouth, which she unsuccessfully tried to slosh out with a swig from a warm bottle of water that she dug out of the backseat.

Her head hurt, it ached from her brow bone to the base of her skull, and made concentration on the road impossible. She flicked open her glove box and leaned into it, fishing with her hands for a bottle of anything stronger than a cough drop. She pulled two bottles out, an off-brand allergy medicine and chewable vitamins – no painkillers. Her head started to throb. She could feel a pulse beat along her temples and tried to massage them with her thumb and forefinger, which made it hurt worse, like she was pressing bruised skin.

She had to go home. It was only three hours to her parents' house. She would park on the street and close her heart to the stale smell of potpourri and the stiff mattress of her childhood bedroom. She would lock the door, tell her mother she was ill and sleep for days. Yes—no, no, she could not go home.

Tiny, white lights began to prick her eyes, like needles, and she blinked, allowing the tears to roll out, praying that they might lubricate the dry sockets. She groaned, it scared her and reminded her of her cat, her abandoned cat, Baboon, who sometimes cried like that at night when he was locked out of the bedroom. It was a painful, guttural sonnet, a poem of desertion, and she felt it rip across her skull in violent, skipping beats. Wildly, she thought that God or the Devil or some divine, supernatural being was punishing her for her cruelty, for leaving Nick and her mother and Baboon.

A horn blared behind her, and her heart thudded in her ears so loudly that she could not think to react. Was she driving too fast? Too slow? She looked at the speedometer – a blurred wall of green and black neon stared back at her. She tried her blinker, but windshield wiper fluid sprayed across the windshield, blocking the street, and she panicked, jerking the wheel to the right. She was on the shoulder of the road, sort of, and cars whizzed by, a line that had been waiting impatiently behind her. Up-north, driving settled around eighty-five mph, not the standard forty-five in the city, and she felt the blast of each car, the trucks especially, as they rocketed by.

She needed air. Her car felt like a sauna, a hot, dry grave, but she couldn't get out on the driver's side as a semi barreled by and shook her car angrily in its wake. She crawled over the seat, the armrest digging into her ribs, her feet kicking at the door behind her to propel her on. She pushed the passenger door open and fell out, headfirst, her hands striking the pebbly ground. She gulped for air, felt it fight into her constricted lungs.

Out of the car, she cried, hands and knees holding her up and the sun gone behind the trees, leaving her in a cold shadow between two ridges of forest. She did not know where she had stopped, but the road stretched out before her and woods lay on either side.

Driving was out of the question. She tried to stand, to balance against the car for support, but her knees failed her. They pooled like jelly and refused to hold. On hands and knees, she crawled away from the road. Her vision tunneled and then became a single tiny spot through which she made out high weeds and fat cattails. She pushed through them headlong, feeling their scratchy flowers on her face and hair. Further in, an eternity of struggling, the forest floor became mossy and soft. She collapsed, her fingers sore, and rested on a bed of red pine needles. Curling into a fetal position, she closed her eyes and rocked against the pain. Her head felt swollen and soft like an overripe melon. She slept.

Chapter 11

Sebastian ripped through the boxes, no longer handling the journals delicately. He wanted answers now, today, not in six months, not in another year. Two years of his life he'd devoted to finding Tobias, to tracking Claire's murderer, to learning about the Vepars, and yet he felt as lost as that first day. That first day after she was dead and the apartment stood empty, with hot blasts of air through the open windows, and him, Sebastian, alone forever.

His hands shook as he gripped each page and stared at it, his eyes willing some new clue to rise from the faded lead writing. Writing, ha! More like chicken scratch. Damn her, damn Claire for her terrible handwriting that left him deciphering each word like hieroglyphs on a cave wall. He flung a notebook against the wall; it hit and smacked the floor, pages splayed, but intact. He wanted to burn it all – to build a fire in Sydney's pit outside and torch the remnants of Claire and her murderers. Maybe then he could sleep again. Maybe he could get on with his life.

He took a swig from an open bottle of wine beside him, gulping the bitter red liquid and caring not that some splattered on the *Book of Shadows*. He didn't give a damn if it was old, let it smolder with the rest of the junk, with his sanity.

He flipped the pages, glancing over spells that he didn't understand and suddenly didn't care to. He'd read the newspaper clippings, read about Aubrey and the fire that had consumed her. It enraged him all the more. Death seemed to be the only constant on his crusade for revenge. He stood and walked again to the window, scanning the driveway for Abby. She still had not returned. Was she dead? Murdered like Claire and Devin? Maybe she had returned to her boyfriend and her family. He hoped for that choice. He prayed that she was making amends with her boyfriend, even if he was an asshole, because it meant that she was alive and safe and he didn't have to face another body, another departed soul.

He had boxes of paperwork, journals and books. He had read more witchcraft books than he could count, but still felt no closer to Tobias, to the Vepar who had stolen his sister's life. He picked up a photo of Claire and sighed; her bright blue eyes peeked from beneath a straw sombrero. It had been her sixteenth birthday, and they had gone to a Mexican Restaurant. She had laughed when they placed the colorful hat on her head and sang *Las Mananitas*. Then she and Sebastian devoured their fried ice cream and went home to watch movies and pretend that their life was normal.

He set the picture aside and picked up a binder stuffed with newspaper clippings. Many were articles from the days after Claire's death as the local cops fumbled with the case and eventually arrested and convicted some poor chap who had nothing to do with it. But what could Sebastian say? My sister was a witch and she was murdered by a group of evil demons called Vepars? Oh, and by the way, the Vepars don't look evil, they look totally normal, but if you stab them, their blood is black? Ha!

He drank more wine and examined each clipping. He had looked at them all, but not closely enough, never closely enough. He found more photos with the detective, Detective Alva, they called him in Trager, but Sebastian found no mention of him in any of the articles, despite his image appearing in more than one picture.

As he looked at the last clipping he saw the detective again, tucked into the scenery like a potted plant. He leaned in and studied the man, his long body and short, stunted arms. He had to speak to him. He knew it was risky, that the detective might be a Vepar, although how could that be? Why would he risk getting so close to the dead?

* * * *

Abby touched her head, smoothing two fingers along her brow-line, but felt no pain. She stared around her at the craggy rock walls, some slick with algae. She was dreaming. But how could she know that? Except – yes – she stood again in the dark cave, and like her previous experience, she did not feel real. No – touching her head was no more than vapor pressed against vapor. No physical body greeted her fingers.

She moved forward, unafraid. She wanted to return to the fire, to the yawning cavern of cloaked figures and the warmth that pulsated around them like a shield. She would be safe there. She took the familiar route, followed the path to the right, and slipped silently along as the passage narrowed and then opened wide. But the fire was gone, and the figures were gone. In the center of the room stood a small, round pool of water – shallow – a puddle really. Had she taken the wrong tunnel? Was she lost? She moved forward, drifting not of her own volition, and she stopped at the water's edge, staring down at the shining surface. It reflected a high, white moon lost in a black universe.

She slipped her fingers into the water and watched as it crawled over her hands and wrists, like a cloth slowly saturated. The water, icy, climbed along her forearm and up her bicep. She shrank from it as it edged up her neck, but it continued, enveloping her head. As it rose over her eyes, she closed them tight, and it covered her entirely.

For several minutes Abby swayed in a state of suspension. The water buried her and then she was moving, flowing with the water, as the water. It raced along the cave floor, snaking along walls and around bends. She could see the fine grains of sand on the floor; feel the smoothed edges of pebbles beneath her. She picked up speed and then exploded into the sky. Water spewed forth in a gush that flowed out of the mountain and rained into the sea. She was every part of the waterfall, the mist, the spray, the thick stream of water like a snake. And then she was whole again, but moving beneath the water like a creature, an animal that must have gills – for how else could she breathe? But then she was not breathing, only moving, slowly now, sifting along the seabed like a current.

As she moved, she gained momentum and felt control return to her. She could direct herself, and she darted up from the floor and then back down again. She reached out with invisible hands and slid her palms along the oily seaweed. Her eyes devoured the sights, the tiny gray zebra mussels and thick-bodied, brown fish. In her mind she laughed, almost expecting a surge of water to flush into her lungs, but none came.

As a child, she'd dreamed of living in the water. For hours she would swim along the lake's edge, goggles and snorkel securely attached, watching the tiny specks of sparkling sand like sea creatures crawling across the lake bed. She would pretend that she'd been shipwrecked on an island, and after years of isolation had grown able to breathe beneath the water, a mermaid with legs. She'd slide her fingers along the shining stones; pretend the large rocks were oceanic monsters stalking her in the summer sun. She got so frightened of her make-believe monsters that she would move close to the shore and swim with her body nearly scraping along the beach bed before returning to the depths. In her case, the greens, because even Sydney would not allow her to swim by herself in the dark, blue waters where the lake bed steeply dropped off.

She propelled her new liquid body forward, gaining speed as she shot across the dark lake. Algae fingers and darting fish parted an open path before her. She could feel the grin on her nonexistent face. She came to the shadow of a small metal fishing boat and drifted directly beneath it, able to see the tiny blotches of rust decorating its belly. She could hear the laughter of two lovers as they whispered in their metal retreat. They had slipped away, seizing the solitude of the shadowy bay, completely unaware of her silent intrusion on their romantic escapade. She moved away, her mind abuzz with a dream so real that she dared not consider it.

Abby turned over in the lake and stared up through the water at the navy sky. Thousands of gaseous balls, only specks to her earthbound eyes, blinked back at her. The moon – no longer full, but still plump and radiant – cast a single streak across the dark water. Below her, a rainbow trout floated lazily in a mass of seaweed, his white underbelly drifting above glossy tentacles. She expected him to dart away, but he remained unmoved, and she slid closer, slipping her fingers over his greenish bronze scales and feeling the prickle of his barbed skin. His yellow eye stared past her, searching for more menacing or appetizing lake life.

As she glided further into the lake, swirling water caught her attention. She dived towards it, watching as the small tornado gained in size, grasping sand and seaweed and spinning them in a white cone of bubbles. The tornado began to burrow, sand lifting from the sea floor, blinding Abby, and she started to swim away, afraid of being sucked into the vortex. But then the sand started to clear, and she saw the tornado disappear into a crevice that started as a black split and grew wider until she looked down into a long, dark hole that ran jaggedly along the sandy bottom. The hole emitted a blue light that became an image, like a movie, and she watched, awestruck.

She could see Detective Alva, his bony fingers tapping thoughtfully on the hood of a waxy black car, recently washed and shining like a beetle's shell in the sun. His eyes scanned the empty dirt road before him, but no cars drove along the dusty street. On either side of the road, woods bore down. It was a three seasons road, clearly not often used, and snakes of green vine crawled across it, smothering the ditches on either side.

The detective cocked his head and smiled. "Is that you, Tobias? Stealthier every day, my son."

Behind the car, a tall man, black clothes sheathing his bone-white skin, stepped from the trees. His eyes looked bloody, red pupils with black irises, and he grinned at Alva, who had turned to greet him.

"My child, you need to eat."

Tobias nodded and ran a slender hand through his black hair, slick and brushed back from his forehead.

"I should have kept Devin for myself," Tobias said, striding to the car. The men did not touch, but stared hard at each other for several minutes, a long time to Abby, who watched from another world, from a dream, she thought.

Tobias scared her. Something sinister leaked from him, but also something familiar. She had sensed him before, in the woods when Devin died, in the grocery store—the man hidden behind the freezer. She was looking at her ghost, at the thing that had been stalking her. She recoiled when his dark tongue darted from his lips and almost lost the image. For a moment, the sea flickered before her, but she concentrated on the men, and the vision returned.

"Well, as luck would have it, Trager City appears to be a coven in itself. Just today I met another young witch, more pure than any I have seen in a long time." Alva's smile grew wider as he spoke.

"Yes, yes, I thought so," Tobias said, leaning against

112

the car, oblivious to the hot surface. "I've been following someone."

"Of course, your senses are improving. Can you find her easily?" Alva asked.

"Yes."

"Good, then do. The ritual will be stronger if you hold it in the same place."

"And you? Do you need her, father?"

Alva lowered his eyes to his fingernails; they looked sharper than Abby remembered.

"No, I am full now. But do not consume her all yourself. Save some for the collective."

"Yes."

Tobias slipped back into the trees, barely a rustle as he disappeared into the forest. Two more people waited for him, but they wore thick, black robes that concealed their faces. One of them lifted a hand, and Abby saw pale fingers. The middle finger, long and slender, was encircled with a simple silver band, in its center a fat, white pearl balanced on the precious metal.

As Abby watched, her view changed, it moved away from the three figures and sped across the forest. She watched trees and shrubs and roads rush by and then she was staring at herself asleep on the wooded floor, at her body curled into a ball, her hand thrust into her chopped hair cradling her head.

* * * *

Abby woke with a jolt and scrambled to her feet, spinning and searching the woods around her. Tobias was not there, nor were the others. She stood alone, returned to the woods, her dreams receding. Her head no longer ached. Instead, her brain buzzed electrically, like she'd been plugged into an outlet and recharged. She flexed her hands and then bent her knees, grateful to have her body back, but terrified of the visions that followed her.

Why had she dreamt of the detective and the strange man that he called Tobias? Why had she returned to the cave only to be catapulted into the sea—as liquid as the water that surrounded her? Sebastian had mentioned the name Tobias. Were they all in it together?

A car roared by on the road. She moved to the edge of the woods and stared out. Her car remained in place, undamaged, and the road lay deserted except for the back of a white SUV disappearing around a curve. She heard another car approach and retreated to the woods, ducking behind a thick white birch. A small silver pickup truck passed and did not slow.

She remembered Tobias dipping into the woods to meet his friends. He had been following her. She felt sure of it. He had spoken with the detective of hunger and eating. Were they cannibals? The thought terrified her and she wrapped her arms over her chest.

"What if it's real?" she asked out loud. A cricket chirped in response, and a grasshopper took flight near her feet, landing on a Black-Eyed Susan and tipping the flower beneath its weight.

She had to act, to move, but where? She dared not return to Sydney's. Sebastian might be waiting. Maybe there was a whole group of murderers, a satanic cult or something. She also could not return to the police station and risk another encounter with Detective Alva. He had done something to her, hypnotized her maybe. That's why her head ached so badly. She knew that leaving the city was her best plan. She could hit the freeway and drive to Lansing, but what if they sought her at home?

In her car, Abby felt safe. She turned on the heat

despite the scorching day, and her body trembled beneath the blasts of hot air.

When she pulled into the library parking lot, she did not have a plan. She wanted to look up Devin and Aubrey Blake on the internet. She also wanted to search Sebastian, Alva and cannibals in northern Michigan. It seemed ridiculous to expose herself, but the library had always been a safe place to her growing up, and she deluded herself now into believing that it still was. She watched the library door, blinking dumbly as a young man walked out and two older women walked in. When nothing aroused her suspicions, she slipped out of her car and jogged to the door, pulling it too hard and slamming it loudly behind her.

A bird-like librarian sat behind the counter, her dark eyes narrowing as Abby entered. Training her eyes on the floor, Abby hurried by, feeling like a kid stealing candy. What was it about librarians that made you feel so criminal?

She sat down at a computer and began her search. She started with Devin Blake. Over six thousand hits came back and she slowly scrolled the pages, hoping for something that popped out. She clicked on a site called *Velvet Night*, because it not only mentioned the name Devin Blake, but also Trager City, Michigan. The introduction revealed that the site was dedicated to art from the dark side. The number two contributor was one Devin Blake. Abby eyed the list displayed beneath Devin's name: 'The Inferno', 'Bleeding Moon', 'Flight of Night' and 'Into The Cave.' Abby shuddered, sickened by the emotional torrent of a dead girl. She clicked on Devin's name, and a short bio appeared.

Hey, this is Devin, recently Blake, previously Kent – it's a long story and since you're here for art and not my life story, I'll skip it. My drawings come from a well inside of me, these images bubble up and I just draw them. Some are pretty dark and maybe a bit strange, but it's my therapy, my sanctuary and, quite frankly, my salvation. So keep your comments to yourself – I'm not here to please you – just to share.

The bio didn't reveal much, but Abby still read it twice more before returning to the drawings. It was Devin's voice in those words, her bit of self revealed. Abby clicked the image titled 'Into The Cave' – it was dated only three weeks earlier. The image loaded slowly, tiny segments appearing like a puzzle. As more fragments emerged, Abby felt her pulse quicken. The picture revealed gray, craggy walls bending in a tight tunnel, a pinpoint at the end that opened wider. She leaned into the screen. The opening was drawn deep into the background, but Abby could see the speck of orange flecked by black, the fire and the cloaked figures. She shoved away from the computer as if Devin's face had popped from the sketch in a bloody grin.

Abby felt cold inside. She had been in that drawing – traveled the tunnels of clammy rock and seen the blaze. Her world tilted, but she clenched her eyes closed and gripped the chair's arms. The slow drum of the air conditioner, a meek cough from the stern librarian – she used these sounds to ground her. Opening her eyes slowly, she slid back to the computer, clicking other drawings, but nothing jarred her as the first. They were dark, as Devin had said, black shadows crouching in corners, several depicting massive fires filled with screaming faces. One more image was familiar. It was a single, glorious castle suspended above the water. Abby had seen something similar in the palm of one of the cloaked figures from the cave.

Perhaps she was overreacting. There were thousands of caves and castles in the world. Maybe Devin had gone to a bonfire in one that just happened to be strangely similar to her dream. But her head disagreed, it shook from side to side, and her thoughts could not change the truth. Something larger than coincidence was happening. Abby had slipped into a series of events that she could not escape from, down the rabbit hole—so to speak.

She typed in 'Aubrey Blake' and another long list of hits came back, mostly ads for writers, business owners and lawyers. She tried again, but this time added 'witch' after the name. This changed the sites dramatically. She went from normal to fantasy, filing through lists of websites devoted to witches, black magic, love spells and other mystical creatures. The first several sites simply listed Aubrey and Blake among the varying names, no Aubrey Blake.

Frustration edged in. She clicked on a site called *A History of Magic*. The screen flashed black, and lines of falling stars wove down the page. Someone had put a lot of effort into the site. As the black faded, she saw an image emerge. It was a large group of women and men standing in an open field. Their clothes were old-fashioned, deep, drab grays, but their faces were luminous. Their arms were interlinked and in the background hung a massive, white moon. Abby leaned forward, noticing a familiar face, ringlets of hair sticking from beneath a hood. Aubrey, Devin's ancestor who could have been her twin, stood in the group wearing a broad smile on her lips.

Abby grinned, knowing that she had finally found something. She began to scroll the page, searching for names, but, just as they appeared, each letter traveling slowly as if from the gravestones of their bearers, the screen went black. The library door swung in, bringing a burst of sweltering summer air. Abby, too distracted by the darkened screen to notice the incoming patrons, stared at the computer in disbelief. She had seen Aubrey in the photo and now it had died?

Crouching on the floor, she found the power button on the computer, pressing it repeatedly – no luck. The tower was dead. She started to wheel to the computer next to her and stopped – noticing for the first time the two people who'd entered the library. They were distinct, to say the least. Both had white blond hair, the girl's long down her back, the boy's short and spiky. They were dressed in jeans and black t-shirts, their skin shock white against their dark clothing. The woman might have been a movie star; her cat-like charcoal eyes were thick and hooded. They moved through the library purposefully and stopped in front of a rack of DVDs. They did not speak, but when their eyes met, Abby felt icy fingers tickle her spine.

* * * *

Sebastian moved quickly, stuffing papers and journals into boxes and sprinting them in loads to the car he had rented. It was a Camaro, "fast," the dealer said, and dark, so it could be concealed. His black curls stuck to his head, and he packed shirtless, sweating anyway. Abby still had not returned, and panic had given way to rage as he imagined her whereabouts. He had seen Detective Alva, followed him and watched his meeting with Tobias like a shocked bystander witnessing a car accident. He did not attack them like he wanted to, planned to. He only watched, shaking and nauseated as Tobias drifted back into the woods, a demon in disguise. Sebastian was a coward, and the reality of his choice, the choice not to kill, twisted inside his skull until he felt it would explode.

He had heard only bits of their conversation, the rest muffled by distance and wind. He'd had to conceal himself from them, which meant not only hiding, but also blocking their ability to sense him, which he had read in Claire's journal was a faculty of very powerful Vepars. Mother Nature provided the best shield, and Claire had an entry that listed protection plants, two of which, ivy and fern, grew abundantly in Michigan. He had lain down on the forest ground, nestling into a thicket of ferns and straining to hear Alva when he spoke. He had not expected to hear the voice of Tobias, and when the empty sound reached him, he nearly cried out in shock. How could he have been so foolish? He should have known the moment that Abby found the body that the Vepars were near. But it had been two years since Claire's death. Two years of futile searching with little or no result. He had started to wonder if he was insane or Claire was insane and the whole idea of witches had been some elaborate way to deal with their parents' deaths.

On the lake a sailboat drifted, its tall, white sails flaccid in the still air. He kept his ears perked for Abby but heard nothing. He had driven around for an hour after hearing Alva and Tobias, sure that he and Tobias searched for the same girl and that her life depended on his reaching her first. But he did not find her and began to convince himself that she had returned to Lansing, to her family, and maybe would be safe, at least for a little while.

He rented the Camaro and returned to Sydney's to pack his stuff and plan his attack. If Abby returned, he would take her and they would run. If she didn't, he would attempt to kill Tobias and Alva. He might die, he knew that, but the fear did not deter him. Death would be a welcome respite from his crusade for vengeance, so long as they went down first.

* * * *

Abby's hands grew cold; her whole body grew cold, as if someone had just cranked up the air conditioner. As she stood, the girl shot a single glance in her direction, raking her eyes over Abby. Something was wrong. All of the flesh on Abby's body crawled, and she searched her brain for understanding, trying to get a sense of the irrational fears pummeling her. She could see that neither person was looking at the DVDs. Instead they both had their eyes trained downward, focused. She followed their gaze to the girl's slender pale hand, to the middle finger where a white pearl shone from a familiar silver ring. As Abby watched, the pearl flashed black, white again and then stayed black. The pair's eyes shot up instantly, locking on Abby.

She stumbled backwards, her legs hit the computer chair and it spun away, knocking gently against the desk. The ring from her dream, the ring on the hand of the cloaked figure who was with Tobias, was on the hand of the woman in front of her. The woman whose eyes looked dark, black, even; they were inhuman eyes.

Abby watched them, their set jaws, unmoving lips. They did not speak, but she heard them, only for a moment, as clear as if they'd whispered in her ear. "We must lure her out." It was the voice of the woman, low and throaty. The man, just a boy really, gave the smallest nod, almost nonexistent.

Chapter 12

Sebastian slammed the trunk and cast a final, fleeting glance at Sydney's house. Would he ever return? He doubted it. Tonight he would kill Tobias, which made every sight more beautiful, more meaningful than it had ever been. Sydney's house had been a place of joy for him and Claire as children. It would be a place of triumph and perhaps of death that night.

He intended to do a final search for Abby in the city and pick up a few, last minute, items at the store. He did not know how to kill a Vepar. In all of Claire's journals, she did not have a single entry about this one, vitally important, subject. Claire's guide, the witch Adora, had disappeared before Claire's death and most likely had not had ample time to teach Claire to defend herself. Sebastian resented the witch for this single fatal error that might have saved his sister's life.

He laid his gun on the seat beside him. It was loaded, but he did not feel adequately armed. He doubted that guns did much in the world of witches and Vepars.

* * * *

Abby jerked her head toward the librarian, who read a newspaper, obliviously. She straightened up, brushed a hand through her hair and hurried toward the door. They did not immediately move behind her, but she felt their eyes piercing her back.

She burst into the bright sunlight and broke into a run, wrenched her car door open and dived inside. She hit the lock button and turned toward the library door, which was slowly swinging shut. She caught only a wisp of the girl's hair as they disappeared around the corner of the building. They were after her. She shoved her key in the ignition and turned – nothing. She tried again, pumping the gas pedal, but not even a growl emitted from the engine. The battery was dead. She'd left her car lights on often enough to know that lack of sound, but this time it wasn't her headlights that had killed the battery. She stayed low in her seat, peeking over the dash in search of her pursuers.

She could stay in the car, doors locked, and honk until someone came. But would that work? Or would the two killers play the rescuers to the scared girl? She could run for it.

The police station was on the other side of town, too far and too risky with Detective Alva. The closest building housed a string of downtown boutiques. Surely, they would not attack her if people were around. She was separated from the building by an open parking lot. If she ran through it, they would have ample time to get her. Across the street stood the woods that snaked back to the lake. Of course if they got her there, they'd have cover to do whatever they wanted. She felt that time was running out – she had to move. She opened her door, crouched low, and slipped onto the pavement, careful to keep her head below the windows. She had only to sprint across the street. She counted the steps it would take, twenty maybe.

With a final breath, she ran. Her sneakers smacked the pavement, hammering in her ears. She strained to hear movement behind her, but caught nothing. Running at full sprint, she darted into the woods, heading straight for a giant mess of bushes. She ducked behind them, burrowing deep into the branches for cover. At first, she thought that they weren't coming – that perhaps she had imagined the whole ordeal – paranoia at its finest. Then she saw her. The girl moved stealthily along the tree perimeter, her eyes scanning the forest. She stepped into the woods, the sun glinting off her blond hair. Abby could not see the boy. She held her breath, feeling the burn flowering in her chest, but fighting it. *I am not here – I am not here,* she repeated in her mind until she almost believed it.

She gradually became aware of a rustling behind her, but dared not move. Praying that she'd adequately concealed herself, she watched in horror as the boy moved into her line of sight. He didn't appear to see her, but stood close enough that a single breath would not escape his attention. She clenched her eyes shut and imagined a game that she used to play as a child. It was called Statue. She and her neighbor, Cassi, would stand in front of the mirror, both of their eyes trained on the other. The first to move, even a twitch, lost. Abby lost a lot, her patience rarely spanned more than two minutes. Abby reopened her eyes as the boy moved closer to the road; the girl came to meet him.

"She's gone," the girl hissed, her venomous voice ringing in Abby's head.

"I hear nothing," he replied, a look of exasperation crossing his face. "Could she have doubled back to the road?"

The girl shook her head furiously, glaring into the trees around her.

"Your ring is white," he said, grasping the woman's hand in his own and moving it from side to side.

"She's not in here." The woman sounded angry, but also frightened, like she had failed.

"But we can still find her, Vesta. Let's go back to the library and wait at her car."

"You fool," she hissed. "You think she'll return to her car after we chased her?"

He said nothing.

"Tobias was right, of course he was right." She spoke more to herself than the boy, her right eye twitching angrily.

A loud buzzing interrupted them and the boy took out a slender black phone.

"We lost her," he told the caller, running a pale hand through his hair. "Yes, she is aware of something, but I don't know what. We can keep looking…are you sure? Okay we'll be there."

"What is it?" the girl asked, moving closer to him.

"We have to leave. He's being followed, he's sure of it now."

The girl's face contorted in rage, and she raced from the trees, the boy close at her heels.

Abby waited, the seconds crawling. A slow aching had spread from her feet, up her legs and into her lower back. She longed to shift, even just a bit, but could not move. Her fear left her immobilized, like an ice sculpture, frozen inside and out. They could be trying to trick her. As she waited, she heard an engine roar to life. Through the trees she saw a flash of red as a car whizzed by.

Was it them? The minutes crawled. The bushes became stifling and Abby felt her tank-top clinging to her back. She let out a long, slow breath of air and waited. Nothing. No pounding steps through the woods. She was alone.

Pushing branches to the side, she ducked low and then back up, disentangling herself from the brush. They hadn't seen her; she could hardly believe it. Her car was dead, and if they were lying in wait, they would see her leave the woods. She knew the way to Sydney's house on foot. If she followed the path of the woods closest to the beach, she'd be near tourists, but still out of sight. Walking slowly, each foot carefully placed for the least amount of noise, she moved back toward the beach.

* * * *

Sydney's house came into view, and Abby leaned against a tree in relief. She'd been walking for over an hour, and even the shade from the forest could not dull the boiling sun. The air was still and wet, the humidity causing what remained of her hair to frizz and the soft short hairs on the back of her neck to kink into a matted ball. She slid to the ground and lifted her shirt, wiping the bottom across her sweaty forehead.

Her vantage point revealed the front, right corner of the house, the bay window jutting out of the pale blue siding. She could see the long porch that wrapped around the lakeside of the house, the black, wrought-iron lounge chair that Sebastian had sat in just a day and a half earlier. She had hoped for Sebastian's car, but the driveway stood empty. Somehow, in all that had happened, she felt that Sebastian was an ally. She did not understand how he came to have Aubrey Blake's stuff, but Abby could not forget the confusion on his face when she fled. He seemed genuinely confused and not at all threatening.

She waited and watched. If the two strangers had followed her to the library, they might know where she was staying. She pulled off her tennis shoes and massaged her feet. A blister had formed on her left heel and throbbed dully. Even Sydney's tennis shoes were built more for fashion than function. She wanted to wade into the lake, allow the water to cool her down, but of course she couldn't. Even in areas where the stretch of beach was thin, she couldn't risk being out in the open. So, what, then?

Wait, wait and hope.

After a half hour of observation and no discernable movement near the house, Abby decided to go in. She sprinted from the woods to the door, her feet clacking on the wooden planks of the porch. She pressed against the house and slipped forward, shooting a final glance towards the empty driveway.

Fishing her keys out of her pocket, she turned to the house lock. It was broken, the entire knob smashed out. A gaping hole revealed the interior of the house, splinters of door littering the floor. She stifled a scream, an automatic reaction to the invasion before her. They'd been to Sydney's; they might still be in the house. She pulled away from the door, flattening her body, and waited, but no noise sounded, there were no muffled voices. She crept to the kitchen window and peeked inside. The kitchen was empty, but a mess. There were open cabinets, coffee dripping off the edge of the counter, a bottle of wine smashed, leaving long maroon streaks across the small white kitchen mat. She continued around the house, peering in windows, searching for any movement, alert to any sound.

After biting her lip until it bled, she decided to go in, at least to call the police and arm herself with something other than her car keys. She slipped her shoes back on; they felt snug on her swollen feet.

Lamps were smashed on the hardwood floor, books strewn across the living room and nearly every shelf was tipped on its side.

Her hands shook, and she had to balance against the wall to face the destruction upright. Terror unfolded anew as she plodded over shards of glass, images of her childhood staring back at her. Sydney's wall of memories had been annihilated viciously, and for what reason? She bent and ran her finger along a silver-edged frame. A spider web of glass blocked most of the image, a picture of Abby dressed as a fairy for Halloween. She must have been ten.

The living room phone was ripped from the wall jack and lay tangled next to the shattered television. She winced at every crunch of some valued possession beneath her sneakered feet. Sydney kept another phone in her study. This room was not nearly as ravaged as the living room and kitchen. The desk drawers were pulled open and a bookshelf lay on its side, otherwise it was untouched. Abby lifted the phone from the cradle to a dead dial tone, and her stomach dropped again. But even as she faced the dead air, she knew that calling the police was futile. Who would they send but Detective Alva? And he had some corrupt hand in the whole mess, Abby was sure.

She missed her mother, not for the first time that week. Her invasive, overbearing mother, who, in a moment like this, would have some iron clad plan that could not fail. Like the 'family fire strategy' that her mother created after a news broadcast about the frequency of dryer fires. Not only did her mother coordinate the plans with their next-door neighbors, she typed them up, laminated them and stapled them next to every door in the house.

Her mother's tight-lipped smile rose in her thoughts, and Abby knew that her mother was not equipped to face the violence that Abby stood in, ankle deep. People wanted to kill her. They were not normal people and they had already killed once, maybe more.

Abby clicked the dial but there was still no tone. She turned, searching hopefully for her cell phone. It was dead, but maybe if she could get enough time to dial…someone. Her hands flew across the desk, scattering papers, and her eyes roved over the room, but she could not find it. Lowering to a squat, she pressed the heels of her hands deep into her eyes. Everything wanted to pour out.

Abby heard a sound and froze. The study had only a single doorway for escape, no windows. She stood fast, blood rushing to her head, followed by a wave of dizziness. Unsteadily, she tiptoed to the door and slipped into the hallway. Someone was on the deck, their shoes shuffling quietly, but not quietly enough. Abby held her breath and edged up Sydney's stairs; she could not make it out of the house without passing the intruder.

From Sydney's bedroom window, a chilling sight greeted her. The blond woman with dead eyes paced the dock, her hair billowing in the breeze coming off the water. The pale skin of her forehead was wrinkled in thought and her chin was tilted. She was sniffing the air.

Downstairs, the front door groaned. Someone shuffled into the house; the door clicked closed quietly, intentionally. Abby searched the room for a place to hide, but knew that she could not risk getting trapped. Sydney's window was the only possible escape. If Abby climbed through it the blond woman would have a clear view of her; maybe she could already smell her. Her entire body perspired, her already filthy shirt stank. She cursed herself for putting on the sequin tank top. How could she be courageous in glitter?

"Vesta!" The shout echoed from the lower floor.

The blond woman's head jerked up, and she moved toward the house. Abby could see her scowl deepening.

"Shut up, Tane," she growled as she crossed the porch. "What if she's close?"

"She is…"

Abby swallowed, her tongue thick and heavy.

His voice was low and excited. "Look at your ring."

Abby felt her body moving before her brain comprehended the danger closing in. She jerked open Sydney's window as their feet hit the stairs, each explosive smack blistering her thoughts. Tumbling onto the small eave, Abby felt her body thrown forward as she slid down the steep shingles. She hit the eaves trough and shoved her feet in, flattening her back on the hot roof. The ground lay fifteen feet directly below her, a straight drop.

Above her, Vesta was screaming orders at Tane, who had stuck his head out the window. His dark eyes connected with Abby's. She did not wait, but pitched forward and flung herself from the roof, flailing in mid-air before she hit the grass with an audible thwack. A searing pain shot up her calf, but she ignored it, springing to her feet and running for the woods. Tane had followed her down the roof, but Vesta banged out the front door, already running across the lawn towards her, her teeth bared.

Abby reached the woods first and raced in, searching for any place to dive and hide, but there were none. She'd entered a thicket of pine trees, the ground littered with red needles and the trees thick with green. She had only a second before Vesta would reach the woods. Darting ahead, she jumped to pass over a decaying log and sprang into the air. Her legs scissored wildly, but she shot straight up, hitting the bough of a thick pine nearly twenty feet high. Her fingers clawed the bark and she nearly fell back to the forest floor, but with a single heave she looped her bicep around the branch and hung on.

Below her, Vesta rushed into the woods, her muscular arms pumping savagely. She passed beneath Abby, oblivious to her hanging high above. Tane followed, darting past, a slur of inaudible words coursing from his mouth.

Swinging her legs and biting her lip against the noise, she arched back and up. Her right leg hooked the branch and she scrambled onto it, her body flat against it, legs and arms dangling over either side.

She struggled into a crouch and shuffled to the trunk, pressing her back against the sappy bark. The forest floor stretched out below her, and she fought the dizziness brought on by the height; too high, she could not have jumped that high.

She tried not to think of her current dilemma – of the

power that had sent her literally flying into the tree to safety. She'd read about amazing strength during adrenaline rushes, though never anything as bizarre as jumping the height of a telephone pole.

Vesta and Tane moved back into her line of sight. They were arguing, Vesta's face contorted with fury.

"You're a fool, Tane. I knew you weren't ready. If she escapes…" She spoke through gritted teeth, anger banging out every word.

"Come on, Vesta. No biggie. So we lost her…again. Big whoop. We'll get her." Tane was much more relaxed, even joking as he playfully punched Vesta's shoulder.

She caught his fist, and he squealed in surprise, shrinking away from her.

"I will not be shamed by you."

She stomped ahead of him from the woods, her fists balled at her sides. He followed, but his head was cast down. He shot a final glance into the trees, but saw nothing.

Abby wanted to scream at them, "What do you want?" But bit her lip instead. She didn't want to die, but she was tired and scared. She'd done nothing to deserve this. She'd only found the body. Dammit, why hadn't she just stayed out of it? They probably knew that she was investigating, trying to find clues. She had brought this on herself. But what was the alternative? Do nothing? No, it wasn't even an option. Devin had lived, she'd breathed, laughed, probably even loved. Abby could not stand idly by, she had lived that way for too long. Her crusade, however, did little to comfort her as she huddled high in the trees like a raccoon watching the wolves circle below.

* * * *

Ink had begun to dim the smoldering sky, and Abby's

entire body ached. She'd shifted positions on her tree branch a hundred times, but to no avail. Frankly, she didn't know how the squirrels did it.

She had no idea where Tane and Vesta had disappeared to – most likely back to Sydney's to lie in wait. Returning to the house was a death wish, and Abby intended to live. Of that, at least, she was sure. Her only chance was to backtrack through the woods, maybe watch the road for somebody to flag down to take her…anywhere.

When the last of the pink slipped below the horizon, she began a slow crawl out of the tree. Her calf had swollen, throbbed and then stopped hurting. She kept putting pressure on it, but the pain seemed to have vanished. It was probably broken, and her body kept the pain at bay by producing copious amounts of natural painkillers, which might also explain why she felt buzzed, like she'd just drank a pot of coffee on an empty stomach. Halfway down the tree, headlights swept over the forest, pulling to a stop in Sydney's driveway. Pausing in midair, she squinted through the branches at the silhouette of a car. Had more of them arrived?

She heard the door slam and a familiar shape emerged. Sebastian.

She started to call out, but stopped herself, a shocked hand going to her mouth. If she called to him, they would hear her. She hesitated for a moment, considering a final time that he might be in on it, but the thought felt wrong. He wasn't in on it, and she could not allow him to walk into a trap. She had to get to him.

Clenching her jaw against the fear that seized her, she dashed from the trees. He was crossing the porch as she reached the lawn, her arms flailing in a silent warning. Nearing the door, a single hand outstretched, he turned, his wide eyes glimpsed Abby and registered her hysterical gestures, but she was too late. The door flung open and Tane dived out, connecting with Sebastian and driving him to the porch floor.

"Run!" he screamed at Abby, but she stayed rooted in place, her feet like cement boots.

Tane straddled him, holding a hunk of his black hair in a single hand. Sebastian thrashed beneath him, but could not break free.

"Abby, there's a gun in my car," he screamed, twisting to look at her.

She started for the car, but Vesta rocketed from the back of the house. Abby turned, but her foot caught a divot, and she tripped. Vesta was on her, her black eyes flashing as she shoved Abby's face into the grass. Abby tried to lift up, twist her head to get a breath, but Vesta held her in a death grip. Her fingernails dug into Abby's scalp, pushing her face down and down. She opened her mouth to dirt and grass; it pushed in, suffocating her. She felt a sharp poke, like a bite on her shoulder. Lungs burning, her muscles gradually growing slack, twilight shoveled its darkness on Abby's bursting skull.

Chapter 13

Sebastian could not see. He blinked against the fabric covering his eyes and tried to assess his surroundings. His hands were bound tight, legs too, but he was upright. Something that tasted coppery, like blood, was shoved in his mouth, and it scared him to smell the scent so close.

He was bound to a tree, his arms wrapped tightly behind him and around the trunk, which dug into his bare skin. The bark pressed into his back, and his head hung slack on his shoulders. He had been hit hard with something, a bat maybe, and wondered if the blood that he tasted was his own.

He had failed, returned to Sydney's like a fool, hoping that Abby might have come back. Now they would both die, and the Vepars would go on.

"No," he murmured. He had to, to maintain control of his thoughts.

Claire had learned that from Adora. "It is the most important thing," Adora had said, "monitoring your thoughts. It is not the danger that kills you – it's the fear. Don't let the fear in."

He heard movement, but did not want the Vepars to know that he was conscious. He had the advantage if they underestimated him, and he needed every possible advantage. The gun was gone; he'd left it in his car, foolishly imagining that Sydney's house posed no danger. He had kept a knife in his back pocket, but its familiar pressure was gone as well.

* * * *

Abby's head was slick with pain. She registered the

ache and understood that she was still alive, not suffocated in Sydney's yard. She kept her eyes closed, listening closely to the sounds around her. Shuffling feet, something thick dragging across the ground, and a sharp scraping in the dirt. Her hands were bound separately above her head and her legs as well, her form in the shape of an X.

Carefully, she stared out through slitted eyelids. Trees yawned over her, limbs reaching towards each other in a skeletal embrace, leaves thick and green bowing down. Darkness had closed in, but the moon cast a bright tunnel onto the forest floor. Three cloaked figures moved around her, their faces hidden from view. None turned as she opened her eyes fully, followed by a low gasp of fear as she recognized her location. She lay at the site of Devin's body, the rotted log in full view to her right. Twisting her neck, she stared at a leather coated stake dug deep into the earth. She followed a silk cord to where it wrapped tightly around her wrist. One of the hooded figures used a long sword to scrape symbols into the dirt.

Sebastian. His face popped into her head and she jerked against the restraints. No point trying to play unconscious now.

"Sebastian!" she screamed. It was pathetic, her voice, hoarse and sandpapery, barely filling the cavern of her mouth.

"Relax, little girl." Vesta lifted her hood, long blond tresses rolling over her black cloak. She moved toward Abby slowly, a wicked grin stretched over her parted mouth. Riveted, Abby stared at the vicious animal that was Vesta, only moments before the attack. Vesta squatted down and dipped her fingers into a black chalky substance that she wiped roughly across Abby's forehead, pressing hard into her thumping skull.

"Where's Sebastian?" Abby gasped. She craned her

neck upward, but beyond the fissure of moonlight every space stood in shadow.

"Uh, oh, getting upset? We can't have that," Vesta crooned. She crushed a palm hard into Abby's throat and pressed.

Abby choked, her eyes bulging, as the soft tissue began to cave in, cutting off her airflow. Her arms fought against the binds, but they only made small flapping circles, a baby bird fallen from its nest.

"Stop!" one of the cloaked figures barked.

Abby watched the man who'd spoken. His voice continued to echo strangely. It sounded like many voices speaking at once. He flipped his hood back, and Abby recognized the man from her dream, Tobias. He turned on his heel, strode to Vesta and ripped her off Abby in a single flick.

Vesta stumbled back, straightened herself and glared at Tobias in reproach. The third figure, Tane, turned to watch the scene unfolding.

"Yes, Abby, at last we meet…in the flesh." Tobias took a deep bow, his white teeth gleaming.

White teeth that looked wrong, too white in the darkness, too white against his red mouth. He and Alva had spoken of eating and of hunger. She pushed out a trembling breath, it stuck in her throat on a sob, but she swallowed it back.

"Let the ground open beneath me," she thought. "Let it swallow me whole."

Vesta walked behind Tobias, running her hand over his shoulder, her sharp nails fingering the fabric of his cloak.

"Stunning in black, isn't he?" She looked adoringly into his eyes, and he smiled back at her, lifting her hand to his lips.

"Almost there," Tane muttered, as he finished a final

J.R. Erickson

marking to Abby's right.

"What do you want?" Abby whispered, awash in fresh terror. Each emotion came as a wave: shock, despair, confusion, and horror, with an underlying desire—no, obsession—to just wake up. Through the fog of emotion she watched Tobias, his long fingers rubbing together as if in preparation for a tasty meal. Her skin crawled as his pink tongue glanced off his lower lip. His eyes continued to dissect her across the clearing.

"I wanted you to be awake for this, my dear," Tobias whispered as though murmuring to a lover. He knelt beside her, ran a single chilled finger along her arm, wrist to neck. "I could have let you sleep, made you sleep, but this is my gift to you."

He smelled like death, his breath stank of rot and decay. She recoiled, but the foulness stayed, making her gag.

A low moan caught her attention. She broke Tobias's trancelike gaze.

"Sebastian!" she screamed, and fire ripped through her swollen throat.

Tobias laughed, contemptuous. Vesta sneered and kicked dirt at Abby's face. She closed her eyes too late and felt the gritty sting of sand beneath her eyelids.

"Well, well, the entire party has arrived," Tobias said.

Abby blinked hard until she could see again.

"Abby?" Sebastian yelled as if a gag had been removed. He sounded groggy.

"Yes, I'm here. Oh, God, please, just let him go," Abby's voice cracked and she clenched her eyes against the tears.

"You have no power over us, Vepar," Sebastian said in a low, serious voice that shocked Abby to silence.

"You use that name freely?" Tobias snarled, rushing out of Abby's sight. She heard a thud, flesh on flesh and

Sebastian gasped, but did not cry out.

She wanted to scream and protest, but understood that if she wasted her energy, she would surely die. Vesta had moved closer to Abby, taking long, deep inhalations like she wanted to smell her, taste her. Abby panted, terrified, and tried to focus on her breath. She had to calm down.

Tobias returned, his dark lips wet and his eyes glazed. He wiped the back of his hand over his mouth. Abby saw a streak of red on his pale hand.

"Oh, God, help me! Please, someone, help us!" she screamed and started to cry, struggling against her bonds. She dug her heels into the dirt and ground down, but knew that she could not rip free.

Tobias laughed; loud insane laughter that flooded the forest and made Abby's brain feel soft and swollen. She wanted to shove her hands over her ears. The others joined him, their laughter drowning out Abby's cries.

Sebastian began to murmur and the laughter stopped.

"What do you say, human?" Tobias shouted, mocking him. "Do you pray to your God for help? Or do you pray to your sister…Claire?"

"Shut up!" Sebastian's scream pierced the silence, and, for a moment, even Tobias stopped to stare.

Abby shook with fear, twisting into the earth like it might protect her. Her shoulder hit a rock and she winced, wishing she had fingers to grab it. She could murder, she would murder, if given the chance.

"This is phenomenal, really, a phenomenon," Tobias sighed, turning his gaze back on Abby. "I have never met one who did not know, at least in some deeper sense. But you, you, my lovely, are completely innocent, so pure…" He bent down, his icy fingers trailing over her cheek. She jerked her head to the side, but he gripped her chin roughly, forcing her to face him. He leaned down and pressed his face into her hair and inhaled.

Vesta hissed, but made no move to stop him.

"However did you find her, Sebastian?" Tobias asked in his thousand voices. "You are like a magnet for them. Maybe we should keep you."

"Get away from her," Sebastian wailed. Tobias only smiled and nuzzled his face into her neck; she felt a dull scrape as he dragged his teeth across her earlobe.

Abby turned her head away, fighting the urge to face Tobias and bite whatever piece of flesh she could get hold of. Through the shadows, she finally spotted Sebastian. He was not staked to the ground, but to a tree, his arms and legs stretched behind him, concealed by the trunk. He bucked and jerked and howled, but could not break free. It looked painful and Abby lost another shard of hope. He could not possibly break free.

"Let's get on with it," Vesta growled, whipping her hair back angrily. "These games bore me."

Tobias turned and glared at Vesta.

"Patience, Vesta, my killer, or you will not eat again."

Tane fidgeted uncomfortably, glancing from Tobias to Vesta as if a fight might erupt.

"Now, before we begin." Tobias stood and walked to Sebastian. Abby could only see Sebastian in shadow, but his head rose as Tobias neared. "You are already dead. You know that, don't you?"

Sebastian remained silent.

"Though I will hate to finish the man who has hunted me for so long. Such a shame that you had to be wasted this way. You might have joined us, I think, powerful human that you are."

"I will follow you to hell," Sebastian whispered.

"Oh, no, I don't think they'd let you in, but no matter." Tobias waved a hand dismissively. "You still live for one reason. The book. Where is the *Book of Shadows?*"

"What Book of Shadows?"

"Don't toy with me, human," Tobias said, low and quiet. "Where is the *Book of Shadows?*"

"If you're talking about Claire's books, they're gone. I burned them a year ago, when I gave up looking for you," Sebastian lied.

Abby listened, rapt. She had seen the *Book of Shadows.*

"He lies," Vesta snarled, kneeling next to Abby. "But we can help him tell the truth."

Vesta grasped Abby's head in her palm, sinking her fingernails into the flesh of Abby's scalp and forehead. A searing pain shot over her skin, and Abby howled in agony.

"Stop!" Sebastian screamed.

Vesta loosened her hold, but Abby felt the burning gouges. Tears rolled from her eyes and she turned away from the sight of Vesta, who smiled meanly above her.

"The Book?" Tobias asked again.

"It's at Sydney's house. I hid it there. I can show you where."

"Liar," Vesta hissed and dug again, but Tobias interrupted her.

"Stop, you fool," he snarled. "She's bleeding, you're wasting her."

Vesta pulled her nails from Abby's skin, and she felt the warm blood trickle towards the back of her head, weaving through her hair.

"You will take us after the ritual," Tobias said simply. "By then you will be ready to die."

Tobias moved back to Abby, staring down at her, his head cocked to the side.

"It is so sad, my dear, that you will never even get to feel it, not once, because it will all belong to me."

He leaned down and licked the blood from her

forehead. His tongue felt hot and bristly.

Abby did not respond. She could barely feel him. Her ears had flooded with sound, and her head throbbed.

Vesta laughed, throwing her blond mane back, her face tilted to the night sky. She looked evil, and Abby felt the magnetism of that thought. They were evil.

A low wind picked up, washing over Abby and swirling her hair around her face. She could smell the lake water, could imagine the coolness against her face. She was so thirsty.

"It's time." Tobias spoke softly. His eyes connected with Vesta and then Tane. They each nodded and moved out of Abby's line of sight. She could hear rustles, but no one spoke. Sebastian continued his struggle, but said nothing; a strange silence had fallen over the group.

Tobias, Vesta and Tane encircled her. A thick grass rope snaked through their hands and they stretched it into a haphazard triangle as they spread out around her body. The rope looked old, bits of grass popping from the whole, deep charcoal and crimson stains embedded along it. The chants began low, just a murmur, their mouths moving in unison. Abby could not hear the words; they sounded like another language. The three trained their eyes on her, seeing, but not seeing, their pupils like smoky crystal balls. The forest was bathed in a silence so thick that it choked her.

Her brain twisted in circles. How to get away... she tried to cling to those thoughts, but something was happening. Her skull felt as if it were being cracked open, sharp fingernails digging down into the bone and stretching it wide. Then a sensation like hot picks pierced the sensitive flesh all over her body. She pitched and twisted, wanting to rake her nails across her face, rip out her burning eyes, stop the images suddenly flooding her vision. Flashes of death assailed her. Blackened corpses strewn in fields of wildflowers, their flesh rank, stinking in her clothes, her hair and her mouth. In the forest she turned and retched, but nothing came out. The visions continued, blood seeping from open wounds, the glint of a knife as it fell over and over. Abby saw Devin, her face a mask of terror, her arms and legs staked to the earth. Beneath it all, she saw the haze of her captors, their eyes gone from black to hot, red fire, faces of the dead dancing deep in their pupils.

Tobias stood at her feet. His face grew starker in the moonlight, his features changed, his eyes sank deeper and his lips paled to a bleached white. The muscles in his neck elongated and tensed, then flexed into rope-like snakes beneath his engorged skin.

Abby shook her head, but it only brought another surge of terrifying visions. She jerked her face to the right where she encountered the bloated face of Devin, her full lips parted, a teardrop of blood sliding from her mouth. She began to scream, but could not hear it. Only the chants of the three murderers rang in her head. They grew louder. Foreign slurs mixed with English, their voices blending into a single stream of loathing that wrapped erotically around their hunger.

Tremors shook her body, everything vibrated, even her eyes. Fire leapt through her veins, singeing. She had once read a story about a man who was electrocuted; he described it as being burned from the inside out. They were burning her alive without a single flame touching her skin. She screeched, shook, fought, but could not reconnect with the circle and the woods. She was sure that her body was trying to shut down, some defense mechanism to knock her out and end the pain, but they would never get away then. More images slammed into her, but she forced them back.

She searched for solace, some pillar of thought to cling to, and the cave from her dream flashed in her mind. She imagined Devin's drawing of the cave and used it to remember. She saw gray slabs of rock, an impenetrable force. That could be her, a solid wall – a dark, cool mass. She returned to her memory of that dream, a slow trudge, almost liquid air.

She felt the pain subside, but was afraid to end her vision – she concentrated. The cave grew more real and the forest dissolved.

In the tunnel a figure moved forward, Devin. Every surface of her body flickered with tiny glittering lights. She sailed towards Abby, a purple silk cloak billowing around her, fire-red hair flying like buoyant energy in the crammed space of the cave. Abby expected her to sail right through her with a single puff of air, but she slowed and stopped. It wasn't possible, Devin was dead, but none of that mattered.

Am I dead? The thought nearly shocked Abby from the vision and back into the woods, but Devin reached out her hand. Abby felt the touch, fresh, clean, like pressed flour clinging to her fingers. Devin's eyes bore into her, they spoke to her, but her lips did not move.

"What?" Abby wanted to scream, to force the urgent message from Devin's silence. Finally, Devin lifted her hand, her slender fingers opening. Abby stared into her palm; it was filled with water, a small pool cupped there like a precious stone. It glittered and undulated, reflected Abby's face in ribbons. She held her own hand out, thought, *Give it to me.* Devin smiled, extending her arm forward.

Liquid poured in. It was ice cold and thick. Abby opened her eyes to the woods, choking. Tobias knelt over her, a heavy glass bottle clutched in his hand. Spitting and hacking, she tasted the metallic blood as it spilled from her lips and over her chin into the crease of her neck. He was feeding her blood!

The vacant look left Tobias's eyes as he watched the

blood spew from her mouth – replaced with a storm of madness. His face warped and turned wolf-like. His lips shrank back, disappearing beneath a row of pointed teeth, and his eyes narrowed to two tiny black slits. For a second, Abby was sure that he was transforming into a monster – that he would bend forward and feast on her trembling flesh, but his features snapped back into place, the monster was a man again. He squeezed her nose, and the soft cartilage howled in protest as bright stars shot through her head. She gulped the blood, her gag reflex overcome by her empty lungs. He reluctantly pulled the bottle away, and she gasped, the fresh air only a minor relief. The acrid taste coated her lips and gums, the blood smeared over her teeth.

She heard Sebastian's screams of protest, but they sounded far away as if she and the three killers had moved to a suspended plane and he had been left far below. Vesta and Tane were still standing around her, their hands tightly clutching the rope, their lips moving rhythmically.

Abby felt her left palm opening and closing mechanically, her hand empty of the small glassy pool of water that Devin had held. Devin was gone, the cave was gone, but Abby felt a tug, an invisible tendon stretching out, not satisfied with the emptiness that it found. It wanted the lake – wanted to pull it inside of her.

Tobias set the bottle aside, slipping a glinting silver dragon from his bag. The dragon, almost a foot long, flashed in the moonlight. Its head was reared back to reveal tiny ruby fangs. He pulled the tail, which separated from the dragon's torso, and a long, pointed blade emerged. Abby's eyes fastened on the dragon. Its eye, a single black gem, throbbed viciously. Tobias clutched it, but it was as if the dragon held him, a force much larger than the palm-sized, jeweled beast. He placed the dragon on the ground, but held the dagger tightly, wetting his lips.

Abby wanted to fight or scream, any response to the quivering blade lingering dangerously close to her neck, but she could muster none of these things. As she watched, the blade changed color, a subtle pink hue that shaded to a deeper red as he shifted it over her body. Centered above her, directly over the hollow of her rib cage, the blade flashed a brilliant red that momentarily blinded her. She closed her eyes, only for a second, snapping them back open as Tobias gripped her tank top and ripped it up the center, exposing her bare flesh.

The red blade pulsed like a throbbing heart sucking and spurting blood. Tobias's hands shook as he held it tightly, poised over her. The invisible tendon in her palm snapped, her fingers closed on wet coolness, not blood, but water. Her arm jerked involuntarily, but the force was immense. It flew forward, ripping the leather stake from the earth. Her hand connected with the dagger, which sliced into the soft flesh below her thumb, but did not hurt.

For Abby, time slowed, her body moved, but everything else traveled five seconds behind her. Tobias's face registered her free hand, but only as it reached back and ripped her other hand free. He dived towards her, his teeth bared, and she rolled. His face connected with the dirt. The dragon knife spun circles on the forest floor, dirt flying up in small plumes, like a mole tunneling underground.

Abby kicked out and the leather binds around her feet snapped like dental floss. Vesta dropped her piece of the rope, Tobias screamed in protest, but it was too late. The circle, the séance, whatever they had been doing, was broken. Tane looked confused, shaking his head and stumbling forward. Tobias jumped on top of the dragon, which was burrowing into the dirt away from him. The dagger lay on the ground, and Abby snatched it up, feeling it singe and melt into her skin. She jumped to her feet and wheeled around, shoving the dagger out blindly. It ripped across Vesta's torso, cutting only fabric, but she reeled back and fell.

A streak of air whipped by Abby's face, and she gasped, stumbling backwards into a wall of brush that barely held her. Tobias had an arrow in his back. He howled and reached behind him, trying to pull it free.

Abby searched for the source, but saw only darkness in the trees beyond. Another arrow ripped into the clearing. It missed Vesta, just, and lodged in the tree beside her. Her eyes were wide and wild, but she did not hesitate, sprinting to Tobias and jerking the arrow from his back. Abby saw a spurt of black blood pour out from the wound.

Abby ran to Sebastian, who had rubbed the ropes on his hands to frayed tethers that she easily sliced free. She knelt, cut the ties on his legs, wincing at the red, chafed skin on his shins.

The dagger continued to burn, merging with her skin, and she started to cry out as the fire moved up her hand into her wrist. Sebastian grasped the dagger and ripped it free, leaving a welt of raw flesh on her palm.

Behind her another arrow whizzed by. It caught Tane in the leg, and he screamed for Vesta, who ran to him, looking shocked and scared. She grabbed the arrow and pulled it free, screaming and howling like a wounded animal.

Across the clearing, a man dropped from a tree. His blond hair was disheveled, but his blue eyes seemed to laugh at the spectacle before him. He reached behind him, pulled another arrow and let it fly. It missed the fleeing Tobias, barely. The man cursed, immediately reaching for another. The leather strap that held his arrows swung violently as he raced into the forest behind Tobias.

"Go!" Sebastian screamed in her ear.

She hesitated. *Hadn't help arrived?* But Sebastian took

hold of her wrist and pulled her blindly. They left the moonlight and dived into the shadows of the trees. She felt pickers rake across her clothing. Her lungs were strained, and she desperately wanted to glance behind her, but Sebastian made no allowances. She could hear his labored breathing, but he fought through it. At the beach edge, Abby began to turn towards Sydney's house, but Sebastian tugged her roughly in the other direction. They sprinted down the beach, and then he turned back into the woods, moving quickly to a destination that she could not see. They emerged in a small clearing, and she stared at a sleek navy-blue car parked along the wooded edge.

It was not the car that Sebastian had returned in earlier that night, but he bent down, pulling the keys from a magnetic lockbox shoved under the back fender. He unlocked it and opened the passenger door, gently pressing Abby's head down as she slid inside. He climbed in and started the engine – it was surprisingly quiet.

Abby shot a fearful glance toward the window, expecting cloaked figures to surround them, but no one came. He drove from the forest, and the car bounced over divots, its low body protesting the roots that grasped its undercarriage. Abby worried that they might bottom out and get trapped in the woods. Black trees flashed by, and she thought she saw the pale face of Vesta staring at her from the darkness, but then they hit the road with an audible bump and the tires caught pavement, rocketing them forward.

Abby did not question Sebastian as he maneuvered the car onto the freeway, pushing the speedometer past 100. His eyes stayed fixed on the road, his tense face ready for any possible disruption.

"What just happened?" Abby whispered, frightened by Sebastian's haunted features. He looked angry and exhausted, his mouth drooping in a grimace.

"It's okay," he said aloud, perhaps for himself as much as her.

She looked at the raw skin of her hand where a glossy heat radiated.

"Should we have stayed? I mean he saved us. Right? Or was he one of them?" she stammered, twisting in her seat nervously. She didn't even know what *one of them* was.

"They weren't human," she added, remembering.

"No," Sebastian agreed, his eyes straight ahead, the white line a blur, as they fled into the night.

"But what about the man with the arrows? Do you know him? Was he human?"

Sebastian did not look at her and she saw something flash over his face, relief.

A million thoughts rocketed around her head, all encased in a giant aching ball of migraine that had not yet hit full speed. Sebastian leaned forward and opened a small console. Several bottles of pills and a swathe of gauze tumbled out. He lifted a bottle and opened it quickly with his teeth, knocking two gray pills into his hand.

"Here," he said gently, handing her the pills. "They'll help with the pain and a nap."

She stared at the pills, strung between her desire for answers and the throbbing in every inch of her body. What if she took the pills and they were attacked? How would she defend herself?

As if reading her mind, he turned to her, his eyes locking with hers before he turned back to the road. "You're okay, now. I promise."

She took the pills dry and cast a final glance out the window. She thought she saw the man with the arrows sprinting along in the woods, but could not be sure. She shook her head and leaned back against the cool leather seat. The outside world rushed by, the highway void of late night traffic. The trees rose up like ghostly observers on either side of the car – or maybe something worse, much worse. The pills worked quickly. Her head grew light and an impenetrable sleep descended.

Chapter 14

Sebastian gripped the wheel and willed his hands to stop shaking. He felt sick to his stomach and sipped from a bottle of water that had grown hot during the day. Abby snored beside him, and he fought his tiredness, knowing that sleep was not an option.

He knew the way to Lake Superior. He had read Claire's account of the Coven of Ula and the secret island a hundred times in the previous two years. He had even considered trying to reach it, but knew that as a normal man he would never make it. Now he had Abby, a witch, and she would have to guide them there, even if she didn't know it.

He replayed the scene in the woods over and over – a bad record that he couldn't take off. How had he lost control so completely? They had nearly died, and if the stranger had not arrived, they probably would have. The blond man with the arrows bothered Sebastian. He wanted to be the one. He wanted to save Abby and avenge Claire. But how could he resent the man who injured Tobias and allowed them to see another dawn? He couldn't, but he did, and he hated the bitterness that tasted of bile on his tongue. He kept expecting the man to swoop down and land on the hood of his car and laugh at the weak human who tried to defeat a Vepar.

Shame clouded his judgment and chased any lingering fear into the shadows. He would go to the island with Abby and he would demand that they teach him as well. He would still avenge Claire.

* * * *

Abby woke gradually, her head leaning heavily on

Sebastian's shoulder, his hand tenderly clasping her own. A thin line of drool had pooled on his shirt and she tried to nonchalantly wipe it away.

"How did you sleep?" He yawned and stretched his legs in front of him.

She stared out the windshield at a vast body of water. The smooth surface reflected the moon in its glassy face. The dashboard clock blinked three am.

"I feel better." She spoke sluggishly and reached a hand to her forehead that no longer throbbed. Gusts of heat from the vents blew over her stomach, chilling her bare skin. She stared at the blood caked on her ripped shirt.

"I dressed it," he told her quietly, nodding his head toward the small white bandage wrapped around her hand.

"Thank you." She had questions, loads of them, but nothing wanted to come out.

"What's happening, Sebastian?" She watched his face closely, but he did not react. He sighed and rubbed his thumb and forefinger across the bridge of his nose.

"I know and I don't know," he murmured, turning his face to the glowing water. "I—I didn't know about you."

"What does that mean? What about me?" She could not keep the edge from her voice.

"I want to tell you." He pulled one of her hands into his own. "But I'm afraid that I shouldn't be the one. I know this makes no sense and you absolutely deserve to know the truth, but please trust me."

Again, he'd told her nothing, but the jolt of electricity that shot through her hand at his touch washed some of the frustration away. She felt so thankful to be with him, to not be alone and to be alive. What had happened in the woods felt unreal, like a dream.

"Okay." She nodded. "I will trust you and I will let this unfold, so long as you promise that we're not going to run into those guys again."

He laughed and blew a puff of air over his lips. "Absolutely fucking crazy."

"Yeah," she said, remembering, and then trying to forget.

"We're not going to run into them. I think I can guarantee you that. So long as this works, anyway."

"What?"

"This." He spread his hands toward the lake and she squinted through the darkness. Was he kidding?

"I'm sorry, I don't see anything." She stared across the water. In her past life, the water at night had always seemed enchanting, like a treasure box at her disposal. But tonight it looked sinister, deep and black, with the moon's bright light as its facade.

"There's a place in this lake that is hidden." He paused, choosing his words carefully. "Only certain people can find it, and I think you may be one of them. Actually, I'm sure you are, and if we go there, we will find help."

"What if you're wrong? What if I'm not one of the people who can find it?" His hesitation frightened her. "Then what, Sebastian?"

She felt foolish for even asking. Why should she be able to find something that he couldn't?

He threw his hands in the air and shook his head. "I don't know. I would love to tell you I have some brilliant plan, but I don't. I sort of expected to be dead right now."

"Excuse me?"

"Abby." He turned in his seat. "I have been trying to kill that thing for two years. I had planned to finish him last night and…" He pursed his lips and looked at the ceiling of the car angrily. "And he got away again. It's like I'm chasing a phantom, like I'm insane."

"Yes, but he's not a phantom, Sebastian. I can attest to

that."

Sebastian nodded, but said nothing.

Again, a trace of homesickness afflicted her. Never in her life had she felt so confused, petrified, and yet strangely exhilarated. Old Abby bellowed, *Run, get home to mom and dad and Nick. Get therapy, take up pottery, anything to squash these dangerous desires.* But old Abby was calling from a far off place and her voice grew softer the longer she watched Sebastian. He was her connection to something greater, something that she was part of, whether she wanted to be or not.

"What do we do now?" She clapped her hands, startling them both into nervous laughter.

"We row." He stepped out of the car and walked to the edge of the water, disappearing into a cluster of bushes. Appearing a moment later, he dragged a small rowboat, the oars sticking like swords into the night air.

She stepped from the car, welcoming the smooth breeze that poured off the water. Sebastian bent over the boat and flicked away cobwebs. He returned to the car and pulled out a small duffel bag and two towels that he spread over the boat's seats. He loaded the cardboard boxes from Sydney's house beneath the benches and then faced the lake for several long minutes. She noticed, for the first time, that he was dressed entirely in black, as if he'd known that he would be on the run that evening. She glanced down at her own torn tank and dirt speckled pants. A clump of burs stuck angrily in her shoelaces.

"Oh, I forgot." Sebastian smiled, turning to his bag. "I have clothes for you." He returned to the trunk and pulled out a paper grocery bag with black shorts, a black tank top and charcoal slip-ons.

She held them up to the light, but did not recognize them from Sydney's closet.

"I bought them today."

"Why?"

"I saw Tobias and thought...well, not this, but something."

"You saw him where?"

"In the woods with Alva."

Surprised, she looked at him sharply, but did not confess to seeing them also.

She slipped behind the car and pulled them on, discarding her old clothes in the woods. He followed her in and picked them up, swiftly digging a small hole in the dirt and burying them.

"Worried about bears?" she joked, watching his serious features soften slightly.

"Bears would be a treat," he mumbled, returning to the boat and sliding it over a bed of algae-covered rocks. "Here, get in now so your feet don't get wet."

She climbed into the boat, lowering herself in the middle as it wobbled. She stifled a nervous giggle and clutched the sides when it attempted to rock her out. He pushed it further and then jumped into the back, forcing her to the front bench. They were still too shallow to do any decent rowing so he skimmed the oars over the surface and they glided deeper into the lake.

"So, where are we anyway?" she asked, dipping her fingers into the frigid water.

"Lake Superior. Pretty amazing, isn't it?"

It was. In the moonlight Abby could see the lake bed. She watched the plot of rocks give way to long ridges of sand. She felt sure that her water dream had taken place right here, in Lake Superior.

She turned in her seat to watch Sebastian from the corner of her eye. His muscular arms flexed as he pulled the oars toward his body, bending forward and then rocking back with each stroke. He was quiet.

He steered them into the lake and then followed the shoreline. They moved around a point of thick maple and ash trees, their plump leaves like thousands of tiny hands. As she watched, a jutting ridge of sandstone cliffs slid into view, their eroding layers threatening to crumble into the water below. At the top of the mass, a wide rock, shaped strangely like a prickly heart, rested on the cliff face.

"That is incredible," she whispered, sliding forward on her bench for a closer look. The moon painted the jutting edges in white marble, and shadows dug deep into the cliff frame like miniature caves. "Is that where we're going?"

She wondered if the caves from her dreams lay in those cliffs.

"No, but I wanted you to see it," he told her as they drifted. "I came here once and found those cliffs. They were like nothing I'd ever seen and I had this huge desire to share it with someone. To turn in the boat and say, *Wow, look at those.* But I was alone and now you're here with me, so..."

"Thank you." She rotated in her seat, her feet brushing his, their knees nearly touching.

She could almost imagine the previous few days were merely a bad dream. She was just a girl rowing across a moonlit lake with a guy. But then they weren't young lovers on a rowboat ride. They were barely more than strangers, bonded by near-death, and trapped in the same web of reality.

"What are you thinking?" he asked her, his face searching.

"I'm thinking that this is like a dream." She beckoned to the surrounding night.

He nodded, but his features turned grave as he watched the dark woods fringing the beach. He lifted the oars back up and pointed the bow towards the center of the lake, his breath slow and steady, as he found his rhythm.

If Abby had not napped in the car, she knew the placid rocking would have lulled her to sleep. Behind them, the dramatic cliffs shrunk in size until they were barely a white speck in the distance. When the shoreline disappeared completely, Abby finally felt safe.

The water was cold, numbing her fingers as she dragged them over the boat's edge. Despite the arctic chill, she longed to jump in, a bit of cold-water therapy for her bruised and beaten body. Running through woods, tangling and disentangling from multiple bushes, being suffocated, burned, choked and tethered did not exactly do a body good. She reached down and stroked her ankle that should have been swollen, but wasn't; in fact, it didn't hurt at all. She was tempted to tell Sebastian. He knew things that she did not and appeared to be taking them in his stride.

The boat slowed, the bottom scraping on shallow sand and rock, despite their location deep in the lake.

"What's happening?" she asked, spinning around and searching the dark sky.

"Sunken island, no worries," he told her, shoving the oar into the sand to prove that they were on solid ground, not stranded on the back of a giant sea monster.

"I'm going to walk us across. I need to stretch my legs." He hopped from the boat, holding it steady so she didn't pitch over the edge. He released a puff of pained air as he moved forward, the water passing to his waist and spreading out in ripples.

He looked surprised when she leapt into the cold water, fully submerging before bursting back to the surface. She came up heaving, the water like melted snow.

He laughed and dipped beneath the surface, shaking his black curls at her. They stood, their shirts a cold second skin, while the moon cast an opal of light upon them.

"Hurts so good." He leaned back in the water, paddling lightly and facing the sky.

She sank down and gasped when the cold water reached her neck. It was worth the sparkling view overhead. She moved her arms in giant circles beneath the water, slowly adjusting to the temperature. Their fingers grazed, and he reached, clasping her hand for a moment before letting go. She allowed the wave of tremors to pass through her, but stayed riveted to the sky, for a moment becoming a creature of the night.

Sebastian planted his feet beneath him and grabbed the boat by the bow, not wanting to risk it drifting away. They walked it across the sunken island until the lake bed began to recede beneath them.

He dipped below the water a final time and then stood slowly, water dripping down his face and pooling on his shoulders. She knew that he was waiting for her, allowing a few more precious moments to pass before they continued their journey. She stood, grasping her short hair and wringing it into the lake as she waded back to him.

"Quite a cut," he joked. "You might have waited for me and a mirror."

She splashed him. "I wanted to save ten bucks and cut it myself."

"Yes, well, you succeeded."

She grinned, and when he kissed her, it took her by surprise. His lips were cold, like pockets of ice. She wrapped her arms around his neck, the kiss passing from her mouth to every living cell in her body, like poison, or a remedy, or both.

When he pulled away, she felt the heat sucked out and staggered back before he grasped her arms firmly and steadied her. He lifted her into the boat easily, his hands beneath her armpits and she slid back onto the seat, shivering despite the warmth of the night. He climbed in behind her and searched through his bag, hauling out a baggie of trail mix and a bottle of sparkling water.

"Not exactly a gourmet picnic." He held them up.

She smiled back at him, feeling shy. Had they really just kissed?

He handed her the water, and she took a long drink, welcoming the slow carbonated burn.

"So," he started, leaning towards her, his expression grim. "First, thank you for joining me on this—" He rolled his eyes "—satanic adventure. But we can't just stare longingly into each other's eyes all night."

She smiled. They could, but they'd most likely end up dead as a result.

"We have to do something, and it's going to be confusing, and it might be pretty terrifying." He spoke slowly as if she might get spooked at any moment and make a run for it. Apparently he'd forgotten that they were in the center of a lake. "I have directions, sort of." He pulled a tattered journal from his bag.

"Directions?" She watched him flip to a page covered in tiny cursive writing.

"Yes, from Claire, my sister."

"Tobias killed her?"

"Yes," he said quickly and continued. "They're directions to a secret island, but it takes a special person to use them. That's you."

She nodded, beginning to believe him.

He turned another page and passed the journal to her. A large, hand-drawn lake covered both sides with several landmarks scribbled along the edges. A gray area marked the sunken island that they were on.

"You have to use a pendulum," he told her, pulling a small, round crystal suspended from a silver chain from the bag.

She clasped the crystal in her palm, moonlight glittering on its surface.

"Do you understand how they work?" he asked her.

"Not exactly. I've heard of them, but I've never used one."

"Yeah, me neither." He leaned forward and flipped the journal to the previous page. "There's an explanation here." He pointed to a block of writing and Abby read it carefully. It seemed pretty simple. Just hold the pendulum over the map in different areas. If it moved in a circle – they'd found their desired location, if it moved in a straight line – they were at the wrong place.

"What's the island, Sebastian? The lost city of Atlantis?"

"It's meant to be obscure, in case someone finds it, but I know what you mean. It's pretty bizarre."

She sighed in exasperation and leaned forward, resting her elbows on her knees.

"You believe in all this, then? Really?"

"Are you serious?" he asked. "Abby, you were there tonight, right? Those things, the inhuman things, were not a figment of your imagination."

Yeah, she knew that, but still, was nothing simple left in the world? Would every day be a series of discoveries that completely obliterated everything that she thought she knew?

"Listen, what you're feeling right now, I've been there, kind of anyway, and honestly, it gets easier. I mean, it gets harder first, but then it gets easier."

"Wow, thanks," she sighed, re-reading the scratchy writing. She started to feel overwhelmed and tears boiled at the back of her eyes.

He moved close and hugged her, wrapping his arms around her back and squeezing. She allowed herself to feel him with no guilt, no fear. She could hear the rapid thud of his heart through his t-shirt, the intoxicating warmth of his closeness. His lips stayed near her ear, but he did not kiss her, only rested his head against hers and breathed.

She had once read that smell was a direct extension of the brain. Sebastian exuded an enthralling mixture of grass and sweat and, more recently, lake water. Unable to tell whether it was her brain or her heart snuggling deeper into that smell, she inhaled a few more deep breaths, hoping to forever ensnare his scent in the capsule of her mind.

Having Sebastian made it easier to believe in the fantastic. She was not alone with her delusions.

She shivered as the wind picked up around them. The boat swayed, gently and then faster, the water lapping at the sides. Sebastian pulled away, his eyes narrowing into the empty night. The fear, only moments ago abated, settled over Abby as Sebastian returned to his bench. The calm water, moved by the wind, started to form small white caps, then larger ones. They still drifted over the sunken island, but the waves were turning violent and thrusting them towards deep water. Abby peered over the side as the sandy bottom sloped downward and then disappeared.

Chapter 15

Abby fell forward, tossed by a wave. The crystal dropped from her hand and slipped beneath Sebastian's bench. He gripped the boat-edge and reached beneath him, but a shadow of clouds slipped over the moon, and they were cast into darkness. Abby could not see Sebastian, only hear him, as he fumbled along the floor. She wanted to help, but each movement was met by another angry swell that nearly threw her overboard.

"Stay on the floor," Sebastian yelled, his voice nearly drowned in the wind.

They both could swim, but the combination of icy waters and a raging storm left even expert swimmers in danger. They had no life jackets and not a soul, outside the two, knew of their current location.

An instant of guilt surged over Abby at the thought of her parents. She felt the tears bubbling up, advancing on the thread of bravery that she so desperately needed.

"Here." Sebastian thrust the crystal and journal into her hands. A sliver of moonlight seeped through the clouds, illuminating their boat and, worse, the stormy waters.

She shook her head but clung to both frantically as another whitecap smashed against the boat. There was no point trying to use the pendulum, they were in a storm; they couldn't possibly row their way out of it.

"Yes," Sebastian cried, nodding his head and pointing at the journal. "You have to!"

Her hands shook as she flipped the page, pressing the journal flat against the bench as the wind tried to rip it away. She braced her forearm over the center of the book, gripping the crystal chain in her left hand and dangling it over the map. At first it swung wildly and she feared that it would rip from the delicate silver chain.

It didn't, and she watched in wonder as a strange calm settled over the air just above the journal. The tempest continued to thrash around them, but the crystal slowed and then stopped. Gradually, as if with great effort, the crystal began to swing in a straight line. She looked at Sebastian, who nodded vigorously, but continued to clutch the boat as it lurched from side to side. She moved the crystal to another area of the map, but again it swung in a straight line. Three more times she shifted the crystal, three more straight lines. In the distance, a flare of white lightning illuminated the sky, followed by a deafening clap of thunder. Abby jerked in fear, ripping her hand away from the journal, but Sebastian lunged forward and pushed it back.

"Don't stop!" She barely heard him.

She held the crystal behind the sunken island, expecting another straight line. It swung back and then, rather than falling forward, it arched to the right and completed a circle and then another. They stared as it revolved again and again, faster, as if gaining in urgency with each rotation.

Sebastian did not wait, he gripped the oars furiously, turning the boat towards a phantom destination that neither he nor Abby could see. The waves fought them like a battalion of molten soldiers, dissolving and rebuilding with infinite life. The water splashed into the boat; Abby thrust the crystal and journal back into the bag, a flimsy protection from the flooding waves. Behind them, lightning and thunder continued its savage descent onto the lake, but Abby faced forward, preferring the wet spray to the terrifying flashes. Sebastian shifted between grunts and what sounded like prayers as he drove the oars down. As they rowed, the storm transformed into a deafening roar at their backs, and, with a final thrust, they slid from the turbulence into a mass of fog. As quickly as the storm had come, it dissipated. The fog fell upon them in thick folds that strangled the last of the moonlight and swallowed the squall like a black hole. Sebastian stopped rowing as the boat glided into the eerily calm waters.

"What is this?" she whispered, expecting the sound of her voice to be sucked from the air before it could take form.

"Defenses," he breathed, squinting into the mist.

She started to question him, but a strange wail silenced her. She thought of the Sirens of Greek mythology, realizing that Sebastian had done the same, shoving his hands tight against his ears. She lifted her own hands, but paused as the words became clear beneath the howls.

Beware those strangers who idle by
A mishap may befall you
And enemies set to trespass here
Would best to turn away in fear
For death is almost guaranteed
But if you claim your gift a virtue
Stay steady on your path
No friends that meet us on their way
Will face the witches' wrath

She wished for a pen and paper, as if she could even see her hands to quickly scrawl the words. As they drifted along, the song grew muffled, fading like an ambulance siren as it raced into the night. When it was gone, she waved a hand in front of Sebastian, letting him know that it was safe to uncover his ears.

"It's stopped." He sounded surprised and uneasy, as if she might try to steer them into a pointed cliff.

"It's okay. It was just a message, a warning, I think." She repeated the song as best she could, and he listened closely, nodding as if in agreement.

"You could hear them," he said. "I only heard a horrible screeching."

"Yes, but you covered your ears, Sebastian," she argued, not willing to accept this newfound uniqueness.

"No." He shook his head. "We wouldn't have heard the same thing, I'm sure of it."

She didn't say anything because she wanted them to be together, in all of it, no one-sided experiences.

The fog started to lift. It fanned out, moving away from them, and allowing a circle of clarity around the boat. Abby shuffled off the floor, back onto the bench, her feet planted in an inch of water. It soaked through her slip-ons, making her toes squish noisily with each shift.

Sebastian's boxers were soaked. He busied himself scooping handfuls of water back into the lake. They weren't going to sink but the less water the better. The cold wetness that earlier had soothed Abby turned into body-numbing agony, accompanied by constant chafing and discomfort. She joined him, thrusting handfuls of water from the boat. She tried to keep her teeth chattering to a minimum, knowing that Sebastian would be motivated by some gene of chivalry to keep her warm, rather than ridding the boat of excess water.

When he reached a knuckle scraping level, he gave up on the water and switched back to rowing. The moonlit lake, sans storm, had returned – a most romantic scene under more pleasant circumstances. Through the water, she saw that they still drifted above the sunken island, but near the rear, in a place where the sand sat peacefully five or more feet below them.

A long silver fish passed beneath the boat, moving so slowly that she wondered if he was wounded. He circled the boat twice and then swam up to the surface, briefly skipping out of the water.

"It's a messenger," Sebastian said, excited, peering

over the boat edge.

She started to argue, but the fish had begun to swim ahead.

It slid to the right and Sebastian followed, aiming the small boat. The fish picked up speed, and Sebastian strained to keep up, sweat glazing his face and neck as he pumped the oars. The newly calm waters greatly reduced his effort, but the fish kept gaining, darting beneath the water. Abby leaned forward on her bench, pointing and shouting out directions, but in the deep water she quickly lost sight of him.

She could sense Sebastian's frustration, but he remained silent, simply rowing forward in hopes of spotting their small guide. A mass of gray clouds spilled over the moon, casting them into darkness once again.

"Well, so much for that," she broke the silence, giggling uncomfortably. The foreign bark of her laugh echoed over the still waters.

Sebastian leaned forward and placed a hand on her knee, saying nothing, but comforting her immensely.

A gap opened in the clouds and the moonlight streamed down. Abby gasped and nearly fell over the side of the boat as she reeled backwards. Looming ominously before them was a massive fortress, turrets twisting toward the sky, their tips like freshly sharpened blades. The castle, as it shifted into full view, sat atop a mass of sandstone cliffs, like those they'd glimpsed earlier in the night, its bulk perched on decaying hunks of rock. Abby stared, mouth agape, at the familiar palace that had not been there only moments before.

"We found it," Sebastian breathed.

"We have?" Her words were barely a squeak.

As they watched, a small object disembarked from the cliffs and began to move towards them. Abby wanted to row away, to hurry back across the lake and not begin this journey, but of course it was too late for that. She remembered the castle from her dream and knew it to be the same.

As the object slid closer, gliding ethereally, as if floating above the water rather than in it, the shape of a narrow, black boat appeared. Abby could see the outline of a tall, slim figure perched behind an enormous silver steering wheel. It was engine powered, but not a sound broke the still night. Abby's stomach bunched in a knot.

The pilot's gaunt face glowed with the pearl-like quality of a man who not only avoided the beach, but also traveled even short distances beneath a vast umbrella. His long, thin arms moved the wheel effortlessly, pulling alongside their boat with expert accuracy. He wore a black shirt beneath a brown tweed coat, and long, gray wool slacks hung over his rail thin legs.

Strange boating attire, Abby thought. His eyes looked dark, brown maybe, and they hid beneath a mass of bushy, black eyebrows that were considerably thicker than the thin black hair speckling his skull.

"Follow me," he said in a subdued British accent, his pursed mouth quivering. He immediately veered the boat back toward the cliff.

Sebastian did not question him, but pushed the oars into the water.

Abby started to speak, but what could she say, after all? *Take me back to Tobias and the others. I'd rather fight them than this quiet Englishman who looked at us like we were rats caught on the kitchen counter.*

She clasped her hands in her lap, massaging her knuckles like rosary beads. She wasn't a religious person, but the idea of rosary beads had always soothed her, as if they were a tangible link to a spiritual higher power. She repeated the few bedtime prayers in her head that she remembered from childhood, her eyes growing wider as they neared the castle.

The rock wall was a flat sheath, slippery with lake water. Algae snaked up the face like ivy. No stairs or dock revealed their passage to the fortress above, but the weedy man continued on, pointing his boat directly at the cliff.

"Oh," Abby gasped as the black boat nearly collided with the rock, but no explosion boomed. Instead, the man disappeared into the wall as if he were merely a spirit traveling on a ghost ship.

"There's a hole," Sebastian told her, apparently reading the horror in her scrunched shoulders.

And there was a hole, though such a deep black that it blended completely into the cliff and easily tricked the eye. As they sailed through it, Abby looked up at the rock ceiling bearing down on them. Tiny black pearls layered the surface like oil-sheathed bubble wrap.

"Bats," Sebastian told her, looking up as well. "Micro bats."

As he said it, one of them shifted and the entire bed shuddered. Abby shuddered in response. Bats were not a great fear, but considering her only escape from the greasy creatures was the ebony water below, she didn't want to disturb them.

They emerged from the cave into an enormous lagoon that glittered gloriously in the night. A wide stone staircase wound down from the castle, ending at a weather beaten dock.

The strange man docked quickly, leaping from his boat like a gazelle and securely fastening it with ropes. He reached a slender hand toward their rowboat and pulled it in, tying it quickly, without a word.

Abby gazed at the lagoon in silent awe. Lush bushes and flowers fell down the sloping grasses that led from castle to beach. Thick, colorful blossoms bloomed in the moonlight. She saw lilies and jasmine and mounds of flowers that she could not name, but imagined grew in private tropical gardens. The flowers scrambled along the edge of the staircase, racing to the castle, which stood over them like a loving but stern mother.

Sebastian took her hand and pulled her from the boat, squeezing it as they followed the gaunt man away from the water. Up the steps and across a cobblestone pathway, they passed a grand mahogany door adorned with a heavy brass pentacle doorknocker.

They curved around a stone tower and advanced down a short staircase that passed beneath a glassy eyed gargoyle protecting a stained glass door. The man pulled out a long skeleton key and inserted it into the lock. It clicked and a deadbolt slid back. They entered a giant chamber with a cement staircase spiraling up the center. Dozens of doors stood along the stairway; their footsteps clapped loudly as they moved up. The man stopped at the fourth doorway, again inserted his skeleton key, and pushed them into a brightly lit room.

Chapter 16

Sebastian and Abby stumbled in together. Abby blinked around the room, light from the candles leaving pockets of darkness that her eyes could not pierce.

"Our guests have arrived." The thin man addressed several people clustered in chairs.

As Abby and Sebastian moved deeper into the space, she scanned their surroundings. The circular room housed a vast library with bookshelves climbing to the exquisite ceiling. The ceiling dipped and soared in rounded arches, painted with elaborate images of the zodiac, symbolized by pink skinned goddesses and enchanted beasts. It reminded her of the Sistine Chapel, although Michelangelo may have begged to differ.

A woman, with long silver hair flowing over each shoulder, beckoned them to a set of empty chairs near a blazing fire. Her face was lined but lovely, her skin softly worn like nude rose petals.

"Please, sit."

Abby lowered herself into a squat chair upholstered in velvety fuchsia, her legs and butt warmed by the hot seat. Sebastian moved his chair closer to hers and sat down as well, facing the group.

Abby counted seven people, including the gaunt man who had led them in. He took a seat close to the silver-haired woman and stared at them suspiciously. The woman had the same ageless beauty as Audrey Hepburn. Her gray eyes sparkled in the firelight and she clasped her slender hands together as she studied them, her face kind but interested.

Abby wanted to observe the rest of the group, but feared their probing eyes, so stared into her lap instead, which comforted her.

"I'm Sebastian. This is Abby," Sebastian told them, sitting up straighter as he did so. His voice was mingled with curiosity, but no fear. He seemed prepared for the group of strangers.

"Welcome, Sebastian, and welcome, Abby," the silver haired woman began. "We are very excited and quite curious to have you here. Shall I begin with introductions?" They did not speak, so she continued. "I am Elda, and your guide here is Faustine." She pointed to their skinny escort, who grumbled in response. "Across from you, there, is Helena, and then Max, Lydie, and Dafne." Her finger pointed lightly at each face as she traveled around the room, and Abby took a moment to stare. Lydie looked, by far, the youngest, not much older than twelve or thirteen, her eyes bright with interest. "So, please, do tell us how you came to find our rather secluded location? I dare say that *you* found us." Elda's eyes were trained carefully on Abby, as were the others.

Abby cleared her throat, but Sebastian spoke first.

"No, I brought her." Each pair of eyes turned to him quickly, suspicion alighting on some of their faces.

"How is that possible?" the woman called Dafne shrilled, igniting the room with tension.

She was matchstick thin, except where the tiny red bulb would lie was a long plait of purple black hair, so dark it seemed invisible, as if it sucked the light from the room and ate it. Her face, nose and chin were pointed and pale, which should have made her ugly, but somehow worked. She was a dazzling ice queen – only desirable from the corner of your eye. Abby guessed her age around twenty-five, but the severity of her expression made her appear older. Although Dafne's words were directed at Sebastian, Abby felt them herself, like steel wool rubbed over skin. She leaned back in her seat and shot Sebastian a warning glance. She didn't want to enrage a room of strangers. Sebastian met their gazes, not flinching at Dafne, who glared at him.

"What she means, Sebastian," Elda continued slowly, ignoring Dafne's hardened gaze, "is that this is a very special place, and we were not under the impression that you possessed those faculties."

"I don't," he told them, slightly defeated. "My sister did."

Dafne leaned toward Helena and whispered something angrily, but no one spoke.

"Your sister?" Max asked, sliding to the edge of his chair. Max was grandfatherly with a lined, puddled face that reminded Abby of a shar-pei. His hair was short but thick, black and silver making up equal parts.

"Yes, Claire." Sebastian's face looked hopeful as if he expected them to register her name, but no dawning appeared on their faces. "She was like you." He gestured to their group, and fury flashed across Dafne's face.

"Like us?" She acted as if he'd called them a derogatory name, and Helena turned red, embarrassed by her outburst.

"I don't mean it as an insult. She was special, she had powers," Sebastian quickly corrected.

Elda nodded, but Dafne continued to look furious.

Abby shifted uncomfortably. She wanted to defend Sebastian, but felt too lost to contribute – lost, tired, overwhelmed and scared.

The door to the room swung open, bringing with it a gust of cool air and sending flickers through hundreds of candles adorning the walls. The man who followed was soaking wet, and his bare feet left a trail of water in the thick rug beneath him.

Abby stared at him – mouth agape. Sebastian stiffened

beside her. It was the man from the forest, the one who saved them.

"Have I missed the party?" He laughed, striding across the room to Lydie and shaking his hair like a wet dog in her face.

He wore the same clothing – a short sleeved white t-shirt of nylon fabric and loose fitting linen pants. He did not carry his bow, but the leather strap and his arrows still hung from his back.

Lydie squealed and batted at him as the water fell onto her face and head.

He stopped shaking, stood and looked at Abby and Sebastian. "If you'd hung around a bit longer, I would have brought you here myself. Saved you some trouble."

Dafne shot him a look of angry surprise, and he shrugged casually. He smiled at Abby, and small lines creased his full mouth. He was boyish looking, but not a boy, a man.

Abby blushed beneath the pierce of his green eyes as they sparkled in the light of the candles. She glanced at Sebastian who stared indignantly at their savior, his lips a line of contempt.

"Oliver, you've met our guests, then?" Elda asked, but did not sound surprised.

He grinned, unstrapped his arrows and let them fall to the floor, pulling a stool from Lydie's feet and straddling it. She protested, but giggled and let him take it.

"Yes, though I dare say not under the most happy of circumstances. Our friends were in the clutches of Tobias and Vesta and a new one. I didn't catch his name."

"Tane," Sebastian answered, continuing to stare at Oliver, sizing him up.

Oliver nodded dismissively. "He's not a Vepar, just a wanna-be right now."

"And Tobias – did you get him?" Sebastian demanded, fidgeting in his seat.

"What business is it of yours?" Dafne snapped, her face coloring when Elda frowned at her.

Oliver cast Abby a mischievous smile and continued. "I did not kill him. The Vepars have a new lair that I have not been able to track. Twice now, he has escaped me."

"Drat," Helena chimed in, slapping her palm angrily on her leg. Like Elda, she had a strange beauty and a calming quality, though she was younger and reminded Abby of her Aunt Sydney. Her long auburn hair was pushed entirely over one shoulder and her brown eyes were soft and creamy, like a puppy's. She blinked them, and Abby could see light blond lashes against her golden skin. Unlike Elda, who wore a simple floor length black dress, Helena's attire set her apart from the group. She wore a caramel colored tunic that fell mid-thigh over black leggings. Her wrists were nearly covered in bangles of gold and silver and they jangled when she moved.

"Yeah, pretty nasty beasts, those two," Oliver continued, wringing his shirt out onto the floor. "I do apologize for my late arrival," he said to Abby. "I would have liked to reach you sooner."

"How did you find us?" she asked.

"Luck, really," Oliver answered. "I've been visiting the area off and on. We sensed a death there, and Faustine suspected that it was a witch who died."

He paused and cast a questioning gaze at Elda, who nodded for him to continue.

"But Vepars are good at covering their tracks and erasing any signs of the death and of the witch."

Abby listened, bothered by the word 'witch'. Did he mean that literally?

"They usually stay near a ritual scene for several days

to absorb any remaining power, and they picked up your scent and started to hunt you. I found you by chance. I sensed something in the woods the last time I visited and decided to return to the spot, and there you were."

"That's it?" Sebastian asked incredulously. "You sensed something there?"

"And what did you do?" Dafne asked coldly, knowing how to hit Sebastian where it hurt. "Were you planning to save her yourself?"

Sebastian exploded from his chair and pointed a finger towards Dafne, his hand shaking visibly. "You have no idea what you're talking about."

Elda stood, interrupting. "We are not enemies here. We are friends. Sebastian, please, take a seat."

He fell back into his chair, but scowled at Dafne. Oliver looked amused, and Abby saw him gently kick Lydie's chair; she smiled in return.

"I believe that we are better served by privacy now," Elda continued, addressing the group, and Abby wasn't sure if she meant her and Sebastian or the others.

Max stood and coaxed everyone from their chairs, carefully avoiding eye contact with Sebastian, who was clearly miserable. Abby started to stand but Max gestured her back down with a wave of his hand. Dafne looked mutinous and stalled, smoothing her bony hands along her heather gray slacks. Faustine sought her eyes and nodded toward the door, a silent demand.

The young one, Lydie, walked to where Abby stood and stopped before her. "You can't learn to swim without getting in the water." She spoke very matter-of-factly and then strode to the door, her short curls bouncing and her pale, pink pedal-pushers making her appear even younger from the back. She shot a final, knowing, stare back at Abby's puzzled face and skipped from the room.

"She speaks almost entirely in clichés," Oliver told her, smiling at her confused expression. "It's endearing about two percent of the time."

Sebastian stared after him as he walked from the room, following behind Dafne, with Helena close at his heels.

When everyone was gone, Elda returned. She stopped at a shelf of books and pressed a small iron eagle bookend. The books disappeared on a rotating counter, and a small platter with several ceramic pots and black mugs swung into the room.

Abby and Sebastian stared, surprised by the secret compartment.

"Yes, our library comes fully equipped," Elda laughed. "Though, still, I am not sure why we have to hide the tea."

Sebastian smiled, and Abby sank back into her chair, relieved to see his sense of humor returning.

"Tea? Or coffee, perhaps?" Elda placed two mugs on a silver tray.

"Tea, please," Abby told her, the first twinges of sleepiness stirring in her mind. Sebastian asked for coffee, and Elda busied herself preparing, not only drinks, but also small sandwiches and cookies.

Abby sipped her tea. The scalding fluid added to the heat of the room and she blinked away the sleepiness creeping in. She should have gone with coffee. The tea, some mix of chamomile and other herbs, only enhanced her weariness. She nibbled a molasses cookie and sat up straight, watching as Elda pulled a chair closer to the fireplace.

"Are you warm enough?" the older woman asked them, settling into her chair.

"Mmm, yes, fine," Abby murmured.

"More than enough." Sebastian nodded. He scooted his chair away from the fire and sat munching a sandwich hungrily. "I am starving."

"Well, eat up. Those things appear around here like magic." She winked at Sebastian as he grabbed another sandwich and several cookies from the tray.

Abby stared at the room lazily, taking in the soft, luxurious décor. Thick velvet drapes shielded the windows and fell onto tasseled oriental rugs. Thousands of books lined the shelves, many with broad leather bindings, their titles engraved and glinting in the firelight. Dozens of chairs, each one different, were scattered in a loose semi-circle facing the enormous stone fireplace.

"Where shall we begin?" Elda asked gently, moving her chair so that she faced Sebastian and Abby directly. "With you, Sebastian? I think you may be able to shed light for both Abby and myself."

He nodded, looking more alert as the coffee set in. He opened his backpack and pulled Claire's journal out, laying it on his lap. "This belonged to my sister, Claire. She started writing in it when she was seventeen, at the beginning of the change. She'd never been a diary keeper, and I remember thinking it strange, but..."

He traced his fingers along the worn pages and smiled, remembering.

Abby sat up taller in her chair, listening.

"Something happened to your parents?" Elda asked knowingly.

He nodded, staring at the fire. "They were killed in a car accident when I was eighteen and Claire was fourteen. I became her legal guardian." Sebastian's voice thickened. "We received an inheritance, a pretty large one, and after I graduated from high school, we sold the house and moved into an apartment. Things were good. We were happy. Claire gave me a purpose and I never resented that. During her junior year in high school, just after her seventeenth birthday, I saw the journal for the first time. She acted very weird about it, protective. I thought maybe she was dealing with it finally, ya know, our parents' deaths."

Abby tried to pay attention but she had begun to feel strange, sort of dizzy and euphoric, as if she'd had too much to drink.

"Then I noticed this peculiar woman who showed up in the most random places," he continued. "At the grocery store or when I'd pick up Claire at school. She was... I don't know, astonishing, I guess. She had long black hair down past her butt and bright green eyes like cats' eyes. And, then, one day I came home from work and she was at our apartment, just sitting in the living room with Claire, talking crazily like they were old friends."

"Adora," Elda whispered.

"Yes, yes, Adora. You know her?"

"I do, and I will tell you about her later. Right now, I want to hear about you."

Sebastian nodded and continued, taking another sip from his coffee. The cup clattered as he returned it to the saucer. "They began spending so much time together that it sort of bothered me. I was jealous, maybe, because it had been just Claire and I for years. Anyway, we fought about it and she completely broke down. She told me everything." He trailed off, his eyes wandering towards Abby and then the floor.

She fought to pay attention, but her brain felt like a sticky puddle in the basement of her skull. Were they talking about her? No, Claire, they were talking about Claire. She looked at the half filled cup of tea, horror struck, as the room began to swim around her. Had this woman poisoned her? She looked at Elda, whose gracious face regarded her with concern.

"Abby, are you okay?" Elda asked, her brow furrowed.

Sebastian stood abruptly, kneeling in front of her.

"Abby?" Worry paled his face.

"I'm just so tired," she whispered, as the heat of the fire slowly traveled up her legs and into her back. "Did you poison me?" she croaked, looking at Elda.

"Oh, dear, no," Elda laughed, looking embarrassed. She rose from her chair and moved toward Abby. "No, no, it's just chamomile and Valerian root and some other herbs. It was meant to calm you, not put you to bed, honey. It's our home, I would imagine." Elda waved her slender fingers at the room. "It affects... some people, differently."

"Not to mention the night we had," Sebastian added, rubbing a hand on his swollen wrists where the ropes had cut in.

"I'll get something for that," Elda told him.

She held her hands out to Abby, who stood shakily, leaning on Sebastian for support.

"I will call Oliver to show her to her room. It's the energy here, for new witches..." Elda trailed off and moved across the room, pressing a button near the doorway.

Abby stared at her, tempted to ask what exactly she meant by 'new witches,' but too exhausted to go there.

"She's right, Abby. I think it's just shock and exhaustion." He looked tired as well, but she knew that he wanted to continue his conversation with Elda.

Abby trusted that he was right and, strangely enough, she trusted Elda. She needed to rest, to allow the demons of the day to leave, at least for a bit. She would welcome sleep.

Oliver entered the room, and Sebastian bristled.

"I can take her," Sebastian said quickly to Elda. "Just tell me where."

"Whoa, there, friend," Oliver chimed, raising a hand to calm Sebastian. "It's a short walk and I already know the way."

Oliver took Abby's hand in his own and began to lead

her from the room. She cast a fleeting smile at Sebastian, who looked agitated, but Elda was already appeasing him with more coffee and cookies.

"I think bed sounds about right," Oliver said happily, closing the door behind him. "You have had one very long night."

Abby nodded and murmured, "Yes," trying not to trip over her sluggish feet.

"I can carry you, if you'd like," Oliver told her, squeezing her hand.

"Oh, no," she said, though it sounded easier than carrying herself.

He talked amicably as they traipsed down a long hallway lit with golden candelabras. A thick gold rug lay before them; something like the lavish red carpets she'd seen on Hollywood awards shows. His golden hair sparkled in the flickering light, and he smelled sweet like cinnamon. If exhaustion had not been robbing her of logic, she might have questioned the enchanted atmosphere, but instead she struggled simply to stay upright as he led her up a tight spiral staircase. He pushed through a massive honey colored door into a room dimly lit with candles. She stumbled blindly to the bed and collapsed onto it, remotely aware that he'd pulled a heavy comforter up to her neck and made a hasty exit.

* * * *

Sebastian chewed another cookie grumpily and forced himself not to act like a jerk in front of Elda. He should have been happy that Oliver saved them and happier still that he was part of the coven, but he wasn't. For one thing, he didn't like the way Oliver looked at Abby, like she was available. He also found him arrogant and too attractive. Why should he be so attractive?

"Don't worry, Sebastian. Oliver is a wonderful witch. He wishes you no harm," Elda said, shifting her eyes to his.

Her voice was very soothing, and he tried to relax into the sound. He was tempted to question her about Oliver and the coven. He wanted to hear that Oliver was a new witch and not a very powerful one. He wanted to glean some tidbit of flaw that would make their rescuer slightly less heroic. He took another drink of coffee and returned to their conversation.

"Anyway," he started, forgetting about Oliver momentarily. "Claire told me she was a witch and that Adora was her witch guide or something like that."

"Yes, Adora is a keeper of a *Book of Shadows* and thus a guide or helper for new witches."

"Adora started to teach her to use her power. She was an air element."

"I'm not surprised," Elda said. "I sense air in you."

He paused. "Does that mean I have powers as well?"

Elda shook her head sadly. "I wish I could give you such news, Sebastian, but no, you are not a witch. Although you are a very powerful man."

"Can I become more powerful?" he asked urgently.

"Yes, anyone can if they desire it and make it their intention, but vengeance is not a safe place to draw that power out of."

Sebastian did not speak, considering her words. Vengeance had driven him for so long. What else did he have?

"You have Abby, Sebastian."

Sebastian stared at her. Had she read his mind or just guessed his thoughts? He liked Elda. She reminded him of Claire, so kind and gentle, but strong too. He felt safe in the castle, not only safe from the Vepars, but safe from himself, from the murderous desire that had been in him lately. Perhaps at the coven he could rest, find himself again. Maybe he could discover another path.

Chapter 17

Morning arrived well after noon for Abby. Even as she opened her eyes, a flight of longing for her dreamless sleep beckoned her back beneath the covers. She stared at the vaulted ceiling, crisscrossed with enormous wood beams, and thought of the previous night. It was blurry and unreal, but her place in the elaborate bedroom rendered it concrete. Like so many things of late, this, too, was not a dream.

She pushed back the dense, silvery-pink comforter, allowing it to heap at the foot of the bed, and slid off the edge. The room was shaped like a hexagon. A floor to ceiling window stretched along a single wall, facing the choppy waves of the lake. Straight down from the window she could see a small ridge of sandstone cliff that plummeted into the water.

Dazzling sunlight poured over the shining blond wood floors, basking everything in a warm, summer glow. She traveled the room slowly and brushed her fingers along the velvet drapes. Intricate woodwork accentuated each piece of furniture, and she wondered how long it took to carve the tiny spirals and knobs. It all looked alarmingly antique and yet in impeccable shape, not a single scratch anywhere. A salmon colored chaise stretched beneath the window, several sets of clothes draped over it.

Abby picked up a silk blouse, eyeing it warily. They were beautiful and expensive, but definitely not her own. *Dafne's*, she thought, who was around her same size, but slightly taller. Probably not an easy feat – soliciting Dafne's clothes. She chose a pair of cream silk pants and a beige tank top. A pair of brown flat-heel Mary Janes sat on the floor with a note tucked into one of the soles.

Hope everything fits – Helena.

She put them on and cast a final glance around the room before leaving. The spiral staircase led her back to the vaguely familiar hallway, but she was clueless as to where to go from there. She looked stupidly at the blank doorways, curious because the castle held a million intrigues, but also dazed. She understood that another world existed outside of her own and that she was a part of it, but she still did not understand her role, which frightened her. After passing several doors and getting no closer to finding Sebastian or Elda, she started leaning her head against the heavy frames. Three doors and silence, then she heard voices, hushed.

She recognized Dafne's shrill tone followed by Helena, trying to calm her.

"Dafne, you have no authority to cast them out. They have every right to be here," Helena stated in a loud whisper.

"She might, but he doesn't. Not only does he not deserve to be here, but he's a danger to all of us," Dafne declared, sounding alarmingly close to the door.

Abby backed up, afraid that it may burst open and ran into Faustine, who huffed loudly, but put his hands out to prevent further damage.

"I see you've risen," he told her shortly, turning on his heel. "Come with me."

Jogging to keep up with him, she tried to gather her bearings, watching the hall carefully, but not getting much detail. Every door looked the same, and though they passed a few that were open, Faustine walked so quickly that she couldn't see what lay inside them.

He turned left and opened a doorway into a long, rectangular room. Several buffet tables stood in the center, each heaped with trays of food. Small, round café-style tables scattered the wall's edge, their white linen tablecloths brushing the peach carpeting. It looked like a hotel dining room, except for the thick, stone castle walls. Abby expected to see little waiters in tuxedos bustling about.

Sebastian and Elda sat at a small table butted against a movie screen sized window. They both stood when Faustine and Abby walked in.

"She wakes," Sebastian said, sounding relieved.

She gave him a quick, one-armed hug, briefly flashing on their kiss from the previous night, and tried to hide her blush as she sat down next to him.

"Lunch, my dear," Elda told her, steering her towards one of the food-stacked tables.

Abby's stomach moaned with longing as she surveyed the options. Pastries were piled next to a long tray of heavily stacked sandwiches and goblets of juice, lemonade and tea. At the end of the table sat two silver trays heaped with sliced fruit and vegetables. She filled a plate, any attempt at modesty buried beneath her hunger, and returned to the table between Sebastian and Elda.

She watched an enormous, charcoal gray cat jump from one of the tables and pad into a bar of sunlight, slumping onto the ground lazily. The cat spun in an alligator death roll, purring like a tractor and covering every inch of his fur in dust. She thought of her own kitty, Baboon, abandoned in Lansing with Nick.

"How did you sleep?" Sebastian asked, mopping the crumbs from his plate.

"Good, really," she reassured him between bites. "I feel like I've been put up in the penthouse suite."

"So, you liked your room, then?" Elda asked happily, sipping a glass of tea.

"Yeah, liked may be a bit of an understatement." She nodded with the pleasant memory of her view.

"Well, we have had quite a long talk, Sebastian and I, oh, and Kissy over there on the floor," Elda told her, smiling as Abby stuffed a chocolate croissant into her mouth.

"But now, Abby, it's time for you and I to talk, alone."

Abby stopped, mid-chew, and looked from Elda to Sebastian.

"You see," Elda continued, "discussion is not our only task at hand. We are going to isolate your element of power today."

"My element of power?"

"Yes," Elda said and Sebastian nodded.

"It's really amazing," he said.

"You've already done it?" Abby asked, turning toward Sebastian with newfound interest.

"Oh no," Elda interrupted quickly. "Sebastian is not a witch, only you are."

"Wait." Abby held up a hand. "What does that mean, I'm a witch? Everyone keeps talking about witches, and, frankly, I'm confused and a little freaked out."

"And that is precisely our goal of the day – understanding."

The door rolled open and Oliver walked in, looking freshly rumpled, his blond hair swept back from his forehead.

"Food." He grinned, stretching his arms overhead and yawning. He filled a plate and took an empty seat next to Elda. "I slept like the dead last night."

Sebastian, Abby noticed, was pretending to ignore Oliver by stirring copious amounts of sugar and cream into his coffee.

"Morning," she said shyly.

"Perfect timing, Oliver. Abby and I were just going to take a walk to the lagoon, and I thought you might entertain Sebastian for a little while."

Sebastian prickled at this suggestion, scowling into his mug and stirring it furiously.

"Love to," Oliver said, taking a bite of eggs.

* * * *

In the daylight, the gardens surrounding the castle were even more magnificent. Dazzling blossoms encircled the stone staircase, some of them sneaking onto the steps, their petals crushed into the rough stone. They were majestic and strange, flowers that Abby had never seen. Some of the blooms were as large as basketballs, their petals heavy and drooping over their skinny, green necks.

Abby saw their small rowboat tied to the dock. It reminded her of the previous night and she shuddered, wrapping her arms over her chest. The sky held billowing, marshmallow-like clouds that reflected in the calm lagoon water.

"Aren't we going down?" Abby asked, as Elda passed the stairway and continued on.

"No, we are going to another lagoon," Elda told her, gesturing in front of them where the pathway disappeared into a thicket of tall, flowering cherry trees.

As they entered the blossoms, the cobblestone path gave way to crushed shells, bleached bone white. They crunched underfoot and Abby stared, in wonder, around them. The blossoms were so thick that she could barely see deeper into the outer forest or gardens. Although glints of sun peeked through the pale pink blossoms, the trail grew darker as they progressed.

Deeper on the trail, the ground sloped noticeably upward and back down again. Every few yards they passed a stone bench, and Abby longed to sit and stare at the plump flowers bursting around her. It reminded her of the sleep inducing poppy fields in the *Wizard of Oz*. Until then, Abby had never encountered anything remotely similar, but the cherry blossoms brought wafts of air, fat with a hypnotic perfume.

"Abby," Elda began, breaking the silence, "have you ever experienced any strange powers?"

Abby shuffled her feet over the shells, not sure what to say. She tried to search for childhood experiences that stuck out, but found that she could only remember her mother's stifling love. Every moment of her past seemed tainted by her mother's watchful eyes and her mean little mouth, always pressed into a line of disappointment. Sometimes, she had pretended she was special, a superhero or a mermaid, simply to escape the hot, dead stillness of her backyard where no kids ever came to play.

"With Sydney," Abby said suddenly. "Sometimes I felt special with Sydney."

"Who is Sydney?"

"My aunt. She always said she could attract anything she wanted just by thinking about it and that I had that power too. She said we got it from her mother, Arlene. And even though I thought it was a game, I really believed it, and sometimes, I think it actually happened."

Elda nodded.

"Do you think that my Aunt Sydney is a witch?"

"No, if she was, she would know it, and she sounds like the kind of woman who would have helped you in your own unveiling."

"But what if she doesn't know? I mean, I didn't know. In fact, I still don't know."

Elda chuckled and twisted a small silver ring on her pinky as she walked. "You will know soon enough, Abby, and then you will never doubt it again. Your aunt may have some special abilities. The ancestors of many witches do. Take Sebastian, for example. He is not a witch, but he is a powerful man, and when he learns to harness it, you will see that even ordinary people have amazing powers."

"What about my mother?"

Elda stopped and looked at Abby, searching her face.

"Your mother was just a woman, and the power that you give her is just that, it's not real, and you can take it away any time."

Abby swallowed hard, her mouth suddenly dry and sticky. Was that true?

She remembered a day; she must have been no older than seven or eight. She had walked into the kitchen, looking for a snack or some insignificant thing, and her mother had been at the sink. Abby could see from the curve of her back and the steady rise and fall of her shoulders that she was crying. She wanted to ask what was wrong, but her mother had turned and saw her. "You don't even know," she'd said, and her eyes were red rimmed and her face blotchy with emotion. She said nothing more, but stared at Abby as if she loathed her, and Abby had run. She hid in the shed for an hour. When she returned to the house, her mother was ironing and her father was watching television, and they never spoke of it.

Her mother had seemed filled with magic that day, but the worst kind, the sort of magic that worked slowly and invisibly, killing everything it touched.

Abby slowed, almost stopped, but Elda continued on. Abby hurried to catch her. "I have a million questions," Abby said.

"And in time you will have the answers."

"Yes, but what if I need some answers right now?"

Elda sighed. "Abby, this is a gift, not a burden. Don't embark on this journey like you've been cursed and have to dissect it and make a decision about whether to seek a cure. Be patient and everything that you need to know, you will."

They moved out of the cherry trees into another large

clearing that sloped down to a second lagoon. The water sparkled emerald green, kissing the white sand. A massive greenhouse, shaped like a scallop seashell, stood on the far side.

"Wow," Abby breathed, staring at the glass structure in wonder. Abby had never gardened, but always felt a longing to learn. Once, when she was ten, her mother bought her a Venus Flytrap, which had withered and died in a matter of days.

"That is our herb and vegetable garden," Elda told her. "It is one of a kind."

Abby nodded, shuffling along in wonder. Sandstone cliffs stretched up behind the foliage surrounding the lagoon. It felt safe, like a new world.

Elda led her to a pair of old wind-worn chairs perched high on a stone slab, which extended over the water. As they stepped onto the slab, Abby felt a rush, as if someone had blown on the back of her neck. She spun around, but the trail was empty. The only sounds were the waves rhythmically caressing the shore.

"Please, sit," Elda told her. Her voice had changed and she closed her eyes for a moment, reveling in the vibrations around her.

Abby sat, folded her hands in her lap and leaned her head against the overworked chair back. It groaned, but not in protest, it sounded gratified to have its space occupied. For a moment, she continued to ponder her surroundings, but slowly an inviting calm engulfed her, as if she'd slipped into a warm bath, and she closed her eyes.

Neither Elda nor Abby spoke. It was time for silence.

A million thoughts crept toward the edge of her consciousness, but none penetrated, as if held back by an invisible force field. The temperature of her body climbed, the silk pants shifted from cool to sticky. She might have felt guilty or even worried about sweating in Dafne's clothing, but her mind was a blank slate of swirling energy. A tornado of blue light formed in her brain, churning and swelling. It continued to build, like a piece of bubble gum blown to maximum capacity. It pressed inside her skull, too full, and then it streaked down her spine. It awakened her chakras, beginning at the crown and ending at the root. The energy moved like a swarm of bees, stinging her cells to life.

She sensed movement and forced her eyes open. Elda stood on the edge of the slab, her eyes trained on the lagoon, her white shawl billowing behind her like a parachute. Abby turned, with great effort, to follow Elda's gaze. The water was swirling, a jade circle widening in fury. Suddenly it reversed and began to twist upward – a writhing cone raised out of the water. Abby's entire body vibrated, her skin prickling with gooseflesh, while inside her body raged with fire. The chair shook beneath her, the wooden frame lifting and smacking the cement. Surely it would break, splinter into a thousand pieces in an explosion that would deafen their ears and leave them both picking slivers from their burned skin, but it did not. The fiendish power pooled back into the cool blue ball and slipped out, as if Abby was a sponge and someone had wrung her dry.

Chapter 18

Sebastian drank two more cups of coffee, wandered the sunlit breakfast room, stared out windows and ignored Oliver. Oliver chewed too loudly; he slurped his coffee and talked to the cat like it had insider information Sebastian wasn't privy to.

"Kissy," Oliver laughed, "don't you love breakfast at the castle? Man, Bridget is the best cook ever. Here, have another sausage."

Then he dropped a sausage to the already obese cat, who ate it ferociously, darting his eyes toward Sebastian and growling like he might try to steal the morsel of fried pork.

"You tried the quiche, Sebastian?" Oliver asked, holding up a forkful. "Goat cheese."

"No," Sebastian told him and returned to the window.

He couldn't see Abby and Elda, but wished they had invited him to join them. He had observed Claire summoning her element, not the first time, but later when she got better at it. He was curious to see Abby do it, partially because she seemed so rigid. He had to admit that he was somewhat surprised she was a witch, though he didn't have many examples to draw from. However, with Claire it had made sense. She was a hippy child who grew up on wheat grass shots for breakfast and bonfire prayers beneath the full moon. His parents had raised Claire and him to see Mother Nature as the divine, to shirk off regular society and to question convention at every level.

Learning that Claire was a witch hadn't come easy, especially when he realized that no one was talking about a pagan witch who burned incense and read tarot cards. However, her changes left no room for disbelief, and, in the end, he felt that maybe they both knew all along.

He believed that Abby would struggle with the realization and wondered if discovering her element would open the portal of belief that hadn't yet appeared.

"I planned to do a bit of shooting, practice my aim. You in?" Oliver asked, standing and stretching down to touch his toes. He bent to each side and then stretched above him again. "After some yoga, that is."

"Sure, got an extra bow?" Sebastian asked hastily, ready for a challenge. Maybe now he would have a chance to redeem himself.

* * * *

Abby slumped back in the chair, her hands gripping the wooden arms painfully. They felt real, solid, they were not a swirling mountain of liquid water conjured from nothing. Her heart pounded in her ears. Elda had turned and stood watching her, a small smile curving her pink lips.

"Water," she told Abby firmly. "Your element is water."

"My element," Abby choked, her throat hoarse.

"Yes, you did that." Elda was proud of her, nearly beaming. She strode off the cement slab to the water's edge.

Abby stood shakily and followed. The water had returned to its early glassiness, the airborne monster gone from its depths.

"I... how—how did I do that?" Abby whispered, standing close to Elda, comforted by the motherly smell that blanketed her.

"Abby, you are an extraordinary witch, and witches draw their power from an element of this world." Elda took Abby's hands firmly in her own.

Abby watched the flecks of light swimming in Elda's

ashen eyes. They shone with excitement.

"Let us sit," Elda said.

Abby turned back toward the slab, but Elda tugged her roughly away. "No, too much energy there," Elda explained. "Over here."

They walked halfway around the lagoon, moving closer to the shell shaped greenhouse. Abby could see rows of jumbled flowers, pots and bristly plants. They crawled over the glass windows, their branches and petals splayed in obscene vegetation. On the cliff, towering behind the glass conservatory, Abby eyed a swatch of color, so brief that she could have imagined it. As she watched, it flashed again. A ripple of black swelled against the deep green pines jutting from the cliff. Dafne. Abby could see her clearly for an instant, her face stark in her mane of shiny black hair. Abby felt a mean satisfaction that Dafne watched them, that she broke her routine to spy, but then it dissipated as she remembered the cyclone of water. Who wouldn't want to watch it?

Elda guided her to two bronze garden chairs tucked alongside a mass of wild roses that flecked the right side of the greenhouse. A bronze table sat between them. Abby sat while Elda disappeared into the greenhouse, emerging a few moments later with a massive black book bursting with loose pages. She laid it on the table carefully, as if placing an infant rather than a bulky text.

Abby leaned toward the cover, eyes widening in surprise.

"You have seen one," Elda asked her, as if expecting this.

"Yes," Abby murmured. "Sebastian has one."

"Really?" Elda's eyebrows raised in surprise. "Claire must have received it from Adora. That does not bode well for my old friend."

"Adora? You knew her well?"

"Yes, I knew her many years ago. She was an exceptional witch, but she never did well in covens, and it can be dangerous to live without one."

"Why would she give the book to Claire?"

"For safekeeping, I would imagine. Perhaps she believed she was in danger."

"From the Vipers?"

"Vepars, and we will get to them later."

The leather book before them had a single title inscribed in the upper left corner: *Coven of Voda*, the words a deep crimson faded by time and touch.

"Voda?" Abby asked, not recognizing the name.

"It means water in Croatian. This book has been with us for a very long time." Elda looked at it lovingly. "Water is your power, Abby. It is the source of your energy."

Abby nodded and looked at the book, but she no longer needed tangible evidence of her uniqueness. She had seen it with her own eyes. Then again, maybe she was delusional. She was probably in a coma somewhere having crazy dreams, or maybe Tobias had killed her and this was heaven.

"I understand your skepticism, Abby," Elda told her.

"I'm sorry, Elda. I still don't get it." Exasperation flooded her voice and she stared hard at the woman across from her. If this wasn't a dream and it wasn't death, then it needed to be put into words that made some damn sense.

"Abby, think of human life—the way that most people live it—as a simulation. Everyone has their own separate reality. If you lived your entire life as a woman in an indigenous tribe in the Australian outback, and then one day you were picked up and flown to New York City to live in a penthouse with servants, would it seem impossible? Could you watch television, images and voices coming from a box, with anything less than shock and disbelief?"

"Well, of course it would be shocking, but I would be seeing those things with my own eyes. I would have to believe them."

Elda smiled, but said nothing.

"But why doesn't anyone else know about witches?"

"They do, but people rationalize things they don't understand. History and legends and myths and stories are all the same. Were you alive when the Europeans came to America and slaughtered thousands of Native Americans? No, but you still believe in the validity of this historical fact. Much of history has been suppressed. I might even say that most of history has been suppressed. The rest has been manipulated to support the powers that be, whether those are government or church or some dictator seeking control of the masses. Witches had power that regular men did not, and that was scary to some men, scary enough to kill those witches, deny their power and re-write their history as myth."

A vague feeling of recognition stole over Abby. She knew that much of recorded history was loaded with agenda, she had just never realized how much was hidden. She was being given an opportunity to learn the lies from the facts.

"That's right, Abby, at any time, you can know the truth. This is the truth." Elda laid her hand on the *Book of Shadows,* and Abby stared at it, newly mesmerized.

"This book," Elda continued, "is from a coven in Croatia that existed thousands of years ago in the Mediterranean Sea. It is a story that I have come by laboriously and only in fragments, but they were one of the first covens that organized themselves by their element of power. In their case, water."

Abby pondered this, but nodded for Elda to continue.

"Your element is water, as is mine. When you are on the energy table—" Elda pointed back to the stone slab "—your power is drawn out in its purest form. It is a place of indescribable energy, and we use the table to pinpoint the elements of each witch. It has many other uses, but we will skip those for now."

"How do I learn all of this?" Abby asked. "I mean where do I begin with really understanding this?"

Elda smiled and Abby noticed the crisscross of soft wrinkles around her mouth and eyes. She wondered Elda's age, but thought she might not be ready to know the answer. Abby had not known many old people in her life. Her grandmother, Arlene, had died when she was young, and her father's parents had died before she was born. When she talked with the elderly, she always felt a chasm between them, like they lived in two different worlds, but wanted to pretend that they didn't. Now she was actually talking to an older woman who truly lived in another world, and the distance was palpable.

"This is not a crash course in history," Elda said, suddenly sounding tired. "It is only a beginning. When you learn the truth of yourself and believe it, other truths come naturally. Some things we will tell you, and some things you will just know."

"What can witches do? I mean, what can I do?"

"That's better," Elda said. "There are many other powers, beyond the water, that is. Some that we all seem to possess and some that will belong to you alone."

"Which do we all have?" Abby asked, surprised at how easily the 'we' rolled off her tongue. She imagined her mother's narrowed eyes, the way she rolled them when Abby believed something absurd, or not absurd, but simply unappealing to her mother.

"Where did you go just now?" Elda asked.

"To my mother. She's like the little doubtful devil on my shoulder."

Elda laughed, a light sound, like far-off wind chimes.

"Mothers are our portal into this world and the chains that strap us to it."

"Yes, mine was more like a barbed wire fence."

Elda nodded, but did not ask more.

"Before I explain the powers of a witch, you must understand that you may have never experienced them before. Witches manifest their power at different times in their life. I feel that you are only just beginning, probably because you have led a very structured life. Here, with us, these abilities will come much more quickly, which is for the best."

Again Abby wanted to blurt out, "What are they?", but she managed to contain herself.

"Firstly, there is night vision. You will see better at night, although it will not be crystal clear, it will be very similar to watching everything beneath dim bulbs. This is true for even the blackest room, void of all light sources." Elda watched Abby's face closely as she spoke.

"Your physical strength will be magnified, but only in certain areas," Elda continued. "You won't be able to lift cars per se, but you will jump very high, swim faster and run faster. In some cases, witches have been known to exhibit superhuman strength, but it generally only occurs when you have an open connection with your element and your power is especially strong."

"I have jumped very high," Abby whispered, shocked by the realization. "In the woods, hiding from Vesta and Tane."

"I do not know Vesta and Tane, but I know of them. Vesta belongs to Tobias. He is her mentor."

"Are they like witches that have turned bad?" Abby asked, imagining the serpentine appearance of his face as he'd leered over her in the woods.

"No, they are not witches, but we will come to all of

that later." Elda traced a slender finger along the edge of the leather book. "All witches have an astral body, a spirit body, which can move outside the physical body."

The hair stood up on the back of Abby's neck. "Like a dream?"

"Like a dream, but not a dream. I have heard new witches compare it to dreaming, but have you ever had such control in your dreams?"

Abby shook her head and imagined visiting the cave. The only thing that made it dream-like was how little it compared to her waking world.

"Power over the astral body is not the same for everyone. Some witches can use their astral body only to gather with other witches in the non-physical state. Others can move beyond this, traveling through other medians, such as their element. Spells are another universal power among witches and a very important one."

"Spells?" Abby asked. "Like turning someone into a toad?"

Elda laughed and looked at Abby like she was considering a small child. "No, no toads that I have heard of. The spells serve us as manipulators of the elements. They are our protection, our defense and one of the greatest faculties that we possess."

Abby could not help the whimsical fancies that popped into her thoughts: fairy godmothers, white bearded wizards, the wicked witch and her ruby slippers.

It was not easy to separate these fictional characters from the woman before her wearing a white beaded shawl and staring out from eyes as deep as the ocean.

"Don't force it, Abby. Understanding comes with time."

Abby hunched forward and clasped her hands on the table, lacing her fingers together and staring through them at the *Book of Shadows*. She was torn by a willingness to fall entirely into the new life offered her and a scared desperation to cling to old certainties.

"It has taken you years to learn the truths of your current life, and it will take years to learn those same truths about your new life."

"My new life." Abby tested the words in her mouth. They were slow and anticlimactic. Saying a thing did not make it real.

"For many of us, life changes drastically when the power surfaces. Our old lives, well, they fall away." She trailed off, and Abby wondered if she was searching back through her own transition from woman to witch.

"Why do they have to change?" Abby implored, clutching her memories as if they'd ever been more than a thought.

"We all change, Abby. Learning to be a witch is less shocking than some changes in everyday life, like going to war or suffering through disease. All living things have an amazing ability to adapt. I think you've already proven as much to yourself."

"Yes, I hadn't thought so, but I've learned a lot about myself lately."

"And so you will. There is so much to learn, so many amazing discoveries that you will be privy to now. Our coven alone has existed since the fifteenth century and originated in Rome. Faustine descends from the original coven founders. Can you even imagine the history that he has seen?"

"Wait." Abby held up a finger. "Does that mean Faustine has lived since the fifteenth century?"

Elda cocked an eyebrow and smiled. "Would you believe me if I said yes?"

Abby scrunched her features and shrugged. "Maybe?"

"Well, it doesn't matter now. What matters is that our coven has much to offer you as a new witch."

"If it began in Rome, why is it here now?"

"Because Faustine fled here many years ago. He came with the purpose of rebuilding his coven in a safer place. When he found this island, the castle had long since been abandoned, and the area on the mainland was hardly populated. He used his power to hide the island and began the process of re-establishing his coven."

"So he is a witch as well?" Abby asked. "I thought maybe just women."

"Oh, yes, Faustine is one of the greatest witches I have ever known. It is a popular misconception, this idea that only women are witches, but sometimes these misconceptions serve us."

"And why do you have these *Books of Shadows*?" Abby asked.

"A coven compiles a very powerful history in their *Book of Shadows*. Not only is it a record of every witch who has existed within the coven, it is also a compilation of spells, some very old and others that are newly discovered. We call it a *Book of Shadows*, but throughout history it has had many names."

"This is the Coven of Voda, then?" Abby asked.

"No, it's not. You see, these books are much sought after. They have been stolen and hidden from our enemies for many years. They are also transferred when a coven disbands. This came with me from Croatia. The Voda Coven had weakened and we were no longer safe. I was only a girl when Faustine found me, and I guarded this book as if it were my very life." Elda's eyes had taken on a glassy quality and she seemed to be reaching back centuries to retrieve this memory.

"Our coven here is the Covenant of Ula. Ula means

jewel of the sea. We have three *Books of Shadows*. We have Ula's, Voda's and Aepa's. Aepa was a Greek coven whose witches were comprised entirely of the air element. Helena, whom you met last night, spent many years at Aepa, and she brought a wealth of knowledge when she came to us here."

"Why did all of these other covens disband?" Abby asked, trying to keep the coven names straight in her mind.

"The reasons are many, but often arise from some type of danger. If a Vepar discovers a coven's location they will attack or find ways to intercept witches who belong to the coven. If a witch within the coven loses their sense of right, they may use the coven's secrets for personal gain, which puts the entire unit in danger." Elda's face fell as she talked, perhaps revisiting her own experiences. "You see, Abby, our power is both yearned for and hated. Vepars long to acquire it, less capable witches may envy the power of greater ones, regular society views us as a threat. But we must carry on regardless of these perils. Our purpose is to use our strength to help others."

"So a coven breaks apart when they are in danger and relocates?"

"Some of them do. However, many covens have simply abandoned their agreement and the witches have scattered. Covens that have no strong leaders rarely survive when threats arise. Some of the witches may join other covens, some may not."

"There were some very old newspaper clippings in the Astral Coven's *Book of Shadows*," Abby interjected. "They were about this woman, Aubrey Blake."

"Devin's great, great, great grandmother."

"You knew Devin?" Abby demanded, wondering why they didn't save her.

"No, but when Sebastian told me about her, I contacted another coven and I learned of her bloodline."

"Since last night?" Abby could not hide the disbelief in her voice.

"I traveled within my astral body. You see, there is a place where witches meet. It is a cave hidden deep in the mountains. I put the word out that I was searching for history on the name Blake. Within a few hours, a witch arrived from Canada who had followed some of the bloodlines in the Astral Coven because she used to belong to it. When the coven broke apart, she took down the names in the *Book of Shadows*, but the book itself went with another witch. You see Devin's mother died during childbirth and she was adopted. The witch from Canada had been tracking the Blake bloodline, but had believed it died with Teresa, Devin's mother. The father did not want the child and paid the hospital to lie and claim that the baby had died as well. Thus Devin went to a new family, and no one in our world, so to speak, knew that she even existed."

"So this woman in Canada was tracking Devin's family since Aubrey."

"Yes, it is part of our duty to follow the bloodlines and assist developing witches; however, so many covens have disbanded that it has become problematic. Not every child of a witch becomes a witch. Sometimes it skips a generation, sometimes several. In Devin's case, it skipped three. But all of these names are kept within our *Books of Shadows*. That is only one of the reasons that they are so important to us. Each of us here at the Coven of Ula has a list of names that we follow through generations. When a new witch surfaces, we contact them and bring them into our coven or help them into another. But, as I said, several generations may pass without a witch born. Then there are witches who disregard their duties in following bloodlines. You see, Adora had the Astral *Book of Shadows*, but passed it to Claire, a new witch who died a short time later, which allowed the book and the names to end up in Sebastian's hands. Sebastian told me how Tobias insisted on retrieving the book, which means that when Tobias seduced Claire before killing her she told him about the book. If he had gotten it, many witches would have been in danger. It is all quite complex. Sadly, Devin is an example of how ineffective our system can be at times."

Abby imagined Devin, her fiery hair, the wild look in her eyes.

"Do you think Devin knew she was a witch?" Abby asked.

Elda thought for a long time, her eyes roaming across the distant water. Over the mass of cherry blossoms, Abby could see the upper half of the castle straining towards the clear blue sky.

"I believe Devin was just discovering that she was a witch. I think she was undergoing changes, and it was these changes that motivated her to seek her true parentage. I doubt she fully understood at her death what she was." Elda looked sad at this.

"What about me?" Abby whispered, knowing how close her own fate had come to mirroring Devin's.

"I want to give you an answer," Elda said. "But I don't have one. We will trace your bloodline, but sometimes it is a difficult process. I happened to get very lucky with Devin. But, as I said, so many covens have broken apart over the years, and when that happens the *Book of Shadows* is passed and the witches responsible for each bloodline scatter. Some travel to new covens, others choose not to. Certain witches are responsible for following bloodlines, some of them die and others just disappear…"

"Where do they go?"

"Some choose to live the human way, as if they are not witches. It is rare, but it does happen. Others will simply disappear, hide in remote locations."

"When was the last time a new witch was born from the names that you guys follow here?"

"Oliver," Elda answered happily. "He came to us fifteen years ago. His great grandfather had been a witch. Oliver was part of a bloodline that Helena was following from her former coven, the Coven of Aepa."

"So, if he came here fifteen years ago, that makes him how old?" To Abby, Oliver did not look much older than Sebastian or her.

Elda cocked her eyebrows and took a moment. "Well, he started exhibiting powers when he was seventeen and he entered the coven at eighteen, so he is thirty-three."

Abby imagined Oliver, his firm, muscular shape and young laughing eyes. "He looks really good."

"Yes, well, physically we are different, Abby. Most witches retain a youthful appearance for quite a long time. Not only do we have differing physiology than normal people, we also have elixirs that work miracles, so to speak." Elda looked at the greenhouse as she said this.

Abby followed her gaze to a small white barked tree with funny cactus shaped leaves covered in little yellow spots.

"Do you mean like a fountain of youth sort of thing?" Abby asked in wonderment. Could it be true?

"Not exactly a fountain of youth, although in regular society some of our potions are construed as such. You see, some of the potions we create are designed for witches and others for regular humans. A witch who takes steps to stay younger should not do so out of vanity, but in order to be more beneficial to the world in general. Whether that is by fitting in more appropriately or simply by living longer."

"Living longer." Abby shuddered, imagining her old body wrinkled and sagging, but the years continuing to idle by.

"Not all witches live past the typical life expectancy for humans. It is a choice..." Elda trailed off and Abby suspected that information was being left out.

"Where are witches from?" Abby asked, wanting desperately to fill the many voids drifting through her thoughts.

"We have always been," Elda replied, her hands smoothing over the *Book of Shadows*. "There is no distinct creator or first witch that is recognized. Our very ancient ancestors were generally known as healers or sleuths. They understood, even then, what they were, but it was much harder to exist in secret. They often lived amongst the public, but then it became dangerous."

"Witch burnings?" Abby asked, imagining the photo of Aubrey Blake's fiery demise.

"Those were the least of our problems." Elda told her gravely. "The Vepars began to hunt us, they had discovered how our power could help them, and they would stop at nothing to attain it."

"Tell me about them. The Vepars, I mean."

Elda scrunched her forehead, tiny lines furrowing her brow. She looked tired. "I will," she paused, "tell you some things, but this discussion is best saved for Dafne or Oliver. The Vepars are connected to a form of evil. Is it dark magic? Maybe. They have a link with demons or dark spirits. The act of becoming a Vepar is not completely clear, but there does appear to be lineage involved. Vepars descend from other Vepars. However, they are not born this way, but inducted into it. As non-Vepars or humans, they have little power over us. As Vepars, they are stronger, faster, and they can often smell witches. Their saliva contains a venom that is like a tranquilizer to a witch, and the potency varies across their people. They can damage humans."

"Damage how?" The excitement and astonishment had

begun to fade. To learn of witches was one thing, but evil beings connected to demons?

"They are manipulative. By this I don't mean just charming, although many are that way as well; they can enter some people's brains, sort of confuse them and worse." Elda whispered this last part.

Abby recalled her experience with Detective Alva and the splitting headache that followed.

"Why didn't they just break down Sydney's door and kill me?" Abby asked, thinking aloud.

"Well, that is one of our advantages. Vepars must perform the ritual sacrifice to absorb our blood as power." Elda looked sourly across the lagoon. "They must use very specific tools to enchant the ritual and open the darkness in them to the light in us. It is an intricate process and one that you already have far too much experience with. Suffice to say that they cannot murder us easily if they want to gain anything from the death."

Once more Abby began to feel overwhelmed by the overload of information – the covens, the powers, Vepars, she felt weary as if from a long walk.

"You are getting tired," Elda told her gently. "And hungry, I'm sure. Let us return to the castle to rejuvenate ourselves."

Abby yawned in agreement. She wanted to ask more questions, but hunger and exhaustion plagued her. And, quite frankly, talking of the Vepars terrified her. How could she choose to believe that witches existed and not their enemies?

Elda stood, her fingers lingering on the *Book of Shadows* a moment longer, before she pulled it to her breast and swept back into the greenhouse. When she returned, she beckoned for Abby to follow, and they began their journey back to the castle. The sun's intense rays made Abby's eyes ache, and she shielded them as she walked.

"Is Dafne unhappy that we've come here?"

Elda took her time answering. The shells crunched beneath their feet and Abby thought of bones.

"Dafne is very protective of our coven and she has experienced things that have frightened her so greatly that every thought is tainted by those memories. You see, Abby, some people are the history that haunts them, and Dafne has some especially difficult ghosts to rid herself of. She welcomes you, I am sure. It is your Sebastian that she fears."

"But why should she fear Sebastian?" Abby asked angrily. "He's wonderful. He led me here." She had no intention of giving up her only friend and link to the other world, the one that still made sense.

"Well, that is part of her fear, Abby. He is a basic man and he led you here. His sister gave him very critical information about us, what we are, where we live. Dafne fears who he could lead here and how easily he could be manipulated by the other side." Elda had slowed as she spoke and Abby slowed as well.

"You mean Tobias?" Abby was incredulous. "Sebastian would never help Tobias."

"No, I agree with you, Abby, but, as I said before, Tobias and the other Vepars have powers said to seduce any regular man or woman, such that natural people do not stand a chance."

"How is that possible?" Abby asked, wanting to believe that Sebastian could somehow deflect these powers, but remembering all too well Danny Kent, Devin's brother, who supposedly confessed to her murder.

"Abby, Vepars are like demons. Forget what you know about villains because you must always believe that you are underestimating them. Never think that you know their intentions or their abilities."

"Demons," she puffed the name out in fear. Tobias had

looked like a demon in the end; he had looked as if he might drag her into hell. She shivered violently. "Sebastian knew what he was."

"Oh, yes, Sebastian knows more than most other commoners that I have met. I apologize, I know that the word commoner is not pleasant, but I use it simply to distinguish between witches and non-witches."

Abby did not like the sound of that. Could Sebastian be ripped away from her because he was a commoner?

"What other kinds of things can the Vepars do?" She had a few ideas, but had not exactly been lucid during much of her encounter with them.

"That is Dafne and Oliver's area of expertise. They are much more capable of properly explaining Tobias and the others."

They departed from the blossoms back onto the cobblestone pathway. The young girl, Lydie, was circling the lagoon in a rowboat. She didn't touch the oars, but it continued to move gracefully through the shimmering water. Her curls blew in the wind, a crown of spirals billowing around her head. Abby wondered if she was lonely, she looked so young, so fragile.

Chapter 19

Nearly everyone that Abby had met the night before was seated at a long dining table that stretched down the center of a vast dining hall. Two glorious chandeliers, covered in hundreds of lit candles, flickered above the diners. Thick, embroidered, chocolate drapes blocked the early evening sun, and Abby noticed that only Oliver was absent.

Sebastian gave a small wave, and she hurried across the plum carpeting, her feet sinking in. She sat beside him and he squeezed her hand, leaning over to kiss her on the cheek.

"You look great. Everything go okay?" His blue eyes glittered and she felt caught up in his excitement. He'd even donned a navy blue and white striped button down in lieu of the usual t-shirt. Abby was happy to see that he and Oliver had not killed each other.

A short, plump woman with frizzy red hair and glossy pink lips entered the room carrying a silver tray almost longer than her arms could stretch. Her long, knit sleeves nearly covered her hands and she shimmied, attempting to slip them further up her forearms. Her cow neck sweater dipped, revealing sparkly, bronzed cleavage, and a small turquoise stone dangled between her hefty bosoms. The tray was piled with food, and the aroma silenced the conversation.

"Sebastian, Abby, this is Bridget," Elda told them, standing at the head of the long table and gesturing to the wide, smiling lady.

"Hi y'all," Bridget chirped, somehow curtsying behind the massive tray. She slid the tray onto the table, pushing each platter down with the ease of a body builder. Abby realized that this miniature woman, with her southern drawl, was a witch.

Large, gleaming platters were passed down the table, Abby's wide eyes taking in a feast that appeared far too enormous for the nine stomachs awaiting it.

"Want me to do this?" Sebastian asked her as he tonged hunks of gravy-covered turkey onto his plate. Apparently he'd noticed her glazed expression and didn't trust her with large serving utensils.

"Yes, please." She slid her plate down.

Sebastian sat to her right, and to her left was Helena, who talked animatedly with Abby between spoonfuls of mashed sweet potatoes and grilled asparagus. It seemed to be Helena's personal goal to ensure that Abby and Sebastian felt welcome in the castle. When Sebastian rubbed the back of his neck absently, Helena leaned over and told them about a whole drawer full of tinctures that Bridget placed in every room for all kinds of ailments.

"From back pain to chicken pox," Helena laughed conspiratorially. "I once took one labeled sweet dreams and spent the best six hours of my life riding flying ponies over a giant sea of Jell-O. Imagine that, Jell-O!"

Sebastian guffawed and winked at Abby.

The room, which should have been drafty, was strangely warm and snug. Abby ate slowly, savoring every bite and listening to Helena who spoke incessantly about food. She listed her favorite appetizers, entrees and finally desserts and then coaxed Abby and Sebastian to do the same.

Everyone else carried on separate conversations. They sounded curiously uninvolved, as if afraid to embark on their so-called normal topics in front of the strangers. Only Dafne remained silent, staring at her food, but barely touching it, her dark eyes occasionally shooting towards Sebastian and Abby. No one else appeared to notice, least of all Sebastian, who ate like a cat at a tuna buffet and somehow still managed

J.R. Erickson

to carry on with Helena as if they were old chums.

Abby studied the other witches. From outside appearances, Elda led the pack, but Abby wondered if Faustine was not their true leader. He often looked irritable, distracted and stared at his food, picking absently, while Lydie chattered in his ear. Abby could not hear her, but wondered if she was simply babbling a long string of clichés into some barely sensible conversation. Max, Elda and Bridget talked about the weather, the food and the gardens – never alighting on a single topic that piqued Abby's interest.

As time ticked by, Abby desperately wanted to wrap up dinner and have time alone with Sebastian. She felt as if the threads between them were fraying or perhaps being burned by Dafne – the fire breathing dragon across the table. Would the conversation be different if Sebastian were not at the table? Were they simply harboring their secrets because there was a commoner in the room, a non-witch?

Abby felt the dormant flower, the angry bloom, ignite in her chest, a brief eruption of fury at the unfairness of it all. As the flower unfurled and her chest tightened, every water glass at the table exploded. Shards of glass blew outward, but before any piece could strike, Faustine stood, shouted an incantation and a rush of air swept the microscopic shards into a miniature tornado of glass, which flew out of the room like a swarm of mosquitoes.

Abby gasped and Sebastian knocked over his wine. The others, except Dafne, quickly sopped the spilled water.

"Not a worry, doll, happens to the best of us," Bridget sang down the table from her place at Elda's elbow.

Everyone was looking at Abby, they all knew that she had created the explosion, everyone except her, that was.

Strangely, no one except Sebastian looked shocked and they surely did not look afraid, despite their near impalement by water goblet. Lydie smiled and gave Abby a thumbs-up.

Sebastian rotated slowly in his chair and stared at her, his eyes wide with excitement.

"Hey, no biggie," he whispered and clutched her trembling hand.

She forced her mouth closed and smiled tightly, staring at Faustine. He had returned to his dinner, not looking at her. How had he reacted so quickly? Almost as if he sensed it before it occurred.

The table talk resumed, other than a few reassuring smiles aimed her way. Bridget disappeared into the kitchen and reappeared with a tray covered in miniature chocolate lava cakes. Abby's usual inclination towards chocolate was squashed by her outburst, but she forced her dessert down anyways. Embarrassment was not the right word, more like shame.

"Don't sweat the small stuff," Lydie leaned across Helena to tell her loudly before moving back and diving into her cake.

Elda finished her dessert and then stood at the end of the table, clinking her fork against a fresh water glass until the room silenced.

"Just a few things before we part for the evening. First, thank you again, Bridget, for a truly magical meal." She winked at Bridget. "Thank you also Abby and Sebastian for gracing us with your presence, it is a great pleasure to have you in our home. Finally, Abby and Sebastian, if you could remain after for a few minutes so that we could chat?"

"Of course," Sebastian said quickly, checking for Abby's nod of approval.

"Should we help?" Abby whispered to Helena, gesturing to the dishes.

"Oh, no, Bridget has her own way of taking care of things," Helena replied, smiling cleverly.

Everyone began to shuffle from their seats, Abby

taking pains to ignore Dafne's glowering looks. Lydie hummed obnoxiously, skipping around the room to swipe the lingering bites of chocolate cake from each plate. She had to hurry because the dessert plates were sliding slowly down the table. Abby spied Bridget at the end, her hands waving in large sloppy circles, beckoning the dishes to her.

"A candle has burned out," Sebastian said nonchalantly, pointing to the chandelier directly above their table.

His were five words that changed everything. Dafne flew out of her seat, knocking the chair clear back to the wall. Lydie gasped loudly. Abby followed the horrified expression of every witch to the small, black wick – flameless – above.

"Oh, dear," Bridget murmured, looking immediately to Elda for guidance, whose eyes were locked with Faustine's.

"Oliver?" Lydie's voice, meek and tearful, seemed to state what everyone else in the room was thinking.

Abby stood dumbfounded; it was just a candle after all. She looked to Sebastian, but he appeared equally confused.

"I apologize." Elda looked at Abby and Sebastian. "The snuffing out of a candle is a very bad omen for us. We will have to postpone our meeting until tomorrow."

Elda, Faustine and Dafne withdrew through a door at the back of the dining area.

The remaining group stood for another moment before Bridget piped up and began to hustle them all out. Her face looked falsely chipper and a significant glance passed between her and Max as he followed Lydie from the room. He placed a hand on Lydie's back, guiding her down the hallway.

"Lessons," Helena told them, nodding towards Max and Lydie and smiling over the anxiety that had lined her face moments earlier.

"Listen," Sebastian started. "I don't want to be a snoop, but…"

"No, of course you have questions," Helena cut in. "Let's go to the library and we'll talk. Sometimes it's difficult for the others to be entirely open, but I'm a firm believer that knowledge is power."

Abby felt a mixture of relief and gloom. She had hoped to get some time alone with Sebastian, but she also wanted to know what was happening.

A fire radiated in the vast stone fireplace when they trailed in, each pulling a chair closer to the blaze.

"Those are beautiful," Sebastian commented, pointing at the zodiac murals on the ceiling.

"Aren't they?" Helena agreed. "They were painted long before I arrived here and yet they have not changed a bit."

"Is there anything to it? The Zodiac?" Sebastian asked.

"Oh, yes. We can understand a great many things through the Zodiac. For instance, I know that you, Sebastian, like me, are a Scorpio, and you, Abby, are a Cancer."

"How do you know that?" Abby asked.

"Well, some of it is your personalities. Sebastian, I can see your sign through your secretiveness and your passion, which is almost uncontrollable. Cancers, Abby, are led by their feelings, and at times they are a prisoner to those feelings."

Abby and Sebastian both nodded, but neither asked for further insight into their identities. It was enough that she could so easily discern their signs. Abby had never been a huge fan of horoscopes; it felt too invasive. How could one tiny paragraph provide insight into her life or even her day, for that matter?

"Let me tell you about the candle," Helena began. "When a candle flickers out, here at Ula, it is not the wind. You see our candles are lit by a spell that enforces a constant

J.R. Erickson

flame in our presence. When a candle extinguishes, it is an omen of death."

"Where was Oliver tonight?" Sebastian asked gravely.

"He has gone again after Tobias," she told them calmly, speaking over their groans. "Oliver is a hunter. That is his place in our coven. He is a powerful witch, and it would take a great force to defeat him. That being said, he had to pursue Tobias. If he didn't, the Vepars might sense weakness in our coven. They have murdered one witch and almost claimed a second. It is our responsibility to stop them."

"But is he?" Abby choked. She barely knew Oliver, but felt sick with grief and guilt.

"No, it is an omen of death, a warning. It does not mean that anyone has died, and it certainly does not mean that Oliver will die," Helena assured them.

"Who else, then?" Sebastian asked.

"Someone that he is near. You see, our spells are meant to encompass our coven, however, death is a violent event and greatly affects an area much larger than a single individual."

"What about Tobias? Maybe he killed Tobias," Sebastian asked eagerly.

"No. Believe me, Sebastian, I am as eager as you for that moment. However, the spells that reveal the state of our coven are not impacted by Vepars."

Sebastian's face fell, shoulders sagging as he slumped further into his chair.

"Do not worry," Helena soothed. "You are not in the presence of ordinary individuals. Having faith in each other is an important practice within our coven."

"Are Oliver and Dafne an item?" Abby asked, thinking that she might understand the venom behind Dafne's earlier scowls.

"No. Dafne, like Oliver, is a hunter, and they are very close. Dafne mentored Oliver when he originally entered the coven. Usually they would hunt Tobias together, but we felt it safer to keep Dafne here with us in case Tobias continued to pursue you, Abby."

"But is that necessary?" Sebastian asked. "I mean, there are so many of you here already."

"Yes, but Dafne and Oliver have certain instincts as hunters. Instincts that are especially strong if Tobias is near because they have stalked him for so long."

"Why do they target Tobias?" Abby asked.

"Proximity," Helena stated simply, fingering a green glass bead around her neck. "He belongs to a pack that began to murder here about ten years ago."

"Pack?" Abby asked. "Like wolves?"

"Well, that is how we define them. I'm sure they choose much loftier classifications for themselves, but to us they are merely animals."

Sebastian tilted his face towards the fire, watching the pointed shadows on the carpet.

"Tell us more about them?" Abby asked, slipping into the thrall of the mysterious world unfolding.

Helena hesitated as if she preferred not to indulge the visitors in a Vepar Q and A.

"Yes, please," Sebastian added.

Abby looked at him, but he trained his eyes on Helena, willing her to open up.

"Okay," she decided. "This is usually left to Oliver and Dafne. It is not that we do not all know and understand the Vepars, but they are constantly changing. It is only Dafne and Oliver who truly know them. It is their skill, not only to hunt the Vepars, but to become them, in mind only, of course."

To become them? Abby could not stand the thought.

215

"The Vepars are our greatest enemies. They, like witches, have descended from an ancient bloodline. They are not born with natural powers, but they have the capacity to unite with darkness. I have heard them called demons, and others say that they communicate with demons, but it is almost impossible to know. They seek to destroy witches because it greatly increases their power. The witches that they gain from the most are new witches, purest in their magic and weakest in discipline. New witches do not have control of their energy, which is both to their detriment and benefit. The uncontrolled energy is unbelievably strong, and a Vepar absorbs this power if he or she does the proper rituals."

Abby followed closely, remembering the ritual and her conversation with Elda that day.

"They are nightmares, not only to us, but to regular people as well. They have been known to control minds, to kill without any actual contact and to commit unspeakable acts in their quest for power."

"What power does it give them when they kill a witch?" Abby asked.

"There are many," Helena conceded, watching them darkly. "But I believe killing becomes intoxicating and supercedes the powers gained. Evil and the strength that accompanies it is always the goal."

"So where have the others gone? To find Oliver?" Sebastian blurted as if ready to join the fight.

"No. They will try to contact him first through Faustine. Faustine is telepathic."

Abby's eyes widened in surprise.

"Faustine has a constant line of communication with each of us at the coven, but there are many earthly elements that block these signals. There is a tower in the castle that is designed for this purpose. He goes there, alone, and attempts to reach Oliver through his mind."

"And if he cannot reach him?" Sebastian asked on the edge of his chair, his feet tapping rapidly.

"Then we wait. We cannot send Dafne and allow our defenses to be weakened if Oliver has fallen. Likewise, we cannot search for him ourselves because he may still be hunting Tobias and we would only alert the Vepars to Oliver's presence. You see it is much easier for them to sense us than to sense Oliver."

"So we're helpless? We do nothing?" Sebastian clambered to his feet and patrolled the room nervously.

"We are far from helpless, Sebastian," Helena replied, looking suddenly tired. "We have fought and survived here for a very long time."

"Are many witches telepathic?" Abby asked, wanting to change the subject.

"That is a very hard question to answer because there are many witches I have never encountered or even heard of. The diverse powers exhibited by our kind are innumerable. Some come naturally while others must be created or invoked."

"Invoked, how?"

"By performing a ritual that directs your power toward a very specific goal."

Abby started to ask more, but Helena held up her hand.

"I understand that you have questions, but we have ways to teach you all of this in a more streamlined fashion."

She nodded and busied herself unraveling a string from her sleeve. Sebastian sat silently, his face a shadow.

"Can Faustine communicate with me?" Sebastian asked.

Abby knew that Helena had grown reluctant to offer more information. She wondered if Sebastian's interest bothered her, if she could be counted among the witches who subscribed to an 'Us vs. Them' mentality.

Her mind prickled at this thought, and again the tiny bloom began to unfold. She could feel Sebastian's anguish, his desire to bring Tobias down, his grief, so why couldn't they? How could they imagine that his knowledge could ever damage them? She considered pushing her chair closer to his, a silent show of support, but didn't. He needed to stand alone, she was sure of that. He seemed reluctant to fully give in to her, as if he feared that falling for her would only suck him deeper into a world that he could never be a part of. What scared her was that he could be right. Had she even been accepted into the world of witches yet? Or would it take years of overcoming people like Dafne before admittance became a reality? She bristled at Dafne's image, her scowling face across the table, her accusatory eyes. How could she blame them for Oliver? Abby suddenly wished that Dafne were in the room with them so that she could confront her. Ask her why she thought that it was okay to pass judgment on them so quickly. The flower fed on her anger, growing larger as she imagined Dafne's scowling face.

Helena and Sebastian both gasped, and Abby whirled toward them, realizing that her thoughts had taken her elsewhere. Sebastian had ripped the arm off his chair. He held the arm of golden wood in the air as if he could not imagine how it had gotten there.

"What just happened?" Abby asked, staring from Helena back to Sebastian.

"I…I don't know," Sebastian stammered, continuing to stare at the wood like he'd never seen it before.

"You just ripped it clear off," Helena breathed, her voice tinged with awe. "For no reason…" But her eyes drifted toward Abby as she spoke.

"Was it loose?" Abby asked, walking to his chair and shaking the other arm, which held firmly in place.

"No, I didn't even know I had my hand on it," he said, turning to stare at the jagged piece still sticking from the chair back. It had not ripped clean, and the leftover arm looked lethal.

"Well, must be time for a new one," Helena joked, continuing to eye Abby and Sebastian strangely.

"I'm really sorry about that," Sebastian told Helena. He stood up and dragged it deeper into the room, selecting a simple beige ottoman to sit on instead. "I hope it wasn't an antique."

"No apologies necessary, Sebastian," Helena laughed, waving her hand dismissively. "I do, however, have to go now." She gave Abby an especially long smile. "It is after ten pm and it is best that I join Faustine."

She stood, without saying more, and began to brush from the room, her red skirt swirling out behind her. A mad tapping at the window stopped her, hand poised above the doorknob, and she turned, her eyes seeking the tall dark window on the opposite wall. Abby and Sebastian turned as well. A purple-black raven clutched the castle ledge, his beak rapping on the thick pane, his feathers oily in the moonlight.

"Oh." Helena's hand flew to her throat, seizing the green bead that hung around her neck.

"What, what is it, Helena?" Sebastian asked.

"A raven," she whispered, "carries the spirit of the murdered...I have to go." She did not continue, but instead glided from the room, her eyes blank.

Abby and Sebastian watched the Raven as it fell from the edge in flight, its long wings stretching to catch an updraft. It soared away, and neither of them spoke for a long time.

Chapter 20

Abby and Sebastian left the library and walked side by side, his hand on the small of her back. The pressure felt good and she longed to turn, stand on tiptoe, and kiss him hard on the mouth. Instead, she ambled beside him in silence, afraid of potential rejection, still fighting old ghosts.

At the foot of the spiral staircase he stopped and turned her towards him.

"Sweet dreams, my Abby." He kissed her feather-like on the forehead and pulled away, his eyes crystal clear, alert. He was not tired, and would not sleep.

She wanted to hold him, make him stay with her, but he turned and strode down the hall, his long legs pumping in his gray slacks. She wondered who he borrowed clothes from. Oliver most likely. Poor Oliver.

She stood on the bottom step of the staircase, her hand clutching the metal rail, her eyes absorbing the castle hall. The ceiling arched high; thousands of tiny iridescent circles reflected the hallway candelabras, as though the entire ceiling were imbedded with golden opals.

In a remote place in her mind, bed sounded nice. She could climb beneath the warm duvet and surrender another day of commotion to the night. But how could she sleep? Was Oliver dead? Would Sebastian be alone in his room, brooding, angry and despondent?

She was a witch after all; couldn't she provide some sort of help?

She slipped off the step and started down the hall. There were so many doors, each with a tiny skeleton keyhole. She did not know the castle layout and wished for a fluorescent mall map with a little arrow that said, 'You Are Here.' Instead, she opted for snooping, creeping to each door and pressing her ear gingerly against the thick wood.

At the end of the hall, two more small sets of spiral staircases drifted upwards, probably to bedrooms. The front door lay ahead and the hallway branched to the left and right. The halls were nearly identical, the floors covered by the same gold rug, the walls adorned with candelabras, every waxen tip burning with a bright orange flame. At the end of the hall to her right stood a blank wooden door. No door closed the end of the left hallway, instead a dark archway led down.

She chose the left, reaching the end and staring into the darkness, which revealed a dimly lit stone staircase that curved and disappeared out of sight. Beginning down the stairs, she stopped abruptly at the loud clack of her shoes. She reached down, slipped them off and clutched them in her hand. The stone was cold on her socked feet.

Moving into the castle's belly, she was not afraid, but exhilarated. She might have had her palm pressed flat against a plasma globe with the hot pink streaks of electricity tickling her fingers and surging out into the air around her.

She stopped abruptly when voices drifted up the stairwell, echoing off the stone walls.

"Lydie, focus please." She heard Max reprimand, but in an entirely mild manner that his feisty counterpart would probably ignore.

"That is as likely as a snowball in hell," Lydie sang back to him and Abby could hear her dancing feet as she skipped about the room.

"Now, Lydie, is that at all appropriate?" a slightly sterner Max asked.

"Half a loaf is better than none, Uncle Max."

Uncle Max? Was he really her uncle?

Abby crept further down, her eyes adjusting quickly to the darkness. When a trickle of light appeared along the wall before her, she slowed. A faint sulfur smell tinged the air, like fire, but no crackling greeted her, or warmth.

"Let's return to the goal at hand. Your astral body. Come, sit." Max sounded tired.

"All work, no play," Lydie moaned.

Abby had come to the open archway now, but remained in the shadows.

Max and Lydie were in an enormous vault-like room, nearly empty except for two green, velvet-backed chairs sitting on a raised stone slab. Max stood behind the chair that Lydie had plopped into, a grimace on her delicate face. Behind the other chair sat a small, wooden table, balancing precariously on two legs. A small, rose colored bowl sat in its center, flames leaping out.

"Now," Max encouraged gently. "Focus on the flames, Lydie. That is your power, and it is your way to the cave. Your astral body can connect directly through the fire."

Lydie's element was fire. Abby didn't know why, but it made sense.

Lydie's eyes closed, their lids like the white wings of light-struck moths. Her hands hovered above her lap, moving in small circles like a cat held over a pool of water.

Max spoke softly. Abby could not hear him, but saw the slight stirring of his lips. Edging forward, she smacked into a low table. It struck her shins and sent searing pain up her legs.

"Ouch," she howled, instantly sorry when Lydie's eyes snapped open.

Max turned towards her and the brief glower that fell over his face disappeared almost instantly. He hurried across the room to aid her.

"Abby?"

"Yes, sorry, this is embarrassing," she stammered, bending to rub her sore shin.

"Not a worry," he interrupted, pulling a jagged purplish rock from his pocket. He leaned down and rubbed it over her shins.

The pain subsided, cooling to a dull ache and then vanishing.

"Wow, how did you do that?" She watched in wonder as he held the stone up.

"Amethyst."

"Better to have and not need than to need and not have," Lydie chirped loudly from her chair.

Max shook his head and slipped the rock back into his pocket.

"I dare say you have properly met Lydie?" Max asked, as Lydie stood from her chair and bowed dramatically.

"More or less," Abby agreed, walking further into the room. She shivered at the coldness of it – like a meat freezer.

"It's cold enough to freeze the balls off a brass monkey, isn't it?" the girl twittered.

Abby bit back a laugh and Max shot Lydie a scathing look. She grinned and spun in a wide circle, her knee-length periwinkle dress fluttering around her like she was the belle of the ball.

"Best not to even acknowledge it," he said curtly and returned to the table on the slab. He raised his hands above the rose bowl and the flames extinguished.

"Not burning the candle at both ends this evening?" Lydie asked, with a quick giggle, before darting across the room.

Abby's mouth fell open, she'd moved faster than Abby's eyes could follow, covering the dungeon's length in seconds.

"She's a bit of a show off," Max told her with a pleased smile that he unsuccessfully tried to muffle.

"I'm sorry I interrupted your lesson," Abby told him

guiltily, brushing a stray hair behind her ear, an old habit, that didn't exactly work since she'd chopped her hair off.

Their room for lessons felt damp, musty. Cold rivulets snaked through the air and made Abby shiver.

"Hardly a lesson this evening, my dear." He gave her a warm, fatherly smile. "Cold?"

She tried to shake her head no, but nodded instead.

"Here." He cast his hands towards her, like Zeus sending a lightning bolt, and a wave of warm air washed over her. She expected it to vanish, get sucked into the stone walls like a sponge made of rock, but it hovered, raising the temperature where she stood.

"We're so used to it down here, I don't even notice."

"How did you do that?" Abby asked eagerly.

"Starting to get used to the idea, eh?" Max asked, his eyes twinkling. "Well, let me show you a bit."

He walked over to her, slipping his brown corduroy coat off and slinging it over the back of a chair. He flexed his fingers a few times and bent his arms in a bicep curl. He stopped next to her, standing shoulder to shoulder.

"First, Abby, my element is air, and therefore I have a much easier time manipulating it. That means wind, tornadoes, temperature, even clouds."

"Clouds?" she whispered, imagining a rolling cloud shaped like a dragon as it chased screaming beach-goers along a shoreline.

"Yes. Now you are a water element and will find that when you direct your energy, water is what changes. That means rain, lakes, oceans, streams, ground water, even ice cubes. Not to say that you cannot influence other elements, but it takes many years of practice and focus. The stone slab here," he explained, pointing at the small island of stone sitting peculiarly in the room "—pulls and focuses your energy. That is why we train with it. In a sense, it forces your power out, even if you yourself are not focused on the task at hand." He glanced at Lydie and she smirked, feigning interest in her fingernails.

Before Abby could respond, he shot his hands out, as if pushing an invisible ball towards Lydie. The air around her swirled, causing her hair to fly and twist and her skirt to whoosh up around her head. The mini cyclone lasted only seconds, but left Lydie sputtering and forcing her skirt back around her legs.

"Max," she whined, but with a challenging gleam in her eye.

"Don't even think about it," he told her shortly. "That was simply an example for Abby's sake."

Abby laughed and shook her head in amazement. She wanted to do that.

"Could I do that here?" she asked.

"Not just yet," he told her, slipping back into his coat. "You have not exercised your power enough for that type of activity. However, you could have a go in the chair."

"A go?" she asked meekly, staring at the chair as if the back might open to reveal saliva-dripping fangs.

"Yes. You see this place helps draw the energy of your astral body specifically. When you sit in one of those chairs and focus your internal power you can access your non-physical self."

"Where would I go?" she asked, conflicted by her desire to seize the newfound power and yet frightened by its potential.

"Go along for the ride, Abby." Lydie stretched a comical grin over her face and twirled around the slab.

"You might not go anywhere, well, your astral body, that is. Your physical body will remain right here with us, safe. Your astral body could go any number of places. Some witches can travel in their element. You may visit the cave of elders or other meeting places. You may even travel through other elements – air, earth, fire, there is no way to know, right now, where you could go."

"The cave of elders?" Abby asked.

"Yes, it is a cave where many of our elders congregate."

"Is it dangerous?" Abby asked, ignoring the sneer that passed over Lydie's girlish features.

"Not here," Max appeased her. "But it can be very dangerous for a witch to leave her physical body in the open. If an enemy were to stumble upon it, you would be virtually defenseless."

It frightened her, the uncertainty of it, but appealed to her as well.

"Okay," she gave in, taking a tentative step towards the slab. As she stepped up, she felt an instant shock of energy, like she'd placed her finger on a low wattage live wire.

"Go on," Max encouraged, the fine wrinkles around his mouth pressing together when he smiled. Lydie stood perfectly still, watching with the glassy, blue eyes of a porcelain doll.

Abby took a seat, running her hand along the smooth velvet, like green moss on the forest floor. She looked to Max for guidance, having only experienced her astral body in what she thought of as a dream state. She had never self-induced it.

"Just close your eyes and relax. If it's going to happen, it will come naturally. If not, do not fret, this just isn't the right time," Max directed her in a calm voice.

She pressed her head against the seat, silently telling herself to relax – no needles, this was virtually painless. She felt the soft, slightly prickly texture of the velvet through her hair, and then as if the chair back had dissipated behind her, she felt herself falling back, out of the chair and down through the floor.

Her body stopped its lightning free fall and she felt hard ground beneath her. She opened her eyes slowly, seeking clarity through the dim fog that materialized into a dark tunnel. Somehow the familiar craggy walls did not come as a surprise, instead she welcomed them, understanding that she had done it. She was moving in her astral body. Her physical self was back in the dungeon with Max and Lydie, but she had returned to the cave.

She reached a hand toward the wall, but could not feel the cold stone or the algae-like mud that clung to it. She moved deeper into the cave, twisting in circles as she had that very first time. She came again to the three tunnels.

She believed that witches met in the far off cavern to her right, but something drew her towards the middle tunnel, she felt the power surge inside of her and the need for familiarity melted away. She had to discover what lay in the center tunnel.

As she advanced, the tunnel sloped down and severely left. It grew wide and then narrowed as if teasing the traveler who dared roam its depths. The cave grew wider and the ceiling, before only inches above her head, steadily rose, two feet, five feet, ten feet and then more. It gave way to a spacious grotto. She could see light and then an underground lake at the back of the cavernous space. It glowed a brilliant sapphire blue. Above the lake, a small hole let in a beam of moonlight and a dazzling waterfall cascaded into the lake. The water fell in a wide spray of tiny mirrors, splashing into the water and spinning away.

The lake drew her, grasping her arms with invisible hands and pulling her forward. She began willingly, but as she neared the gossamer pool, delicate like layers of ice-blue chiffon, she felt a fine terror sweep down her spine. It bit with razor sharp teeth; it shrieked that she should not take a step closer, but even as she attempted to slam her feet onto the stone floor, the invisible fingers sank into her flesh and dragged her on. She came to the pool and then was thrust over the small rock edge. For a second she tipped, like a porcelain vase rocking on a table's edge, and then she fell. Her arms splayed out, but no painful smack of water on skin occurred; instead she just drifted into the shiny water, like a balloon floating from a building top.

She wafted down, her eyes wide and searching. Around her, tall, coarse stalagmites jutted skyward, their tips pointed and menacing. The water felt like nothing, as if she floated in space, an underwater astronaut. The sinking did not frighten her because she understood that she was safe, that her body sat in the castle's dungeon and that whatever hid in the lake's glistening depths could not harm her.

Slipping deeper, she saw someone else, another person in the water. But as she reached for the form, the person shifted, drifting to face her. Abby opened her mouth in a silent shriek as the body of her Aunt Sydney floated inches from her face. Sydney's bright blue eyes bulged at her, passed through her – her red mouth twisted in a hideous smile, a final smirk at death. Abby reached out, but her hand could not grasp the familiar shape, a pale pink sun dress billowing around it, blond hair floating in the gem colored water. The waxy skin stretched over the bloated organs left Sydney's beautiful body a distended bag of slippery flesh. Her corpse refused to stop and slid by with ease, as if trying to say, "Gotta run – I'm late for a date."

Abby continued her silent scream, spiraling up, away from the body, toward the surface.

She burst from the water, but instead sprang out of the green velvet chair and flung herself across the long stone room, slamming hard into the opposite wall.

Distantly, she heard Max's yells and Lydie's screams

of fear. The stone floor felt cold, but her eyelids were heavy, she couldn't open them, and then the room was gone and she drifted down.

Chapter 21

What had once been an oratory (place of worship) in the castle had long ago been transformed into a special meeting place for the coven. Here the witches gathered to create the Magic Circle, an especially useful ritual that drew each of their individual energies into a single extraordinary sphere of power. The room's ceiling was a maze of red brick arches shaped oddly like a starfish. From the center of the starfish drooped a heavy iron chandelier twisted into a crooked spiral with hundreds of candles dotting its warped frame. The center of the Magic Circle lay directly beneath it, marked by a single X, denoting the runic symbol for sacrifice and generosity, which was coarsely etched into the stone floor. The outer circle was a smooth fissure, approximately one foot deep, that ran the circumference of the circle, and when the Magic Circle was called, involved each of the four elements: air, water, earth and fire. Three of the room's four walls revealed curved stained glass windows set deep into the stone, their bright images set afire during the noonday sun.

Helena found Elda sitting quietly in the room, a *Book of Shadows* open on the table before her.

"Elda," she sighed, brushing into the room, her silver bracelets jingling on her wrists. "Something strange has happened."

Elda smiled and leaned back in her chair, stretching her legs out and rubbing the tips of her fingers into her tired eyes. She closed Ula's *Book of Shadows,* satisfied that she had updated Bridget's most recent plant creations.

Helena pulled out a chair and sat down, resting her hands squarely in her lap.

"I witnessed something tonight that I believe deserves our attention," Helena continued, absently fingering the corner of the heavy book that Elda had closed.

In one corner of the room, shelves were built into the stone wall, each piled with books and ritual tools.

"What is it, Helena?" Elda asked with a yawn.

"First, tell me if Faustine has reached Oliver?" Helena asked.

Elda shook her head slowly and then spoke. "No, however, he feels certain that the raven does not belong to Oliver. He can still feel him."

Helena nodded, relieved.

"It's about Abby…" Helena began, staring intently into Elda's glossy pupils, like tiny mirrors in the candlelight. "I believe that she controls Sebastian."

Elda looked at her quizzically. "Well, of course, Helena, it's obvious that they are extremely attached, so it's only logical that he would act in accordance with her."

"No," Helena waved her hand dismissively. "That is not what I mean. I believe that I witnessed her thoughts activating a physical response in him. Elda, he ripped the arm off the walnut Victorian chair."

Elda shifted uncomfortably, pursing her lips. "He ripped it off? Was he angry?"

"No, that is what I am trying to explain to you," Helena said perching on the edge of the desk. "He and I were simply discussing Faustine's telepathy, it was a very controlled conversation, but Abby, well, she was sort of staring off, thinking about something else, obviously. I noticed her frown and then, out of nowhere, Sebastian ripped the arm off the chair."

Elda took in a long breath and stood. She walked along the outer perimeter of the Magic Circle, staring at the small cones of flame dancing on the chandelier.

J.R. Erickson

"Elda, it's like..." but Helena did not finish. The door burst open and Lydie rushed in, her pink cheeks streaked with tears.

"It's Abby, come quick, she's been hurt," Lydie wailed.

Helena jumped from her chair and the three of them ran from the room, leaving the circle abandoned behind them.

* * * *

Abby came to slowly, swimming up from the depths of her dreams. She smelled currents of lavender and rose, which spun above her, a silken spider web wrapping her tightly in place. She focused on her eyes, on the doughy lids that lay like anvils on the soft flesh of her cheeks. Swollen? Maybe, but she didn't think so. Somewhere hushed whispers drifted towards her, but they merged and disappeared beneath the sounds of trickling water and something else, a vibration.

With great effort, her eyelids lifted and she stared at a glass dome ceiling high above her. Thick gold beams curved up the glass, interfacing at a single gold hand. Turning her head, she saw sheer white drapes, the fabric, a hybrid of mosquito net and silk. She reached a hand out, wincing as if she anticipated horrible pain, but felt nothing, only a cool numbness that started at the tips of her toes and traveled up to the crown of her skull. Brushing her hands over the drapes, which she only barely reached, she realized that her fingers were wrapped in moist linen cloths. Her entire body was wrapped in the cloth, and as she blinked she felt her eyelashes brush the fabric that covered her face.

"Oh," she cried out as a chamber opened in her mind and Sydney's face came swirling back to the surface.

Before she could make another noise, footsteps pounded across the room and the shroud was ripped back.

Sebastian stood before her, his face eroded with worry.

"Abby." He leaned close, but did not touch her.

Elda, Max and Helena huddled behind him, watching her closely.

"I was in the cave…" she started, but Elda hushed her.

"Abby, you've been injured very badly. I know that you feel okay right now and you are healing rapidly, but the process is not complete. You cannot strain yourself at this time." Elda's words were final, a command, and Sebastian nodded vigorously that she must comply.

Helena walked around the long bed, pulling the drapes away. Abby appeared to be in an infirmary, but like none she had ever seen. The room was round, the walls directly opposite her were glass, and she could see panoramic views of the lake beyond a stone terrace. The walls were made of thick, sandy bricks, but ended abruptly at the glass dome above. At the foot of her bed stood a long wooden altar with candles flickering from its hollowed center. To her left, she could see more beds, like massage tables draped in thick cream coverlets. To her right, freshly oiled wood floors ended at a rim of red bricks, which outlined a colossal circular tub filled with water. Sunflower sized candles floated on the glassy surface. Around the room candles flickered, illuminating a long workstation with neatly organized glass bottles, vials, and nylon bags of crushed flowers and herbs.

She licked her lips, which felt sandpaper dry, and tasted blood.

Helena passed a long glass bottle with a straw to Sebastian, and he held it to her lips. She sucked eagerly, feeling a burst of pain in her raw throat and then soothing coolness. It tasted like water and something else, flowers or perfume, but so faint she barely detected it.

"It will help you heal," Elda told her sternly as if she

might spit it out.

Abby only nodded, finishing the drink and sighing back against the bed. She could feel the elixir reach her stomach and spread with a warming intensity. Her limbs grew heavy, and her eyes started to droop closed. She turned to Sebastian and began to mouth Sydney's name, but already she was gone, drifting back to her dreams.

* * * *

She slept a drugged sleep. Phasing in and out of consciousness, never entirely aware of reality or fantasy. She saw Sydney on the end of her dock, blond hair billowing, a delicate hand giving Abby the Miss America wave. Sydney melted into Vesta, who pointed at her with malicious glee. In the infirmary, Sebastian's face moved in and out of view, replaced by Max, Helena, Dafne, Tobias, Sydney and the moon. Sometimes her body felt heavy, like bags of wet sand, and other times she was as light as a dandelion blown into the night sky.

She came to, fully and lucidly. Sebastian snored beside her on a vacant bed, a tangle of hair drifting above his open mouth, the tendril gusting out with each puff. She wanted to crawl onto his bed and lay her head against the rise and fall of his chest.

She rubbed her fingers together, expecting to feel the linen bandages, but her hands were bare. Lifting her head onto her chest, she scanned her body. No more bandages, just a thin sheet tucked to her waist. She wore a pink, silky robe, probably another of Dafne's. Hopefully, she hadn't bled on it.

The vision of Sydney sat in her mind, a boulder lying heavily on every thought. The tears came then, slowly at first and then harder, until snot ran from her nose and she couldn't bite back the hiccupping sobs.

Sebastian woke and came to her, his hands warmly rubbing her arms.

"Hey, it's okay. You're okay," he whispered as she cried harder, her whole body joining the event.

When she could manage her breath, she whispered Sydney's name. His eyebrows lifted in confusion, but he waited for her to speak.

"Syd...Sydney's dead." She let it out with another low wail that brought Elda into the room, looking wide-awake despite the early morning hour.

"Are you sure?" he asked.

She nodded and shook jerkily, her cries like hands rocking her back and forth. He leaned onto the bed and pulled her to his chest where she quickly soaked his gray t-shirt with tears.

Elda stood quietly beside them, her eyes kind and apologetic. "I'm sorry, Abby, I hate to pester you right now, but I think I should hear this." Elda looked troubled.

"Yes," Abby said as Sebastian lowered her to the bed.

"Max told me you came to the Training Room while he was giving Lydie lessons," Elda continued.

Abby nodded. "He told me that I could use one of the chairs and try to travel in my astral body."

"And you did?" Elda asked, taking one of Abby's hands in her own.

"Yes. I... I returned to the cave. I've visited it before." Elda nodded and Abby continued. "But this time, instead of taking the tunnel to the right, I went to the middle. I felt as if I needed to. I came to this underground lake with light shining down on it from an opening above." She paused, a lump forming in her throat as she imagined Sydney's face. "I started toward the water and then something scared me. I didn't want to go, but I was pulled toward it and then I fell in. Sydney. My aunt, Sydney, was dead in the water. Her corpse was in that pond."

Sebastian did not make a sound, but his face fell, followed by a flash of anger.

"Could it have been a dream?" Abby asked hopefully, but she could see in Elda's face that it was no dream.

"The center tunnel is a place of truth. The lake reveals things. I have never met a witch who visited that tunnel and did not receive very difficult news. You see, the tunnel draws you because there is something for you to see. Some truth that you are denying or that you have not yet discovered." Elda squeezed Abby's hand as she said this, as if trying to reconcile the hard reality that she had to deliver.

"The raven?" Sebastian asked after a long silence.

"Yes, I imagine so," Elda told him sadly.

"Then, where is Oliver?" Abby asked, her heart aching as she remembered the raven's beating wings.

"We have had no contact. Faustine has been in the tower all night, but he has not been able to connect to him." Elda did not look frightened as she said this. Instead, she appeared to stand a bit taller, her faith in Oliver unwavering.

"Do you think Tobias…?" But Abby couldn't finish the question, couldn't say, "murder", because then it meant it was her fault. That Sydney was dead because of her.

"I don't know that, Abby," Elda consoled.

"Of course it was Tobias," Sebastian broke in angrily. He looked like he might continue, but stopped at the stricken look on Abby's face. "I'm sorry," he told her.

"I think," Elda proceeded, "that we should assume Tobias is behind this and that we should prepare accordingly. However, first we must see to it that you are fully healed, Abby."

"What happened?" Abby asked. "I remember the cave and then surfacing in the room, but nothing else."

"Well, you gave Max and Lydie quite a start. When you came to, in the chair, you flung yourself out, and, remember, you don't have much control over your strength yet. You jumped clear across the room and hit the opposite wall."

"Was it really bad?" Abby asked, knowing that it was. Knowing that without these new powers and the help of the others, she would probably be dead.

"Yes, it was very bad. But before we even got you to the Healing Room, you were healing on your own. It was remarkable. I don't think your body could have healed completely without the tonic that Helena created, but many of your wounds were already closed when we got you here." Elda looked mystified.

"Can't all witches heal themselves?" she asked. Elda had never mentioned this as a power, but surely she wasn't the only one.

"No. Some witches can heal themselves, but usually only minor wounds and abrasions. Abby, your bones were mending themselves." Elda held her gaze steadily.

"I had broken bones?" Abby was incredulous. She didn't feel as if she had broken any bones.

"Yes. It is a wonderful gift," Elda told her.

Abby considered this and, moreover, considered the glint in Elda's eyes.

"Well, then," Elda added finally, giving Abby a stern, but kind, look. "That is a revival bath." She pointed to the candlelit bath that looked more like half a swimming pool. "It will help to calm any inflammation left in your body. You'll need to fully submerge at least once, head and everything."

"Okay," Abby replied tentatively. Could she walk to the bath? Would she stand up only to realize that her newly mended bones snapped immediately under pressure?

"Can I walk?" Abby asked, staring at her pale, skinny legs.

"Oh, yes, you are fully healed now," Elda said in her grandmotherly way, as if she were not just telling, but thanking some divine entity for Abby's healing. "Besides, you didn't break any bones in your legs."

This made Abby feel better and she sat up, feeling a slight dizziness as the blood rushed to her head. She swung her legs over the side, and Elda handed her a pair of feather gray satin slippers.

"To keep your toes warm."

Abby smiled her thanks and dropped them to the floor, stepping into each one slowly as if testing cold lake water.

"Dafne brought you some more clothes." Elda pointed to a pile near the bed. "I will leave you now, but do take your time. No rush. Let the bath do its work."

Elda left the room, her long black skirt trailing over the shining wood floors.

"Need to lean?" Sebastian asked, offering his arm. She took it and trudged to the bath, pressing on him heavily, though her body felt fine.

Sebastian turned his head and Abby slipped off her robe, foregoing the brick stairs and climbing over the edge. The water rushed up to her waist and then chest as she stepped fully in. The pool was over four foot deep, the water hot, but not scalding. She sat on a marble bench, water reaching almost to her neck. Submerged jets forced a current along her spine.

Sebastian turned and sat on an edge, letting his fingers slip into the water. He made small circles on the surface and Abby stared at his reflection.

"I don't know what to say," he started.

Abby blew a long breath out of her mouth, cupped some water in her hands and splashed it over her face.

"There's nothing to say," she said, leaning her back against the brick edge. "Sydney is gone."

"Gone," he repeated.

"It never seems real, death."

"Yeah, I know, believe me."

Abby caught his gaze in the water and held it. He moved along the brick edge until he sat just behind her and lowered his hands to her shoulders, massaging gently and scooping water onto her neck and back.

His hands felt good, she needed touch and she bent her head forward as he pushed his fingers into the hair at the base of her skull.

She turned and tilted her face and he leaned down to meet her, his mouth pushing into hers. They kissed, and she felt the cold of the room when her wet body lifted out of the bath. She pressed against him, soaking his t-shirt, and he swung his legs over the bath edge, ignoring his pants as the water crawled up his shins and over his knees. She did not mind her nakedness against him, his hands roaming from her shoulders to her breasts and then back to her buttocks. Her grief wanted him as much as her body did. His fingers made her skin feel alive, and she knew that she was healed completely and tugged him towards her into the water.

He sat on the marble bench, the water above his chest, and pulled her onto his lap, kissing her ears, her neck and her collarbone. She leaned back, his hands holding her waist, and let his mouth sweep over her shoulders and arms.

She stood in the bath and reached beneath the water, fumbling with his pants. Wet, they would not come off, and they laughed as he kicked and struggled out of them, finally shoving them off with a splash. He pulled her back and, as she lowered onto him, she gasped and bit his shoulder to muffle her moans. They rocked in the water, and she tilted her head back, feeling him inside her, but also feeling the warm caress of the water and the strange pulses as her body continued to heal.

They made love, and they did not think of death or witches or evil.

* * * *

"Ahem." The interruption startled Abby and Sebastian, who stood draped with towels, walking idly around the healing room.

Faustine stood in the doorway, apparently indifferent to their practical nudity.

"This is for you, Abby." He set a small amber colored bottle on a long table. "And Sebastian, Elda had hoped to retrieve the *Book of Shadows* in your possession."

Faustine waited.

"Right now?" Sebastian asked, clearly annoyed.

"Yes, right now."

Abby felt chastised, but when she looked at Sebastian he grinned.

"Until we meet again," he whispered, his socked feet squishing as he left the room. Faustine turned on his heel and followed him out.

* * * *

In her bedroom, Abby watched the dark lake crashing far below the castle walls. It looked turbulent and unsettled, the way Abby felt. The storm blacked out the stars and sent shrieks of thunder into the night.

Her body felt strange, her muscles like very firm jelly. She could almost feel atoms silently connecting inside her, bounding together to create an army of strength. A body that would take less time to heal when the next injury occurred and even less each time after that.

She laid her head against the pillow and watched as rain pelted the window, sending fat drops racing down the glass. Flashes of thunder sent white streaks zigzagging across her eyes, and she pulled the comforter up snugly beneath her chin.

Rainstorms in Abby's previous life were greeted with anxiety and distress; searching out her slicker and umbrella, driving down rain slicked streets, fighting the steering wheel against the dreaded hydroplane. All to sit at her cheap metal desk, the sky a black mirror of her mood, while her boss, Doobie Duvall, paraded the office in some clingy new velvet bell bottoms, circa 1969. The rain was different now – it charged her.

Energy buzzed beneath her skin, a gyrating sheet of electricity as powerful as the lightning outside.

She forced her eyes closed and concentrated on sleep, which of course was useless. After leaving the infirmary, it had taken almost twenty minutes to find her bedroom. Twice she stumbled into strange green rooms, hot and sticky, and filled with enormous plants basking under giant fluorescent lights. Luckily, she ran into Bridget, who guided her back to her bedroom and asked her a million times if she felt okay to walk.

She had wanted to find Sebastian, but then she also wanted to lie in bed and remember every kiss and caress. She felt overwhelmed by her desire for him, but torn by all of the other thoughts vying for her attention. Sydney was dead and Oliver was missing.

Her thoughts bounced wildly around until, finally, she leaned over to her nightstand and pulled open the drawer. Helena had told her about the stash of herbs that Bridget placed in every nightstand, tinctures for ailments of all kinds.

Abby fingered the small glass bottles, each labeled with

black marker: 'Headaches,' 'Nausea,' 'Cramps,' 'Full Moon Neurosis,' 'Nightmares.' She couldn't believe the supply; she'd never have trouble sleeping again. Choosing the bottle labeled 'Brain Overload,' she squeezed a single drop onto her tongue. It tasted like cinnamon and cherries, a strange but pleasant flavor.

The results were instantaneous. Abby's mind slowed, as if it were a train approaching its destination, the wheels grinding slower as the platform came into view. A long, slow sigh erupted, but Abby barely heard it, already disappearing into her dreams.

* * * *

She awoke to darkness, and her mind buzzed with some unseen force that had yanked her from sleep. Despite the black sky outside her window, Abby could see clearly. The rain had slowed to a steady drizzle, the lightning and thunder long faded into the dark. She sat drowsily, pushing the covers down and staring around the room. Something had woken her, she could feel a presence, but could see no one.

"Hello?" Abby asked the room, afraid of what, she did not know. The mere cutting of silence made her jump in her bed and she laughed at her own cowardice.

"Hello," a voice spirited to her from the darkness, easily dismissed as a rustle of the wind, but Abby knew better.

She was not alone.

Chapter 22

"Who's there?" Abby asked, straining into the shadows.

For a moment nothing stirred, not even a breeze to trick her distressed ears. She waited, her inhale caught in her chest.

"Abby," it came in a breath, a whoosh of cold air across her face.

Abby reeled away, pushing herself with her palms until her back was flat against the wooden headboard. Still, no person jumped from the shadows.

"Please, just go away," she cried out, wanting to dive beneath the covers and hide. Her mind careened. Why should she be afraid? She was a witch!

But then the face appeared, gradually, as if gathering dust particles to create some image of solidarity.

Abby watched the pale white cheeks, the wide set green eyes, the mass of red tendrils as they came into view, each curl fighting to appear. Devin's body was slow to take form, her long, slender shoulders outlined beneath a purple cloak. She hovered beside Abby's bed, a small smile on her slightly parted lips.

"Abby," Devin whispered again, and this time Abby saw the breath crystallize around Devin's word, as if she exhaled frigid air from her dead lips.

Abby shook her head in disbelief, her eyes like saucers in her sleepy face.

"Yes," Devin said. A nearly transparent hand drifted out from her cloak and hovered over Abby's own, which instantly grew cold. "I've come to help you."

The "you," was almost lost, as if Devin were stealing

the air to speak and the air was fighting back.

"Help me?" Abby asked. She glanced toward the door to her room, quietly willing someone to burst in.

"Don't be…" Devin breathed and Abby knew that she wanted to say, "afraid," but the word died before it could form.

"Help me with what?" Abby repeated, her fear ebbing away, but not entirely. Devin would not hurt her, right?

"With your life…" Devin shimmered; her body disappearing and reappearing like a television losing its connection.

"I don't understand," Abby whispered, moving onto her knees in the bed.

"Danger." Devin's voice was faint, almost gone.

"Who's in danger? Me?" Abby leaned toward Devin's faint shape.

"Hold my hand." Abby barely heard it, but she felt the cold just above her fingers. She reached her hand up, and the air thickened and froze like she had dipped it into ice-cold water. The cold moved along her wrist, her forearm, slowly seeping into her torso and neck. When it reached her head, she let out a single, strangled breath.

She was no longer looking at Devin's transparent spirit. She was inside Devin looking back at herself. Her own body was statue still, her skin ashen, and her lips nearly white. As she watched, she faded with Devin, falling back through the castle wall and into another place and time.

* * * *

Devin sat on rotted driftwood, her toes sunk into the wet sand, the tide floating up and cooling her feet and ankles. She stared out at the lake, at the sailboats and jet skis, the sun looking down merrily on all of the happy tourists. She herself did not feel happy. She was changing and felt it on the surface of her skin, in her limbs, even deep inside of her. She had wondered if she had cancer or been stricken with some horrible disease that slowly consumed her from the inside out, but then it had begun to change. It stopped feeling like death and started feeling like life.

First there were visions and then strange abilities.

She reached into her pocket and pulled out her lighter. It was a tiny bronze goddess with exquisitely crafted features. The goddess held a sword that, when pushed, released a sharp blue flame from the goddess's head. It was old, very old, and Devin had stolen it from her adopted father. Technically, it was hers. She found it in a stiff white envelope that contained her birth certificate, a single photo of her biological mother at the hospital, and the lighter. It was the goddess that instigated her search for her birth parents. She wanted to heal, to be strong like the miniature warrior, and they would help her do it. Or might have, if they weren't dead.

A week earlier, she'd been absently clicking the fire on and off when it had suddenly leapt out and raced across her apartment floor, igniting a picture of her and Tobias. Before Devin could put out the flames, Tobias's face had been singed to a deep black, the photo curling in. Somehow the fire had not touched her face, but had completely snuffed out Tobias. She had cried, feeling overwhelmed by the changes and frustrated by the picture.

Tobias hadn't called her in two weeks. He had been her entire life and then suddenly vanished as if they hadn't been madly in love. She had called the number that he had given her, but it was disconnected. Worse, she thought she saw him only days earlier, driving around with a beautiful blond woman.

She stood from the driftwood and kicked it brusquely,

angrily. Continuing down the beach, she bubbled with resentment for all of the teenagers enjoying the beautiful summer day. They leaned their tan faces back, laughing and showing off their dentally straightened teeth. They were on summer vacation from high school or college; they drove expensive leased cars and looked forward to beach bonfires and lakefront house parties. What did she have to enjoy? No family, no Tobias. And now she was turning into some kind of mutant that would probably be sprouting scales and tentacles.

Devin turned back, heading for her car, which was over two miles down the beach, parked at a campground. It was Friday, and she had no plans, no friends and an empty apartment occupied by her cat, Sam, and a few goldfish that managed to stay alive despite their very dirty tank. She thought about calling her adoptive brother, Danny, but decided against it. Since she had begun the search for her birth parents, her adopted siblings had given her the cold shoulder. They'd never been close, but she was lonely and suddenly wished she had put more effort into the relationships.

She left the beach and cut through the woods. Behind her, the sun was setting, the orange burning into the back of her head with ferocity, as if in warning. She stopped abruptly as she came upon her old, pea green Volkswagen. Tobias was leaning against it, a sly smile on his perfect face. He wore black slacks and a charcoal polo, his skin the same ivory porcelain that she loved.

"Hi." She stood back, wanting to run to him or scream at him or both.

"I've missed you," he replied, cocking his head to the side and giving her a 'forgive me' look.

That was enough. She rushed in to him, wrapping her arms around his lean waist and breathing his musty cologne.

He held her tightly, pushing his hand into her thick red curls and tilting her face toward his. He kissed her long and hard, and she forgot her anger and hurt. As they kissed, he opened his mouth wider and she felt a sharp pain on her lip. He'd accidentally bitten her. Before she could pull away to wipe the blood seeping from her lip, she went slack in his arms and darkness moved in.

Devin awoke in the woods. Her hands were bound tight and stretched out, as were her legs. Through groggy eyes she saw leather straps tightly secured to her wrists and ankles. At first she felt alone, but then she saw Tobias. He wore a long, black, hooded cloak, the hood resting on his shoulders. He watched her carefully with an interest that frightened her.

"Tobias?" she asked meekly.

He was playing a game, some sort of prank. But then she heard more movement and strained her head up. Two more cloaked figures moved around her. One of the figures turned and she recognized the blond woman she had seen Tobias driving with.

She twisted toward Tobias and he smiled wide, his teeth white and shining in the light of the moon. The trees rose up around them and she stared straight into the branches, surprised by the silence. Where were the squirrels and owls and even the crickets? Since when were the woods this quiet at night?

"What is this?" she asked Tobias finally, pulling, for the first time, against the ties.

"I'm releasing you," he told her simply.

Another cloaked figure bent beside her, and she stared at his face. He looked even younger than she, maybe seventeen or eighteen; his close cut, white blond hair soft like a chick's baby fur.

"Who are you?" she asked, but he gave her only a comical grin that turned his baby face ugly.

The three moved around her, each of their hands clutching an old dirty rope. They began to chant, and Devin screamed at Tobias, demanding an explanation. He ignored her.

She remembered the goddess in her back pocket and struggled to look downwards, if only she could get it, she could stop them, she knew it. Their eyes were closed; they were not watching her. She shifted her hips back and forth, like a horizontal belly dancer, focusing her thoughts on the lighter. It pressed against her butt, but shifted. In her mind's eye, she could see it tucked tightly against the fabric of her jean shorts. It was coming out; as she careened from side to side, she felt it dislodge and flop onto the forest floor. She began to lift her butt to help push it upwards, but a horrible pain smashed into her skull. She screamed, a long gurgling cry that ripped through the silent forest. They must have hit her, but no, they had not moved. Tiny needles began to poke her flesh everywhere, her arms and legs, even her eyelids seared in pain. They were burning her alive, but no; there was no fire, nothing. She thrashed and screamed, clenching her eyes against the pain, fighting to stay conscious. The forest and night sky disappeared above her and visions of death closed in. Demonic faces dancing around charred bodies, long black coffins, knives dripping with freshly spilled blood, the images advanced on her.

Suddenly, Tobias was above her, but it was not Tobias. His face had changed. His eyes were sunken, black and burning, his forehead broader. She turned her head, not able to look at him. He gripped her face hard and ripped it back, sticking his fingers into her mouth and clenching it open. She tried to bite down, but his grip was machine-like. With his other hand, he lifted an old, dusty bottle above her and poured. Ice-cold blood flooded her mouth and spilled out over her lips and chin. She swallowed, choking, and saw a disgusting smile split his face.

He laid the bottle aside and pulled out a silver dragon, its eye a single black jewel. Tobias pulled the dragon apart, revealing a knife, the tip sharpened to a deadly point. He waved the knife over her body and grunted in delight as it glowed red near her arm. Before she could plead or protest, he drove the knife down. She felt it pierce her side, just below her armpit. No scream came, only a white-hot pain that shot through her. He did not pull the knife back, and Devin felt as if it were eating her. Blood began to drift upwards from her legs and torso towards the spot of penetration, as if the dragon were drinking it greedily. She opened her mouth in horror as Tobias motioned to the blond woman, who lowered her face towards the wound, her tongue slipping out like a serpent's.

Time was lost then, Tobias's face melded into a white blur and Devin drifted. She was in the cave staring blankly at the figures around the fire, and then she found herself floating lifelessly in a deep aqua colored pool with moonlight shining above her. Finally, she was back in the woods, but looking down at her body, rather than out from it. Her eyes were glassy, her mouth open. They'd stripped her clothes away and stuffed them in a black trash bag. Tobias left the clearing. His face had returned to its original handsomeness. His skin seemed to glow from the inside, she might have believed it was simply a reflection from the moon, but she knew better. It was her energy, her power inside of him – he had taken it. The mouth of the blond woman was red and wet; she glowed like Tobias, but brighter, her whole body shimmering in the moonlight.

As she watched, Tane dragged her dead body forward, discarding it near a dead log and pile of thick bushes. Vesta had wiped away the designs etched in the dirt. She bent down, her fingers clasping the goddess lighter, and shot a glance towards Tobias's retreating frame. Safe that no one was looking, she slipped it beneath her cloak and departed the forest, Tane followed quickly behind.

* * * *

The cry was far off, muffled, and when Abby sat up in bed, she wondered if she had imagined it. She scanned the room silently but in the brisk morning light she could not even imagine Devin's ghost – let alone find her. Had it only been a dream? No, she was certain she had witnessed Devin's death.

A wail sounded again, and this time she recognized Lydie, the screams of a child.

She rushed from her room and down the spiral staircase, smelling something charred. It blew in gusts, and as she ran down the hallway, she saw that the great oak door stood open and wind thrashed the entryway, blowing out candles that immediately reignited in tiny bursts of blue flame.

Out the door she skidded to a stop, colliding with Helena, who stood on the stone steps, her hand flat against her mouth.

Below them, at the lagoon edge, the other coven members had gathered. They were huddled, except for Lydie, who stood to the side, bawling like an infant with fat tears rolling over her blotched cheeks. The wind whipped around them, turning the lagoon into a pool of thrashing tidal waves.

The burnt smell hit her again and she wrinkled her nose, shielding her face with the sleeve of her robe. Below her, the group parted. Faustine held something in his arms, a black shriveled form that seemed to be alive. As Faustine grew closer, Abby saw the burned blond hair, melded to a red, black scalp. Oliver.

She gasped and stepped back, making room for Faustine, who did not look at her, but rushed by, his face grim.

Abby could not see Oliver's face, which was pressed into Faustine's chest, his arms looped around his neck like a child. Dafne sprinted behind him. Elda and Max carried a leather satchel, still smoking, with a single singed arrow sticking out from it.

When the group had disappeared into the castle, Helena crept down the stone steps to Lydie, who had not moved. Her eyes were clenched tight and her hands balled at her sides. Helena wrapped an arm around her quivering body and gently led her away from the castle, towards the cherry trees, their blossoms ravaged by the wind.

Abby stood and gulped the fresh air; the only remaining smell was the poignant flowers as they danced in the gale. Her robe blew up and exposed her legs, but she didn't care. She wanted to erase Oliver's image from her mind, make his body complete again, give him back his handsome, smiling face, but she saw only his seared head, the flesh slick.

"Abby?" Sebastian stood behind her, looking dazed. She could see that he had just woken and run from his room in a pair of blue boxer shorts and nothing else.

"Oliver," she said, shaking her head and looking around numbly. "I think he might die."

Sebastian stepped closer to her, peering past her toward the lagoon. Nothing remained of where Oliver lay, but Abby could still see the spot.

"What happened?" Sebastian whispered, turning to Abby and taking her shoulders in his hands.

She looked at him, mute. Her body had begun to shake violently, and he pulled her against him, crushing her face into his bare chest.

"I don't know."

* * * *

How many hours had passed? Abby could not guess, but she sat perfectly still, her legs folded beneath her on the carpet, a book splayed before her. There were no clocks in the library and she had stopped caring, counting the passage of time by Oliver's improvement, which was slow, if at all.

She and Sebastian had retreated there after they visited his room to get clothes. Now he read as well, hungrily devouring pages of heavy books that he propped in his lap, his eyes frequently lifting to the doorway, then to Abby and then back to the page.

Helena had visited them twice, both times carrying mugs of tea from Bridget and news of Oliver from Elda. Oliver, she said, was in the infirmary and healing slowly. He had been bitten and burned, but managed to escape the Vepar who attacked him. The Vepar, they discovered, was Detective Alva.

"It says here," Sebastian started, "that Vepars have a pouch just beneath their heart that contains their blood sacrifices and their power. They have to be stabbed there to die, but their ribcage is like steel."

Abby stood, happy for the interruption, and padded across the room. She slid onto the couch next to him and looked down at the images on the page. A tall man who looked part animal—wolf maybe—stood clutching his chest. Black blood leaked from a wound there. Another man held a long sword, the tip thrust into the wound, a look of triumph on his pale face.

"It also says that Vepars have venom in their teeth that immobilizes witches. Depending on how hard they bite and how powerful they are, it can cause total incapacitation for minutes, hours and even days."

"Vesta bit me," Abby said, rubbing a hand on her shoulder. "I think, anyway."

"She did," Sebastian said, flipping the page. "I saw her."

He didn't add more and Abby didn't ask. Neither of them were ready to relive that night.

Abby read over Sebastian's shoulder.

According to the book, the first discovered and slain Vepar came from Greece in 8000 B.C. His name was Gorzen, and he lured a young witch to a cave high in the mountains where he murdered her and consumed her blood. As his power grew, he began to seek more followers attracted to his promises of power. He not only sought out humans, but also witches who desired dark magic and who wanted absolute power. He spoke with demons, he said, and they promised him great gifts. He branched beyond witches, sacrificing humans to provide violent souls. With every murder, his strength grew. He was eventually slain by a witch who he had attempted to draw toward his cave.

"I feel like we should do something," Abby sighed, leaning her head back against the couch.

Reading was too still – she needed movement, action. The part of her that wasn't terrified wanted to find Alva and kill him.

"We are doing something," Sebastian said absently. "We're learning to defend ourselves. We're learning how to kill these bastards."

Abby returned to her own book, lifting it from the floor and setting it back on the shelf. She picked along the titles and pulled out another called *The Defiance of Death*. The cover was freaky, a long white face with a giant black mouth, open – as if screaming. She flipped through the pages, trying to concentrate, but distracted by every noise, hoping each time that Helena returned with news.

She crossed a bold headline that said 'Surviving Death' and did a double-take, immediately thinking of Devin. She glanced at Sebastian to see if he was watching her, but he wasn't, so she leaned in close to read.

Death is a transfer of energy. The energy moves from the physical vessel into the energetic world, but this process can be complicated when a witch focuses her energy at the point of death on a powerful object. The object, known as a relic, is a physical manifestation of her element and may take on part of the soul, or energy, and keep it until it is released.

Abby read it again, imagining Devin's death and the small goddess lighter in her pocket.

Had Devin defied death?

The book offered an example, a witch, known as Egon, who was murdered by a Vepar during the 1400's, but transferred his energy into a nearby stone. As Egon lay dying, he focused on the stone, which embodied his earth element. His body died but a portion of his energy entered the stone and allowed Egon to remain in the physical world without a physical body. The Vepar who picked up the stone created a bridge between his own mind and the dead witch. When another witch later found the stone, he was able to see, not only thoughts of the slain witch, but thoughts of the Vepar as well, which ultimately aided him in slaying the Vepar.

Abby moved her face away from the book. Was Devin still alive? Had she transferred her energy into the lighter? Vesta had picked up the lighter; Abby had seen it in Devin's memory. But how could Abby retrieve the lighter without first finding Vesta?

She considered telling Sebastian. It was far fetched, sure, but he would believe her. He had to. She started to get up, taking the book with her, but the door swung open.

"He's awake," Helena breathed, rushing into the room. "He's conscious and he's going to be okay." She talked fast, describing Elda's brilliant salve that seeped into his organs and repaired the burned tissue. Abby tried to listen and understand, but could not follow when Helena got into different herbs and incantations, waving her hands wildly about the room.

Sebastian just smiled and nodded, clearly relieved. Abby wondered if he felt guilty for his cool treatment of Oliver in the previous days.

"Bridget made some lunch, and, Abby, Oliver has asked to see you."

"Me? Why?" Abby asked, surprised.

Sebastian was forcing his smile now, some of his joy eroded by the strange request.

"I don't know, but I can take you down."

Chapter 23

The infirmary felt different to Abby than it had the previous night. Many of the candles had been extinguished and long, dark drapes covered the skylight ceiling, blocking the daylight.

Oliver lay on one of the many beds, shrunken beneath a thin white sheet. His face was heavily bandaged with small holes for his eyes, nose and mouth. Lydie snored softly from another bed and Dafne stood rigid at a long counter, crushing herbs in a mortar and pestle, and then adding them to a tall glass bottle.

She drew herself up and stared meanly at Abby, who averted her eyes and hurried to Oliver's side, wishing that Helena had accompanied her all the way to the infirmary.

"Oliver," she whispered, staring at his burned skin, his eyelashes gone.

His eyes cracked open and she saw the slits of green, like tiny jewels.

She grasped his hand. It was bandaged and she recoiled, thinking that she had injured him.

He shook his head with effort. "No, it's okay, feel away. Let me know if I've got any skin left down there." His voice was hoarse, but stronger than she expected.

She smiled and leaned closer to him. "Oh, I'm so happy that you're okay. We thought…"

"Nope, still alive. Barely, but still alive."

"Can I get you something—water?"

Dafne had stopped mixing and moved closer to the bed.

Oliver noticed her from the corner of his eye. "Relax, Daffy," he called. "She's not dumping acid in my peepholes."

Dafne looked angrily at Oliver and then turned, leaving the room without a backward glance.

"She's still touchy," he said.

"Yeah," Abby agreed. "I don't think this helped."

"Help me sit up, babe," he said, groaning as he tried to lift his head.

"No, stop," Abby gasped, startled as some of his bandages ripped from his arms.

She braced her hands under his back, stuffing several more pillows beneath him.

"Don't worry, it doesn't hurt anymore. Bridget makes a mean painkiller."

"Yes, I think I've tried it."

"I heard."

"You did? How?"

"Faustine sent me an image while I was on the hunt. I'm sorry about your aunt."

Abby sighed and perched on the edge of Oliver's bed where he had made space for her.

"This world is shocking in the beginning," Oliver continued, his eyes anguished. "People die for us."

"Why, though? Why do other people have to die?"

"Because our enemies don't simply want witches, they enjoy killing."

Oliver spoke flatly, and it hurt Abby to hear his hardened tone. Had his family died for him?

"Oliver, why did you want to see me?"

He turned toward her and smiled, but his lips were burned, and they cracked when he opened his mouth.

"Because you're new and I know how that feels. I knew that you were hurting about your aunt, probably about me and I wanted to tell you that it's okay. I'm okay and you will be okay."

Lydie shook beside them, her leg jerking and then

settling back down.

"Must be chasing cats," Oliver said.

"She's sweet."

"Yes, and a monster."

"Have you been here longer than her?" Abby asked him, helping lift a straw to his lips so that he could drink.

"Technically, yes, but she was born here at the Coven. Her parents were both witches, and they lived here for a few years because a Vepar had discovered their home. Prior to that, they avoided covens, but they knew Faustine and wanted to be safe. So they came here and Lydie was born and we all loved her, but then they grew tired of being part of the coven and the castle. They wanted their life back, so they left and found a new home. The same Vepar tracked them down. They were powerful, but he had his entire clan and they murdered them."

Abby's chest tightened painfully and she gripped Oliver's hand too hard. He pulled it gently from her fingers.

"Luckily, they had enchanted a crawl space for Lydie, who was too young to be detected by the Vepars anyway. Faustine found her a few days later when he hadn't heard anything from her parents. She's been with us ever since."

"How did Faustine know she would be a witch?"

"He didn't know for sure. But it didn't take long. She started exhibiting powers when she was three. She lit her own birthday candles without a match. It was brilliant, I still remember it."

Abby smiled and looked at Lydie, who seemed tiny beneath the fuzzy pink blanket someone had thrown over her. A small bubble rose from her lips and popped.

"I just want you to know," Oliver said, pulling her hand back into his own. "That I'm here for you, no matter what. Okay?"

* * * *

The cold of the stone seeped into Sebastian's pants and he stared down at the small spider webs that cracked the surface. There were a million tiny paths, each flowing in a different direction, a minute change with completely different results. He wondered what would have happened if he had not gone to Sydney's house. Would Abby still have found her way there, discovered the body and been subsequently murdered? Or would everything have been different? Maybe she would have arrived at Sydney's, gotten lonely and returned home to her boyfriend. He did not have the answers, and trying to meditate, to visit his spirit pool, proved unproductive in the castle. He couldn't concentrate. It was like the walls constantly hummed.

He kicked a pebble, watching it skid down the stone steps and disappear into a tangle of bushes, raspberry or blackberry, he wasn't sure which. Abby had gone to visit Oliver – Oliver who had nearly died. Would he have survived if Sebastian had spoken of Detective Alva, explained his suspicions that Alva was a Vepar?

He hadn't liked Oliver, and, if he was honest, he still didn't want to chum around with the guy, but the guilt had settled in the back of his mind like a stone dropping to the bottom of the sea. It might get kicked around, shift on the currents, but it would still lie there – solid and heavy on his thoughts.

"I'm guessing you're not thinking about clouds right now," Helena said, startling him.

She looked happy, relieved that Oliver was well, and her smile was contagious. Sebastian smiled back.

She settled next to him on the step, lifting her heavy skirt, so colorful that it was hard to look at.

"Sparkles," he said, lifting a piece of the fabric.

Sparkles rubbed off on his fingers, and he held them up to the light. They glittered in the sun.

"That would be Lydie's doing. She's learned to make them by crushing stones. My entire wardrobe is sprinkled with the stuff. I kind of like it, though."

Helena wiped some of the sparkles off and painted them on her cheeks.

"What happened to Oliver?" Sebastian asked.

Helena plucked a wilted pink rose and pulled the petals off one by one. "He loves me, he loves me not," she said, letting the flower fall. "Oliver was ambushed."

"By Alva?"

"By their clan. He picked up Tobias's scent in the woods and began to track him, but the Vepars knew when he appeared at the ritual that he would be back. They created a false trail to Abby's Aunt Sydney's house."

"Sydney's?"

"Yes, he walked right into a trap. You see, Oliver didn't even know of Alva. None of us did except Faustine, who believed that he lived west, Washington or Oregon, but apparently he's here now."

"He has been. I saw him when Claire died."

Really?" Helena looked surprised. "I wish you would have mentioned that to Elda."

"Yeah, I know." Sebastian was crestfallen. Helena had verified his fear, that he could have prevented the attack.

"Oh, no, you don't." She poked Sebastian in the side. "Don't be taking this on yourself. Oliver is a big boy. He knows he's walking into danger when he goes after those Vepars. We all live with that knowledge every day. You, Sebastian, have to liberate yourself from all the guilt swirling around in there." She tapped the side of his head with her finger.

It felt good to joke with someone. It reminded him of

his mother. It had been a long time since someone told him he wasn't responsible for all the bad befalling the people in his life.

"Do you think I brought this on Abby?"

"Ha! Abby's a witch, you fool. Whether she met you or not, that's what she is. We just thank Mother Earth that you got her here safely."

"Thanks to Oliver."

"Sebastian, you played a part in saving her and you know it. Your worst enemies are those thoughts. You'd be smart to check them at the door."

"Yeah, that was Claire's advice too. A lot of good it did her."

"People die, Sebastian. We all do eventually. Stop believing it's so final."

They both stared at their feet for several minutes, and neither spoke.

"Does that mean you know what comes after this?" he asked, hopeful.

"Nah, not really. But I've chatted with enough of the dead to know there's something."

"Really?"

"Yep, but don't start badgering me about that just now. I'm starving." She got up and turned back to him. "You coming?"

He grinned, hopped to his feet and followed her back into the castle.

* * * *

Faustine stepped onto the stone slab, his black robes swaying, and Abby sensed his enormous strength. It was not only the dark rising sky, nor even the air of power that drifted like a tailwind behind him. He was a sorcerer, and

J.R. Erickson

everyone in the group silenced at the sight of him.

Behind him the full moon climbed. It was a gleaming red ball that would grow orange and then yellow as the night wore on.

All of the witches and Sebastian stood on the beach, surrounding the second lagoon. They wore black robes, their pockets heavy. Abby did not know what each witch carried. The drooping pockets of her own robe held amber – for physical protection, bloodstone – to protect against the evil eye, dried elderberries – for banishing negative energy, and dried raspberries – for protection of the home. Helena had provided her the stones and herbs with descriptions of each. Sebastian's robe sagged especially low.

Faustine stood on the raised stone slab and faced the group. He held an enormous tattered book in his arms, the pages blowing in the wind. Only Oliver was missing, still in the infirmary where he would stay for several more days.

"I have nightmares about that book getting snatched by a turkey buzzard out here," Helena whispered to Abby from the corner of her mouth.

Abby looked overhead, but the violet sky held only the faintest flicker of stars.

Sebastian stood on Abby's other side, his arms swinging, his fingers occasionally clinging to hers and then releasing.

Elda and Bridget carried several brooms, which they passed to the group.

"It is time to prepare our circle. We must sweep the negative energy away." She looked pointedly at Abby and Sebastian. "Follow my lead."

All of the witches began to vigorously sweep sand and grass outward, creating a wide circular space of raked beach.

"Out, out negative. I sweep you away," Elda murmured and everyone followed. They repeated the line until Faustine raised a hand.

Elda then walked around the circle's perimeter three times. First she carried a bowl of water, next a bowl of salt and finally a small stick of burning incense.

"She is consecrating our circle with representations of the four elements," Helena whispered to Abby and Sebastian.

"Separate," Faustine said. His eyes were closed and his hands hovered above the book, which floated on air, lifting and settling like gentle waves drifted beneath it.

"Earth faces north, air east, fire south and water west," Elda called, but she sounded far away, like she'd already vacated the beach.

Abby followed Elda, who stood facing west, toward the castle. Faustine turned west from the slab. Helena and Max walked to the other side of the circle and stood looking east. Bridget had taken Sebastian's hand and led him to the northern end of the circle; they faced the lake, though the island's high dunes blocked the water. Lydie and Dafne faced the lagoon, their arms entwined.

Faustine began, "I call to the Watchtower of the west, my ancestor. Protect us with your blue spirit, the flow of your positive energy that surrounds our island. Lift up that water to cleanse us of negative spirits and to provide a barrier between us and the evil that wants to come in."

Elda started to repeat it and Abby hurried along with her, tripping over words, but getting the gist.

Faustine turned and faced the lagoon. "I call to the Watchtower of the South, my ancestor. Protect us with your fiery red spirit. Spark our powers within and let those fires burn so brightly that no evil dares venture here."

Lydie and Dafne repeated his words.

He continued with each direction, calling upon Watchtowers to the east and north. As he spoke, his book shook violently, the pages whipping back and forth. The sky overhead grew darker and then brighter and when rain started to fall, Abby did not get wet. The circle that Elda had created was a dome, a bubble that the water fell onto and slid off, pooling on the sand.

Soon Faustine faced west again and this time everyone chanted with him. Their voices rose and Abby felt her robes lift as if gusts of wind blew from below. She tilted her face up and let the power wash through her. The chant tickled each vertebra of her spine and small portals opened for energy to flow through her to every muscle and fiber. She shook with delight and noticed that the others did as well. Even Sebastian and Dafne held similar smiles of ecstasy. Their energy built within the circle and Abby felt the pressure. She stared as the bubble pressed out, the rain pinging against the invisible surface.

"I release you!" Faustine bellowed, and the bubble burst, the energy rushing into the rain and momentarily driving it back.

Abby felt the storm descend then. A deluge of water spilled over them and she laughed, choking on a mouthful, but swallowing it and gulping more. The moon continued to shine; no clouds hid its dusty face. Helena and Bridget started to dance, slowly at first, turning in circles and swaying down so that their bodies became like pendulums, swinging closer together with each rotation. Dafne, Lydie and Elda joined, their bodies wet and heavy beneath their robes, but they moved gracefully. Abby did not look to Max or Faustine, not even to Sebastian. She closed her eyes and tilted her neck and let the wind and rain dictate her dance.

Thunder clapped overhead and behind the sheer veil of her eyelids, Abby saw white streaks of lightning. She felt her feet sink into the mushy sand of the lagoon's edge, but she continued into the lagoon. The water rose up to her knees and then her waist. She fell backwards, allowing her body to let go, and felt the water wrap her in, enfold her. It covered her face and when her shoulders hit the sandy bottom, she willed herself up. She did not push her feet beneath her or scramble back to the surface. She simply put all of her attention into the image of coming back up above the water and then she did. The water rushed by and she burst out of the lagoon and into the night, her body flying for several seconds above the water.

The others turned to watch, but she could only feel their stares, not see them through the sheets of rain. She hovered for a second and then crashed back into the water, feeling it explode away from her and then close back in as she sank down. She did it again and then again. She flew out of the water with only her thoughts. She felt the fingers in the water gathering beneath her and then flinging her out, a geyser that she created.

* * * *

When Abby awoke to Devin beside her, it was nearly 2:30 am and she'd been asleep for only two hours. No tremor of fear stole over her this time, only a perplexing calm, as though she had expected Devin in the dead of night. She should have been exhausted, but the ritual on the beach had awakened something within her. She had known Devin would come that night, had felt it the moment her head hit the pillow.

Devin did not speak, but cold seeped from her like condensation and settled on Abby's skin.

"Hi," Abby said, not afraid – not even surprised anymore.

"You understand now?" Devin whispered, her red hair flickering and disappearing for a moment, leaving only her pale face and large green eyes above her purple robe.

"I read about relics. Is the lighter a relic?" Abby asked.

Devin smiled and moved her head up and down. It was a gesture consumed by effort and Devin flickered out briefly.

Abby wanted to sign up for the task, but her heart had moved into her throat. She had seen Vesta with the lighter, and the fear coiled around her thoughts. She wanted to help Devin, but she wasn't ready.

"You must get the lighter."

"Yes, and I will. Tomorrow I will tell Elda, and we will find a way."

Devin shook her head violently and vanished. Abby waited several seconds, and when she reappeared, her eyes looked empty, but her mouth was twisted in warning.

"Your family is in danger."

"What?" Though Abby had heard her clearly.

"You must get the lighter."

"But I can't, don't you see that? I can't take on Vesta alone." Abby stood from the bed and paced the room, glancing back at Devin, who seemed to be moving towards her with great difficulty. She reached slowly towards Abby, her hand an iridescent vapor with little shape.

Abby understood and lifted her own to meet it, the cold quickly enveloping her.

* * * *

Again she peered through Devin's eyes. They had returned to the woods on the night of her death. Devin stared down as Vesta left the forest, Tane scurrying behind her.

"I'll take the car," Vesta barked at Tane, who nodded, but did not speak. "You know where to meet me."

Devin watched Vesta slide behind the wheel of her Volkswagen, and the car grumbled to life. Vesta drove fast, faster than the car liked. It groaned and shook on the freeway, her hands vibrating beneath the gyrating steering wheel. While Vesta drove, she pulled out the goddess lighter and lifted it to her face. Staring at it closely, she rubbed her fingers over the surface, her long nails blocking the goddess's tiny metallic features.

She took an exit and Devin stared hard at the sign, 'Devil's Bend', in white lettering against green metal. Vesta took the turns fast, laughing maliciously when the car squealed in protest. Jerking the wheel hard to the right, she turned down a dirt trail that wound through trees. The car bumped over exposed roots and deep grass, threatening to get stuck, but somehow forging on, an unwilling participant in Vesta's joyride. The trail ended abruptly at a small bluff that overlooked a large, mossy pond. Cattails and weeds poked thickly from the grimy surface.

Vesta stepped from the car and walked to the dune edge. The drop was no more than fifteen feet, but it would be plenty to get the car moving. She pulled the lighter out again and this time flicked it on, watching the flame, mesmerized.

Suddenly the fire jumped from the goddess and snaked around Vesta's wrist. She shrieked and threw it to the ground, shaking her arm in pain. A red ring surrounded the flesh, already blistering. Vesta cursed and kicked the lighter hard, sending it over the dune embankment into the water below, where it splashed once and disappeared.

Vesta returned to the car and began to push. With very little effort, the car wheeled over the edge. It smashed into the dune once with its nose, then flipped onto its back in the murky water and began to sink. Vesta waited until the wheels slipped below the water, then turned and trotted back to the woods and out of sight.

* * * *

In the castle, Abby moved away from Devin with an audible suck, as if she had pulled her hand from a bowl of gelatin.

The lighter was in the pond.

"I still don't understand," Abby whispered, scared. She was teetering on the edge of belief in herself and hated the small sound of her voice.

"You... your family is in danger." Devin's voice had begun as nothing more than a low raspy draft, but now it grew loud and urgent. "With the lighter...you can see her."

"No," Abby interjected. "Why would they want them? Not to get to me. No, I don't believe it."

But she did believe it. Her heart pounded in her head and she had to sit on the edge of the bed, feet planted, to steady the blood pulsing in her ears.

"There's no time," Devin breathed.

No time? How could there be no time? But her mind reeled back to Sydney and she understood that if there was any time at all, she had to act now.

"Yes, now," Devin breathed and then she was gone. A light mist lingered in the air, but before it faded completely, Abby had left the room.

Chapter 24

The castle slept. Abby crept down the hallway and slipped out the door without notice. She fought her brain's cries to seek help. At the lagoon, she stopped. The rowboat that Abby and Sebastian had used sat motionless on the beach, its weather beaten bow hardly the trusty steed that she hoped for. Would it be fast enough?

She jumped into the boat, pushing hard with the oars and pointing herself towards the black hole that would take her out to the lake. The muscles of her arms did not burn and she exercised her power, pushing harder and faster with each stroke. Her forearms were a blur as she thrust and pulled, not needing to pause to find her way because her body did it for her. Muscle memory took over her confused and frightened brain.

When she saw the black headlights of Sebastian's discarded car, she veered towards it, rowing harder. She did not pull onto the shore, but leapt from the boat, planting her feet hard in the sand. The keys still clung to the back bumper and she accelerated in reverse, whipping the car around and almost losing control.

"Relax," she commanded herself. She was exhibiting the lack of control that Elda had warned her about.

The trees whizzed by, the road laid empty, no late night cars.

She watched road signs, reading them easily, despite driving by at eighty-five mph. She might have missed the exit for Devil's Bend, but a puff of frigid air blew against her neck and she instantly let off the gas. The exit drew up on her left and she took it slowly.

Her confidence started to teeter. Sure, she'd left the

island and made it here on her own, but what now? What if Vesta was waiting for her in the forest?

For a split second she considered turning the car around, racing back to the Coven and waking Elda or just crawling back into bed, but then her mother's voice drifted into her ear. It was not her mother's voice now, but from when Abby was a child. She was singing to Abby, who lay snuggled in her lap, her fingers gently massaging Abby's scalp. "Baby's boat's a silver moon, sailing o'er the sky, sailing o'er the sea of dew, while the clouds float by…"

As her mother's voice sang gently in her ear, Abby started to cry. The car had nearly stopped, but Abby didn't care. She stared through her tears and the windshield at the dark night and allowed thoughts of her mother to rain down, but when the guilt at leaving started to ebb in, she resumed her search.

She pressed the gas and turned right as the dirt trail came up beside her. Tree branches scraped and grabbed at the car. She knew that they were not sinister beasts trying to take hold, but she couldn't kill the thought. She pulled to a stop on the embankment edge that Devin had showed her.

The sand and rock sloped down, while the cattails climbed up, both fighting in the opposite direction. Abby hesitated, then slipped off her pants and shoes and dropped over the edge, stumbling and falling down the dune and splashing into the water. It was warm and murky, impossible to see beneath the thick, hairy lily pads and piles of floating brush.

She stood for a moment, waist deep, hoping that Devin might point her towards the lighter, but nothing happened, no spirit guide or whispered words. Finally, she waded out. Another foot in and the pond sloped so steeply down that Abby could no longer touch the bottom. She trod water, then dived, opening her eyes. Amazingly, she could see, though her view was no better than smudged goggles.

Deeper she went, searching the tangles of seaweed and thrusting her hand into the muddy bottom, which suctioned her fingers and threatened to hang on. Her sodden clothes hung below her, and as her air ran out, much slower than usual, she pushed back to the surface. Gulping another lungful, she dived back below. Near the pond's center she spotted Devin's car, the roof and windshield completely submerged in mud, only the body and tires visible through the swampy water.

Tendrils of slimy weeds swayed lazily on the pond floor and made her think of corpses stuck in the earth. She swam closer to the car, kicking her legs and propelling downward until she could reach out and touch the rubbery tires.

Around the car she moved, hands scraping up billows of dirt, but no lighter. She could see the cracked leather seats in the Volkswagen and several items floating in the cavity: a bag of potato chips, a headband, a t-shirt gone from white to mud.

Swimming up for more air, she paddled back near the sand dune edge. This time she remained in the shallow area, standing and shuffling her feet along the slimy bottom. Mud caked between her toes and lodged beneath her toenails. Twice she hit a rock and thought she'd found the lighter. Frustration barged in, followed by defeat. She plopped into the water, mud oozing along her legs, but she didn't care. The water reached her chest and lapped her shirt, creating a distinct line of muck that she didn't bother wiping away.

Mosquitoes buzzed in her ears, swimming on the humid air that smelled of rotting vegetation, like the compost pile her mother kept by the backdoor. She slapped them away and swore under her breath and couldn't imagine how she'd gone from a magic castle to a rotting swamp alive with parasites.

She started to doubt her plan, even to doubt the vision of Devin, but a massive bullfrog drew her eyes. He sat on a gargantuan lily pad, his throat ballooning white and then deflating with a loud call that ricocheted off the forest walls. She stood to look at him closer; she had never seen such a large frog. His long, gummy tongue lashed out and caught a fat mosquito buzzing overhead, bringing it into the soft pink belly of his mouth. His shining glass eyes lowered into the folds of his body, but Abby felt him looking at her and then he leapt, the fat body extending into a long white stripe before disappearing into the water with barely a splash.

She stared at the tiny ripples of water and then returned her gaze to the pond. The ripples fanned out and when they reached her legs, she felt them. "Ha!" The laugh erupted out of her, sounding like the bullfrog's croak. Her fingers trailed the top of the water, her element, black water bugs skittering by.

Abby clenched her eyes closed and concentrated. The water hugged her, plastering her shirt to her stomach, dripping in muddy rivulets from strands of her hair. In her mind, hope gave way to the blue ball of energy. It grew larger, vibrating, shaking Abby's body and flowing out into the water. She imagined the water lifting, all in a single unified mass, simply floating above the squishy floor.

Opening her eyes, but holding steady to her vision, the water began to rise around her. It moved up, washing over her torso, then neck, then head, momentarily submerging her from the waist up. Then it was above her, hanging like a low, wet cloud. Shifting her gaze to the pond bottom, she was greeted with a treasure trove of discards. Her eyes passed over keys, sodden towels, hubcaps, and the skeleton of a Christmas tree.

The goddess stuck straight up from the mud, her

metallic body vibrant against the dark browns and greens, an easily overlooked bit of rubbish in a water-filled junkyard. Abby moved forward and squatted down slowly, her mind concentrating on the wet beast dangling overhead. She clutched the lighter in her fist and rose upward. For a moment she stared at it in disbelief, not quite ready to celebrate in case she realized she was holding a gum wrapper or discarded bottle cap instead. But no, it was the goddess lighter, surprisingly clean in its boggy home.

Abby let out a loud whoop and felt her tether to the pond snap. It crashed down, not painful, but shocking, and for a terrifying moment she felt the lighter begin to slip in her moist hand. Her body fell forward and she clutched it before it could slither out. She landed roughly on her knees in the muck. Pressing the lighter to her breast, she waded and then ran back to the car, struggling quickly into her pants and shoes.

She drove from the woods slowly, stopping at the freeway on-ramp. The lighter balanced on the dashboard in front of her, but she didn't know what to do.

She picked the lighter up and pressed her thumb along the tiny sword that the goddess held; a small blue flame erupted and then flickered out. She did it again; this time the light held and grew steadily. The flame drew her in, and beneath the blue light an image emerged.

Abby pulled the lighter closer, gazing beyond the flame and seeing out through Vesta's charcoal eyes.

* * * *

Vesta stood in a small clearing. The trees on every side of her were dead, their bark black and withering further as she pushed all of her energy at that single goal: death.

Beside her, Tane let in a rush of breath that nearly

273

broke her concentration. She flicked a thought, a mean one, his way and he recoiled, as if pricked by something small and lethal.

The moon overhead was luminous and Vesta felt the full enormity of her power as she stared at the singed trees, their branches curling into their base, trying to hug the life she'd already extinguished.

Tane quaked with envy, and now that she had become a full Vepar, she felt the emotion pouring out from him. It was like a stench, thick and putrid and needling the exposed flesh of her body. Evil thrived on evil, but Tane was not evil. Vesta had made a mistake in offering him as a disciple. But what choice did she have? Tobias had insisted that all new Vepars mentor the next. Those were the rules, and had Tobias not complied, she, too, would not be a Vepar. Though she could have chosen better – darker and meaner. Tane wanted human power. He wanted money and women. He didn't want to feel power by feeding on another's life. She had seen him flinch when she fed at Devin's death. She knew that Tobias had felt it too.

"Can I see your ring?" Tane asked meekly, and she glowered at him.

Her ring. It was a gift from her Aunt Fiona, a Vepar, who'd been disowned by their human family fifty years earlier. Vesta's parents did not know that Fiona still lived and they preferred it that way. As a girl, Vesta had known Fiona only through photos and family lore.

"Evil, she was," Vesta and Tane's father had told them when they were barely teenagers. "Killed her own kid. Axed him while he slept."

Vesta had not believed the tales. She knew Fiona existed, but doubted there was any truth to the gory legends that accompanied her. Later, she discovered the truth when Fiona visited her at school. She was only fifteen then, but

Fiona recognized the black blood within her, waiting to be let out.

"No, Tane," she snapped. "Interrupt me again and you will join them." She jerked her head towards the burned trees.

Fiona, Vesta learned, had killed her only child, a boy. Not with an axe though, she used a hammer because it happened to be lying nearby.

"Those were more barbaric times," Fiona had said, describing her own initiation into the world of Vepars. In those days, it was not enough to kill and consume witch blood. You also had to kill kin, one of your own, to prove that you renounced them and chose the Vepars as your new family.

Not only had Vesta not murdered her kin, she had chosen her own brother to mentor. He would become a Vepar and join their ranks. She looked at Tane, who squatted on the grass, poking at a black beetle with a stick, like a child.

She did not speak to him, but strode from the field. In the cave she breathed deep, preferring the hot, moist air to the cool night. She took a narrow tunnel to the dungeons, stopping outside a heavy black door.

* * * *

Abby returned to the car in a painful flash that sent the lighter flying from her hand into the windshield. Her head ached, and she fumbled to put the car in gear, her sweaty hands slipping over the shifter.

The dungeon door lingered in her mind. It was thick and black and heavy looking. If her parents were in there, would they still be alive? Did Vepars barter for human lives?

"Abby." The breathy voice startled her.

The shimmering image of Devin hovered in the passenger seat. Abby glanced at her, then back at the road.

"My parents," Abby choked. "Are they okay?"

Devin flickered, disappeared, then emerged again. She looked pained. "They're captive," she sighed, waving a pale hand towards the dark night outside her window.

"No," Abby demanded, "please, no." She shook her head as if that might make it go away.

Devin nodded, her nearly transparent curls bouncing in response. "There's a woman, a witch," Devin began, her green eyes glittering suddenly as if a surge of strength had poured in. "She can help you. She can help both of us."

"Who is she?" Abby asked. "Where is she?"

The trees whipped by and a blue sign said, 'REST AREA. 4 MILES.' When it came up, Abby quickly veered to the right and pulled into the empty parking area. The lights shone in the little brick building, but no late night patrons were stopped.

"She is north of here. She is very special." Devin's image was much sharper now.

Abby twisted to face her, studying her white skin and her long black eyelashes. She still wore the purple robe, the sparkling sleeves falling away from her bare forearms as she spoke. Her full lips were parted only slightly as she talked, like a ventriloquist.

"She is called the Lourdes of Warning. She was once a very powerful witch."

"Once?" Abby interrupted.

"Yes, some very bad things happened…" Devin closed her eyes for a moment, as if retrieving this information from some unseen place. "She is still powerful, but she lives in solitude, complete solitude."

Abby nodded and took mental notes, sensing a foreboding in Devin's words.

"The woods where she lives are very unusual, magical, but it is the only way to reach her. You can get there. You are a witch and will be able to move through them with ease. Others would not be so lucky," Devin told her, her face serious.

"Is it dangerous?" Abby asked, self-consciously rubbing her palms on the slick steering wheel.

Devin took a moment to answer, then shook her head slowly. "Not dangerous, but it will be like nothing you've encountered before."

"Okay, what do I do?" Abby asked, realizing that—dangerous or not—she had no other choice.

Chapter 25

After Devin described her task, Abby was alone again, driving recklessly deeper into the wilderness. Thick rows of pines lined the freeway and the sparse small towns became ever fewer, eventually disappearing completely.

The sun began to rise, peeking over the tree line and casting swaths of sunlight across the car's hood.

Devin had told her where to leave her car and enter the forest on foot. In the woods she would find a small gray tree carved with a symbol called the Fate Triad. Three linked half circles carved inside of a bowed triangle. From this place, she would travel west, approximately fifty yards, and come to a very large, very red weeping willow tree. Abby had never seen a red weeping willow, nor heard of one, but Devin assured her of its existence. Beneath this tree, she would find the Lourdes of Warning. The Lourdes would tell her where to find her family, but what's more, she would tell Abby how to destroy the lighter, which, Devin insisted, must be done quickly. Devin repeated the directions and told Abby that under no circumstances should she give the lighter to the Lourdes, not even for a second.

Abby opened her mouth to ask more questions but Devin had disappeared.

Now, she drove through the early morning with fear gnawing anxiously at her thoughts.

She tried to flip the lighter on and see through Vesta's eyes, but it would not light. It snapped and hissed but refused to relinquish the flame hiding inside it.

It took nearly three hours to reach the forest opening. A hidden road of ebony dirt, the kind that farmers coveted, led into the shadowy woods. Tall, needled pines stood in trim rows. As Abby carefully maneuvered her car into the thick brush, the pines gave way to a jumble of other trees. She saw beech, weeping willow, birch and black maple. They clumped together over thick moss and strangled ferns. Tiny streaks of sunlight pestered the shadows. The black dirt road snaked and twisted, ending abruptly at a massive, coffee colored tree flourishing with diamond-shaped, emerald leaves.

She stepped from the car hesitantly, mentally rehearsing Devin's directions.

She hated to travel on foot from the safety of the car. Although she knew that, as a witch, the car was more of a hindrance than help.

Walking, she stared at the tall trees coated with neon green moss that chased up their thick, wrinkled trunks. The ground felt mushy, the twigs and mossy earth squishing beneath her. Minutes passed. She could feel time whizzing by like an untouchable breeze. Nothing could be stopped, the wheels were in motion.

"Oh!" She fell hard on her hands, her left foot jammed beneath a thick root, and her yell ricocheted through the forest, sending a spiral of black crows out of a squat gray tree, its gnarled hands distinct.

Abby crawled back to her feet and approached the tree slowly. There, engraved deep into the puckered bark, was the symbol that Devin had described, the Fate Triad. Glossy sap had seeped into the symbol, shining like a palm sized amber jewel.

She turned and walked directly west, passing beneath the canopies of bushy trees and tangled branches, all fighting towards the skinny shafts of sunlight peeking through. The ground moss began to disappear beneath shin-length ferns of such neon green that Abby bent and touched one. They were real.

She would have spotted the Lourdes of Warning's home sooner, but her eyes kept lingering on pockets of tiny purple and blue flowers that twittered beneath the ferns, as if teasing Abby in her haste.

The cardinal colored Weeping Willow flamed like a brilliant sore against the healthy green backdrop of the forest. Its long, red, skeletal arms brushed the ground. Abby could see nothing of the trunk, nothing of the shadows that lingered underneath its scarlet canopy, and nothing of the Lourdes. She would have liked to have knocked, but there was not exactly a door, or a wall, for that matter.

Instead, she called out, cupping her hands around her mouth, not to lengthen her bellow, but to muffle it.

"Hello," she squeaked, wincing as her voice died beneath the forest din.

No response, not even a ruffle of birds this time to show signs of life. Perhaps the willow had eaten the Lourdes; it surely looked like it could.

She took a step closer and then another. Now she could smell the diseased looking tree. It reeked of patchouli, but not only that. It smelled as if the patchouli was meant to cover something dead, like dried flowers and incense burned at a place that housed corpses.

Abby wanted to turn back, to distance herself from the rotted thing and whatever hid beneath its bloody branches, but she could not. Her parents could die, Sydney was dead, and cowardice was not an option.

With a deep breath, she reached out and grabbed a handful of the weeping willow's branches, which were not dry as she expected, but wet and slimy. They slipped over her palms like long, slick worms, and she shoved them up over her head and ducked under, running forward. Some of the dripping limbs fell across her face and hair as she clambered through, fighting the urge to retch or scream. She wiped her hands on her pants, expecting to leave a red, gooey slime, but they were dry. She stared out at the branches from the awning they created, but could see nothing of the forest beyond. The dark, circular shadow she stood in glowed a dull red, the floor was moss covered like the woods, but the moss was red and sponged down beneath her weight.

She moved around the tree hesitantly, her hands balled in preparation for possible threats. At the back of the thick brown trunk, a gaping hole, the size of a large welcome mat, disappeared into the red moss. Abby could see what appeared to be a stairwell moving down, but it wasn't actually a stairway. Instead, huge hunks of root twisted beneath the tree, creating steps that dropped lower and then disappeared. Abby did not want to place her foot on that first warped root, but she thought again of time. A clock ticking for every step that she took and for every one she didn't.

The first tentative step found her knee length into the hole, then waist deep, neck and then she was below it, walking on the deformed roots of the flaming willow. On either side were thick black walls of dirt that crumbled when her arms brushed them. The tiny white veins of plants poked at her, and shiny beetles scaled the dirt floor overhead as she plunged further into the ground.

The stairwell ended at a thick-carpeted floor that may have been a pale pink at one point, but was now so embedded with dirt and mold that pink only showed through in slightly grayed patches. Not far from where Abby stood, at the foot of the root staircase, was a long brown table with claw foot legs. Candles burned along its length, their waxen bodies melted down to the final inch of life, piles of white wax clumped around them. The table seated ten, and each setting was adorned with a silky red placemat and full dinnerware. The white porcelain plates were piled with decayed food, the mold crawling over it like living things, its furry green back bristling in the candle light. Tall, thin-stemmed wine glasses held a deep crimson liquid that looked like wine. Bugs buzzed around the overripe beverages and crawled across the acrid lettuce wilting in crystal bowls. No one sat in the straight-backed chairs that butted to the table's edge, but far in a back corner of the room, facing a plain dirt wall, sat a woman.

She appeared to be very beautiful, her slender shoulders pointed beneath a pale pink cloak that looked woven from cobwebs. Her white flesh glowed beneath the translucent fabric. Long, almond waves of hair cascaded to the floor and pooled there, as if she had been growing it for centuries.

"Hello," Abby said with more courage this time. The woman was young and beautiful, not a sinister fiend hiding in the woods.

"Come closer," the woman said, her voice like a dry hinge.

Abby did not like the voice. She did not like the way the woman floated a note of youth over the coarse sound below it.

She took a step, repulsed by the smells of rotting food, rotting meat.

"Closer," it cracked again.

Another step and another. The smell was overpowering now, as if she had her face pressed right down to one of the plates, inhaling the spoiled scent and the festering germs above it.

"I…I need your help," Abby whispered as she neared the back of the woman.

The Lourdes sat on a worn wooden bench, the legs cracked and the finish chipped away. Near her, on a small, round black table, rested a cracked hand mirror, the handle an ornately carved golden stem speckled with red bejeweled flowers. Abby glanced down at the mirror, at the reflection in the spider cracked surface and gasped.

* * * *

Dafne shook Elda awake.

"Abby has left the castle."

Elda sat up, her eyes small, and lit a candle beside her.

"She left in the night. I thought for a walk, but she hasn't come back, and her rowboat is gone."

"Wake the others," Elda said quietly, pushing her blankets off.

Chapter 26

The woman sat erect and whipped her head forward, realizing that Abby had glimpsed her face in the broken glass.

The face did not belong to the back of the young woman sitting before her. The face was puckered, the skin gray and twisting around the black hole where a mouth should have been. Tiny, coal-singed eyes glittered in the deep, wrinkled folds of eyelids that were red rimmed, as if she'd been crying for a hundred years. The woman—the thing—looked inhuman, as though her head were merely stolen from a rotted corpse and deposited on the slim, beautiful body.

Abby backed up, her feet tripping over the thick carpeting. She stumbled and turned, accidentally plunging one hand into a thick plate of putrid yams. The gooey mess slid over her fingers and wrist, opening a cavity of stench that poured forth, sickening her. She vomited, water and bile spraying the already reeking food. In different circumstances, she might have apologized, might have cleaned up the mess, but she only turned and ran for the knotted roots that served as the beast's stairway.

"Wait." The voice, as deep as a cave, halted her at the first black branch.

Abby did not immediately turn, but stayed, foot raised. Her mouth tasted bitter and her heart pounded as if the grim reaper stood behind her. She wanted to run, to race out of the underground hole and away from the weeping willow, but a disturbing mixture of desperation and curiosity held her.

"A girl," the woman said suddenly. "A little girl, such a peach, a gem to behold." She laughed, a shrill giggling spasm that shook the bench she sat on. "Mothers love their little girls."

Abby cringed away, but could not move, frozen at the thought of her own mother.

She listened to the sounds of the woman rising from the bench. It shrieked in protest, as if she were a monstrous ogre and not the petite beauty that her body simulated. Abby felt a flutter of gooseflesh prickle her back as the woman shuffled across the carpeting. It did not sound like the movements of a human, not even the slow gait of an older woman. The thing made a slithering noise.

Abby wondered if she turned around, would the woman be crawling towards her on her belly, using only her hands to propel her scaly flesh? That was the sound the thing made, a slow wriggling, like a snake across the carpeting.

A few feet behind Abby, she heard the Lourdes stop and sigh deeply. The sigh went on and on, the woman's lungs stretching into infinity.

"I can help you," the Lourdes spoke breathlessly.

Abby shook her head, but did not move. She didn't want the Lourdes's help. A beetle scuttled across the floor and Abby heard the woman's rough tongue slither out over her lipless mouth.

"You need my help," the Lourdes told her eagerly, her scratchy voice too close.

"I do," Abby agreed with a violent shiver.

The woman snickered behind her.

"I...I have to help my family, they're in danger."

"Yes, and more?"

Somehow the woman knew what she had come for. Abby could sense that, could sense that the Lourdes wanted Abby to voice it, to ask for her help.

"I also need you to help me destroy this." Abby pulled the goddess from her pocket. It felt warm to the touch and shone in the candle light. She realized that she did not want to destroy the lighter. It connected her to Vesta and her family. Once destroyed, the connection was lost.

"A relic," the Lourdes hissed, and Abby felt the hot, acrid breath on her neck.

"Yes, I promised to destroy it…" *But I don't want to*, she thought.

"Of course you don't want to," the Lourdes divined. "You have another soul in your grasp. Her life and death are in your control."

Abby did not like the Lourdes's tone or her words. She clearly longed for that type of power, but Abby didn't want it. She did not want to control Devin's soul; she just wanted to find her family.

"It's not about that," she started, but the Lourdes interrupted her.

"I will help you," she said, teasing, and Abby knew that she had retreated some, giving her a morsel of space.

"Yes, please…" Abby said, fighting her instinct to run—flee from the underground pit of despair and never look back.

"First, you will help me," the Lourdes continued, further away now.

Abby turned, but did not look at the woman's face. Instead, she stared at her claw-like toes, the toenails so long they hooked over the edge of her silver sandals. The sandals were lovely with long straps that crisscrossed, but the Lourdes's feet were decayed and gray like her face.

"What…what kind of help?" Abby stuttered, angry at her fear. She was a witch, why should she be afraid?

"I am sick and there is a potion I must make," the Lourdes pleaded, as if Abby might suddenly change her mind and run after all. "It is easy for you, so easy."

Abby nodded and forced a few deep breaths through

her mouth to avoid the stench. A bit of pity invaded her now, sympathy at the wretchedness that oozed from the Lourdes like bad perfume. She could do this – she would do this.

"You must return to the woods and retrieve two berries from the shrub of a Belladonna. The berries must be black. Not green, black. The shrub is not far, back to the tree marked by the Fate Triad, where you will find these berries at the base. Then, on your way back, you must scoop a handful of the red moss into your shirt. Do not hold the moss in your hand for more than a second." The Lourdes laughed a low, guttural giggle. "Your skin will burn if you do."

Abby cringed at the laugh and again when she heard the papery tongue slip out and rake over the dried flesh. The Lourdes was enjoying Abby's disgust and hating her for it at the same time. Abby could feel the woman's every emotion as it flew out and landed on her trembling skin.

"Do not hesitate, young Abby!" the Lourdes demanded. "The woods are not safe."

This last line came in a rush and prevented Abby's question as to how the Lourdes knew her name. The woods were not safe? But she'd only just walked through them.

"Go now and hurry." The Lourdes spoke no more, but turned, once again revealing her delicate, shapely back.

Without pause, Abby turned and sprinted up the roots. She burst out of the hole beneath the red willow, her shoes sinking into the red moss. Crouching low, she escaped from the willow, feeling the clammy branches slide over her. She reached the Belladonna bush, squatted down and carefully chose two plump berries, their skins black and shining.

She hesitated as she slipped underneath the willow a second time, staring at the blood red moss that carpeted the earth. The Lourdes scared her, and the whole situation felt wrong, dangerous, but what could she do? Devin had said that she was the only one who could help her, who could tell her where they'd taken her family.

With a deep breath, she stooped down and slid her cupped hand into the moss. It pulled away easily, a damp pile of velvety mush. Not holding it even for a second, she pulled out her t-shirt and dumped it in, her hand slightly throbbing where the moss touched, its wetness pressing against her stomach.

Back in the hole, the woman once again sat on her bench facing the wall. A large, gilded silver bowl rested on the edge of the table. Some of the decayed food had been brushed to the floor to clear space.

"Place the berries and the moss in the dish," the Lourdes said, her voice scratchy, but filled with a hope that was new.

Abby did, flipping the contents of her t-shirt out, rather than touch it a second time. The moss made a quiet splattering sound, oozing into the dish.

"Now, lift the dagger," the Lourdes said, shifting slightly on her bench. Abby saw her lift the golden mirror so that she could watch.

"The dagger?" Abby asked, seeing it for the first time. It was a simple piece, sharp silver blade; plain wooden handle stained a cherry red. Against the yellowing tablecloth, the dagger might have been an ordinary piece of cutlery, placed for guests when tough meat was served, but this was no dinner party and obviously the Lourdes had other plans.

Abby did not want to touch it, or feel the weighty knife in her palm. The room had begun to feel stifling. A stench of anticipation seeped from the Lourdes in eye-watering clouds. Abby frowned, pressing her lips into a tight line of disgust; she had to fight the rising bile in her throat.

"You must prick your skin, anywhere, but press deep. Three drops, I need. Three drops of blood." The Lourdes shifted further, her hand angling the mirror as if it were a fragile antique, not a cracked looking glass that harbored the likeness of a monster. Abby could see her greenish profile, and the dripping skin that hung slack from her jaw.

"No, no, I won't," Abby said, for herself as much as the Lourdes.

"You must," the woman hissed, her voice growing deeper still, angry. "Or they will die." The Lourdes sighed the last part, knowing that Abby would hear her, and finish the task.

Tears sprung to Abby's eyes, but she clenched them tightly closed, not allowing even a single one to fall. *My blood, but not my tears*, she thought madly.

She lifted the dagger and swiped it quickly over the top of her forearm, a line of blood twisting across her pale skin. Throwing the knife back onto the table, she pinched the skin and allowed three large drops to disappear into the bowl. She released the skin and it closed instantly. She watched in wonder as it puckered into a thin white line and then faded almost completely.

"Yes, good," the woman whispered, lurching from the bench.

Abby stared at the floor as the Lourdes slithered to the edge of the table. She sank her hands deep into the bowl, mashing and pinching with her fingers. Abby continued to avert her eyes, sickened by the woman's closeness. She reached up to pull her hair from behind her ear, hoping for a flimsy wall of defense, but found only cropped strands.

To Abby's horror, the Lourdes hunched over the bowl and dipped her face down, lapping hungrily. The sounds nearly sent Abby vomiting again, but she fought it down. She could hear the Lourdes licking the bowl, her shriveled tongue scraping its surface.

When she finished, she straightened up and stood gasping, choking down the last of the mixture.

"Here," she whispered.

Abby looked up, avoiding the woman's face, but staring at a small black bottle clutched in her gnarled hand. "For your relic."

"I don't understand," Abby told her, carefully taking the bottle. It was cold to the touch.

"You must drown the spirit out," the Lourdes said. "Soak the relic in this, it will dissolve completely, and your friend will be free."

"Yes, okay," Abby breathed, committing the directions to memory. "And my family, how do I reach my family?"

"Your family," the Lourdes spoke, but her voice had changed. The gravel was gone, replaced by a youthfulness that conflicted with her very nature. "I will show you how to reach them."

Abby had to look at her, could not stop the shift of her gaze to the source of the girlish voice.

The Lourdes was changing, her face melting and reforming before Abby's eyes. Her mouth, the black hole, had sprouted plump red lips. Her gray skin had become milkier, the ashen pallor dissolving into an ivory silkiness.

She's becoming beautiful, Abby thought, and recoiled as the woman smiled, her teeth still yellowed and thick with mold.

"I will draw you a map," the Lourdes giggled.

Abby watched as she shimmied across the room, her hips swinging seductively. The slither had vanished, the entire woman had vanished and been replaced by a graceful beauty whose appearance might have challenged Helen of Troy.

The Lourdes pulled out a long piece of parchment and tore it in half, mindless of the jagged edges. She picked up an old feathered quill from a crumbling desk along one dirt wall. Her writing scratched loudly in the cellar-like room.

The Lourdes to her lair was a diamond resting in a field of manure. A face and figure only observed in the glossy pages of magazines. Abby could not force closed her wide hanging mouth, too much in shock to register the germs probably piling into her throat from the polluted air.

She waited, frightened, as the Lourdes finished, and could not dispute the feeling of dread that plagued her. Somehow the woman's transformation scared her even more than her original hideousness. Perhaps just the mere possibility of a mask so encompassing that it could hide the decayed creature. No, not just hide, but swallow whole.

"The map to your destiny," the Lourdes flirted, holding the parchment out. She extended it just far enough that Abby had to step forward to retrieve it.

As she reached out, the Lourdes clamped her hand on Abby's wrist. Abby gasped and tried to pull away, but the woman held her easily, digging her sharp fingernails into Abby's flesh. Her eyes were two brilliant black pearls shining with desire and triumph.

She wants to keep me or eat me, Abby thought and bit back the scream that rose inside of her. The Lourdes laughed and let her go. Abby sprawled onto the dirty pink carpeting, landing on her side, the map fluttering down next to her.

Without faltering, she snatched the paper from the floor and ran from the hole. The witch laughed behind her, the melodious giggle giving way to her original shrill cackle. As Abby raced from the willow she could still hear the Lourdes, her laugh strangled and hungry.

* * * *

Abby soared through the woods, her feet barely scraping the marshy ground as she sprinted back to the car. In her previous life, Abby had not been a runner, or any type of athlete, unless you counted ping-pong. As a witch, not only could she run like an Olympic sprinter, she didn't even break a sweat. She looked at her limbs and wondered at their strength. The cramps and thirst that should have plagued her, did not.

When she neared the car, she slowed, braced her hands on her knees and gasped. Her heaves came not from exhaustion, but alarm and outrage. How could she reconcile herself and the Lourdes? She wanted to label her as something rotten, a warlock, a monster, anything that cast her apart, but she could not. She was the newcomer, the ignorant student blindly assuming that all magic was good.

Her stomach throbbed dully where the red moss had touched her, penetrating the cheap cotton of her shirt. She used a large maple leaf to rub the area dry, hoping to chafe her skin until any remaining juices faded away.

She spread the map on the hood of the car and pulled out the lighter, flicking it several times.

"Come on," she grumbled in frustration, shaking the lighter as if that might elicit the connection to Vesta.

Her heart leapt when the tiny blue flame appeared, but then died. Two more flicks and the flame grew.

* * * *

Vesta moved swiftly down a long corridor, the stone walls on either side black and shiny, like the slick back of a snake. The ceiling was low, and Vesta's platinum hair flew out behind her, a blinding contrast to the surrounding darkness.

She strode into a large, round room. Several men stood huddled in tight circles, their backs to Vesta as she entered. One man whipped around to face her and she keeled backward, fear clouding her features, quickly replaced by defiance.

Tony, the Vepar whose hate for her boiled beneath his gaze like scorching tar. Their dislike was mutual, though hers was largely mingled with fear.

"Tony." She swallowed hard, but held his gaze.

"Ah, Vesta. Our newest…member." The man sneered, his eyes maliciously raking over Vesta's pointed features. Tony was a grotesque and foreboding figure. He might have stood seven foot tall, but his twisted frame was hunched. The bent posture placed his head below his neck, a giant version of Igor, Victor Frankenstein's loyal servant. Though Tony did not look like anyone's servant.

Vesta stood her ground, hips jutting forward, but Abby could see the slight tremor in her lips as she spoke, and feel the terror buried deep in her core.

* * * *

Devin appeared, flushing the vision away. They were back in the woods and Devin's spirit undulated thickly.

"You must destroy the lighter," she commanded, sending a small robin fluttering from a tree branch nearby.

"I can't. Devin, I could see Vesta. I have to see what's happening."

Abby ran her thumb over the bronze sword rapidly. Devin looked furious, which drained her energy. She disappeared for a second and then returned, surging towards Abby.

Abby stumbled back, her legs hitting the Camaro's grille, and nearly tumbling onto the hood.

"Destroy it," Devin hissed, and Abby felt a wave of cold mottle her skin as Devin brushed through her.

Abby shook her head, continuing to flick the lighter.

"Why are you doing this?" she cried as Devin forced

through her again, causing a stream of goosebumps to appear on her arms. It did not hurt when Devin touched her, but the cold frightened her, and Devin's anger frightened her more. "I thought you wanted to help me."

"We help each other," Devin's voice was low, barely a whisper and then gone.

Abby stood alone, her breath coming in gasps and her lips purple with cold. Why was Devin angry? She wanted to take the black bottle and smash it against a tree. See how Devin acted then, but she knew that she wouldn't.

The sun disappeared behind a mass of gray clouds, casting the forest in shadows.

The map that the Lourdes had provided showed a trail on foot. No roads, just miles of woods. Abby was not worried about the distance. Now that she could run and jump like a jungle cat, she figured long distances were not a problem, but getting lost was something else. A few markers were drawn in, but what if Abby missed one? And how could the Lourdes be sure that Vesta would not move her parents before Abby arrived?

These questions might have plagued her longer, but a long wail sliced through the forest. A gravelly cry filled with rage and mourning. Although the noise sounded more animal than human, Abby knew that the Lourdes had left her lair. She didn't wait to find out why.

* * * *

The first hour of running was exhilarating for Abby, and she grinned frequently despite the lump of fear growing in her stomach. The map showed a clear path that roughly followed the highway north, but stayed deep enough in the trees to avoid detection by passing motorists. She passed over a small stream, barely exerting herself in the jump, and landed in a marshy field thick with cattails. The ground squished beneath her, but she bounded over it in five leaps and found herself again in the woods. This time the forest consisted entirely of neat rows of dark pine trees, and she ran fast, bee-lining a straight path ahead.

In her haste, she nearly missed her next marker on the map. A dilapidated shack sat just outside of the last row of pines to the east. The mostly collapsed roof caught her eye, and she skidded to a halt, sliding nearly five feet along the slippery needles before stopping. The shack, hidden almost entirely by crawling green vines, appeared to have given in to the forest after some effort. A hole gaped from moss-covered boards that the weather had warped, leaving strange gaps in the shack's walls. Abby moved toward it, leaving the cover of pine trees. The sky had grown a dark green-gray, and thick, bulbous clouds raced overhead. Abby could smell the approaching rain.

The hovel had no visible door, but Abby could see the interior through several smashed windows. Vines had found their way in and crisscrossed the floor, twisting around a moldy red couch, coils sticking from its bed. She tried to peer in further, but the darkening sky added to the pockets of shadow inside the shack.

According to the map, she should turn east from the shack until she reached a small pond in the shape of an arrowhead.

Pausing, she decided to give the lighter another try, but no flame erupted. For a moment Devin's form appeared next to her, eyes blazing, but before her lips parted, she vanished again. Devin looked angry, hateful even. Abby could not understand the sudden change. Devin had been her confidante only hours earlier.

As she ran on, leaving the shack behind, she thought of Sebastian. Was he in a panic at the castle? Was everyone wondering where she had gone? Maybe. Or maybe not.

Maybe they didn't realize she was missing; it had to be before noon, they might think that she was simply sleeping in. That thought both scared and calmed her. On the one hand, if no one knew she was gone, there would be no help if trouble arose. What if she couldn't handle Vesta on her own? But then if they knew she was gone, Sebastian would probably risk himself to find her, and Abby surely did not want that.

Through several fields she sprinted, her legs pumping in rhythm with her steady breath. If she'd ever felt it, she might have claimed a runner's high. Euphoria had stolen over her, and trees passed in a blur. The positive feelings began to drain from her gradually, replaced by a burning hunger. Her stomach growled, and above her a clap of thunder snapped her attention skyward. No rain yet, but it was coming.

She squinted at the ground around her. There had to be berries or some other edible plant. The problem was that she knew squat about plants. She was liable to eat some poisonous fern and end up dead before she ever reached Vesta.

She walked a few paces deeper into the woods, scanning the ground and bushes. A few pink flowers poked from the brush, but beyond that lay only weeds and trees. She plucked one of the flowers and pressed it to her nose. A scent of bitter vanilla greeted her, and she might have taken a bite, but remembered once reading about bitter meaning poison, and dropped the flower back to the ground. Too hungry to give up entirely, she bent down, grabbing a handful of chickweed. It tasted a bit like dirt and stuck to her gums, but she forced down three handfuls before giving up. It was something. She couldn't risk meeting Vesta with absolutely no energy.

Overhead, lightning streaked the sky, a loud and bright welcome to the avalanche of rain that poured down.

Chapter 27

The castle lay silent, except for the library, where the small congregation of witches had gathered.

Dafne stood angrily in front of the stone fireplace, her eyes narrowed and her hands waving in dramatic emphasis.

"I saw her go. She left the castle in the dead of night. We can NOT trust her," she shouted as if the other witches were not standing mere feet away.

"Dafne," Elda began, her tone measured. "Abby is a witch, she is part of our coven now. She may be the newest member, but as you know we do not place value according to longevity."

"And how about him?" Dafne hissed, stepping closer to the group and stabbing a single pointed finger at the ceiling above them. "Are we calling him a witch as well, Elda?"

"Dafne, stop," Faustine's voice rose amid the tension and silenced everyone. Even Lydie, who'd been indifferently braiding strands of her curly hair, looked up in surprise.

He moved into the center of their haphazard circle, his glare reserved for Dafne alone.

"I respect your opinion. However, there is a fine line between insight and paranoia. Sebastian is asleep in his room, and Abby is a new witch who has wandered into a dangerous place alone. You," he said, pointing a finger squarely at her face. "Know each of these things as well as I. You are allowing your emotions, and your past, to dictate your decisions and it will not happen. Not here and definitely not now."

Dafne's puffed, proud form deflated, and though her face remained a mask of outrage, she slumped into a chair in silence. The other witches carefully averted their eyes, focusing their stares at Faustine, who had taken control of the room.

"My connection to Abby is weak," Faustine started. "But I will go to the tower and try to make contact. Bridget, I will need you to assemble a store of anti-venom that can travel if need be."

Bridget nodded and exited immediately.

"Elda, Sebastian will rise soon. He must be kept distracted. Perhaps this would be a good time to gather more information about Claire. Max, you have your lessons with Lydie, and those may continue for now."

The three left quickly, only Lydie daring to hazard a glance at Dafne.

"Helena," Faustine commanded. "After I try to reach Abby, I will go on foot. I will need you in the tower. You must try to connect. I know that it may not be…"

He trailed off and Helena reddened. Despite all of her practice, she still had been unable to telepathically reach the others once they left the castle.

Dafne stood up. The straight-backed chair she'd occupied clattered to the floor. "I will go for her, you stay in the tower," Dafne told him, her request both a demand and a plea.

Faustine stared at her appraisingly, lifting his index finger to his upper lip and watching her as if seeking out the lie he feared was there.

Finally, he nodded. "I will be in the tower until you return."

"You mustn't tell Oliver," Dafne added, reaching back to slip her long black hair into a low ponytail. The hunter inside of her was clicking on.

"There is not time to prepare, Dafne," Helena whispered with a smile, meant to be an apology for her unreliable mind reading.

"Fine." Dafne shrugged. "I'm ready."

Faustine and Helena watched as Dafne flung open a library window and dived from the high castle walls. They did not hear the soft splash as her body broke the water and began its hasty swim to shore. Faustine beckoned to Helena, and they left the library to the company of its books.

* * * *

Abby splashed through the rain, puddled in the soft earth. Her sneakers were sodden and heavy, but she barely noticed, searching for the ramshackle hut through sheets of blinding rain. It pelted her from every direction, stinging her eyes and bare skin, drenching her hair and clothes. Thick raindrops slid off the leaves, collapsing the mini structures created beneath the bowing trees. The wall of vines and bushes hiding the shack fought against her, but her strength in the presence of the rain had nearly quadrupled, and she ripped the wiry branches away with ease. She stumbled into the cottage and collapsed onto the dusty floor, cushioned by dead leaves and yellowed newspaper.

She hated to turn back, knowing that her mother and father were held captive, possibly tortured, but when the rain grew so thick that she could not see her hand in front of her face, she'd had to. The hut would provide shelter and time to think. It would only make things worse if she missed a marker in the rain and ended up reaching Canada instead of her parents.

In the silence of the shack, with the storm beating around her, she felt disconnected from the power that she'd held only moments earlier. How easily it could be switched on and off. A simple movement from wet to dry seeped the energy from her limbs.

The shack was a mess, long ago abandoned by its

previous residents. The hole in the roof allowed a waterfall to flood what once had been a kitchen. The water hit a row of decayed plywood cabinets and spattered onto the peeling kitchen counter. There was a black hole where a sink had been, and the window, which might have once revealed a garden view for the dish-doer, was strangled with weeds, a few splinters of glass still hanging in the frame.

Despite the hole and several others like it, the living room was mostly dry. The tortured red couch and a threadbare blue rug sat in one corner facing a small fireplace. Like everything else, the fireplace appeared ancient and misused, but Abby felt a chill settling in her bones. With the storm had come a severe temperature drop, dragging the warm summer day into the teeth-rattling cold of November. She almost expected to see her breath crystallize in the air before her.

She took a minute to survey the rest of the shack. A small, dark hallway led to a tiny bathroom that tightly fit a toilet, stand up shower, and white porcelain sink. Used to be white, anyway. Every inch of the room was covered in a layer of grime, and leaves had blown in clogging the toilet bowl and sink drain. At the end of the hall, she found a closet-sized bedroom. A mattress-less metal frame sat along one wall, and a squat wooden dresser faced it, almost daring the bed to make a run for it. The roof slanted sharply which allowed for standing room in only half of the bedroom.

Returning to the sitting area, she peeked into the fireplace, surprised at the rain falling through. She had expected the chute to be clogged with leaves and maybe even some dead animals, but the flue looked mostly empty. She shoveled in some of the leaves and newspaper strewn along the floor, knowing that she'd need something bigger if the fire were to last more than a few minutes. With no other options, she kicked the arm of the couch until a hunk of the wooden frame broke free, and she shoved that into the fire pit as well.

"Come on, Devin, just a flame," she whispered to the small goddess lighter as she held it near a wad of newspaper. The tiny blue flame peeked and disappeared. She felt vaguely guilty for using the lighter for its actual purpose. It was, after all, a powerful object that housed a piece of Devin's soul, but the cold that had earlier felt like a whisper had become a full on scream. Pressing her blue lips together, she gave the lighter another flick.

The newspaper erupted into flames, and at the same moment Abby saw Vesta.

* * * *

The Vepar was moving through a thick tangle of woods, skeletal branches snatching at her long hair, wet from the rain. She thrust her forearm in front of her and muttered a slur of profanities. A deep, condescending chuckle snaked behind her, and Abby saw the Vepar, Tony, his hunched face grimacing in delight at Vesta's obvious frustration. The branches scraped him as well, but he paid no mind, more interested in watching Vesta as she hurried ahead of him, her stride a mixture of rush and apprehension.

"I had an omen today," Tony whispered meanly, boring holes into Vesta's back with his dark gaze. "A black hound in the forest."

"Sure that wasn't the mirror?" she snapped.

"Oh, no, little girl. Though in your naiveté I understand the confusion. It takes time to learn the black world – time and something else. Something that you do not have."

She turned her head and noticed that he had moved closer. She pulled a branch out of her way and let it fling back, but he caught it before it struck his face.

"I ate the hound, and you know what I saw?"

She ignored him.

"I saw you, Vesta. Ripe, fresh, Vesta. I saw you, and I think that today you will die."

She stumbled, fell to her hands and knees and then stood, hurriedly. He reached her, but did not pass, falling back. She did not like him behind her.

"The Lourdes has news for you," Tony hissed.

"So what," she cut him off, not bothering to turn around. "The Lourdes is deranged, and this is a prank." She hoped, but no, hope was for the weak, and she was strong.

"Tisk tisk," he told her haughtily. "Tobias has used her guidance many times. I must wonder why you're so quick to disregard her. Unless, of course, it's jealousy."

Vesta's shoulders stiffened at this comment. "Jealous?" she spat. "Of a disgusting old witch? Hardly."

Not jealous exactly, but afraid. Afraid because the witch had powers that surpassed hers, and the witch yearned for Tobias. Whether to love him or devour him, Vesta did not know.

"Au contraire," he continued, his skinny lips crackling into a smile to reveal blackened teeth. "I have seen her looking most delectable."

Vesta did not retort, but spat rudely into the bushes as if trying to remove the taste of the Lourdes from her mouth.

The Red Willow appeared before them. Water gushed over the long tentacles and flowed onto the ground, pulling some of the slimy redness into rivulets that cut through the green grass. Vesta stepped around these, but Tony sloshed through them, the red water splashing onto his faded black jeans.

They ducked below the willow branches and moved quickly down the root steps into the Lourdes's rotted home. Vesta wrinkled her nose in disgust, more to insult the

Lourdes than out of true revulsion.

The witch no longer sat on the wooden bench. She had moved into the head seat at her table and faced them as they entered. All of her ugliness had been stripped away. Her long, almond hair flowed over each shoulder, tumbling down the front of a silky red gown that clung to her slender frame. Her black eyes sparkled in the candlelight, and she smiled at them hard, not opening her mouth, but winking seductively at Tony, who lifted his eyebrows in return. Despite the alarming attraction that seeped from her, the Lourdes still felt wrong. As if a monster lurked just below the pink skin, waiting to tear it away and reveal itself.

"You have news for us?" Vesta asked evenly.

"Oh, yes," the Lourdes purred, resting her elbows on the table and clasping her slender fingers before her. She cocked her head to the side and placed her small, slightly pointed chin on her knuckles. "I had hoped Tobias would come…"

Vesta sucked in a breath, but plastered a hateful smile on her face. "Tobias has more important things to do…" Vesta's words seemed to have no impact on the Lourdes, who continued to watch Vesta merrily.

"I don't doubt that he's busy elsewhere," she whispered, tracing a finger along her red lips. When she pulled her hand away, a single line of blood remained on her fingertip. Blood that Vesta doubted was her own. "In fact, if my powers are not mistaken, he has no idea that you are here at all."

Vesta glowered at her, but did not confirm.

"Get on with it," Vesta told her angrily, no longer able to hide her contempt.

"If you insist." The Lourdes stood from her chair, her long angular body poking through the flimsy dress.

Tony grunted his approval, but did not speak.

"I was visited today by a young witch," the Lourdes spoke very slowly, watching Vesta's face carefully. "She was looking for her family. She believed that you had taken them…"

Vesta's face remained impassive, but her right eyelid twitched, her thoughts blank and guarded.

"And she believed this because she had something in her possession. A very special—"

"What?" Vesta's annoyance clouded her features, and the Lourdes flicked a blackened tongue over her lips.

"A relic."

Both the Vepars reacted instantly. Vesta moaned as if she'd been socked in the stomach. Tony gasped and then hooted noisily, apparently happy at this bit of information.

"A relic from your last kill, I believe."

"Yes," Tony whispered, rubbing his big meaty hands together. "This is your end, little girl."

Vesta turned on him, baring her pointed teeth, her features twisted; a scared animal ready to fight. He only smiled and she faltered, her face returning to its previous form.

"Where is she?" Vesta turned back to the Lourdes.

"Well, that all depends…" the Lourdes trailed off, leering at Vesta's distress.

* * * *

In the shack, Abby collapsed onto her hands and knees, and the lighter skidded several feet away.

"I knew she was bad. I knew it," Abby whispered aloud, the panic in her voice scaring her more.

The Lourdes had contacted Vesta, and now they would come for her. Vesta was mad about the relic, mad because she could be watched now, watched without her knowing.

She rose shakily to her feet and looked around the dingy shack. There were no weapons, no phones to call for help.

Why hadn't she tried to learn more? Why hadn't she practiced her powers?

Devin appeared suddenly, startling her backwards toward the tiny fire that crackled behind her. The newspapers had burned and the couch arm let off billows of greenish smoke that smelled like chemical sealers, probably toxic to breathe.

"Destroy the relic, now!" Devin shrieked, hurtling her vapory frame across the room.

Abby stumbled further back and then stood her ground, shoving a strand of wet hair from her face.

"You sent me to her," Abby accused, pointing a finger at Devin. "And now she's given me to them."

Devin's eyes flashed, the effort causing everything except her eyes to disappear and then return, this time less solid than before.

"Why did you do this?" Abby pleaded, anger giving way to desperation.

"You must destroy it now. They will come for you…"

"No," Abby shook her head. "No way."

Devin lunged toward her, and Abby expected the impact as their bodies collided, but she felt only a rush of cold and then nothing. Devin was gone again.

Rain continued to beat on the roof, and wind howled in the trees like haunted wind chimes. Abby was trapped. The shack groaned and shook with the tempest.

Still cold, but too nervous to sit in front of the fire, she paced the room, avoiding the water cascading into the kitchen. She picked up the lighter and flicked it repeatedly, swearing and then crying when it refused to light. The Lourdes would have directed them right to her. But would they think to check the shack? Or would they continue to the map's final destination? A destination probably no more significant than a patch of weeds. She had been tricked.

"Think, think," she murmured to herself, flexing and extending her fists.

Elda had shown her some basics on manipulating water. But how could that help against two murderous Vepars? In the few conversations she'd had about them, the details were blurred. When it counted, she had nothing useful to go on. Were they stronger than her? Faster? Could they move things without touching them?

Time flew and dragged in unison. Her body ached with the effort of trying to move objects about. She had succeeded in lifting the ragged couch an inch, before it dropped back to the floor, vomiting a stream of stuffing into the air. She had opened and closed the door twice, levitated a sheet of newspaper and turned a puddle of rain into ice. Each activity took mounds of mental and physical strain, all of which left Abby feeling exhausted and headachy. At least twenty minutes had passed since seeing Vesta at the Lourdes's lair, and though they had not arrived, intuition told her that they were coming. She considered leaving the shack, but feared their paths crossing in the open.

Her body felt hot, feverish even, a result of her heavy concentrating, and she'd put the fire out long ago, fearing that the Vepars would track her by the smoke in the air.

Bursts of uncontrollable grief plagued her, thoughts for her family, who might already be dead, for Sebastian, who she might never see again, even for Nick. His watery eyes swam before her, and she shook the thoughts away, afraid that they sucked even more of her quickly dwindling energy.

She should not have left the castle so abruptly. If she had gone to Elda, a better plan would have been concocted.

Perhaps Elda would have come with her. Instead, like a fool, she had run away, intending to fight the unknown evil on her own. Now she would probably die for it.

Outside, the rain slowed to a dull trickle. The steady stream pouring into the kitchen faded to a drip…drip that grated on her nerves until they felt raw and exposed.

She picked the lighter up and stood near a window, staring out at the glistening forest. It would not come to life, and each frustrated flick rubbed against the tender skin of her thumb. She knew Devin was controlling the image in the lighter. She did not know when the realization hit her, but it had. Devin was angry and intentionally preventing her from seeing Vesta's whereabouts. Her compassion for Devin had all but died, and just as she prepared to fling the lighter across the room, a voice drifted through the open window.

"You see, Vesta, she was telling the truth, there is the shack," Tony's booming voice rang in Abby's ears, and she clenched her eyes shut in a spasm of fear. They were close, very close.

"Just because the markers are true does not mean we will find the witch. The Lourdes likes to play her games. I'll believe it when I see it," Vesta's voice was strained, and Abby knew she was afraid. Not afraid of Abby, but afraid of the repercussions awaiting her.

"Oh, we'll find her all right. I'd bet your life on it." Tony's laughter rang out at his own joke, but Vesta did not retort.

Abby pressed herself against the wall and moved to the glassless window nearest the voices. They were so close that she could smell them – one of them anyway. An odor coppery like blood and something more bitter, animal sweat maybe, poured into her flared nostrils. She could hear their shuffling feet, the variations in their breathing. She wondered if they could smell her as well.

"Don't ya have your little ring, Vesta?" he taunted her. "You know they only give those tools to Vepars in whom they sense weakness?"

"Tobias will make you pay for this disrespect," she growled.

"Oh, no, my dainty moth, it is you who will pay…" he trailed off, laughing under his breath.

"Let's check that dump," Tony said, his heavy footfalls silent.

"No, we have no time to waste on juvenile exploring," Vesta snapped, not slowing.

"I'll catch up with you, then. Of course, alone you might not make it," he told her, mock uncertainty in his voice. "It'd be a shame to let the witch get to you before Tobias."

Vesta did not reply, but Abby knew that she had stopped. She could hear her shallow breathing only feet away from Tony's.

"Fine, then, I will wait, but hurry up."

Abby's skin crawled, danger flaring in her brain like a never-ending fireworks display. She moved back from the wall, planting each foot gently, careful to avoid dried leaves or newspaper. She could hear Tony circling around the shack, searching for the door.

"Looks to me like we got some pretty recent footprints here," he called out hungrily as he closed in.

Chapter 28

Reluctantly, Sebastian handed several of Claire's journals to Elda.

"Don't worry, I will give them back," she said. "Also, I wanted to show you something in the Astral Coven's *Book of Shadows*."

She flipped the book open and pointed at the line of names. "Blake and Daniels, both here," she said, running her fingers along the page.

"Devin and Abby are in that book?" he asked, surprised.

"Yes. Abby's grandmother, Arlene. Amazing, it only skipped a generation."

"Arlene, she knew my grandmother."

"Yes, though I do not believe that she was a witch. In fact, it's possible that Arlene was watching your family's bloodline, but she died before your sister was born."

Sebastian looked up as the door opened, but it was only Bridget with coffee.

"Abby's still not awake?" he asked.

Bridget, avoiding his gaze, left the room and Elda continued to stare at the book.

Sebastian had a strange feeling – something was off.

"Is Oliver still doing okay?"

"Oh, yes, he is well." Elda smiled and pointed at a page. "Here is your great grandmother Isabelle."

Sebastian had seen the name already. Claire had shown it to him, though neither he nor Claire knew their great grandmother.

"I think I should wake her," he said, leaving his coffee untouched.

"No, Sebastian," Elda said suddenly as he neared the library door.

He turned to face her, but found that he did not want to look too closely at her eyes.

"What happened?" he asked.

* * * *

Abby did not wait for the door to burst open. She moved quickly and quietly into the tiny bedroom, seeking not refuge, but a means of escape. There was a small hole where a window had once been. Branches poked into the room. As the front door banged in, she leapt, using all of her strength to pummel herself out of the shack. The bushes caught her, slowing her hurling body, but the strength of her jump ripped them from the earth, leaving a few tangled around her calves and waist. She landed with a wet thud on a patch of soggy grass, adrenaline causing Vesta's scream to die out in her ears.

Her legs instantly sprang forward, almost leaving her torso behind in the rush to flee from her chasers. She felt a hand, for only a second, clasp her shirt, but jerked away before they could take hold. The trees rushed at her like the jumping adversaries in a 3-D movie, but she dodged them easily, throwing her weight from side to side, sometimes pushing off the thick trunks to propel herself onward.

Behind her, Vesta and Tony crashed through the forest. He snarled as he ran, plowing over the smaller trees and occasionally banging against the larger ones, removing massive hunks of bark in his wake. Vesta, much more agile, sprinted, leaping high and fast like a carnivorous deer.

Abby wanted to jump and searched frantically ahead with her eyes for a branch, but feared their strength. What if they leapt easily onto the branch beside her? What if Tony caught her in midair and pulled her to the ground? No, she had to run and pray that she could gain some distance.

Overhead, the rain picked up again, abandoning the gentle pitter-patter for a torrential downpour. The leaves and pine needles became dangerously slick, but Abby could feel the energy as it built inside of her. Every muscle and fiber in her body twitched excitedly, and she sensed the gap growing as the two Vepars fought to maintain her quickening pace. Blinking furiously, she watched the trees up ahead. The pines gave way to wide-berthed elms and oaks, their ripe green leaves flapping as the rain beat against them. The sound of Vesta and Tony died, leaving only the bawling rain and her pounding feet as noise.

As she moved into the thicket of elms and oaks, she spotted a thick branch twenty yards ahead of her and at least forty feet into the air. She did not know if she could spring that high, but felt a glimmer of hope in the image of that branch. Ten feet away, she focused all of her energy into her calves and thighs, swinging hard with her arms as she jumped. The branch moved toward her swiftly, but almost five feet below it, too far to reach with her outstretched arms, her jump ran out of power. Her legs flailed wildly in the air and she fell back to the earth with a hard smack and an audible crunch as the bones in her left foot shattered. She did not know if she screamed, aware only of the awful explosion of pain that snaked through her foot and up her leg.

Wanting to lie on the ground and howl in agony, she overcame the pain and rolled across the forest floor into a pile of weeds that barely reached over her head. The pain slowed, but the rain beat on. Within seconds, Tony and Vesta sped by, their bodies a blur in the downpour. Abby held her breath as they passed, fearing their ability to hear her, or worse yet, sense her pain.

* * * *

The rain released its stronghold and returned to a monotonous drizzle that gently pelted her throbbing limbs. Within minutes of her crash-landing, her leg began to heal. The bones made a soft grinding sound like gnashing teeth, but the pain of their recovery burned with the ferocity of a California wild fire. It did not merely cling to her foot and ankle, but traveled up her thigh, into her stomach and eventually her head. Unable to watch for the Vepars through the agony, she clenched her eyes closed and focused on invisibility. She had no idea if it were even possible, but could think of no other option.

The crash of branches and bushes deeper in the woods taunted her. Not sure if they were moving towards her or away, she waited, her face slick with rain and sweat. The muddy grass below her felt was slippery and reptilian, as if thousands of tiny wet snakes writhed beneath her.

"Abby?" The whisper slid beneath her discomfort and penetrated; it was familiar, but so faint.

She struggled onto her elbows, her stomach still planted firmly on the ground, her legs splayed out behind her. She searched the woods, her eyes narrowing on every tree and shrub, but nothing popped out. Were they trying to trick her?

"Abby, where are you?" the voice came again, closer now and mad.

Through the mist to her left, Abby watched in wonder as Dafne's reedy figure emerged. Her long black hair was wet and plastered to the pink tank top that hung loosely from her bony shoulders. Her eyes were narrowed, searching, but she had not spotted Abby hidden in the weeds.

Dafne walked closer and Abby could see that her jeans were soaked, slowly sagging down to reveal two very pronounced hipbones.

"I'm here," Abby croaked, poking her head above the weeds and lifting an arm to wave.

"What happened?" Dafne demanded, moving to Abby's side and staring down at her with disapproval.

"I—" But Abby was silenced by Tony as he barreled out of the woods and plowed into Dafne. Her body flew like a rag doll and smacked into a tall oak tree, coming to rest at its base.

Abby felt a scream bubble inside of her, but did not release it because Tony did not seem to see her. He stood, a crooked grin on his grotesque mouth, surveying the damage that was Dafne. Dafne struggled feebly, her head like a rag doll flopped at an awkward angle.

Vesta sprinted from the woods behind him, her long, talon-like fingers curled as if ready to fight. She slowed as she saw Dafne crumpled on the forest floor.

"Dafne," Vesta hissed in delight.

"She's mine," Tony roared, pushing his ugly face close to Vesta's. She drew back and bared her teeth, but said nothing.

"Where is the other?" she asked, as Tony circled the fallen Dafne, licking his lips as if he could already taste her.

"Not my concern." He knelt down beside her and ripped a handful of black hair from her scalp, shoving it to his nose and breathing deeply. Dafne let out a weak squeal and attempted to fight him groggily, but her arms went limp. He lifted Dafne's thin wrist to his revolting mouth and sank his teeth into her flesh. Any movement from Dafne ceased as the venom took hold and carried her to unconsciousness.

Abby felt tears begin to stream over her cheeks, followed by annoyance at her fragility. She stared at the two Vepars, her blood hot with shame and anger. Concentrating her rage upward, a thick, leafy tree branch above them split and fell. The branch struck Vesta in the shoulder and sent her onto her knees in the dirt, but Tony leapt out of the way. He looked around wildly, searching for the source of power that he knew was there. Abby felt his eyes rove over her, once, twice, but no dawning appeared. He could not see her, almost as if her prayer for invisibility had worked, but Dafne had seen her.

Before she could give it further thought, Tony buried his hand in Dafne's hair and started away, dragging her limp body through the forest. He looked like a Neanderthal, lugging his club through the dirt behind him. Vesta struggled to her feet, shook her head once and followed.

* * * *

For several excruciatingly long minutes, Abby waited for her foot to heal completely. Finally, only a dull tingling remained where shattered bones had been. She stood, placed weight on it gingerly, then more when no pain alighted. Ahead of her, she could hear Vesta and Tony and, more importantly, Dafne – the wet crunching of her body dragged across the forest floor.

The branch that she had amazingly snapped with her thoughts had been the very one she'd attempted to jump to and missed. "That's vengeance for you," she thought wryly and stared up into the trees, looking for a more suitable match. A bit further ahead, a long, thick branch snaked between two trees. It was at least ten feet lower than her previous choice, and she went for it without thought. Her recently injured leg sprang easily, her body shooting up. Branches and leaves slapped at her face, but this time she did not miss, landing on the branch with two feet firmly planted.

Any remaining fears of height dissipated as she leapt across the tree limbs. Her sneakers slid on the wet bark, but she did not fall. Not only was she more powerful as a witch, but her balance had improved tenfold.

A small red squirrel began to keep pace with her. He leaped from branch to branch in a group of elms to her left, his bushy tail shivering in fear and delight. A risk taker, she imagined. One of the squirrels that defended his turf at all costs. She was so distracted watching him, she nearly passed right over the enemy, but Tony's low gravelly voice caught her attention and she slowed, trying to quiet her movement above them.

"You need to finish her," Vesta snapped, her fingers balled into fists. She paced the forest floor, shooting distrustful glances at Dafne's slumped figure.

"Not yet," Tony told her quietly. "We have no tools. The ritual is the most important thing. Plus—" He grinned. "I want her to be awake. I want to see her eyes when I sink my teeth into her flesh."

Abby could only see the top of his head, the reddish brown hair a snarled mass on his uneven scalp. His hunched frame heaved up and down with excitement. He took a few lunging steps towards Vesta, who quickly jumped out of range.

"Stay back!" he howled, rushing at her again.

This time Vesta stood her ground, her fists clenching and unclenching. Something was happening. Abby could feel it, like electricity in the air. Overhead, the dimming sky began to darken. The sun had set far in the west, and the remaining orange caresses had slipped away, leaving a slowly blackening dusk. Abby knew that night stalked them now. The summer sun would set, releasing a navy mask poked with thousands of tiny sparkling holes. Long shadows slowly enveloped the forest floor, but Abby could still see the scene below clearly. Her night vision improved daily.

In front of her, the small red squirrel chattered loudly.

He placed a tiny, clawed foot carefully before him and pressed his bulbous nose into the air. He could smell the Vepars below, and more than that, he could smell danger. Abby watched the skin of his back crawl with fear. He looked at her for another moment and then fled, his twig-like legs sending him into the black trees beyond.

Both of the Vepars growled now. Abby could see Vesta's sharp white teeth bared in an inhuman snarl. Her pretty face peeled away, replaced by a creature with bulging eyes and sharp skeletal cheekbones. Abby could not see Tony's face, but had no doubt that it had transformed as well. Below them, Dafne moaned, her head slowly lifting from her chest and slumping to the side.

Tony took a step toward her, but Vesta lunged, a gurgling cry ripping from her throat as she landed on his hunched back. Dafne, awakened by the screech, started to backpedal on the forest floor, her bare heels digging into the muddy ground, her sandals lost. Her face, disoriented, fought to understand the chaos into which she'd awakened, but could not clear the fog that the venom had created.

Abby, sensing a moment of weakness, dropped from the tree. She landed with a thud next to Dafne, bent quickly and swept her up over her shoulder like a knight in a medieval romance, though Abby felt only terror. Dafne was light, flimsy, like well-worn fabric, and Abby sprang back into the trees as Tony grasped her arrival. He had broken away from Vesta, leaving a gaping hunk of his shoulder in her mouth, and reached for Abby.

For both the Vepars, the sight of Abby broke their murderous spell and they lunged after her as she leapt across the tree branches. They easily kept pace below her, but neither attempted to scramble into a tree behind her. She did not know if they could jump and grab her, but dared not slow and find out.

Ahead of her, a clearing of trees appeared, and she faltered, feeling Dafne's weight shift, and almost plunged back to the forest floor. Abby bent quickly, Dafne rolled slightly down her back and then she readjusted her, wrapping her like a silk scarf around her neck. Though Dafne had initially felt weightless, Abby's shoulders began to ache and her legs trembled beneath her.

I have to set her down, she thought wildly, but knew that she could not. The Vepars circled hungrily below her, like sharks frenzied by the taste of blood.

For a moment, a splitting pain shot through her head, and she saw Faustine's frantic face floating there. His mouth moved but no sound emerged, and then she was back in the forest, the vision and the pain gone.

Vesta had begun to crawl up the tree, and Abby realized, with relief, they could not simply jump and retrieve her, but they could climb. Vesta's long nails sank deep into the bark, her teeth grinding as she propelled herself upward.

Abby turned to her right and jumped into another tree and then another. The balls of thick leaves made her transport more difficult. On her back, Dafne groaned again, painfully. A tall tree stood in the distance and she felt if she could just reach it, she might be able to climb high enough to lose them. As her feet left the branch another sharp pain shot across her head. This time it was not a vision of Faustine, but a hard blast to the back of her skull. Her body bucked in the air, Dafne tumbled from her back, and she felt a spurt of blood spray onto her neck. They'd hit her with something. As she pummeled toward the ground, she knew that, and, worse, she knew that Tony waited anxiously below.

Chapter 29

Abby came to and felt the hard ground beneath her. Time had lapsed, most likely a result of the slow moving venom that the Vepars carried in their teeth like anatomical warfare. Slimy walls rose up on either side of her, dark torches burned in black iron holders, and shadows slid across every surface. Her mind felt coated with a thin layer of fuzz, and a low buzzing droned in her ears. She turned her head to the side, a bout of nausea washing over her. Dafne was nowhere in sight; no one was. She lay alone in a cavernous room all too familiar. The same place where she had seen Vesta during one of Devin's visions. Vesta and many other Vepars. They had taken her and Dafne home.

Far off, behind a heavy wooden door, a shrill cackle rose into the air, echoing wildly off the walls and making Abby break out in a clammy sweat. The laugh sounded like the kind of psychosis played in carnival madhouses to scare children as they walked through mirrored rooms. Abby did not recognize it, but sensed it belonged to a Vepar and that there were many nearby.

She struggled to a sitting position, ignoring the warnings of queasiness. Although she felt dazed, she could function and think. She could see a mark where one of them had bit her hand, but already it was almost healed. Their venom was not as strong in her. She knew it, not only by how she felt now, but also by watching Dafne. Dafne had been almost completely unconscious, but Abby was not. Her legs were shackled to the cave floor, thick metal chains wrapped around her shins, but nothing held her arms. Nothing, because they did not really believe she would wake up anytime soon. They had discarded her, knowing that their venom circulated in her blood.

Now what? Abby asked herself silently, studying the mostly empty room. A few other metal chains lay strewn across the floor. She tried to pull on the chains, rip them free, but they did not budge. There was no available water source, which meant she'd be weaker here, and she couldn't afford to waste time. They would hear her and they would come.

Lying back against the dirt-caked floor, she closed her eyes and thought of Faustine. He had appeared to her out there in the trees, his face frantic and searching. Why?

If only she could get some water, some extra source of energy. What was Dafne's sign again? Fire, the south facing Watchtower. But what did it matter if Dafne was unconscious?

She carefully retraced her time at the castle again, searching out any information that might help her get free, find Dafne and then escape. She remembered Max telling her that some witches could travel through other elements while in their astral body.

Closing her eyes, she forced herself to relax. She imagined moving easily through the slab-like walls around her, passing through other caverns. If she could find water…

Her body began to feel weightless and she focused her energy on that, mentally reciting the adolescent magic, 'light as a feather, stiff as a board.' She did feel light as a feather, but not stiff at all. In fact, she began to feel malleable, like pudding.

When she opened her eyes, she was still inside er body, but it no longer felt finite. Instead, she knew that if she sat up, she could step out of her body completely. Max had told her that it was very dangerous to leave her physical body while enemies were present, but what choice did she have?

Sitting up was more like oozing out. She floated across the floor and entered the wall at its base, expecting a pinch or pressure, but feeling nothing. Within the wall, it was dark and claustrophobic. She waved her arms in large loopy circles, dog-paddling in the walls, she thought humorlessly. Through the wall, she entered another cavernous room, same as the last, but totally empty except for shackles that hung from the walls rather than the floor.

The next room was not empty. A long wooden table, stained with streaks of red, probably blood, stood along one wall. Old, weathered chairs surrounded it, the paint peeling from the chair-backs. Two people, one a Vepar, occupied them. The other, Tane, had his feet propped on the table. He picked vacantly at his teeth, his blond hair soft and fuzzy in the firelight. His jeans were wet and streaked with mud. Abby wondered if he'd rushed out to see Tony and Vesta's successful hunt. Next to him sat an extremely thin woman, her skin so pale that tiny blue veins streaked like cobwebs beneath it. Her hair was black, short and spiky and stood on end. She wore black leather pants and a clingy red halter-top, the bones of her chest jutting out like an accordion. The title *Satan's Stripper* crossed Abby's mind, and if she'd had a mouth, she might have laughed. Tane whispered something in the Vepar's pointed ear and she cackled excitedly, the cackle that Abby had heard a short while ago.

In the next room, Abby found Dafne. She hung limply, her body shackled to the wall, a small bucket beneath her. It collected a thin pool of blood that dripped ceaselessly from her right arm. The blood, which appeared to be coming from the bite mark on her wrist, trailed over her palm and down her middle finger, dropping noiselessly into the container. Tony sat across the room, saliva trickling from his scaly red lips, his glassy eyes trained on Dafne's immobile figure.

As Abby passed before him, he looked up as if he sensed her, but quickly turned back to Dafne, engrossed in his prey.

Drifting up, she entered a thick slab of rock that stretched on and on as if the Vepars lived in the solid rock core of the earth that scientists were always trying to penetrate. Finally, the rock began to give way to dirt, and here Abby struck gold. Well, not gold, but water. It dribbled in a slow stream, meandering through the clay and sand like a snake in the grass. She followed it eagerly, passing earthworms and ant trails, long, skinny white vines and thick tree roots. The water began to quicken and the stream grew, flooding forward as if drawn by an unseen magnetic force. She found the force moments later, a long spraying waterfall that fell out from the cliff. The cliff jutted steeply down to a black ravine, the water thick and shining like oil. The waterfall itself grew as it neared the cliff edge and spurted out in a cascading torrent that looked, to Abby, like heaven. If she could have dived, she would have, but instead she drifted lazily through the water, feeling nothing, but a low vibration inside.

A loud thump brought her back to her body and she nearly snapped her eyes open in shock. Remembering, at the last minute, that the Vepars believed she was unconscious, she held perfectly still and prayed that they had not seen the flutter of her eyelids as she'd reentered her body.

"I got her good." Vesta spoke loudly, boasting about the seemingly unconscious Abby on the floor.

"Yeah, you did." Abby recognized Tane's voice. "You gonna wait for Tobias?"

"Yes, of course," she snapped irritably. "Tobias is my creator, my...my everything."

"Yeah," Tane agreed, but he did not sound convinced.

To Abby, Vesta sounded like a battered woman, in love out of fear more than anything else.

"I doubt Tony's gonna wait," Tane joked.

"Then he is a fool," Vesta spat, and Abby heard her

feet as she stomped from the room. Tane scurried behind her and Abby opened her eyes slowly.

She lay alone again, but Tane was probably right. Tony did not look like the patient type.

The Vepars had said that Tobias was on his way.

She did not have time to dwell on the possibilities. Instead, she focused hard, seeing the water that flowed far above her. She imagined the rock walls were sponges that the water seeped down through. At first, she felt nothing, no pull beyond her body, only a murmuring self-doubt that turned every second into ten. Then the vibrations began, a reenactment of her first encounter with the stone slab. Perspiration broke out on her upper lip, but she ignored it, needing desperately to keep the connection forming within her. The tiny blue ball of light materialized in her head, pulsing like a lung. In her mind's eye, the rock walls cracked, creating a tiny seam that the water quickly leached into. The pressure within the cracks grew, producing even larger fissures that flooded with water. In the room, Abby's entire body had begun to vibrate, the blue ball slipping down her spine. She could hear the water, the hiss as it fought its way toward her.

She focused on the water, reaching out with invisible hands, pushing it mechanically toward the cavern where Dafne hung, her captor greedily awaiting his chance to devour her. The water pooled above the ceiling, toppling upon itself, the weight growing exponentially. If it had been anything but rock, it would have bowed down, giving the Vepar some warning of the danger that lay above. Instead, he saw nothing and heard nothing, too immersed in his fantasies of death and power. When the water had reached what Abby believed to be maximum capacity, she forced the entirety of her energy against it.

The ceiling over Tony shattered, water and rock

flooding into the room. He had not even thought to blink when the first slab struck him hard in the back, pitching him out of his chair and onto his hands and knees. He cried out, but too late, water poured into his mouth and throat, cutting off his cries. Within seconds, the entire room was submerged and the water, close enough to heighten Abby's strength, gave her the intensity needed to rip the chains from the ground that she lay shackled to.

She burst from the room and into the dark hallway beyond. A single yell of surprise echoed in the distance as the water began to fill the hall and give away the mutiny occurring within the cave's depths. The chains, still hooked to her feet, clanged metallically as she sprinted through the flood, finding Dafne's cavern easily, as the entire door frame spouted water. She wrenched it open, the outpouring of water not slowing her, but providing her with another burst of raw power. Tony thrashed wildly beneath the surface, he might have been suffocating, but Abby knew that he would not drown. He could not be killed that way. Dafne, still unconscious, floated at the top of the water, her head barely above the surface, the binds keeping her tightly against the wall. Soon she would go under completely, but Abby had to go for Tony first.

She did not have to swim, moving easily in the submerged room, her feet planted on the stone floor. She searched the murky water and spotted what she needed, a long, pointed piece of rock, maybe a foot in length. She grabbed for it and missed. Tony took his shot and dived into her back, but he was weak and panic-stricken with the water thrusting him down and she merely shrugged him off. He turned and swam frantically for the doorway, water still pouring from the hole above. She grabbed him, pulled him beneath and found another shard of rock, this one dull, but maybe if she shoved hard enough…

He jerked and turned, his face bulging as she allowed him above the surface. Her fist was wrapped tightly in a swath of his shirt. She was disgusted by the proximity to his swelling eyes and writhing body as she slipped the slice of rock into the hem of her pants. Panic leaked from him, making his retaliation loose and unsuccessful. He grabbed at the hand that held his shirt and pressed hard. Abby felt her bones bend and then something cracked, a blinding pain that somehow focused her attack, giving heat to the boiling energy within her. She dragged Tony toward his chair and struggled onto it, jerking both their heads above water while he kicked at her futilely, his legs rarely finding their target.

"Where is my family?" she shrieked, her face only an inch from his, and the reek of his breath acrid in her nose.

He flung his head toward her, snapping his teeth and narrowly missing her chin, which she jerked away swiftly. She brought up her right hand, the one that was most likely broken and also most likely healing itself, and wrapped it around his neck, her small fingers digging into his flesh. It was like molding playdough. He scowled and struggled, but she held fast.

"My family?" she screamed again.

His face was purple and his rapid head shakes were turning into giant sways like a ship in a stormy sea. She loosened her hand, but only enough to allow him a single gulp of air, sufficient for the breath to answer.

"No family," he croaked. "We don't have 'em."

It crossed her mind not to believe him, to continue squeezing until the truth popped out like a cork from a champagne bottle, but Dafne distracted her. Her head had dipped below the water, and the brief diversion gave Tony the chance that he needed. He lunged away from her, ripping free of her hand and planting a solid side-kick to her stomach. Even in his terror, his aim was spot on and she felt his foot sink into the softness of her flesh and connect. A breath rushed out and she doubled over, her head back below the water, a good place apparently, as it instantly brought her attention back fully to Tony and away from her pain.

In a single movement, she pulled the rock from her pants and seized a wad of his stringy hair. She did not hesitate, even as Tony tried to buck away. Her good hand moved swiftly, slicing across the water and forcing the blunt stone sword up and into his stomach. It caught in the thick sinewy threads of bone and muscle encased there, but she had aimed with precision and missed the hard steel-like grate that protected the evil within. Black blood poured out, filling the water like spilled ink, but she shoved harder, further and felt the moment that she reached the pouch deep inside of him. It burst like a ripe grape and howled as if it had a life of its own. Tony's face twisted in hate and then agony and then nothing. His eyes shrank like pitted prunes and his lips turned in, shriveling into the black hole of his mouth. Abby turned her face away, sickened and fighting to see through the blackness that had swarmed out of him.

Dafne's head was beneath the water and when Abby saw her she remembered Sydney, her dead, bloated face. Time was running short. Soon the others would reach the room, or worse yet, Dafne would drown. Abby reached her, and rather than grabbing Dafne's body, she grabbed the thick black chains that held her. With a single fierce tug she ripped them from the wall. Dafne floated lazily towards her. Abby grasped her tight around the waist and kicked hard against the floor, pushing herself back towards the open doorway. The hallway had flooded. Abby waded through waist high water, some of her energy lost as she dragged Dafne away from the room of swirling black blood.

In the hallway ahead, Vepars yelled. She saw one emerge from the room where she'd been held captive. A long, stone stairway appeared on her left and she took it, running despite the chains that still hung from her legs and Dafne's weight in her arms. The stairs were slippery and Abby fell once, feeling a shot of pain in her elbow as it struck the step above her. The Vepar chasing her screamed words she did not understand, or perhaps did not want to understand. The ball of blue energy had disappeared and Abby knew that she now worked on sheer willpower. Up and up she went, ignoring other tunnels and hallways, praying that she'd break the surface soon, searching for any sign that daylight lay ahead. The Vepar behind her—the pixie-ish girl Abby had seen with Tane—was gaining on her. The loud slaps of her feet echoed loudly in Abby's ears and sounded much faster than her own steps that dragged with each lift.

Suddenly she felt a force—a sort of sixth sense—pull her to a tunnel on her left. Afraid that she might be running right into the Vepars' arms, but too exhausted to continue up, she took it. It twisted endlessly, but Abby did not slow, even when her feet left the rocky ground and she was airborne, she still kicked as if running on the air. A second of disorientation grasped her as she flailed in the wide, open sky. She had let go of Dafne, and they were both falling fast. She felt the rush of the waterfall and spotted the black ravine below, before plunging in feet first.

Chapter 30

A gentle slap against her cheek brought Abby's world back. She struck out, narrowly missing Dafne's jaw, her face leaning worriedly over Abby's own.

"It's okay, it's just me," Dafne said, her voice strangely apologetic.

Abby sat up and looked around. They were on a patch of rocky beach that hugged the foaming river. Tiny gray pebbles marred the white sand. Tall, rocky cliffs hugged the beach on all sides; they sat in the small canyon that it created. She searched frantically for the waterfall, but it was nowhere in sight.

"Don't worry, we drifted quite a ways, I think." Dafne's own eyes wandered along the cliffs and then came to rest on Abby's. She looked as if she was struggling to say something, but Abby had a pretty good idea what it was.

"Thank you, you saved me," Dafne finally blurted.

Abby nodded, but did not speak. The memories of their near death were too raw to touch, so she shrugged instead. Her head felt water logged, no, her whole body did, bloated times a million. She imagined if she pinched her skin, river water would trickle out.

"Are we safe here?" she asked suddenly, her eyes darting to the cliffs overhead.

"I think so," Dafne murmured, wincing as a breeze lit across the wounds on her arms and legs. The shackles had dug deep red welts into her skin that had not yet healed. "I did an invisibility incantation, but I don't have any tools, so…"

"So, will it work?" Abby asked, again searching the cliffs, the sky and the river for signs of trouble.

"So far, so good," Dafne said feebly.

"How do we get out of here?" Abby asked finally, noticing for the first time that her shackles were gone as well.

"I removed them," Dafne told her. "And my own." Dafne held out her wrists, and Abby grimaced at the puckered flesh. "Faustine will be here soon."

"Faustine?" Abby asked in disbelief. How could he possibly find them?

"He sent me. When we were both captured, he came for us," Dafne explained. "Telepathy, remember?" She pointed at her head. "Anyway, his connection with me is much stronger than yours, and while I was unconscious he lost us, but when I came to in the river, he reconnected. He's close by now, I can feel him."

Abby nodded and struggled to her feet, feeling weak and nauseated. She had almost thought that the nearby water would give her another surge of strength, but she felt only drained and exhausted. She tottered and nearly fell, but steadied her legs wide apart for balance.

"It happens sometimes," Dafne told her. "The dizziness, when you've really drawn on your energy, it just totally wipes you out."

"I'm starving," Abby said, listening to the angry rumble that stirred in her stomach.

"Yeah, me too." Dafne gingerly touched the pink spot on her scalp where Tony had ripped out her hair. "I wish I healed as fast as you."

Abby gave her a small smile and walked down to the water, staring at her disheveled appearance in the surface. Her hair had dried in what her mother would have called a rat's nest and stuck mostly to the right side of her head. Black streaks that she knew were Tony's blood stained her t-shirt.

"You killed him," Dafne breathed, noticing that Abby

was studying the blood on her shirt. Abby heard a mix of awe, envy and maybe even annoyance in her voice.

"Yeah," she said gravely.

"How did you know—?"

But Dafne did not finish, because on the cliff directly in front of them, Faustine had appeared. He moved down the cliff face easily, his heavy boots knocking hunks of stone and dirt into the river. He was dressed for hiking in green windbreaker pants and a gray Capilene shirt. His face was lined with worry, but he forced a polite smile and offered a curt nod before striding across the beach toward them.

* * * *

Abby, Dafne and Faustine received a warm but concerned welcome on their return to the castle. Sebastian kissed her on the head, but he seemed anxious. They were all bubbling with questions, but none would be answered that day. Instead, Abby slipped silently to her room, barely settling on the bed before sleep stole her from their curious faces.

Sebastian, desperate for reassurance that Abby was in fact okay, settled in a chair beside her, refusing to leave until she woke. Unfortunately, Abby slept for nearly fourteen hours, unaware that every gasp and toss evoked in Sebastian the bitter memories of his sister's death and the constant fear that he would lose Abby as well. When she finally came to, in the early morning hours, Sebastian, exhausted, had drifted off as well. Abby watched his peaceful face, unshaven and grisly, the flutter of his lower lip as he snored. He lay cockeyed on the edge of her bed, his right leg dangling over the side. His red Lake Superior t-shirt looked rumpled.

Abby crept from the bed into the bathroom, scowling at the face peering out from the mirror. Her skin looked sallow, and every surface of her body was coated with blood, dirt or grime. She turned the faucet on the claw footed tub, allowing the water to reach near scalding level, and slipped out of the nightshirt she didn't remember putting on.

As she slid into the water, she allowed her brain to retrieve the memories of the previous few days. Her hands shook as she meticulously scrubbed black smears off her forearms and palms. She had killed Tony, had murdered him. Or perhaps murder was the wrong word. But was self-defense the right one?

She did not know and might have felt guilty, but she could not. Her new mind would not allow the shame that had so closely followed the Abby of her previous life. She was a witch now, and he was an enemy. He intended to kill Dafne, and surely intended killing her if given the chance.

When Faustine had first begun to lead them back to the castle, "back home," as he referred to it, Abby had fought him.

"My parents!" she'd shrieked. "They might still be inside. The Vepars have them."

That was when she had learned the truth. Vesta did not have her parents. No one had her parents. Faustine had already placed a protective barrier around their house after he had learned of Sydney's death. The barrier, according to Faustine, prevented the Vepars from getting closer than the sidewalk and cloaked them when they left the house. If they found a way to reach her parents, he would physically feel their passing and know to act. Devin had only fabricated the story to lure Abby to the Lourdes, who frequently tormented lost souls or witches trapped in relics. The Lourdes was known for using the dead to lure witches and other victims to her lair.

Abby had cried then, and though Faustine had attempted to soothe her, his naturally cold demeanor had fallen flat. He explained the horrible existence for Devin, a witch residing in what he called the middle world. A place of shadows; of existence without life. He told her not to blame Devin, because, despite her wrong actions, her motives had not been all bad. Abby had wanted to believe that, to seek out some good in Devin, but she felt nothing except a cold anger towards her.

Abby knew that Faustine was trying to console her for what had happened. He did not want Abby to fear the new world she had entered.

Faustine talked throughout their trip back to the castle. For the first time, Abby had not cared to hear the information offered so freely. Abby and Dafne had nearly died. Abby had killed. She was now a killer.

She dunked her head beneath the hot water, trying to wash away that thought, but it stayed. A tiny tap sounded on the bathroom door.

"Abby?" Sebastian murmured, his voice sounding groggy.

"Yep, I'm here, Sebastian. I'll be right out."

* * * *

Elda sat in a tall walnut chair, her arms resting easily in her lap. She smiled when Abby walked into the library, but did not speak until she had found a seat. Abby chose one nearest the fire, a thick, rounded chair covered in blush chenille fabric with small gold tassels brushing the floor.

"So," Elda began, lifting a finger to her chin and studying Abby across the room.

Abby maintained eye contact, though it hurt to do so. Guilt gnawed at her insides, creating a constant barrier to any feelings of euphoria that the whole ordeal was over. She felt she had let everyone down, and though no one had said as much, how could it not be true? Dafne had nearly died. Worse, what if they had tortured secrets of the castle out of her? What if, in a state of delirium and pain, she had led them all back to the Coven of Ula?

"Abby, I know you are battling yourself right now," Elda murmured, her long coppery dress shimmering in the firelight. "But those thoughts you're having come from within, only from within."

Abby listened, almost unwillingly, her head bowed as Elda spoke. "But I put everyone in danger," she whined, a juvenile ploy that immediately embarrassed her.

"No, you did not. You trusted your instincts, and right now those feelings still have one foot in your previous life. The life where you don't want to burden anyone with your problems. The life where you don't fully understand the powers we all have individually and as a unit. Dafne saw you leave, Abby. When she alerted the rest of the coven, we took action. She volunteered to find you. We all made choices."

Abby sighed and gave a short nod that hardly reflected belief in Elda's words.

"Listen to what I am saying, Abby." Elda's voice was sharper now. "You are one of us. There is no blame, no single responsibility. Every weight is shouldered by all of us, not one. Never one."

Tears dripped down Abby's cheeks and she pulled her legs up to her chest, hugging them tightly.

"You eliminated an enemy who has killed savagely for over thirty years. Antonio, you killed him, Abby. Do you understand how important that is?"

Abby didn't. How could she? All she had done was follow the directions laid out in a book in their very own library, information that every one of them had access to. Not to mention she killed him to save herself, to save her family, or so she'd thought at the time.

"Abby, of all the witches in our coven, only Oliver, Faustine and Dafne have ever successfully killed a Vepar."

"How is that possible?" she asked in disbelief.

"It is possible because they are very difficult to murder. They're evil, their power and their desire for our blood makes them the most horrific of enemies. To kill them means to get close enough to taste their scent, feel their fingernails on your skin." Elda shuddered. "We have found that they kill us more frequently than we do them."

Again, Abby stared incredulously at Elda, fighting the urge to shake her head, "no."

"It's true," Elda confirmed. "That's why we created Covens. That's why we band together. Only our hunters, Oliver and Dafne, seek out the Vepars and only if threatened."

"But why?" Abby demanded. "Why not just rush in and attack? Take all of them down in their cave or hole or whatever it is they live in?"

Elda sat up straighter and rotated a smoky quartz ring on the middle finger of her right hand. Finally she spoke. "Abby, the Vepars surpass us in some ways. Not all of them, of course, but enough. They have a direct link to the darkest magic that exists. They can conjure the dead. They can bring people back."

This final remark sent a strip of chills down Abby's spine, and she burrowed further into the chair, pulling her thin black cardigan more closely around her.

"How?" she croaked.

"That, I do not know," Elda replied, standing and moving towards the fire. She rested a hand on the mantle, fingering a small silver picture frame. In the frame, a sepia colored photo revealed a row of smiling faces. They may have been ordinary people, but Abby doubted it. Their clothing dated them, maybe 1920s or 30s. The men wore tuxedos, the women slinky flapper dresses, and the children, three boys, were dressed in matching white tuxedos, their hair combed flat against their melon shaped heads.

"Who are they?" Abby asked, fishing.

"They are a story for another time," Elda whispered, sweeping away from the fire and back to her chair. "Let's talk about the Lourdes."

Abby frowned, but bit back the gurgle of disgust that threatened.

"She was horrible," she told Elda, unconsciously rubbing her palms along her pant legs, as if still trying to remove the red moss that had momentarily pooled within them. "And I think I helped her."

"Perhaps," said Elda simply. "But that is of no matter. What I would like now is for you to understand what the Lourdes is."

"Isn't she a witch?"

"Yes, she is a witch, but she is also one of the Depraved. The Depraved are witches who are seduced by dark magic and choose to align with Vepars."

"Why would they do that?"

"Because Vepars cross lines that ordinary witches will not. You see, Abby, it is part of our contract with the earth to do good with our powers. That is a sacred belief in the witch community, 'Harm None.' The Vepars have no such convictions. If anything, their supreme goal is to murder, maim and destroy anything with even an ounce of good residing in it."

"But why the Lourdes? Why did she go bad?"

Elda paused and stared across the room. Abby saw her eyes settle briefly on the picture over the fireplace.

"Because her child was murdered by a Vepar and she wanted her back," Elda spoke so casually that Abby almost misunderstood.

"Wait, the Vepars killed her kid, and she joined them?"

"Not exactly," Elda hurried on. "You see, the Lourdes was one of the most powerful witches in the world. She could see things, the future, in a way. She was clairvoyant, could tell fortunes, and concoct potions that have never been replicated. The Vepars wanted her badly, and there are witches who are also Vepars, who choose that black world. One such Vepar, Ira, was a man who had a very strange ability. He could block witches who read minds. Not just telepathy, but tarot readings, astrology readings, even dream analyzers. His mind was impenetrable, however, he also had the ability to create thoughts so that a witch attempting to discern him would get whatever message he intended to send. He befriended the Lourdes, and she began to fall in love with him."

Abby shook her head slowly from side to side, almost afraid to hear more.

"Just imagine that? Is he true? Does he love me? Yes, loud and clear and passionate, yes. That's what she heard from his thoughts every time. So she fell for him, and when her daughter, Delphia, was murdered, the Lourdes very nearly went insane. Only her new lover, Ira, consoled her. He conjured thoughts of grief and devastation. Then he showed her a false memory that involved glimpsing Delphia with a group of human men. A group of men supposedly luring her to her death. The Lourdes wanted to kill them, to burn their village to the ground, but Ira convinced her there was another way. 'A Vepar,' he said. 'One whom could help them.' Not only would the Vepar drive mad the men who had murdered Delphia, they would bring her back from the dead. The Lourdes, in her grief, obliged."

Elda stopped, waiting, and Abby slid to the edge of her seat, enraptured with the heinous tale.

"Why couldn't she do it herself?"

"Because our oath is to 'harm none'. It is sacred, and it comes with sacrifice. Sometimes that means losing people you love because revenge is dark. To think it is one thing, but to act it out, that's something else…"

Abby remembered the Lourdes speaking of mothers and daughters.

"Abby, to cross to their side, to become entwined with their evil, is permanent. There is no coming back."

Abby nodded. She did not understand, but wanted desperately to hear Delphia's story.

"The Vepar did as promised. He caused the men to go insane, to kill their own families, to wreak havoc until their own village hanged them. Then he brought Delphia back, but it was not the same Delphia. Her soul, her very nature was gone, replaced by a blackness that permeated her to the core. I will spare you the details except to say that the Lourdes was forced to kill her own child to save herself, and worse yet, to save Ira. This affected the Lourdes as nothing before had. Her abilities disintegrated, they become haphazard, nearly useless. When Ira finally abandoned her, she banished herself to the woods. She used the powers still available to her to make the forest a magical place that constantly shifted between poisonous and enchanting. The Vepar, to whose service she had committed herself, cursed her for weakening. He told her the truth. That he had killed Delphia, that Ira had done his bidding, that the village men were innocent. He told her that, because she had allowed her power to spoil, her physical self would as well. He cast a spell that rendered her physically hideous and which caused everything around her to decay and die. Only in her hole can people be near her and live, but food, plants, even animals, wither within minutes."

When Elda finished, she closed her eyes for a moment, a brief silence for the horrors told.

"I…I don't know what to say," Abby said at last,

J.R. Erickson

battling a storm of emotions. She had hated the Lourdes, hated her, but now…how could she?

"I am not asking you to change what you have seen, but only to truly understand it. That is what absolute truth provides for you, Abby, a light to cast away the shadows of every story. The Lourdes of Warning, as she is now known, was once just Milda, the name her mother gave her after the Lithuanian Goddess of Love. The Lourdes was Milda, a witch and a mother, and that was all."

Abby licked her lips and watched Elda cross the room to the large window that faced the lake. Her hand trembled as she pulled back the French pleated draperies, their caramel color shimmering with the morning sun. Elda looked older then, her face drawn and her body shrunken in her dress. Her smallness scared Abby. It stole the comfort that she sought in the older witch's presence.

* * * *

Oliver placed the arrow against the string and pulled, watching it slice straight up into the sky and then dive back down, landing in a circle of sand he had drawn on the beach.

"Good aim," Faustine said, surprising him from behind.

"Trying to confuse them."

"Yes, I'd say it will work."

"I can't believe she killed Tony."

Faustine nodded and drew a smaller circle inside of Oliver's. He took the bow and an arrow, lined it up and pulled. The arrow drove skyward and then arched, landing directly in the center of his target.

"I learned from the best," Oliver complimented him.

"Not best," Faustine said. "I don't believe in best, but good, now that is something. Abby is a good witch. We are lucky."

338

"Yes." Oliver looked at the earth, at his feet, anywhere but at Faustine.

"It's easier to tell me now," Faustine said.

Oliver cast his eyes around the lagoon, then up at the castle. They were the only two outside.

"Don't worry, we're alone," Faustine reassured him.

"I killed Sydney," Oliver said quietly.

"An accident?"

"Maybe."

Chapter 31

Two weeks after her narrow escape from death, Abby stood at the top of the cliff that jutted above the lagoon furthest from the castle. Below her stretched the choppy Lake Superior waters, the gray black swells tossing like a baby seal in the mouth of a killer whale. Behind her, she could see the shell shaped greenhouse, and if she looked closely, Bridget's fiery red hair as she tottered back and forth among the plants.

Abby was alone, had asked to be alone, and everyone complied. In the weeks since the Vepar encounter, Sebastian had lapsed into himself. He had sat on the edge of her bed that first night, his mouth agape, his eyes a haunted well of sorrow as she told him the tale. When she had described killing Tony, he had squeezed her knee so hard she'd actually gasped in pain. He frantically apologized, and Abby knew that it was more than shock that caused that squeeze. He wanted that blood on his hands, though Tobias was the Vepar that consumed him.

The warm September breeze blew Abby's hair back and she faced into it. Her hands shook as she pulled the small goddess from the back pocket of her jeans. It was smooth and warm and though Abby had fought the idea of ever touching it again, she had eventually come around. Devin's life had been stolen from her, her life as a woman and as a witch. And worse yet, her death had been stolen when Vesta plucked the lighter from the forest floor.

In a small glass bowl, sealed tight, was the elixir that the Lourdes had given her. When Abby had mixed it earlier that morning a pungent aroma had wafted out, followed by thick tendrils of red smoke. Lydie, enthralled by the strange smoke, had almost reached in to touch it, but shrank away when Max had bellowed from the hallway that it was time for another lesson. Now it was only Abby and the goddess, maybe even Abby and Devin, she did not know. Devin had not appeared to her since that day in the woods. Elda believed Devin was afraid that she had angered Abby and did not want to risk eternity in the middle world by further tormenting her. In a way, Devin would have been right, but now Abby felt differently. Time, even a very short amount, could soften wounds that felt too deep to heal.

Abby set the bowl down and then dropped to her knees beside it. Before she pulled off the lid, she gave the lighter a final flick – a farewell perhaps. Before her, the tiny blue flame winked and erupted.

* * * *

Vesta. The Vepar was naked except for a dirt-smeared sheet draped over her emaciated body. Vesta had been thin before, but now she looked skeletal. Her hands, bloodied and bruised, were raised to her face. Black tears streamed from her eyelids and stained the matted, white-blond hair hanging over each shoulder. She knelt on a dirt caked floor, one that Abby recognized nauseously. Vesta looked up and let out an animal wail. Before her, chained to the wall, was Tane. His head drooped onto his naked chest, so thin, the bones stuck through his translucent skin. His hair had fallen out and all of his limbs dangled. Several gashes on his chest and legs were caked with dried blood, red blood because Tane had not yet become a Vepar, and he never would. Tane was dead.

From a black doorway, Tobias emerged. He looked healthy. His tall figure moved gracefully into the room. He looked down at Vesta, his black eyes narrowing in disgust at her wasted body. She looked up at him, a fresh surge of oily tears streaking over her face. She started to speak, but as her lips trembled apart, the vision dissipated and Abby was back on the cliff edge.

She rocked for a moment on her knees, unsteady and shocked by the sight of Vesta and worse yet, of Tane. No amount of hatred for their kind could have inhibited the pity she felt for them in that moment. Vesta's brother had been murdered, and she had been forced to watch and suffer with him.

"Abby," the whisper, thick with misery, caught her and she looked up.

Devin drifted, her faint image flickering, her eyes cast toward the water.

"Devin…" Abby murmured, unable to recite all of the things that she had planned to say, were this moment ever to come. She wanted to tell Devin it was okay, that she understood, that Tobias would pay, but nothing came out. Instead, she smiled and before she could speak, Devin vanished for the last time.

Abby pulled the lid from the glass bowl, recoiling at the scent of moldy meat and dirt that assaulted her. The liquid, a rusted orange color, swayed in the bowl, as if beckoning to the goddess that lay in Abby's palm. She dropped it in, watching the goddess's face disappear. She did not know if anything would happen. After nearly three minutes, the elixir began to boil softly. A thin coil of steam rose up and out, disappearing almost instantly in the breeze. After five minutes, Abby turned the bowl on its side, dumping the remains into the grass, but the lighter had disintegrated. Not even a fleck of metal remained.

Chapter 32

The funeral was lovely, if they ever could be called that. It took place on a sandy bluff that hung suspended over the choppy waters of Lake Michigan on a clear blue day.

Abby attended alone, at least she appeared alone, but Oliver and Dafne crouched nearby, their bodies sensitive to every shift, every energy that beat on the air. Her parents had hugged her briefly; her mother sobbing into her hair and then breaking away. They stood now, arms linked near the dune edge. Her mother stared out at the white swells and remembered a whole lifetime of Sydney that Abby never knew.

Abby pulled her sleeves down over her hands, protecting her skin from the autumn breeze that blew down the lake shore. A man Abby did not know read the words that Sydney had prepared years earlier. The woman couldn't plan a weekend, but had somehow prepared her funeral. A simple ceremony at Old Baldy, a steep dune backed by miles of Sleeping Bear forests. Abby's mother, Becky, read a poem about sisters and then she held a small wooden box to the breeze and let Sydney's ashes rush away.

Abby bit back her grief, knowing that strong emotion often manifested in physical changes, and she didn't want a rainstorm to begin with her tears.

The police had found Sydney's body nearly three weeks after Abby and Sebastian had escaped to the castle. She had been badly decomposed and, without any leads, the Trager police decided that Rod could be the only culprit. Of course, no one had seen or heard from Rod since he and Sydney left for their vacation. He had vanished without a trace, and Abby did not allow herself to consider the possibilities of his demise.

"Sydney, we release you from this earth," the man continued as Becky tilted the box and the last of Sydney's ashes pulled from the corners and caught the wind.

Abby watched the ashes, so fine that she could not connect them to her once vivacious aunt.

"We begin as dust and end as dust," the man continued.

Dust. Abby imagined Sydney's bright blue eyes, their mischievous gleam, and a tidal wave of pain tried to rush over her. Her chest constricted and a sob caught in her throat. She swallowed it back and imagined neutral things: sailboats, upholstery, kitchen appliances. It was a work in progress and Abby had not mastered it, but Elda insisted on its importance, especially in the presence of regular people: i.e. Abby's family. She stared at the horizon, and when the howl of pain that wanted free died away, her eyes drifted to Nick, who stood next to her dad, his hands shoved into his gray blazer.

She had suspected he would attend the funeral, though she was surprised to learn that he rode north with her parents, which meant that he, too, would be spending the night at Sydney's home. She dropped her gaze to the sand, which blew in sheets up over the dune and caught in the prickly grass.

Sebastian had stayed at the castle at Elda's bidding. She insisted it was not safe for Abby and Sebastian to both attend the funeral and cited far more important tasks for him at the coven. Sebastian had been distant since Abby's harrowing Vepar encounter. He stalked the castle and complained about Tobias's continued freedom. Twice he demanded that they allow him to return to the mainland to search for the Vepar's lair, which Abby had mistakenly described to him in detail. Only after Abby begged him to stay did he agree, moodily, but with the promise that he would destroy Tobias whether the other witches assisted him or not.

Abby was relieved that Sebastian had been asked to stay at Ula. She was exhausted processing Sydney's death and seeing her parents without the additional stress of Sebastian trying to hunt down Tobias. She had ridden to Trager with Dafne and Oliver in Oliver's blue jeep. He didn't drive the freeway, but seemed to understand an intricate trail of seasonal roads that snaked through the woods and allowed the three witches to travel the 200 miles with little detection. Excluding, of course, crossing the Mackinaw Bridge, which Abby examined excitedly after Oliver mentioned diving off of it.

"Hey, Abby pants," her dad said, clutching her elbow and surprising her from her thoughts.

She looked up to see Sydney's small group of friends and family breaking apart and picking their way through the woods back to their cars.

"Go apologize to your mom, honey," her dad continued and nudged Abby towards her mother, who stood at the bluff edge as if she might like to drop over the side.

Abby went to her, knowing that the apology was not only inevitable, but invaluable at that moment.

"Mom, I am so very sorry," Abby whispered into her mother's ear, wrapping an arm around her back. "For everything."

Becky sniffled and nodded, but she seemed unable to speak. She sank slowly to the sand and Abby sat with her, leaning her head on her mother's shoulder, bony beneath her black cardigan.

* * * *

Abby did not immediately get out of the car when her

dad pulled to a stop in Sydney's driveway. She took a deep breath and closed her eyes against the flood of memories that the house ignited. In seconds, she flew over years of catching fireflies in Sydney's yard and eating pancakes on the patio. She stumbled over meeting Sebastian, finding Devin, and landed finally, with a jolt, on Sydney's bloated face in the pool of truth.

When she blinked the image away, she realized that Nick had taken her hand and he was talking. Her parents had already gotten out and moved slowly, side by side, across the porch to the front door.

"I'm sorry, what?" Abby asked Nick.

"I was just saying that I've missed you. I mean, I do miss you, and if—"

"Stop." She held up her hand. "This isn't the right time, Nick. I can't have this conversation right now."

He seemed to take this as progress and nodded eagerly. "I totally understand, you're hurting, and I'm here for you, no matter what, okay?"

She smiled weakly and pushed the car door open before he could go on.

As she walked toward the door, she considered the will that Sydney had left – the will that left everything to Abby and her mother. An estate worth nearly two million dollars, not including the lakefront property, which Abby's mother alone inherited.

Abby was now independently wealthy. The thought skidded across her thoughts, but could not find footing. She lived in the coven; money barely made an appearance and the quick thump that resounded in her chest at the figure – a million dollars – had more to do with fantasy than reality. A fantasy that dulled in comparison to the one that she was now living in a castle surrounded by witches. Additionally, Helena had already hinted that witches rarely wanted for anything, least of all money, and had a myriad ways of making it when in need.

Her dad held the door open and Abby followed him in. The house smelled strongly of lemon disinfectant – a scent left over from the cleaning company that scrubbed the house after Sydney's body was discovered. They had fixed the rampage of the Vepars; a mess that the police assumed was created by Rod in a passionate outburst when he murdered his wife. Of course, Rod's body was never discovered and Abby had not considered the possibility that he was still alive.

Chief Caplan had even called Abby to ask for her whereabouts when Sydney died, but he did not remember her as the girl who found Devin, nor did he bother checking her story that she'd spent only a couple of nights at Sydney's home and then traveled into the Upper Peninsula to enroll at Lake Superior State for graduate school. It was an easy lie, one that Caplan and her mother both ate up readily. Abby didn't mind telling it, but it did pain her that Rod was the scapegoat for her and the Vepars, not to mention Devin's brother, Danny. Although Faustine had said the previous week that he intended to exonerate Danny soon; Abby made a mental note to ask him more when she returned to Ula.

Like Danny, Rod's name had been in all of Trager's newspapers along with a grainy mug shot taken when he was sixteen and caught with a bag of marijuana. In the image, he was young with a mischievous smile and wild blond hair. He didn't look like a killer, but the small-town media of Trager was making an example out of Sydney. They seemed to be saying: This is what happens when you leave your husband (and gated community) for a younger man!

"Ugh, get this out of here," Becky groaned and thrust a photo of Sydney and Rod groping each other on a beach towel into Abby's dad's hands.

Becky then dropped onto the couch, her frail body heavier somehow. She leaned her head back and struggled blindly through her purse, finally pulling out a wrinkled pack of menthol cigarettes.

"Are you smoking?" Abby asked, incredulous.

"I figure I've abstained for twenty years. I've earned a few." She knocked one from the pack and lifted it trembling to her lips.

Nick, desperate to get good marks from Abby, scrambled to the fireplace and grabbed a box of matches. He lit one and dropped to a knee in front of Abby's mother, who didn't bother leaning forward, but gestured impatiently for him to come closer.

She drew deep and held the smoke.

Abby's dad returned to the living room with a bottle of wine and four glasses. He cocked an eyebrow at Becky, but she ignored him, taking another drag.

"I'll do it," Nick said, snatching the cork and setting to work on the bottle of Cherry Wine. He seemed unnerved by Becky's smoking. She was usually as square as he.

"So, what do we do now?" Becky asked suddenly, eyeing the room. "Do we sell this place?"

Abby bit her lip and tried to focus on the strap of her left sandal. Her throat constricted, but she refused the building tears.

"Yes," she blurted. "Sydney died here. There are too many bad memories."

And there were – but what was more – she didn't want her parents in Sydney's house. The Vepars knew of the house and they could return anytime.

"I agree with Abby," her dad added. "This place has never been our style."

"And what's our style, Rich? Drab and boring?" Becky inhaled again, blowing the smoke through her nose and challenging him with her eyes.

Abby's dad shrugged. He was not used to his wife's flippant behavior and found silence to be the only safe response.

"Maybe you should buy something downstate. I hear property on Lake Lansing is hot right now," Nick lied. Property on Lake Lansing was never hot, but Abby knew he hated not speaking. The quiet embarrassed him.

Abby snorted. "Sorry," she laughed. "But Lake Lansing? Come on, Nick, have you seen that water?"

"Sewage," Abby's mom drawled, downing the last of her wine and tapping her glass for a refill.

Rich frowned and looked at his watch. He had spent most of his life adhering to the motto that time was money. As a realtor, he didn't vacation on holidays because that was when buyers vacationed. Now, he and Becky were rich, and he felt lost, as if his watch had tethered him to the earth and the strap had just broken.

"Maybe you and Nick should go into town and get takeout," Abby suggested.

Her mother was sinking deeper into the couch and appeared to be on the verge of a complete meltdown. When Becky broke down, everyone was safer at a distance.

"Yes, great idea," her dad enthused, immediately jumping from the couch.

Nick, happy to be included, sprang from his own seat, quickly wiping the crease from his slacks.

"Want me to run you a bath?" Abby asked her mother.

Becky lolled her head to the side, and Abby reached forward, quickly catching the ash hanging from the tip of her cigarette.

"Yes. Maybe I'll drown and then your dad can worry about this house."

* * * *

"Psst, hey, you guys here?" Abby whispered.

She walked further into the woods, glancing back at Sydney's house, hoping that no one would see her. Her dad and Nick had gone for burgers, and her mother was drunkenly soaking in the tub. She had insisted on taking a second bottle of wine in with her.

"Gotcha!" Oliver cheered, landing on the pine-needled floor with a thud.

Surprised, Abby stumbled back, but Oliver caught her hand before she sprawled on the forest floor.

"Sorry, I've gotta get my thrills somehow," he laughed.

"Right, as if your life is lacking thrills," she said dryly, her eyes narrowing on the flesh of his hand, still raw and red from his former burns. His body had almost entirely healed since the night that Alva had doused him in gas and set him on fire. A story that Oliver had regaled to the witches by firelight one evening, forcing Lydie to play the part of the evil Vepar by standing on a chair with a navy blanket thrown over her head.

Oliver held his hand close to his face.

"Looks a lot better, though, if I do say so myself." He grinned and jumped onto a low tree branch.

Abby hopped onto it behind him, and when he sprang to the next, she jumped higher, catching a branch in two hands and swinging herself up and over it. They raced up the tree, not easy with the tightly woven branches and stiff needles.

At the top, they each held the trunk, and Oliver parted the needles so they could see the lake. It was barely eight pm and the sun had begun to set, leaving a flame-soaked horizon. Abby leaned into the light, already longing for the receding summer.

"I smell bonfires," Oliver said softly.

In the fading light, Abby could see some of the scarring on his face. She reached up, unconsciously, and touched his jaw where the skin still puckered slightly. It was very smooth, and he leaned his face into her hand.

"That feels good," he said.

Her fingers started to drift. She wanted to rub her thumb along his lower lip, but then her eyes saw a dark shape and she was instantly elsewhere, pulling back into the trees – spooked.

Oliver moved to her branch and peered out.

"It's only Dafne," he said quickly, letting the needles fall back into place.

Car headlights turned into Sydney's driveway, and Abby realized that Nick and her dad had returned.

"Damn, I've gotta go," Abby sighed. She started to climb down the tree, her face burning. She felt a little ashamed, touching Oliver in any way when Sebastian waited at the castle alone.

"Hey." Oliver caught her arm in his hand and she turned, looking back up at him.

"Don't give it a thought, okay? This is a strange time for you and I've found it's best if you let things unfold organically."

He was referring to her blush, of course, and she smiled, shaking her head. "Stupid to feel guilty about something you didn't do," she said.

"Exactly," he laughed and dived from the tree, somersaulting twice in the air before he hit the forest floor and tumbled forward, coming to rest at Dafne's feet.

"Wow, graceless as usual," she said, lightly kicking leaves at his face.

He rolled and grabbed her legs, buckling her. When Abby reach the bottom of the tree, Dafne was laughing and snarling at Oliver to release her pant leg, which he held in his mouth.

"Say please," he told her, but it sounded more like, "thay fleas."

"Please," she snapped, and he let the fabric fall from his mouth.

"How's everything going, Abby?" Dafne asked her coolly, brushing pine needles from the seat of her pants.

"Good. I'm just heading back, actually."

Dafne nodded. "We'll be patrolling the beach and the forest, but if you sense anything, anything at all, use your amulet."

The amulet, given to Abby by Elda, held the symbol of the witch's claw or woven triple moons. It was a powerful pendant, which Abby held on a chain around her neck, and was connected to two other identical amulets. When squeezed in her hand, the energetic heat traveled to its duplicates; one of each hung around the necks of Oliver and Dafne. They would feel the hot metal against their skin and know that Abby was in need.

Abby reached up to the amulet beneath her shirt and nodded. "I will."

She turned, but before she was out of the woods, Oliver caught up to her.

"Hey, I forgot to give you this." He placed a thick, cream envelope in her hand. In the upper right corner her name was stenciled in tiny, red calligraphy. "Elda wanted me to give it to you here on the mainland. Away from prying eyes."

"What is it?" she asked, holding the envelope up.

"You'll see when you open it." He leaned in and kissed her on the cheek and then jogged backward into the woods, giving her a final salute before disappearing into the trees.

* * * *

Abby snuggled under the covers in Sydney's guest bedroom. She had hoped the sheets would still smell of Sebastian, but the cleaning crew had apparently stripped even the beds and pillowcases. She was greeted with lavender detergent.

In her backpack she found the shell that Helena had given her. It was a large pink conch shell, the kind you could hear the ocean in if you listened closely, but Abby knew that hers could do far more than that. She tapped it three times with her right pointer finger and then whispered 'Sebastian' twice. Nothing happened, then just as she started to feel foolish, she heard his voice.

"Abby," he bellowed, and she shoved the shell beneath the comforter.

"Sshhh, you're yelling," she whispered.

It had sounded so clear, as if she might peer into the shell and see a tiny Sebastian lounging on the mother of pearl edge.

"Sorry. I'm not used to this yet," he said, lowering his voice.

"You and me both," Abby giggled, resting her head against the shell and wishing Sebastian were lying in bed beside her.

At the castle, he often crept into her bedroom late when all of the witches had retired to their rooms. It wasn't necessary, of course, both she and Sebastian were adults, but it added to their late night jaunts, and they both wanted to take it slow, not allow their identities to get lost in their desire for each other.

"I'm in your room," Sebastian said. "Your pillow smells like you."

She heard him taking a deep breath and groaned aloud.

"I miss you," she whispered. "A lot."

"Me, too," he said. "This place is like a tomb without you."

"Oh, come on."

"No, really. Lydie barely comes up from the dungeon where Max has her on some deadline to astral travel. Elda and Faustine are busy. I had lunch and dinner alone with Helena today. So much for needing me here at the castle," Sebastian said bitterly.

"I'm sorry you couldn't come," Abby told him, and she was sorry as she stared at the smooth, plastered ceiling. She wanted to feel his breath on her neck, snuggle into him and forget about the funeral.

"Me, too. I shouldn't have listened to them," he muttered.

She started to interrupt, but a knock sounded against her door.

"Oh, I'm sorry, I have to go," she whispered and stuffed the shell back into her bag.

She hopped from the bed and trotted to the door. Her mother stood on the other side, a third bottle of wine clutched in one hand and two crystal glasses in the other. Her eyes were red rimmed again, and she had changed from her black cardigan and skirt into a pair of gray silk pajamas.

"Can I come in?" she asked, but she didn't sound drunk anymore.

"Yeah, of course." Abby opened the door further, and her mother walked in, perching on the edge of the bed.

She pulled the already loose cork out with her teeth and filled them each a glass.

"Are you okay?" Abby asked, gently touching her mother's hand.

"Okay? Am I okay?" her mother asked, tracing the rim of her glass with a finger. "I'm alive and that counts for something. But I feel...alone now. My whole family is dead."

"No, we're still here, Dad and I," Abby reminded her.

"I know, and I'm very grateful for that, but even so, my parents and now my sister are gone. They're gone, and I am the only one left to remember..."

Abby thought of Sebastian then and understood a little more his loneliness.

"I'm sorry, Mom. I'm so sorry about Sydney."

Becky nodded, took another sip and then slipped a canvas bag off her shoulder. She reached inside and pulled out a large wooden box, setting it on the bed between her and Abby.

"This is for you, Abby. I don't know if I ever told you, but my father, your grandfather, was a novice wood worker."

Abby lifted the box; it was heavy.

"He carved this for your grandmother as a wedding gift. It's a sewing box, and God only knows why he chose a sewing box because she never sewed a day in her life." She laughed and waved her hand dismissively. "But that's all dead and buried, no pun intended, and I believe this box really belongs to you."

Abby looked closer at the image carved into the surface.

"That's her, your grandmother, sitting in that boat."

As Abby drew the box closer to her face, she saw the woman who sat in the boat. In the wood, her features were blurry, but Abby could see a massive cliff in the background. At the top of the jutting cliff, a castle twisted and disappeared into the sky.

Abby gasped and nearly dropped the box, which her mother caught easily.

"I should have given this to you years ago. My mother told me to," Becky continued, ignoring Abby's eyes. "But I was afraid of my mother's strange life, and when she requested that on your twelfth birthday I give you this box and then take you to her, I completely – well, I flipped out and I told her no. I told her not to come around anymore, that my family didn't need her, and she died less than a year after we had that conversation."

"I was five," Abby said, tonelessly.

"Yes, you were five, and I hid the box in the basement, and I never looked at it again. Until about a month ago, the day that you left Lansing, this box somehow found its way onto the kitchen table."

"What?" Abby asked, shocked.

"It was just there, and I don't need to wonder how because I used to know that those things happened. Living with my mother, you just learned that. And I knew then that you were already gone. I just tried to deny it and I tried to make you come home, but I knew…"

"What did you know?" Abby asked, wondering just how much her mother understood about witches.

"Oh, not much," Becky said quickly. "And please don't judge me when I say that I don't want to know any more than I already do. It's not my life, it's yours, and it was my mother's. Sydney wanted it, I always felt that, but it wasn't hers either."

Abby smiled and laid her palm against the face of the wooden box. It felt warm and vibrated subtly; Abby knew her mother could not feel the energy the box housed.

"Open it," her mother urged.

Abby flipped up the lid and looked at the jumble of contents inside. She saw a worn journal that said *"Arlene's Book of Shadows"* in dull pencil on the cover. She touched a strand of blond hair, several small jars of dried herbs and sticks of broken incense.

"I know that Rod didn't kill Sydney," Becky went on.

"But that's not to say I want to know who did or even that I think you know who did."

Abby started to interrupt, but her mother waved her to silence. "I just want you to know that I love you, and I support you, and I will not ask questions, and I will hear what you need me to hear, and that will be it."

"I'm sorry for lying to you, mom," Abby said, but she was suddenly very confused. Did her mother want the truth or not?

"No, don't be sorry. That's what I'm saying. I understand, and I don't want to know more. Maybe that makes me a coward, but I just don't."

Abby nodded and set the box aside, moving closer to her mother and hugging her. She hugged back and then started to cry softly, finally tearing herself from Abby's grasp.

"Goodnight, honey," she whispered and left the room.

Abby stared at the box for a long time. She wanted to open it, to read her grandmother's journals and sift through the contents, but something told her not to. Finally, she stuffed it into her bag beneath several t-shirts. Her hand brushed the envelope that Oliver had given her earlier that evening and she pulled it out.

Her fingernails had grown long in the past several weeks and she easily ripped along the envelope flap, pulling it open. Inside, she found an invitation.

All Hallows Eve
To: Abby Daniels
What: The Ritual Celebration of All Hallows Eve:
When the veil between the living and dead vanishes
Where: Bordeaux, France
Hosted by: The Coven of Sorciere
When: October 31st

About The Author

J.R. Erickson has always loved to write. However, like many young women, she gave in to the pressures of college and full time corporate work before realizing that life without dreams is no life at all. This epiphany spurred J.R. to leave her job and, with her husband, escape to Northern Michigan where she spends her days writing, reading, hiking the Sleeping Bear Dunes and being eternally grateful for the ability to pursue her passions full time. Prior to her great escape, she received a Bachelor Degree in Psychology from Michigan State University. She has published nonfiction articles at The White Pine Press, Michigan Nature Association and Demand Studios and short fiction at Story House. She is also a member of Michigan Writers.

Ula is her first published novel.

CPSIA information can be obtained
at www.ICGtesting.com
Printed in the USA
FFOW01n0253280715
15439FF